Praise

Fräulein

Struggle for Identity

Published by Piscataqua Press

32 Daniel St., Portsmouth NH 03801

www.ppressbooks.com

ISBN: 978-1-950381-73-9

Printed in the United States of America

Fräulein

Struggle for Identity

Jeffrey T. Leonards

About the Author

Jeffry T. Leonards is a retired psychologist living in Maine. He is the author of numerous scholarly publications and the former editor of *The Maine Psychologist*. His lifelong interest in man's inherent capacity for cruelty inspired extensive study in the fields of sociology, politics, existential philosophy and history, particularly 20th Century. When not engage in cycling, hockey, and Nordic skiing, Dr. Leonards devotes full-time to writing. He is currently crafting his second novel.

Dedication

The story that follows is a fictionalized memoir to a 20th century tragedy, global in scale yet earth-shattering to the individuals caught in its crosshairs. World War Two was an epic conflagration involving three utopian ideologies: Hitler's, Hirohito's, and Stalin's. Each was spawned within a cult of personality espousing superiority of its own people at the supreme expense to outsiders.

In only a matter of years, sixty million people lost their lives to xenophobia and racism; millions more were maimed or permanently displaced. Whether in Germany, Japan or the Soviet Union, these had been people who worked and loved, who worshipped and raised children, people who did all the things that normal folk do. Nationalistic demagoguery was to change all that, persuading everyday citizens to sign Faustian bargains exchanging morality for wild-eyed, shallow promises of a 'new world order.'

Ovid said that "in our play, we reveal what kind of people we are." Social upheaval, as depicted in this story, can expose the very same latencies. Almost overnight, ordinary citizens would align somewhere between heroism and cowardice. The most rabid killed and tortured with unrivaled ruthlessness, while the more passive stood idly by with some, especially corporations, even profiting from theft, slavery, and murder.

It may be tempting to think of Germans as inherently evil, but doing so overlooks the reality that Hitler ascended to power with only a small percentage of the popular vote, an approval rating eerily close to Donald Trump's in the run-up to the 2016 election. Many people in Germany and throughout Europe actually detested the *Führer* and the ideas he espoused, but that didn't stop the rhetoric of nihilism from washing over the masses like a blinding fog. Millions would perish in 43,000 concentration camps, and entire cities throughout

Jeffrey T. Leonards

Europe and beyond would be laid waste for many years thereafter. Hitler, of course, was not unique. In the east, a similar scenario played out with additional millions falling victim to the grandiosity and paranoia of the man once revered as "Uncle Joe."

We know that history does repeat itself, though often in ways that are unclear- until, of course, it is too late. While acknowledging the 130,000 women incarcerated at Ravensbrück, especially the 50,000 who tragically died there, it is to the resistors- the models of integrity and bravery, those willing to stand up and risk imprisonment, torture or even death in fighting against tyranny and injustice- it is to them and their sacrifices that this poignant story is dedicated.

Silence in the face of evil is evil itself.
Dietrich Bonhoeffer

The first country to be occupied
by the Nazis was not
Austria or Czechoslovakia.
It was Germany.

Sebastian Haffner

Prologue

*Because I remember, I despair. Because I remember, I have the
duty to reject despair.*

Elie Wiesel

New York City: July 30, 2016

Slumped over a dated blue wheelchair and largely ignored in the
far corner of the cavernous, 1950s-era dayroom sat a motionless
centenarian whose presence was announced only by the orange
bandana encircling her small head. The few strands of bluish-gray
hair peeking out from the cotton gave the appearance of a waning sun
on the horizon – in this case, fading twilight in life's ebbing tide. The
ancient woman's wizened frame might have been lost under her white
institutional robe were it not for the brown hand-knit shawl draped
unevenly across her bony shoulders. Gray, lifeless eyes hid behind
the smudged lenses to her wire glasses, an ensemble incomplete were
it not for the roadmap of wrinkles navigating the contours of her
sallow, weather-beaten face.

Annika Tritzchler, sitting amidst an ensemble of mismatched
furniture, at 102 was the oldest resident of thirty-five warehoused at
the Bayshore Nursing Home – a low-cost facility in Queens almost
entirely dependent on Medicare funding, and a place where true
nursing care masqueraded more as fantasy than reality. She had been
sitting uncomfortably for the past hour, waiting stoically for
assistance which had been promised, but which as usual was slow in
coming. Nodding off in short bouts interrupted by startled

awakenings, she needed help transferring to the well-worn recliner facing the television set, her favorite spot. She sat quietly, like a dog that might lay for hours staring longingly at an empty food bowl. Annika was said to have the patience of a monk, even while tethered to a urine bag so often filled to capacity.

With staff turnover high at this facility, little effort was expended in learning the names of the residents. Instead, they were more likely to be identified by nicknames – sometimes irreverent – or simply by their room number. Annika, for example, was "the woman in room twelve," or to some, "the Fräulein." If no one knew much about her, it was partly their own lack of interest, but also because she was not given to talking about herself. Aches, pains, the weather, the day's menu – even empty toilet paper rolls – these were the topics of everyday conversation. Gone was any inclination at cultivating friendships; she had seen too many come and go, and not just at Bayshore, but all throughout her life. Instead, her primary attachment was inanimate, a notebook inexorably cleaved to her chest. Ostensibly a journal, it was more than that, a place where her mind lived, where she could emote in private – a virtual therapist some might say. But even more, it was a confessional, as worthy as any priest or rabbi, and as much a part of her as an arm or leg. To the many who didn't know her, the notebook was nothing more than idiosyncrasy, a quirk of "the foreigner."

The "foreigner." Indeed. Annika had an accent, for sure, and to some it sounded quite strong, but having lived in New York for over six decades, she rarely thought of herself as an immigrant, unless, of course, it was brought up by others, which, when first meeting her, often became an ice-breaker. Today was a perfect example. After Annika's prolonged wait, one of the aides, a young, robust African-American woman dressed in white blouse and brown slacks came over to assist.

"So what can I do for you, little lady?" she asked.

Annika opened her eyes. "Ah, thank you." Then noticing that she had never seen this aide, she said, "You must be new here, *ja*?"

2

"That I am. Started a couple days ago."

Annika explained that she simply wanted some help getting into the recliner.

"Well, I can help you with that," the aide replied, pleasantly. As she leaned forward to scoop Annika out of the wheelchair and into the recliner, her identification card, dangling from a lanyard, brushed Annika's face, slightly dislodging her glasses. "'Scuse me," she said, taking a step backwards. Beads of perspiration dotted the woman's forehead. Rolling the wheelchair out of the way, she exclaimed, "Jeezum, is it *hot!*" Mmmm-*mmm!* Lord have mercy! You hot?" she asked Annika.

"No, I'm fine," Annika replied. She struggled to adjust herself in the recliner, while the aide straightened her gown along with the thin blanket in her lap. Responding to the comment about the weather, Annika said, "But, *ja,* it's been a hot summer. They're saying, though, that . . ."

Before Annika could finish her statement, the caretaker stopped what she was doing and stared as if her patient was from a different planet. "Say *what?*" she asked, her head cocked to an angle.

"What I said was that the weather *is* quite warm. But the weather people are calling for rain. It's supposed to cool down later in the week." With Annika's accent, every word beginning with a "w" was pronounced as a "v," so "weather" sounded like "vetta."

The aide, fumbling with the urine bag, said, "Girl, where you from, anyway? Sure cain't be from around here, talkin' like that. You French, right?"

Annika noticed the woman's nametag, and instead of answering her question, said, "Your name . . . Jasmine, *ja?*"

"That would be me," the aide responded, and then, holding up one hand as if testifying in court, said with a flourish, "Guilty, as charged!"

"Ah, very pretty name . . . *Jasmine.*" Annika repeated it, showing a thin smile. Names were important to her. "Well, Jasmine, thank you for helping me. I appreciate it. And in answer to your question, no,

I'm not French. I was born in Germany . . . long before your time."

Jasmine's life experience up to that point had mostly centered around the Bronx, so to her Germany was some far-off place where there had been a war – nothing of any consequence to her life in the here-and-now. Shrugging her shoulders, she said, "Aha. Well, I guess you like it better here, then, right?" She straightened out Annika's thin white blanket, and before Annika could answer, Jasmine's beeper began to vibrate. "Oops. Gotta go. Call me if you need anything . . ." To Annika, that was a familiar refrain – empty, but familiar.

The recliner she had been transferred to was a perfect location for someone with failing eyesight. Where many in the facility had succumbed to senescence, Annika feasted on a steady diet of cable news, making her as up to date with current events as anyone, staff included. And if the TV was in some ways a lifeline, it was also her sleeping pill. Over the past couple of years, she had come to rely on its white noise to lull her into somnolence, which proved more comforting out in the solarium than being isolated in her bedroom where, for reasons unknown to staff, she was often prone to nightmares. The solitude of "Room Twelve" had a way of opening her mind to fears that even sedatives failed to assuage, so it was almost expected that Annika could be found in the dayroom, even into the wee hours of the morning.

On this particular night, when most of the other residents had gone to bed, Annika was curled up by herself in the darkened room surrounded by dark silhouettes of furniture. She would have been lost over in the corner if not for flickering light from the TV dancing strobe-like across her body. The few staff on duty were socializing in the adjoining room where their muffled banter and occasional peals of laughter joined with the newscast into a semi-hypnotic monotone. In no time, Annika was asleep, still clutching her notebook.

An hour passed, then another, and just when it might have seemed that the night would pass like any other, the din from the television changed in both tenor and volume. The cable news network was replaying a raucous campaign rally featuring an upstart Republican candidate, Donald J. Trump, a man known as much for his flamboyance and bombast as for his overtly racist views. Annika, still asleep, stirred in the chair.

"We're going to Washington to drain the swamp!" came Trump's raspy voice, ". . . and we're going to make America great again!" the would-be president proclaimed. Reluctantly, Annika opened one eye. Trump's message was greeted with pandemonium and booming chants of "U-S-A . . . U-S-A . . . U-S-A . . ." Like a sleeping puppy with one furtive eye open, still not lifting her head from the small pillow, she watched the smiling célèbre saunter back and forth on the stage, all the while applauding himself, basking in the limelight.

She was now wide-awake. This was a man who had always disgusted her, a man she thought so unhinged and unscrupulous that to think of him as a serious candidate seemed hyperbole in the extreme. What she knew of Trump was that his persona had been crafted decades before when he achieved notoriety for grandiose real-estate deals, including big-named casinos in Atlantic City, high-rises in major metropolitan areas, and lavish golf resorts, all bearing his name. Annika had read that behind all the glitz were a string of bankruptcies that his billionaire father had repeatedly bailed him out of, not to mention allegations of money-laundering and ties to the mob. Like most people, she knew that his grandiosity was buttressed by a reality-TV show where he aggrandized himself by insulting and denigrating his fawning guests, especially women. She had learned of his dalliances with porn stars, his three marriages, and the scores of allegations of sexual improprieties against women, including the alleged physical abuse of an ex-wife.

In contrast, Annika had long admired the current president, Barack Obama. Aside from what she felt was his intelligence and diplomacy on the world stage, she appreciated him as the first President of color. To her, such diversity represented all the best in American democracy, not quite Horatio Alger, but damn close; in fact, a perfect illustration of why she had immigrated to the US back in 1949. So, it was only natural for her to feel repulsion toward a man who had launched himself into the political arena by spearheading a shameful publicity campaign to de-legitimize Obama, proclaiming his election to have been invalid because, according to Trump's "research," Obama was purportedly born in Kenya and therefore not eligible to be President. The media had been quick to prove that claim wrong, but the invective gained traction with a growing sector of the far-right electorate.

"They all 'crackers,'" Shontaya, one of the other aides, had said. "Them white boys cain't stomach the idea of a black president."

Annika agreed. She saw Trump's popularity as rising in direct relation to his outlandishness, particularly his bent for white supremacy, and dismissed him as both a clown and a fraud. "He's like Professor Harold Hill, the huckster in *The Music Man*, selling out his own community for personal gain," she had heard one of the other resident's remark. ". . . a real buffoon." It was inconceivable to her that he could be taken seriously, much less as a nominee for President. Those thoughts were about to change.

The TV cameras panned across the crowd as chants of "U-S-A," those heard at every international sporting event, suddenly morphed into a more sinister, "Jew-S-A . . . Jew-S-A . . . Jew-S-A . . ." Annika was wide-eyed. A wave of panic washed over her. To hear "Jew" juxtaposed with the letters "S-A" flooded her with reminiscences of jackbooted, Jew-baiting Nazis. "S-A" in the 1930's was a moniker to be feared, an abbreviation for the brown-shirted *Sturmabteilung*, the ruthless Nazi "storm troopers."

That wasn't all. Trump's catch phrases about "draining the swamp" and "making America great again" were slogans that Annika recognized from her childhood in Berlin. Sitting up in her chair, she began to see the man in a different light, one which cast a foreboding shadow on established democratic norms. His implicit racism mimicked the xenophobia of pre-war Germany, and the authoritarian rhetoric that was igniting his rapt audience seemed to parallel the fascism that swept through Europe in the 1930s.

Fräulein

She scribbled in her journal:

Like Hitler, he's become the lightning rod for everything wrong in the lives of Trump's followers. He proclaims himself a savior, the answer to not just some, but all of society's ills.

The televised rally had become deeply disturbing. Part of her wanted to shut it off, but another part felt it a duty to see where this was all heading. She didn't have to wait long. Richard Spencer, the founder of the American white supremacist movement, was at the podium slurring the American press with a resurrected Nazi term: *lügenpresse*. "The lying press is not to be trusted," he screamed, while he referred to Trump's political opponents as demons, part of a malevolent conspiracy now identified as the "Deep State."

Another familiar tactic, Annika recalled. Back in the 30s there had been over a hundred newspapers in Berlin alone, but under the guise that they were spreading fake news, Hitler shut them down one-by-one, substituting instead only a few state-regulated news outlets. What the people would know was only what the state wanted them to know. Spencer concluded his oratory with something that shook Annika to the core. "Hail Trump," he bellowed. "Hail our people. Hail victory!" A surge went through the crowd. "America," Spencer continued, "is a white country that belongs to *us*!" At that point, many leapt to their feet with outstretched arms in the Hitler salute, chanting "Hail Trump . . . Sieg Heil . . . Hail Trump . . ."

That was enough. Annika, visibly shaken, called to the staff, which brought Danisha from her coffee break.

"You OK, hon?" she asked. It was a voice of true compassion, not the usual fare at Bayshore.

"Ah, Danisha. I'm happy to see you. I didn't know you were on tonight."

"Yeah, Doctor T. I'm here. So what's going on?"

Annika's face was flushed. "I-I feel a little faint . . . think I need to go back to my room."

Danisha checked Annika's pulse, which she found faster than usual. She looked over at the TV broadcast. "You gettin' all worked up again from that garbage on TV, aren't you?"

"*Ja,* I think so," Annika conceded.

"I thought we talked about that. You're watching too much of it, Doctor T." She adjusted the urine bag to avoid tripping over the long plastic tube. "Me, I limit myself. All that talk about immigrants and white supremacy and violence and stuff. It's aggravating. Scary." She gently helped Annika out of the recliner and into the wheelchair, and from there, wheeled her down the hallway to her bedroom. Once situated in bed, Danisha called one of the other attendants to come in with a sedative, which Annika washed down dutifully with a few sips of water.

"You should be okay now. Just rest up. I'll be back to check on you in a little while."

"Before you go, Danisha, would you mind bringing me the large paper bag from the closet? It's on the top shelf."

"Sure. No problem." Danisha pulled down the bag, which was heavier than she anticipated. "Weighs a ton. What have you got in here, anyway?"

"They're just my notebooks. I want to take a look through them. Just, if you will, put 'em on the bed beside me."

Annika liked Danisha. She didn't know much about her, but there was something comforting about her presence, something Annika couldn't put a finger on, but which almost felt like a kinship. She always found it easier to relax when Danisha was on-duty, so it was not surprising that once the aide left the room, Annika's anxiety returned. Her stomach felt unsettled, and made its displeasure known in gurgling sounds that in any other setting would have called forth a plumber. The rally on TV had brought forth unbidden images that flashed through her mind like an oscillating current regulated by the frenzied tempo of her dysrhythmic heartbeat. Even with the medication, she was certain to be up the rest of the night.

She reached over to the bag and pulled out the stack of notebooks, all of varying ages and sizes. One by one, she sorted through them so that within a few minutes, they were piled in reverse order next to her on the bed. The one at the top appeared to be the oldest. The cover, frayed and wrinkled, was bound together by a thin, brown string tied in a small bow at the center. Loose, dog-eared papers poked out from every side. Annika had to look closely to make out the faded inscription centering the jacket.

Annika Tritzchler 1925

Recognizing the handwriting as her own, she took a deep breath and began reading, and as she did, Annika could see her whole life passing before her eyes.

Part One

Street Fight

Children are educated by what the grown-up is and not by his talk.

Carl Jung

<u>11 February, 1927: Wedding District. Berlin, Germany</u>

"We oughta be getting home now," Annika said, finishing the last of her ice cream soda. It was only a little after four, but in the waning autumn sunlight, she knew that her parents, who knew nothing of her whereabouts, would start to worry. Sitting across from her, lips curled around a straw to his own soda, was thirteen-year-old, Rolf Müller, a friend since childhood. She and Rolf had spent the afternoon at the Rehberge Park, and it was the first time they had shared any time together since Annika had switched schools earlier in September.

"OK," Rolf said. "One more sip." He directed his straw in circles around the bottom of the glass making a prolonged slurp that was loud enough to turn heads at the opposite table. Looking up at Annika, he wiped his mouth with the back of his hand, and followed up with a deep, guttural belch. "Done!" he exclaimed, as if he had just won a contest.

Annika turned crimson with embarrassment. She gave a nervous glance at the diners seated nearby. Scooping up her books, she said, "C'mon. Let's go." It wasn't that she was unaccustomed to Rolf's coarse manners. After all, their mothers had been close friends well before either of the kids were born, and with the two families living within a stone's throw of one another, Rolf and Annika could have

13

easily been brother and sister. But now, as a budding adolescent, it was harder to overlook some of Rolf's idiosyncrasies that in the past she simply took for granted. And plunking down a Deutschmark for the ice cream was something grown-ups do, not children who slurp and burp and laugh at inane jokes. Maybe having been apart from Rolf the past few months made her aware of how different they really were.

Stepping out into a brisk November wind, Annika zipped up her jacket. She looked at Rolf, who was clad only in a long-sleeved tan shirt (*badly stained at that*, she observed) and asked, "Are you gonna be warm enough, Rolf?"

"Yeah, sure. I'm fine," he said, thrusting his hands in his pockets. He hugged his arms at his chest for warmth. It was obvious he was cold.

Annika humiliation at Rolf's behavior was not without a certain sympathy. Little things like stains, inadequate or torn clothing, hand-me-down shoes and the like had always been there, but of these things too she was beginning to take more notice. For the first time, she wondered if Rolf even had a jacket. Unlike her, he was from a working-class family, though even that was in name only as his father, Hermann, was shiftless more often than not. He also drank heavily, and more than once, Annika had overheard her parents whispering about Hermann's temper, commenting that he was physically abusive to both his wife and son.

In fact, the Tritzchlers and the Müllers couldn't have been more apart; everything about them was different. Unlike Hermann, Annika's stepfather, Otto, was a kindly, well-to-do physician, highly respected throughout Berlin where he enjoyed a busy, successful practice. Her mother was not just formally educated, but maternal and energetic in community affairs. Her parents' personalities were tied to strong religious backgrounds, even though Otto was Jewish and Eva devoutly Protestant. They provided Annika with a strong moral upbringing. The contrast between the two families stood out even more now that Annika had been accepted into the *gymnasium*, an elite

14

track for high-achievers. Rolf remained in the public school, which meant that even with some effort on his part, which was unlikely, the most he could aspire to was work in the trades.

Dusk was upon them as Annika and Rolf hurried down the Müllerstraße en route to their homes. Street lamps blended with neon lighting from stores, and for kids not used to being alone in the city at night, the artificial illumination gave the area an almost alien appearance. The sidewalks were abuzz with people, none showing the usual calmness of shoppers and diners. Instead, an electricity quickened everyone's pace, and it was obvious even to the kids that something was amiss; this was no ordinary night. The farther along they walked, the more chaotic things became. They passed men in uniform, some carrying flags or banners. Some of the passers-by in plainclothes were armed with placards.

"It looks like some kind of political rally," Rolf said. These were common in Berlin, and even though the kids had never attended one, they were quick to notice the lack of uniformity in the colors and the flags. Even the insignias were different. One of them, the hammer and sickle, Rolf recognized from his father's paraphernalia, but he had no idea what it all represented.

"Maybe we should take a different street," Rolf suggested.

Annika looked around, almost stumbling on the sidewalk which was difficult to see amidst the throng. "There are tons of people on all the side streets, Rolf. I don't know if it would be any better. We could try."

"I-I'm . . ." Rolf began, looking nervously to each side. ". . . I'm not sure I even know the way home if we get off this street." Just then he was bumped from behind by a large man hastening to the gathering up ahead.

"Out of the way, Sport!" the man said as he brushed by them. Rolf was out of his element, and worse, Annika knew it.

There were two distinct groups assembling near one of the buildings in the distance. Most of the crowd was in normal attire, so whatever persuasion they had was discernible only in terms of the crowd they assimilated with. Two lines consisting of young men clad in brown shirts, leather belts, shoulder straps, and black leather boots formed a path from the road to the door. Some held truncheons and most had knives attached to their belts. Interspersed among them were numerous flags, most bearing a cross-like symbol. Several soldiers also had armbands with the same mark.

"That's the Nazi flag," Rolf said. Annika had heard her parents talking about Nazis, and while she didn't know much about them, she had been warned to avoid them. "Steer clear of them," her stepfather had advised. "If they approach you, just walk away – *quickly*." His words echoed in her ears, and now caught in this boisterous web, she began to feel threatened.

The soldiers formed a two-sided barricade enabling ticketholders to enter the building unscathed. On either side were boisterous protestors, many wearing red garments, some with red armbands bearing the inscription "KPD." Whoever they were, they seemed to the kids to be at odds with the Brownshirts. There was yelling and more profanity than Annika had heard in her whole life. Before they could do anything about it, Annika and Rolf found themselves the only young people in a crowd that towered over them. Worse, people were growing meaner by the minute. They were pushed and shoved, and at one point, Annika lost sight of Rolf.

"Rolf!" she screamed.

"Grab my hand," came his reply. As she reached for it, they were separated again. Rolf pushed a woman aside, who responded by slapping his arm. Ignoring her, he caught a glimpse of Annika moments before she would again disappear in the throng. "Here!" he screamed, and Annika's hand was now firmly in his grasp. The atmosphere was a powder keg, ready to explode at any moment.

Just then a large Mercedes rolled up and was quickly surrounded on the street by more men in brown uniforms. The front door of the limousine snapped open and out jumped a soldier who promptly unfastened the rear door. Standing rigidly, he directed a straight-armed salute as the short, well-dressed man in the back seat slithered out onto the sidewalk. No doubt this was the individual everyone was waiting for. The crowd grew so loud that Rolf could barely hear Annika yell, "Let's get out of here, Rolf. Hurry!"

Cheers blended with taunts and catcalls, as red-shirted bystanders disparaged the man with assorted vulgarities. The apparent dignitary, distinguished and unfazed, made his way through the path cleared by his entourage. Draped in a full-length, black leather overcoat, he walked with a distinct limp, yet carried himself with both confidence and even flamboyance. *"Sieg Heil* . . . Heil Hitler,"* came the chants, as the crowd on Müllerstrasse grew both in size and unruliness.

"Go back to the hole you crawled out of, Goebbels," screamed someone in the back.

"You fucking Nazis don't represent Germany," bellowed another. A rotten vegetable smashed against the front windshield of the limousine as it sped away, which triggered a retaliatory response from the enraged paramilitaries, who began using batons against the Reds. This merely emboldened the Nazi followers. Arms sprang forward in salutes that mimicked the ancient Romans. Cries of "Heil Hitler . . . Heil Hitler" rang out, and the situation became volatile.

"Go home, kids," a man dressed in ordinary street clothes shouted. "This is no place for you. Go on! Get out of here!" It was as if he was yelling at a dog. Another chimed in, telling them, "It's not safe for you to be here. Leave!" Rolf looked at Annika, then back at the man.

"You hear me? Scram!" the man persisted, which he followed up by giving Rolf a shove.

Rolf did not take kindly to authority, nor did he appreciate an affront to his budding masculinity, especially in front of Annika. Just as he was readying to defend his honor with an insolent response, a tall man suddenly emerged from the shadows. Looming over him, much like a lion about to devour a field mouse, was none other than Rolf's father, the only person in the world whose appearance alone was so intimidating that it had caused Rolf on one humiliating occasion to lose control of his bladder. Like so many of the men around them, his father had a red armband with those same letters: "KPD." And, as with many others, Hermann was carrying a steel pipe, obviously ready for trouble. If Rolf felt a rush of fear at the immense presence before him, he was simultaneously awed by the power his father's countenance exuded.

"What the hell are you doing here?" bellowed his father.

Rolf felt his legs tremble. "Annika and I were over at the new park. We stopped for a soda and were on our way home. We . . ."

"Don't lie to me! You know damn well the park is nowhere near here." His father was livid. Rolf knew that he wasn't supposed to venture any farther from home than the park across the street. His father kept tight constraints on him, much tighter than warranted for a twelve-year-old. Rolf feared his father's temper, especially the consequences meted out for any infractions, however minor. Hermann was a man who demanded obedience. He had cut his teeth in trench warfare during the Great War and, from what Rolf had once overheard from his mother, Hermann had been exposed to indescribable atrocities. His intimidating personality, at times downright terrifying, suggested to Rolf, even at his young age, that his father may have even perpetrated some of that barbarity. All Rolf knew was that whatever traumas his father had experienced in war had become invariably displaced onto him. The beatings he doled out had long ago made Rolf feel that he, not the French, not the English, but *he* was his father's enemy.

Hermann slapped his son across the face, almost knocking him down. "I've told you not to leave our area, yet you disobey me, over and over again." The metal pipe in his hand was trembling as if he expected to use it on his son. But just then one of Hermann's cronies pulled him back. "Hey, c'mon, Comrade. He's just a kid. Let him be." But Hermann, furious at having been disobeyed by his son, pushed the man aside without even looking at him. The friend backed off.

Then pointing to Annika, who was hiding behind Rolf, Hermann barked, "And what do you think her parents are thinking, her being out with *you*? Why do you think she's in a different school now?" Rolf's face was beet-red. "I'll tell you why." He bent down so that his face was inches away from his son's. "To get her away from *you!*" he said, poking a finger into his son's ribs. "And *us!* They think we're lowlife trash." He was so enraged that spittle pelted Rolf's cheek. And then, looking wild-eyed at Annika, he demanded, "Right?"

Annika was frightened beyond words. She had always been afraid of Hermann and did her best to keep as far from him as possible. But now, here he was, larger than life, a frightening figure zeroing in on her as if she herself was somehow the cause of his misery.

He turned back to Rolf. "Now get home, little man, and take her with you. You can bet I'll deal with you later." With that, he gave his son a forceful shove.

Rolf regained his balance more quickly than his composure. "Y-yes, Father," he stammered, his eyes filled with tears. He grabbed Annika's hand and together they hurried away, darting in and out of the crowd to get as far away from the mayhem as possible. He looked back once to see his father standing his ground, hands on his hips, glowering after them. Eventually, he disappeared in the shadows.

The frenzy of the crowd was no match for how terrified Rolf was of his father. He knew that getting home would offer little sanctuary. His father was a man of his word, especially when it came to punishment. Rolf had tried to mask any display of weakness, but with his father now safely behind them, he dabbed at his cheeks with both hands, already tasting the saltiness of tears on his tongue.

Their effort to get away from Hermann didn't come fast enough, as the street scene had grown more turbulent. Men from both sides were pushing and shoving, and within seconds a fight broke out. A short distance away was another one. A man's voice rang out above the crowd. "Kill the fucking fascists," he screamed, as one of the Nazis was knocked to the ground. The kids snaked through the crowd, but not before seeing the man on the ground being kicked and stomped. He was writhing on the sidewalk, arms flapping wildly above his head trying to protect himself as one blow after another rained down on his defenseless body. A kick from a bystander landed squarely in his face, which to Rolf made it resemble a cut of meat at the butcher's shop where his mother worked.

"We gotta get outta here," Rolf exhorted. By now, he was no less frightened than Annika, maybe more so. An afternoon which had started out as so promising had devolved into a slice of reality that neither could have imagined. Annika wanted to cry, but she grabbed Rolf's arm and rushed off, just as two police vehicles, sirens wailing, came roaring to the scene.

They reached Rolf's house first. All he could bring himself to say was, "See you around, Annika." She expected nothing more and was left to walk home alone. It was only a couple of blocks, but unnerving to be out on the street so late, particularly with strangers of all types eyeing her as she hurried along the sidewalks.

When she finally came through the door, Eva burst in from the kitchen, tears in her eyes, obviously frazzled. "Where on earth have you been, Annika? We were so worried about you."

That was all it took. Annika broke down crying and within minutes was telling her mother everything that had happened. She couldn't shake the image of the man's blood-stained face. The day had ended on a traumatic note, and it would shape her world for years to come.

... I felt like Rolf and I were going to get killed. I hate to think what his father will do to him when he gets home. {11 February, 1927}

Coming of Age

Out of your vulnerabilities will come your strength.
Sigmund Freud

April, 1929. Großer Tiergarten, Berlin

Annika couldn't have been more excited. Schools were closed for the Easter recess, and this was the long-awaited day that she and a cadre of classmates would be spending at the Tiergarten, Berlin's largest and most picturesque park. The day had blossomed exactly as she had hoped. The sun was peeking in and out of big, fluffy clouds, and although it was only early spring, the temperatures were unseasonably mild. She met two of her friends at the U-Bahn, which took them to Kleistpark, where they hopped on the bus to the Tiergarten. There at the gates were four more of the girls, all dressed in light clothing apropos to the weather.

"Where should we go?" Lena asked.

"Wherever the boys are," quipped Ingrid, eliciting a chorus of snickers. The girls were all close to sixteen and the topic of boys had become a common theme in their discourse. Elke hooked her arm into Annika's in a quick display of camaraderie as they walked along the tree-shrouded pathway past walkers, bicyclists, families, some with strollers, and more than a few young lovers. Everyone, it seemed, was intoxicated by the early spring warmth. Lush green foliage had begun to appear on branches high above, while fruit trees twinkled in pink and white blossoms. Everywhere they looked were gardens of daffodils and multicolored tulips.

Annika squinted her eyes as she took a deep breath. "Wow, I can smell the lilacs," she crooned.

"You sure that's not Ingrid's perfume?" joked Elke, and they all laughed. A spirit of levity pervaded the park on a day where troubles ceased to exist.

Not long into their foray, the girls came upon a wide field where young people, mostly teenagers, were engaged in a variety of activities. A group of boys, four on a side, were playing soccer, yelling and waving to each other for a pass. Another group, this one younger, was trying without much luck to get a kite airborne. Most of the others were simply sitting on the grassy hillside looking down at the action. Behind them, on the pathway, were vendors hawking everything from greasy kielbasa and cold, sugary beverages to pendants and assorted souvenirs.

Annika was in the midst of a story about one of their teachers when, quite without warning, two hands gave her a quick tickle under the armpits. She gasped and jumped, all at the same time. Everyone's head turned.

"Hey, Anni. How are you doing? I thought that was you." It was Rolf. Out of nowhere. She couldn't even remember the last time they had seen each other.

"Rolf," she stammered, trying to regain her breath. "Where'd you come from?" Annika hadn't seen Rolf for two years. Where she had qualified to attend the *gymnasium*, an elite preparatory school, Rolf, who had never performed well academically, remained in the public school, tracked at best for a future in the trades. Now she wasn't even sure she was all that happy to see him. "Girls, this is Rolf," she said. "He and I have known each other since we were kids."

No longer the gangly kid she remembered, Rolf had grown considerably, in some ways unrecognizably, especially now that he sported a trace of dark peach-fuzz above his lip. He was clad in rumpled khaki pants, a brown sleeveless T-shirt that boasted fledgling musculature, and a tan, herringbone Gatsby cap pulled rakishly to one side. He wasn't particularly handsome, but he *was* a boy, and this made him immediately interesting to Annika's classmates, especially because of the attention he was showing towards Annika. If nothing else, here was grist for the gossip mill.

Bolstered by her friends, Elke drawled, "Hiii Rolfff . . ." stringing out each word in a coquettish singsong, which sparked a round of giggling from the girls.

22

"Hey," he responded, glancing only fleetingly at Elke while shifting back and forth on his feet. Turning to the group as a whole, he said, "Great day, huh? How're y'all doing?" Somewhere in that brief attempt at buying currency with the girls, his voice cracked – that dreaded abomination of male adolescence, causing the school girls to nudge each other, wide-eyed and smiling, trying to hide their amusement. Embarrassed, Rolf fumbled for a cigarette to cover for this too-obvious betrayal of affected machismo, but there too he fumbled with three matches before finally lighting the cigarette.

The girls were not sure what to make of him. Lena was next to speak. Looking up at Rolf with a coquettish smile, she said, "Nice hat," which was more of a joke than a statement of admiration. Rolf wasn't used to being the center of attention, especially by girls, and at that moment did not know how to respond. Instead, almost involuntarily, he took his cap off to give it a quick glance. His nervousness, now rather obvious, sent Lena into hysterics, which she tried unsuccessfully to cover up by putting her hand over her mouth. Her giggling set off another volley of titters as the girls leaned into each other while keeping their eyes fixated on Rolf.

Annika sensed her old friend's awkwardness and quickly came to his rescue. "Don't pay attention to them, Rolf. They're just kidding around." Rolf nodded. "So, anyway, it's amazing seeing you here. Have you ever been to the park before?"

"Oh sure," he boasted, exhaling a plume of smoke. "A bunch of times. How 'bout you?"

"No, this is my first time," Annika replied.

Lena nudged Margrit, who sat next to her. Trying to avoid laughing outright, she said in a whisper loud enough for everyone to hear, "Her first time. Get it?" She then turned to the group, silently mouthing the word "virgin" in a way that everyone could read her lips. There was a renewed round of laughter, even from Rolf, who was in on the joke. Now it was Annika's turn to be embarrassed.

Rolf was emboldened by the girls' attention. "Well, hey," he said to the group, "you want me to show you around? The park is amazing. A few weeks ago, over in the woods, I saw a deer and her fawn, and I've seen a bunch of red foxes. Over there," he said, pointing, "is a pond with ducks and swans. C'mon, I'll show you."

The girls looked at each other. Elke said, "No, you and Annika go."

Annika stiffened, not wanting to leave them. She had no interest in going off alone with Rolf. Too much time had elapsed since they last saw each other, so she demurred. "Oh, let's all go."

This was not an option as far as the girls were concerned. Perhaps it was their age, or the mischievousness of adolescent girls, but they were less interested in discovering the park than with prodding Annika into what for all of them were uncharted waters – spending time alone with a boy. Ingrid pushed Annika forward towards Rolf, saying, "No, Annika. We're fine. You go with Rolf. He wants to show you around. We'll catch up with you at school tomorrow."

Rolf, beaming with the unexpected approval of Annika's friends, grabbed her hand enthusiastically, as if any hesitation would destroy his big moment. "Yeah, let's go, Anni," he said triumphantly. "You'll love it!"

Annika felt tremendous pressure from her friends. "Go on!" Elke said. The pressure was too great. She couldn't back down; it would make her look immature, scared to be alone with a boy. She was hoping one of her friends might stop them. They didn't.

"Ok, girls," Annika said. "I'll see you all Monday." As she walked off with Rolf, she looked back over her shoulder and saw her friends laughing and pushing each other. She knew she was being set up.

Being with Rolf was the last thing I wanted!. {21 April,1929}

They walked in awkward silence for several minutes before Rolf broke the ice. "So, how are things with you?" he asked. Annika began talking about the *gymnasium*, but it became quickly clear that Rolf didn't want to hear anything about the school, or even the new housing that her parents had relocated to. Instead, he changed the topic. "Let's go over there, Annika. By those trees near the water."

"Why. What's over there?" she asked.

"That's the pond I told you about. It's awesome. It's where the swans are. Last time I was here, there were two huge ones."

24

Annika relaxed a bit. The idea of seeing wildlife, particularly inside the city limits, was captivating. They hadn't yet spotted any deer, but with the thick undergrowth and trees, she could easily imagine them being around. So, she followed Rolf. They navigated through a stand of bushes, which grabbed at their feet, occasionally entangling them in vines. "They're right around the bend," he said, encouraging her to continue.

For a moment, she had a feeling of panic. She was not accustomed to wading through brush like kids in the country, and was beginning to feel out of her element. Then suddenly one of the vines ripped at her dress. She looked down. It was only a small tear, but upsetting nonetheless. "Hey, maybe we should do this another day," she said. "I shouldn't be wearing a dress in this jungle."

"Oh, c'mon, Anni. Not a big deal. Besides, we're almost there."

Annika had a bad feeling. She wasn't accustomed to being ignored. Maybe this wasn't such a good idea, she thought. But before she had a chance to be any more insistent, they rounded the bend, where they could easily see the swans not too far from shore. Annika was instantly transfixed; she couldn't take her eyes off them. Their statuesque physiques bathed in the fading sunlight was a scene right out of a story book. She watched them slip contentedly through the calm water, creating soft ripples of orange and purple from the late afternoon sky. Regal in their splendor, the waterfowl looked as if they should be gracing a castle moat. It was easy to overlook the hesitancies of only a few minutes ago.

Rolf was quick to notice. He took her hand and guided her to a small embankment overlooking the small pond. "Let's sit and watch them," he suggested. As they took a seat on the cool, damp ground, the two large swans, equally enraptured by their audience, made their way through mirror-smooth water, headed directly towards them. They came within about fifty feet of the shoreline, pausing to keep a safe distance yet close enough that every stunning detail, each ruffled feather, stood out to Annika. It was like a work of art. She marveled as the birds circled, occasionally dipping their heads below the water, but constantly staring, expectantly.

Annika was unexpectedly delighted. The struggle to get here had been worth it. "Oh, Rolf," she said, in a soft voice so as to not scare them away, ". . . they're beautiful." Just then one of the swans made a deep-throated "*glock glock*." "Listen," Annika whispered. "They're calling each other."

Rolf himself was taken with the scene, though more by Annika's presence than the swans. Her excitement was exactly what he was hoping for. "I told you," he said. "They're beautiful. Maybe if we throw them some food, they'll come a little closer." He and Annika were sitting side-by-side. As she reached for her knapsack, she rubbed lightly against Rolf. He made no effort to avoid the contact. She retrieved part of her sandwich and broke it into several pieces, which she tossed to the birds.

"Wow! Look at their reaction," Annika said, her face a picture of excitement. Even Rolf seemed enthused at how quickly the swans glided through the water to salvage the morsels. Once in their mouths, they raised their beaks skyward, rapidly shaking their heads to swallow. It was a delightful spectacle.

"I think they're a male and a female," Rolf said. "Probably married. You think?"

She couldn't tell if he was serious or not, so with a chuckle, she said, "I don't think birds get married, Rolf."

Rolf looked back at the swans and threw them a small piece of bread. Taking a quick peek at Annika, he saw a broad smile animate the constellation of freckles above her cheeks. Whatever guardedness she exhibited earlier seemed to be gone. That was his cue. Smiling, himself, he looked back to the pond while surreptitiously slipping his arm across her shoulders. Before she could react, he pointed to the pond and said, "Look. That one's diving underwater. You think he's got a fish?"

Annika didn't know what to do. She turned to look at the birds, but froze under Rolf's unforeseen touch. She had only recently turned sixteen and had never experienced any affection from a boy. Sitting perfectly still, Rolf pulled her closer.

"I think we should probably go now," Annika said. Her body was stiff as a board.

Rolf tried to be reassuring. "It's OK, Annika. We're not that far from home. Let's just stay for a little longer."

Annika was almost paralyzed by fear and uncertainty. It didn't

26

take an expert in the art of love to sense Rolf's true intentions. Growing up in an upper-class, religious family, she had only the most rudimentary understanding of sex and at this stage of her life had no interest in rushing into it with anyone. She was tempted to leave, but didn't want to offend him or appear naïve. Instead, she sat rigidly as Rolf's free hand moved slowly up her side to her ribcage. No one, outside of her doctor, had ever touched her body, and these advances made her feel self-conscious, even embarrassed.

Rolf had been reared in a home where open displays of sex between his parents were commonplace and always the one-sided prerogative of his father. He had never observed true intimacy, so he knew almost nothing about affection, even less about personal boundaries. As such, it felt entirely natural for him to expect that Annika would simply yield under his touch. He began to coax her backwards, using his weight to steer her onto the hard ground. Annika felt a small stick dig into her back, but before she could say anything, Rolf's free hand was working its way to her chest.

Annika froze as Rolf leaned forward in a clumsy attempt to kiss her. That was it. Everything about him, at this point, was nauseating: his breath, his insensitivity, his selfishness, and above all his intruding himself into a carefree day she had wanted to spend with her friends. She turned away with his lips landing coarsely on her cheek.

"I need to go, Rolf," she said, arching her back in an effort to extricate herself. "C'mon. Let me up." She had tears in her eyes.

"What's wrong with you, Annika? I thought we were friends."

"You're not treating me like a friend!" she said, leaping to her feet. "I'm going home." The swans bleated in full retreat calling an end to the bucolic calm.

Rolf's pride was in tatters. Annika got to her feet – cold, red-faced, and disheveled. She began straightening her clothes and dusting herself off as Rolf watched incredulously, not knowing what to do next. The years of rejection and humiliation, first at the hands of his father and later by teachers and classmates alike, was now being repeated, and by someone he would have least suspected. Clueless, he pleaded with her. "What'd I do wrong?"

Annika wiped tears from her cheeks, but she turned away in an

27

effort to keep her emotions private. "I'm leaving," she bawled, and began to hurriedly walk towards the park exit.

"OK. OK. Wait up. Please. We'll walk together." He too brushed some dirt and leaves from his clothes. He cast a quick glance back at the spot where just moments ago it appeared that he was to finally experience the acceptance he craved, where he would leave behind not just his virginity, but his self-doubt. But instead of inauguration into manhood, what looked back at him in that fleeting moment was failure. The honking from the swans, now far off on the pond, sounded to him like laughter. As he trotted to catch up with her, he felt desperately alone. He had no idea why she had acted that way, but he was determined, if at all possible, to salvage her friendship. But Annika was walking at such a fast pace that Rolf found it difficult to keep up.

"Annika, can you slow down a little?"

"I'm going home, Rolf. Alone!"

"I'm sorry, Anni," he persisted. "I didn't mean to upset you. C'mon, can't we just forget it?"

"I *said*," she barked, turning to face him directly, "I want to be alone!" She quickened her pace, as Rolf stood speechless. All he could do was watch his former playmate recede in the distance, eventually swallowed by gray, amorphous buildings. Annika never looked back.

... He violated my trust. I never want to see him again.   {21 April, 1929}

𝔄 𝔜𝔬𝔲𝔫𝔤 𝔖𝔠𝔥𝔬𝔩𝔞𝔯

...if a woman succeeds in withdrawing from the mass, or rather raising herself from above the mass, she grows ceaselessly and more than a man.

Arthur Schopenhauer

Friedrich Wilhelm University (Berlin): September, 1931

It was late summer and a balmy afternoon in downtown Berlin. The late day sun cast long shadows on the grounds of Friedrich Wilhelm (Berlin) University, where Eva and Annika were walking arm-in-arm, flanked by Otto, her beaming stepfather.

"So, this is where I'll be spending the next few years," said Annika, raising her arms in the air. She turned a full circle, her head tilted upwards, and surveyed a campus distinguished by hoary buildings, mature trees, and an assortment of plaques and statuary. It was everything one would expect at a university dating back almost two centuries. It wasn't the first time she had been on campus, but in this primal moment, it took on brand new meaning. Annika had graduated from the *gymnasium* just three months earlier, and now here she was, an entering freshman at Berlin's oldest and most esteemed university.

"What a wonderful opportunity, Annika. If anyone ever deserved to be here, it's you," Eva replied wistfully. She was filled with rueful memories of her own years on these same hollowed grounds.

"Here, here," said Otto. "This has been your dream, Annika, and you've made it all come true."

"No," she replied, turning to hug them. "*We* have made it all come true. I wouldn't be here if it weren't for your support." It was a touching moment, one that Annika would never forget.

The trio paused at the imposing statue of Wilhelm von Humboldt, founder of the university, looking down from his stentorian perch. It was as if he was scrutinizing those daring enough to enter his vaunted sanctum. Even after so many years, Eva was filled with awe. "You have no idea how proud I am of you, darling. I wish Vater could have been here to witness his little girl going to college. He would have been so happy."

Annika knew what her mother meant. Her biological father, Martin, had been a successful, well-respected physician who was employed in the research department at Schering, the large pharmaceutical firm in Berlin. It was in the early spring of 1916 when, walking home from work, he staggered and fell in the street. From what Annika had learned from her mother, her father had been suffering from headaches for quite some time prior to that incident. At the hospital, he came under the care of Otto Baumann, now her stepfather, who at the time was a family friend and colleague. X-rays revealed that her father had a substantial brain tumor, which was thought to have been caused by long-term exposure to the chemicals he worked with on a daily basis. After a poignant struggle of several months, Annika's father died. She was too young to have anything more than vague memories of her father, though she did recall a solitary life with her mother for the interval leading up to Otto's courtship. Back then, he was young, had never married, and was extremely well-liked. Their discrepant religious backgrounds – her being Christian, him Jewish – were apparently inconsequential to their relationship, and in the long run seemed to give Annika an even more solid grounding in her own faith.

Annika had been told many times of Martin's dedication to scholarship. He had also been a benefactor to the university, which he too loved. "I'm sure if there is a Heaven above, he's looking down on us right now with a big smile," Eva said.

Annika looked over to Otto and, grabbing his hand, said, "My father *is* here, Mutti . . . and you're right; he looks very happy." The reply was perfect. Otto put his arm around his stepdaughter's shoulders, while Eva pulled a handkerchief from her purse and dabbed at her eyes.

"I just don't want you to forget Vater," Eva continued. "He was a great champion of women's rights, and always felt that women were just as smart as men . . . that they deserved to be educated in exactly the same way. I feel like . . ." she paused. ". . . like, in some ways, you have become the incarnation of his beliefs."

"Yeah, well, it's hard, Mutti. I never really knew Vater, other than what you've told me about him."

"I had great respect for your father," Otto said. "You know, I wouldn't be surprised that if he were here right now, he'd be encouraging you to follow in his footsteps and study medicine."

Annika knew that she, as a woman, was fortunate to be attending a university, especially one so steeped in tradition and achievement. Most women her age felt compelled into a life of *kinder, küche und kirche* (children, church and kitchen); in short, raising a sound family – nothing more. Professional work was understood as the province of men. But Annika was different. She had studied hard, and having graduated from the *gymnasium* with high honors, all of her childhood aspirations – helping the poor, the mentally challenged, even animals – were now possible.

They made their way over to a food kiosk, where they ordered sandwiches and drinks. The weather was still summer-like, perfect for eating at a small outdoor table. Otto adjusted the umbrella to keep the sun out of everyone's eyes. After a few bites and a bit of small talk, Annika said, "Ya' know, since we've been here, I haven't seen one person wearing a brown shirt," an allusion to the conspicuous absence of stormtroopers.

Eva looked to Otto. "Praise God for small favors," she said.

Annika continued. "Papa, where do you think things are headed with the Nazis? There's so much talk these days about Jews, comparing them to vermin and talking about getting rid of them. It really worries me."

"Don't be concerned, *Pits'l*," Otto responded, using the nickname he had called Annika since early childhood. It was a Yiddish term meaning something like "small" or "adorable." There were times growing up where she felt embarrassed when he used it, especially in front of her friends, but now, in her early adulthood, she welcomed it as a term of endearment, something special to their relationship. Otto continued, "Even with the recent elections, Hitler's

31

a crank and still a minority figure. His followers represent only a fringe element. They're freaks. No one takes them seriously."

Somehow Otto's response didn't sound overly encouraging to Annika. Just two months earlier, the Nazi party had garnered almost forty percent of the popular vote in the Reichstag elections, making them the largest political party. Their rhetoric had become more virulent and bigoted, especially their flagrant antisemitism. "You say that, Papa, but the streets are dotted with brown-shirted henchmen beating up people and scaring them half to death. And look at all the children who are entering Hitler Youth organizations. To me, it's all very unnerving."

"No need to worry, hon. Everything'll be OK. I think it's safe to say I'm well-regarded at the hospital and probably here in the community, as well. Nobody seems to want me gone. And remember, Annika, your mother's not even Jewish, so things are going to be fine."

"I hope you're right, Papa. I worry about you, both of you, and now living on my own, I'll probably be that much more worried."

Eva broke into the discussion. "Well for now, can we just enjoy the moment? I mean, look around, honey. Don't think about us. Think of *you*, and your future. Imagine. Here you are, being able to study at the very same university that spawned some of Germany's greatest thinkers." Eva continued in what to Annika was sounding like an advertisement. "I studied here at the same time Max Planck and Albert Einstein were in residence. I'm sure I must've told you . . ."

Before she could go on, Annika rolled her eyes while finishing the sentence for her. "I know, Mutti. They each went on to earn the Nobel Prize. You've told me that many times."

Eva blushed. "Well, all I'm saying is, maybe you will be fortunate enough to be influenced by men of similar stature."

"Or maybe *women* of similar stature," Annika shot back, which triggered a loud belly laugh from Otto.

"Touché!" he said.

". . . or maybe women." Eva agreed.

The afternoon came to an end. Too quickly, Annika thought. She found it difficult to see her parents off, but any melancholy faded rapidly as she set out to explore the campus on her own. After all, this was to be her home for quite some time; no time like the present to get a feel for it. If to some a building was nothing more than a structure, to Annika these old, ivy-covered buildings were edifices of greatness. It was awe-inspiring to walk down two-hundred-year-old pathways and pass through the same venerated portals as Germany's elite before they went on to greatness. Men like Feuerbach, Fichte, Hegel, and Marx. Inside, the empty classrooms came alive before her eyes. There, she thought, might have sat Schopenhauer, maybe Kant. Over there, perhaps physicists, like Einstein. They were all giants who imagined the world in ways that no one else could. Just when she thought she had seen it all, Annika heard chamber music coming from the window of an adjacent building. It enabled her to imagine an earlier time when melodies from the great composer, Felix Mendelssohn, floated through the same air. By the end of the day, hers had been nothing less than a journey through a German *Who's Who*, which she found meaningful and inspiring. Life at that moment seemed alive with opportunity – her future so full of promise.

Maybe Papa is right. We're way too advanced as a civilization to think anything could come of all the Nazi propaganda. {11 September, 1931}

Make Germany Great Again

Nothing is so difficult as not deceiving oneself.
Ludwig Wittgenstein

<u>Berlin: November, 1932</u>

Annika put her spoon down and looked directly at her stepfather. "You told me not to worry, Papa . . . that the Nazis were a passing fad. An oddity. Wasn't that what you said?" Otto had taken a few hours off to have lunch with his stepdaughter. They were seated in the far corner of a small café, well away from other patrons, yet Annika looked around to be certain no one could overhear their conversation.

"You're right," Otto agreed. "I did say that. And I believe it. The thing is, *Pits'l*, Germany doesn't belong to just one group. It's not just for Nazis in the same way it's not just for Communists, or Buddhists or Christians, or any other group. This is a republic . . ."

"Papa . . . *shhh*," Annika said, glancing at the waiter who had just walked by. "You should keep your voice down."

Otto wasn't one to be upbraided, particularly in his defense of his own rights. Nevertheless, he hunched forward, only inches away from Annika, and in a stage whisper said, "Okay, I'll try to be quieter, but listen," he began, his voice several octaves lower, "Germany belongs to all of us. I fought for Germany. I put my life on the line in the last war, so Germany is just as much my country as anyone else's."

Annika listened, wanting to believe her father, yet thinking he was not fully cognizant of the massive changes taking place all around him. She wondered if he truly believed everything he was

34

saying. It was as if he was trying to convince *himself* with all the talk about democracy, rule of law and the like. She found it difficult to pay attention as he droned on. In some ways, he sounded like a salesman who knows more about a product's downside than what he's willing to let on.

". . . and remember, honey, that many of Germany's greatest accomplishments in art, music, literature, and even medicine wouldn't have been possible without Jews."

"I know that, Papa, but you never hear people acknowledging that today. Instead, it's all about an international Jewish conspiracy, right? . . . to take over the world."

"Yeah, yeah, yeah. A bunch of poppycock. I know all about that . . . It comes from those *verdammt* writings they're always pointing to, *The Protocols.*

"The what?"

"*The Protocols.* You know. *The Protocols of the Elders of Zion.*"

A look of recognition came over Annika. "Okay. Sure, I know what you're talking about."

Otto's face reddened. It was obvious he was getting worked up. "They try to make it sound like they're a revelation handed down from God. Nothing but fabricated horseshit. Anybody of reasonable intelligence knows that *The Protocols* are a fake.

"You really think so, Papa? You really believe that people have enough interest or even enough intelligence to research their authenticity? You think people really care if they're forged documents?"

"What I *think*, Annika, is that the people who believe in that kind of nonsense are in the minority. They're xenophobes . . . people too ignorant to be open to immigrants or people of different religions or ethnicities. They're nationalists, people bent on keeping the country white and Christian, even though their attitudes are anything but Christian. They feel too threatened by ideas which run counter to their own limited worldview." Annika nodded. "In my opinion, though,

Annika," Otto went on, "they're the minority. They don't represent the average citizenry."

Annika didn't want to argue with him, but privately she was dubious. "I really would like to believe there's no real threat."

"Good. So, what's your worry?"

"Well, to start off with, I've seen a lot of Jewish people being openly harassed – insulted and humiliated." Now it was Otto who nodded. "But not just insulted, Papa. Actually threatened! For example, in the library last night, I picked up a newspaper. Was just planning to thumb through it for current events. It turned out to be *Der Stürmer*. Have you heard of it?"

"*Ja*, I'm familiar with it. It's one of those anti-Jewish rags. I've seen them being hawked on the street, usually by the SA fanatics. It's just trash, *Pits'l*. That kind of stuff has been around since the time of Abraham."

"Papa, you know, you make it sound so insignificant. It's more than trash. It's full of the most disgusting stereotypes about Jews. It has repulsive cartoons that show them with long hooked noses; says they're out to take over the world . . . It even says Jews practice infant killings as part of their pagan worship." Otto looked away, as if by so doing he could negate everything his stepdaughter was telling him. "And, Papa, it's not just a fringe minority. People all over are reading it, being influenced by it. Hitler claims he intends to abide by the existing laws . . . work within the government. But it's a lie. Face facts! His people want to purge Germany of all its Jews, maybe even all of Europe."

"Maybe the *whole world*!" Otto snapped in a vain attempt at making her observations sound ridiculous. He was not blind to what was happening on the streets as well as in the Reichstag, but he didn't want to give any fuel to his stepdaughter's fears. Better to consider them irrational. He also found it difficult to imagine, in spite of the Nazi rhetoric, the idea of exterminating all the Jews, which numbered in the tens of millions across Europe; it was pretty much impossible, even if only from a practical standpoint.

"You know, honey, that propaganda about mass extermination, or even deportation . . . it sounds a little far-fetched, don't you think? Putting aside that there are just too many of us, I think we can rest assured that the majority our neighbors, most of them Christian, would never tolerate such bestiality, much less participate in it. C'mon, think of it. It's not the Middle Ages anymore . . ." Annika closed her eyes and slowly shook her head. She wasn't buying. "And besides," Otto went on, ". . . with me being married to a genuine German . . . oh, excuse me, I guess I should say, 'an Aryan' . . . right? . . . well, anyway, I'd have to imagine that me being married to your mom makes me pretty safe, wouldn't you agree?"

Annika found herself increasingly frustrated by her father's cavalier dismissal of her concerns. He seemed out of touch, as did so many of the older generation. And she had good reason to worry, even though the Nazis *were*, as her father pointed out, still in the minority.

She was no student of social movements, but in school she had learned about the Russian revolution, and the consequences of Germany's defeat in the Great War were all around her.

"I'd like to think so, Papa. But to be honest, there's so much discontent out there . . . people struggling financially . . . a lot of anger."

"There's always been anger . . ."

"Like this? I mean, look what happened in Russia. People were hungry, there was mass unemployment. Next thing you know, they revolted . . . right?"

"Sure. But that's Russia. A long way away, and an entirely different people . . ."

"You say that, but how about Italy? Look what's happening with Mussolini. The whole fascist movement."

"I don't know. He can only go so far with social change. Don't forget. He's got to work with the Church. I can't imagine the Pope would blithely sit back and allow him autocratic rule. After all," he said with a snort, "who would be subsidizing the bloated Vatican if Mussolini became the supreme ruler? What a joke."

"I think you're being dismissive, Papa."

"Not dismissive, honey. I just wonder if your professors are throwing too much at you too quickly. It's scaring you . . ."

30 January, 1933

Annika was studying for an upcoming chemistry exam when she began to realize that the streets outside were teeming with commotion. She got up from her studies to peer out her window. Throngs of people, mostly well-dressed men in long wool coats and fedora-style hats – some walking, others on bicycles – had swollen the sidewalks where all seemed headed in the same direction. A crescendo of disparate shouts, police whistles, bicycle bells, and automobile horns blended into a disparate symphony resembling an offbeat jazz band in some sort of herky-jerky dance revue. Maybe the Berlin football team had just won, Annika wondered. But football season was over, as was New Year's, and it was way too early for Easter. And the gray, raw days of winter were certainly nothing to celebrate, nor was the periodic table of elements, which at that moment she was trying to memorize. So, what accounted for all the excitement?

Abruptly and without warning, her door burst open. It was Magda Schering, one of her friends. "Annika, C'mon. Hilter's being sworn in as Chancellor. He's on his way right now over to meet with Hindenburg. Everybody wants to see him."

"Where?"

"At the Reich Chancellery. It's only a few blocks from here. We can make it if we leave now. Let's go see him."

As much as Annika might be tempted to join the melee, if only out of curiosity, she needed this time to study. "You go ahead, Magda. I've got too much to do."

Magda pulled at her arm. "No! C'mon Annika. This is history in the making. Let's go witness it."

Reluctantly, Annika, who hadn't made her politics known outside of her family, looked up at the exuberant classmate, paused, and agreed. "OK, but I need to get back to scan my notes one more time before bed."

They hadn't as much stepped out the door before the young women were entwined in the fast-moving hordes making their way down Unter den Linden, the venerable, tree-lined boulevard in the heart of Berlin. It was as if a tidal wave was sweeping them forward. "Annika, grab my hand so we don't get separated," screeched Magda as they squeezed through a crowd multiplying by the minute. Wending their way to the Reich Chancellery, the hordes became even thicker, and over the din were shouts of, "He's at the Hotel Kaiserhof." Within minutes, Annika and Magda were on the Wilhelmstrasse, where the mass of spectators was so dense as to be almost impenetrable. Traffic had come to a standstill. Some were there out of curiosity, some drawn by excitement, but most were enthusiastic supporters of the self-styled redeemer who promised to bring Germany out of its current miasma. It wasn't world domination people sought, and war was indeed the last thing they wanted. No, their enthusiasm for Hitler was all about his promise to improve the economy: jobs, affordable housing, health care, in short, *making Germany great again.*

The revelers took up an entire city block as they swarmed the luxurious hotel. Annika and Magda were well back from the fashionable entrance, but had arrived just in time as Hitler had not yet made an appearance. People pushed and shoved, trying desperately for a peek at their hero. Annika and her friend could hardly see above the bobbing heads and were close to abandoning the effort when suddenly Hitler appeared in the entryway. Looming above the crowd, his words were drowned out in a chorus of cheers and *"Sieg Heils"* as thousands of arms shot forward in choreographed obeisance. From Hitler's perch, the semi-circular sea of outstretched limbs took the shape of a Japanese folding fan. The crowd's jubilation was a bit less sanguine for the girls, who found their heads sandwiched between jutting arms and maniacal screams of adulation. Magda's hat was knocked from her head, and as she bent to retrieve it, Annika caught a glimpse of women in the front being restrained by police from reaching out to touch their leader.

It was as if touching him was somehow curative, like Christ with the lepers. {30 January, 1933}

A cameraman was standing on a makeshift platform about six feet above the crowd, presumably situated to capture the occasion for one of Berlin's many newspapers. Hitler was surrounded by an entourage of officials, including policemen, bodyguards, and black-uniformed officers of the SS. It took almost fifteen minutes before he and his staff made their way to an awaiting limousine for the short ride to the Reich Chancellery. Like Moses at the Red Sea, the crowd parted to allow the luxurious, retrofitted Mercedes to pass unmolested. Whether they wanted to or not, Annika and Magda were swept up in the surging crowd that followed the limousine to the government building.

They remained outside the government complex for what seemed like hours, being pushed and jostled by what Annika perceived as acolytes thirsting for a glimpse of their messiah. It was mass hysteria, and if nothing else, being a part of this event convinced Annika at that moment that Nazism was no "passing fad," as her stepfather had put it. It was huge, cataclysmic, and spreading like wildfire – a revolution by anyone's definition and no less real than any of the other uprisings that she had read about. Worse, it reeked of malevolence and there seemed to be no stopping it. As she thought this, a wave of dread overtook her, one which turned quickly to panic, and she no longer wanted to be part of it.

"Magda, I've got to get back. I have a huge exam coming up."

But before her friend could respond, someone yelled, "Look! There he is," pointing to an upstairs window. There, silhouetted against the orange hue from the room inside, was *der Führer* himself,

Adolf Hitler, waving to an enraptured discipleship. Down below at street level, a parade took shape. Hundreds, perhaps thousands, of delirious celebrants, many carrying torches, marched down the street, all singing in unison the Horst Wessel song. It was jubilant homage under the watchful eyes of, first, Hitler and then Hindenburg.

To Annika, the ceremony with its singing and pageantry screamed of paganism, everything that she had grown to revile. What scared her most, though, was that it was so eerily infectious. She suddenly realized that, as ardently opposed to Nazism as she was, *even she* had the capacity to get drawn in. Maybe it was the energy, or the feeling of connectedness. Whatever it was, something became abundantly clear. This was the antithesis to the Weimar regime. It was the Hegelian *Volksgeist* coursing through the national consciousness in a thundering dialectic of social change. This spirit was dark and seductive with the power to lull the disaffected with avaricious desire to participate. Annika could see it. It was all about belonging to something larger and greater than oneself, a path to individual meaning for those without purpose even if the trade-off was unequivocal allegiance and suppression of selfhood. This, she reasoned, was cult-like camaraderie offering mind-numbing salvation to its enraptured acolytes. On this night, everyone belonged – to this group and to this moment, a moment when free-will was abandoned and blind trust transferred to their would-be savior. It must feel wonderful, she thought – a drug like none other. Were it not for her love and undying commitment to her Jewish stepfather, Annika sensed that she herself might be as mesmerized as the others. That awareness alone made the entire scene disturbing, and, *God-forbid*, a portent of evil to come.

Then something totally unforeseen happened. Towards the front of the procession, illuminated briefly by a street lamp, she caught sight of something familiar. It was a man, not just any man, but someone who for all the world looked like . . . *Rolf*. He was on the far side of the pageant and mostly hidden in the dark columns of marchers, but in that brief moment his face and swagger bore all the earmarks of the boy Annika had spent so much of her childhood with. As quickly as she saw him, he disappeared into the flock of revelers, leaving her panicking, wondering if he might have seen her. It had been years since their ill-fated encounter in the park, and Annika would have been just as happy to never see him again. But even more troubling was that if the person she saw actually was Rolf, he was wearing the brown uniform of the SA.

. . . Tonight's events were unnerving. What luxury to not have to think, to let others make decisions for them. To let others tell them what to believe . . . Did I really see Rolf? Is he one of Hitler's stormtroopers? {30 January, 1933}

True Believers

Let me control the textbooks, and I will control the state.
Adolf Hitler

<u>30 January, 1933</u>

Annika and Magda returned to the women's dormitory where the mood was anything but the usual melancholy that tended to pervade their antiquated surroundings. Young women, a few already in nightclothes, were dancing and flitting about in what, for the time, was a most unladylike fashion.

"What's going on?" Magda asked, showing no signs of concealing her own excitement.

"We're celebrating!" boasted Frieda. She held up a partially consumed bottle of Riesling, like Perseus, the conqueror, holding high the severed head of Medusa.

"Yeah, haven't you heard? We're celebrating the change in government." Renate's eyes were as bloodshot as Frieda's. It was obvious that more than that one bottle had been consumed. "Where were you girls?"

"Where were *we*?" Magda gloated. "We were at the Chancellery. We saw it all. Hindenburg *and* Hitler!"

"You *saw* him?" Herta asked excitedly. "What was he like?" Two other girls quickly gathered around making Magda the center of attention. To the residents, she had prized information – maybe gossip – that would otherwise have been totally unavailable. Annika stood back, content to listen, even as Magda treated her rapt audience to the most unlikely embellishments ("He waved to *me* . . . and *smiled!*"). It was as if Hitler was the coveted star of the football team, someone

43

every woman, young and old, dreamed about.

Not Annika. The entire evening did little more than undermine her sense of security. It wasn't just stressful; it was traumatic, because it seemed to be confirming her worst fears.

Sleep did not come easily that night. It was fragmented and riddled with stressful dreams involving her stepfather and Nazi thugs. For the first time in her life, she came to the realization that everything she had known, and everything she was banking her future on, was now uncertain. In fact, she reasoned, her only certainty was that her life was going to change.

The morning sun shone brightly, but instead of luster and opportunity, Annika gazed out her window to an environment that no longer seemed familiar. The buildings were the same, the street was no different. People continued to scurry about as always: men headed to work, women pushing children in strollers, buses and automobiles passing to and fro. Amidst it all, however, at least for Annika, was an ineffable pallor; something dramatic had changed. Maybe not physically, at least not yet, but definitely psychically.

I had so hoped nothing would come of Hitler, and now here he is, a whisper away from the presidency. And people seem so happy. How can they be so stupid, not to see the danger? {30 January, 1933}

She wished it had remained just a nightmare – that morning would come, and everything would return to normal. But it didn't. It only brought uncertainties and worries. Eating was out of the question; she had no appetite. Her eyes were red and felt like they were burning from lack of sleep. But she needed to study, and maybe doing so would bring distraction. She opened her chemistry notebook to begin reviewing neatly-penned chapter summaries. Twenty minutes elapsed before she realized that she had been reading some of the same sentences over and over again. She tried to force herself to focus, but her mind was elsewhere.

Fräulein

Maybe it was lack of sleep, she told herself, or maybe not having eaten. Maybe it was not living with her parents and feeling alone for the first time. Whatever it was, everything she was working towards suddenly seemed meaningless. She wondered why even bother to study when nothing seems stable anymore? Such thoughts were not just unusual for Annika, they were utterly foreign, threatening to void everything that she had worked towards and fantasized about throughout her life. How could she, a perennial optimist and overachiever, entertain negativity? Doubts began to quickly envelope her.

All at once, she broke into a cold sweat as her breathing accelerated into short, shallow gasps. She looked furtively from side to side, not sure what was happening to her. It was terrifying, and it all happened in a moment. Annika's fear spiraled through the roof, causing not only intensified breathing, but quickened pulse, pounding heart and light-headedness. It was overwhelming; the walls were closing in. For a fleeting moment, she wondered if she might actually be losing her mind, a thought which did nothing but add to her hysteria. At that point, instinct took over. She ran to the window and opened it with such vigor that it banged the casing above and caused the single pane of glass to rattle as if ready to break. She leaned out and retched, repeatedly, though it was nothing more than dry heaves.

Hanging out of the window several floors above street level, her torment slowly abated as blood returned to her head. The cold air was like smelling salts to an exhausted boxer. She pulled herself from the windowsill, ambled over to her bed and propped herself against the pillow, now feeling totally drained. None of this was what she had expected in her first year as a student. Reality was changing before her eyes, and she knew it would take great fortitude to handle it. She closed her eyes, rubbed her head slowly with both hands, and began to softly weep. Within minutes, she had fallen into a deep slumber.

A few hours elapsed before Annika was awakened by a flurry of footsteps thundering down the staircase. She sat bolt upright. Still groggy, she was confused by the commotion. Once again, her door pushed open, and now it was Ursula's voice. "Annika. Get up. Hitler's on the radio! Let's go."

"Go where?" she asked, rubbing her eyes.

"Down to the lobby. Hitler's giving a radio address. Hurry." Annika blinked and slowly rose to a sitting position. As much as she hated Hitler, maybe it was wise to hear the speech in order to have at least some idea of what the Nazis were up to. Plus, not going would make her stand out, and she wasn't ready for that. Mechanically, she brushed her hair to the side before following her classmate down to the large foyer, where five other women had gathered around a radio.

"Has he started?" Ursula asked. She was clearly excited.

"Shh . . . shh," they yelled, almost in unison. Several other women clambered into the room, and now a throng had assembled, all craning their necks to hear the Führer. "Turn it up," one of them demanded, which prompted others to wave their arms in a desperate effort to quiet the crowd, lest no one could hear. The women, now standing perfectly still, listened as the radio crackled with Hitler's impassioned voice. He started by praising fellow Germans for their spirit and support, and progressed to promises of needed changes that would ramp up the economy and make Germany into the strong, proud land of its forbears.

"*. . . In the appalling fate that has dogged us since November 1918 we see only the consequence of our inward collapse . . . The misery of our people is terrible! The starving industrial proletariat have become unemployed in their millions, while the whole middle and artisan class have been made paupers. If the German farmer also is involved in this collapse we shall be faced with a catastrophe of vast proportions. For in that case, there will collapse not only a Reich, but also a 2000-year-old inheritance of the highest works of human culture and civilization.*

"*All around us are symptoms portending this breakdown. With an unparalleled effort of will and of brute force the Communist method of madness is trying as a last resort to poison and undermine an inwardly shaken and uprooted nation . . . But if Germany is to experience this political and economic revival and conscientiously to fulfill its duties towards other nations, a decisive act is required: We must overcome the demoralization of Germany by the Communists."*

The students listened in restrained silence until the speech ended, at which point one of the women broke into loud applause. "He's incredible . . ." chirped a woman in a high-pitched voice. "Absolutely spellbinding," swooned another. And then came a voice far more disturbing to Annika. *"Sieg Heil . . . Heil Hitler!"* boomed the young man. Annika hadn't noticed him in all the excitement, nor had ever seen him. Maybe a boyfriend of one of the girls. He stood statuesque in the regimental brown of the SA, his right arm thrust forward, ramrod stiff, in the new Nazi salute. His voice echoed through the foyer, down corridors, off the ceilings and into people's psyches, where it blasted like a soundwave from an explosion. Everyone turned to look just as one of the girls, infatuated with the moment if not the young man himself, retorted with her own full-throated outcry. *"Heil, mein Führer!"* she shouted, waving a miniature red flag. Were it some other circumstance, she might have been cheering on her favorite team at a regional sporting event. In the merriment that followed, any thoughts of schoolwork were once again subsumed in a stupor of nationalism.

A Resistor

The whole problem with the world is that fools and fanatics are always so certain of themselves, and wiser people so full of doubts.
Bertrand Russell

<u>27 February, 1933</u>

Doctor Bonhoeffer was in the middle of a lecture on Christian ethics when Annika raised her hand. "Yes, Fräulein," he said, encouraging her to speak. "Please."

Annika stood up, looked around at the fifteen or so students, and said, "To me, Professor Bonhoeffer, social morality, at least the way I think you've described it, is something that evolves with society. So, I'm wondering. Are you saying that the more advanced a society becomes, the more sophisticated its ethical structure needs to be to keep it together?"

Doctor Bonhoeffer smiled. "Well, in so many words, yes. That's basically what I was implying, Fräulein . . ." he paused to look at his roll book. ". . . hmmm, let's see . . . Fräulein . . . Tritzchler, yes?"

Annika nodded, feeling unusually conspicuous that the professor was taking the time to identify her, especially with her being the only woman in a class made up mostly of men. She started to sit back down, but then a thought crossed her mind and she abruptly returned to her feet. Looking squarely at the professor, she asked, "Well, sir, if morality advances with society, can you tell me what accounts for moral *decay* in an advanced civilization?"

"Ah," said the professor, tapping his index finger to his temple. "Excellent question, Fräulein. You've actually presupposed my next lecture, but let me take the opportunity, if you don't mind, to ask what

48

you might be thinking of when you say, 'moral decay in advanced civilizations.'"

Annika was not prepared to have her question answered with a question. She looked around at the faces staring at her and wondered if she, as a woman, might have spoken out of turn. "Well . . ." she stammered, not sure that she wanted to continue, "maybe it would be better to wait for your next lecture."

She pulled in her dress to sit, when Doctor Bonhoeffer stopped her. "No, no. Please. I'd like to hear your thoughts," he implored.

The first thing that came to Annika's mind was her stepfather. And then images of local Jews she had seen being harassed. She suddenly felt emboldened to respond. "Well, Professor Bonhoeffer. I don't think anyone would argue that we are at a privileged university, one that owes its legacy to scores of prominent educators that came before us. In every field – philosophy, mathematics, medicine, and many more – Germany is at the pinnacle of civilization. So, when I think of ethics being a cornerstone of every cultural advancement, I can't help but wonder how bigotry and other immoral behaviors can simultaneously compete. I would think, according to what you've taught us, that immorality would weaken as society moves toward greater and greater advancement."

"Thank you, Fräulein, for that question." Annika sat, as Bonhoeffer addressed the class. "Fräulein Tritzchler brings up a most important point. Before returning to Germany two years ago, I studied in America under the Reverend Reinhold Niebuhr. Last year, Doctor Niebuhr published a book of great importance, one that speaks to exactly this issue. It's titled *Moral Man and Immoral Society.* Write it down. Unfortunately, the book is not yet available in German, but I have an English version and will be lecturing on some of his major tenets."

Just then the campus chimes sounded out the hour. Bonhoeffer looked at his watch. "Oh, I didn't realize we were out of time. Well, let's pick up right here next week. Class dismissed," he said, causing a flurry of activity as students snatched up books and notepads before heading off to their next class. Annika was about to join the stampede when Doctor Bonhoeffer called out, "Fräulein Tritzchler. Could I have a word with you?"

Annika looked back, not sure what to think. Had she spoken out of turn? The professor singling *her* out? She walked over to Bonhoeffer, her books clutched at her chest as if she was nursing a baby.

Bonhoeffer wasted no time in getting right to the point. "I must say, Fräulein, that I found your question most stimulating. You seem very committed to this class, not just today, but some of your contributions throughout. Forgive me if this sounds forward, but I can't help wondering if there's more to your question than just intellectual curiosity."

At first, Annika didn't know how to respond. What she knew of Bonhoeffer, she greatly appreciated. He was young, charismatic, and showed great interest in nurturing his students not just intellectually, but spiritually. Like her, he was a Lutheran, but unlike the majority of Lutherans throughout Germany, he was far from doctrinal. He spoke out openly and often against what he called "German Christians," those who abandon Scripture in their support of the Nazis. As such, he was a controversial figure on campus, lending deep concern that his outspokenness could run him afoul of the Gestapo.

"Herr Professor," Annika began, "I am afraid of what I see taking place all around me. All the fighting. Democrats fighting Communists . . . Communists fighting Nazis. I find myself wondering whatever happened to stability? Maybe it was just artificial . . . being sheltered as a child. Maybe it's been there all along."

"Well, you're right. To one degree or another, it's always been there. Isn't that what led us into the Great War. It wasn't that long ago, right?"

"I realize that. But we talk in class about liberty and free-will, and yet so much of what seems to be happening here in Berlin is not freedom, but repression. The great ideals we talk about in class

50

doesn't really relate to what's going on . . ."

"Well, you're exactly right," Bonhoeffer conceded. "And that's why it's so important for us to look at ideologies and how they relate to utopian thinking. In an introductory course, we need to start with ideals in order to have a benchmark against which to measure the realities of a given society . . . you know . . . the ways in which societies fall short of the mark . . ."

Annika interrupted. "I understand that, and I find this education to be really stimulating. I never imagined learning so much." She studied Bonhoeffer for a few seconds before continuing. He seemed so genuine; she felt that she could trust him. "To be perfectly honest, Herr Professor, my stepfather is Jewish, and I stay up at nights worrying about him. I see such hate-mongering out there. All this talk about Jewish conspiracies . . . and purging society of all the Jews. It scares me half to death, and I asked those questions in class, because it makes me wonder how advanced we really are."

"And you're right to be thinking that way, Fräulein. Changes that we see every day, if one chooses to look, are subtle, but have dire implications. You show unusual insight in being able to recognize them." Annika blushed. "As I think you know, I am very much opposed to the National Socialists. When I lived in New York City, I taught Sunday school in a Negro church. It was in a very impoverished slum. For me, it was a blessing. I learned a great deal about oppression and how so-called 'people of the cloth' have used the Bible to justify racism in America. The misrepresentations continue, even today, to seduce white America into believing that Negros are inferior, and that God encourages both slavery and annihilation."

"Pretty much what we're seeing here in Germany . . ."

"Well, yes and no. The lies and duplicities that spawned racism in America have also set the stage for their own wave of anti-Semitism. Believe it or not, there are many in the States who subscribe to the same policies as our own Nazis. What I'm concerned about are the Lutherans here in Germany who have by and large thrown their lot in with the Nazis. They're supposed to be leaders, people who model resistance against oppression. But sadly, too many churches today fail at following Scripture. The Nazis, on the other hand, are fundamentally atheists, despite any lip-service they may pay to religion. They are pretty much manipulating the pastorate to preach the Nazi gospel to their congregations. That is a gospel that neither you nor I would subscribe to; it's a gospel of exclusivity, one which justifies any actions that true followers of Christ would consider immoral – lies, slander, imprisonment, even murder."

Annika studied the professor with admiration. He was so different than other German lecturers she had met. Most of them were rigid, stentorian, and condescending, especially to women. Yes, he too was preeminent in his field, and certainly deserving of deference, but he treated students with respect, regardless of religious affiliation.

She looked Bonhoeffer in the eye and said, "I heard you speak out on the radio a couple days after Hitler was sworn in. You were warning people about him, how dangerous he is and how much a threat the Nazis represent to our country . . . and to the world." Bonhoeffer nodded. "But, I'm sorry to say, something went wrong with our radio. It went dead part way through."

Bonhoeffer looked at her solemnly. "There was nothing wrong with your radio, Fräulein. The Nazis cut the broadcast. They don't want to hear any opposition."

Annika was stunned, almost speechless. "B-but . . . what about free speech?"

"I think you'll find that many of the freedoms we've enjoyed under the Weimar regime are one-by-one going to disappear. It's already started. This new Reich that Hitler talks about, his so-called utopia . . . it's nothing but an illusion. It will only be possible by quashing most of the freedoms made possible over the past decade, maybe several decades. If allowed to persist, the Nazi version of utopia will be one of exclusivity, a society limited to those privileged enough to participate. Everyone else will be left out." Annika brushed the hair out of her eyes and adjusted the load of books she was carrying. "But enough about that for now," Bonhoeffer continued. "Listen . . . I know you have to get on your way, but I'd like to invite you to join a group of Christian students who meet with me once a week off campus. We discuss a whole variety of issues like these: theological, political, and social. The kids in the group are committed Christians and quite active socially. I think you'd fit in really well."

Annika was flabbergasted at being invited. "Absolutely," she said. "I'd love to take part. Thank you."

"So, let me ask. Would you mind if I called you by your first name?

"Certainly not. Please. My name is Annika."

I saw a painting yesterday. It was of a mariner, solitary and lost at sea with not even a moon to guide him. I stared at it, thinking that this is how I have been feeling here at the university. But maybe that's going to change.

Today Professor Bonhoeffer invited me to be part of a Christian fellowship he has with select students off campus. {27 February, 1933}

This was the breath of fresh air Annika had been hoping for. Until that moment, she had felt cut off from her peers. It hadn't been that way when she first arrived on campus, but now, within less than six months, she recognized that the students opposed to Nazism were increasingly in the minority. It was beyond her comprehension how anyone studying to be an intellectual could fail to grasp the dangers of fascism. She found it appalling how quickly anti-Semitism was spreading, but even scarier was the violence it spawned. To her, nationalism sounded almost tribal, a sinister throwback to pre-civilization.

Annika wasted no time in attending Bonhoeffer's extracurricular meetings and found great comfort in her companionship with his select group of theology students. Eager to learn more about him, she struggled with his book, *Akt und Sein*, but marveled at Bonhoeffer's courageousness in speaking out against the perils of fascism. She watched him throw down the gauntlet to church leaders throughout the country, challenging them to stand up boldly for Christian ethics, rather than hiding behind hollow words in their artificial Sunday sermons. Here was a man who didn't just pray, but actively applied his faith in advocating for social justice and responsibility. And he did so in a way that put his life in peril. Bonhoeffer gave Annika hope at a time when life felt like it could easily spin out of control.

Rally

The scum, which exists in every society, comes to the surface during troubled times.

Fyodor Dostoyevsky

10 February, 1933

It was Friday afternoon, and the Bonhoeffer group was meeting at the small parish off-campus. Annika was last to appear. Ten of their group were already sitting around a conference table. Several of them welcomed her as she pulled up a chair and began removing her coat.

"You might want to leave your coat on, Fräulein. We're all headed downtown," Matthias announced.

"Why? What's going on?" Annika asked.

"We're going to the Sportpalast. Gonna hear the *big speech*," Matthias drawled, making no effort to disguise his sarcasm.

"Where's Professor Bonhoeffer?"

"We're not sure," Lukas answered. "He may be out of town. Anyway, we figured we should represent the opposition."

It had only been two weeks since Hindenburg's transfer of power, and already the new Chancellor was to host a marquee event at Berlin's famed Sportpalast, the fourteen thousand seat sporting arena in the very heart of the city. Highly publicized, the speech was billed as Hitler's "Proclamation to the German Nation" and was to be broadcast on all German radio stations as well as many throughout the world.

"I don't understand. Why would you want to attend a Nazi rally? Isn't that just showing support for everything we stand opposed to?" Annika was confused.

"Yeah, maybe to them," Matthias responded. "But we're thinking there'll be some resistance groups there. If so, we can join them. Isn't that what Bonhoeffer has been preaching?"

Edmund spoke up. "Right . . . and if nothing else, our attendance proves that not everyone at the rally is a Nazi supporter."

Annika was nervous. She wanted to be true to her faith, but she wasn't ready to risk her already tenuous status at the university by engaging in resistance activities. "Is the professor going?" she asked.

"Not sure. We haven't heard from him. He may be out of town, but we're going anyway. If you want to come along, let's go."

Annika had no interest in attending the rally. In the short time since Hitler's appointment, Berlin had witnessed an unprecedented display of violence out on the streets, especially from the communists, and with Hitler's unexpected ascension to power, the SA stormtroopers had become increasingly bold and vicious, disrupting opposition party meetings, beating up rivals, and even arresting innocent civilians. Several people had been killed, and even among his supporters, the public had started to feel insecure, knowing that the *polizei* were tending not to intervene.

Despite that, Annika joined her friends out on the streets, where they hopped on a tram for the brief journey down to the Schöneberg section. They were lucky to get on, as it was jammed with rally-goers, all speaking at once. Hope, expectation, and fulfillment were written all over their faces; this was nothing short of a pilgrimage to see the man who was to save them, if not from outside forces, then maybe from themselves.

Once they arrived, though, Annika wished she had stayed back at the dorm. The ceremonials proved even more disturbing and incendiary than expected, so it was actually a twist of good fortune that seating inside was sold out. Her group, along with hundreds of others who couldn't get in, were all relegated to an outdoor plaza where loudspeakers had been placed so that no one would miss a word, even amid the clamor.

Doctor Goebbels, the opening speaker, began with an attack on what he called "the enemy press."

"Before the meeting begins, I would just like to take notice of a few articles from the Berlin press which assert that I shouldn't be allowed to broadcast over the German radio, since I'm . . . too much of a habitual liar to address the whole world . . .

"And if the Jewish press today believes that it can make veiled threats against the National Socialist movement . . . one day our patience will reach its end and the Jews' insolent lying mouths will be shut for them! . . . The Jewish insolence has lived longer in the past than it will live in the future. And soon we will teach (them) a thing or two they have never been taught before . . ."

He eventually got down to business, regaling the enthusiastic crowd with sleight-of-hand descriptions of Hitler as a near-mythical figure, a phenom who emerges *maybe* once a millennium or so.

"Yeah," whispered Annika to Edmund, "he's a phenom, alright. Like the asteroid that killed the dinosaurs . . ."

She turned to Edmund but was immediately silenced by his penetrating stare. He looked around nervously, hoping no one overheard her. And then, in a voice just loud enough for her alone to hear, said, "Annika, please! You want to get us beaten up? Keep those thoughts to yourself."

Annika was embarrassed, but the upbraiding was well-timed, as she and her friends were surrounded by passionate supporters of Hitler and this was not the stage for speaking out. Goebbels' introduction had an electrifying effect on the audience, which inside and out burst into cacophonies of *"Sieg Heil!"* Many waved the Nazi flag, which in such a brief period of time had begun to show up in public places all throughout the city. Goebbels had done a masterful job in firing up the crowd, stoking them for the main event.

When it was Hitler's turn to approach the podium, the crowd was wild with expectation. They watched his every movement as if this was a once-in-a-lifetime opportunity to witness a divine event, and

Hitler wasn't about to rob them of their beliefs. He stood at the dais not saying a word, allowing their excitement to build into booming chants and thunderous ovations. Only when he sensed their passion to be on the brink of overflowing did he break his silence, at which point his voice, crackling through the loudspeakers, began softly, even sounding somewhat meek and tentative. The crowd quieted, not wanting to miss a single word. Hitler was a master of oratorical foreplay, and in no time, he had the adoring crowd in the palm of his hands. He was like an orchestral conductor, measuring his rhythm while teasing his audience with small gestures that would progress into raving gesticulations, making him appear, if only for a moment, unhinged. His voice spanned many octaves fluctuating from softness to bellicosity and back again, so loud and so intense that the loudspeakers might have burst in his crescendo of his maniacal zeal.

Hitler's speech culminated on a climactic note. When it was all over, the crowd basked in ecstasy as if a powerful orgasm had just washed over them. Maybe Hitler was taking a page from Freud. The Nazis' forbearance in rooting out the sexual permissiveness of the Weimar regime seemed to be tapping that same collective libido for the energy it needed to militate against Jews, homosexuals, and *Ausländers* near and far. Here was sex by proxy.

Whatever their motivation, it was lost on Annika's coterie. "I would have preferred seeing Max Schmeling, to be honest with you," Edmund said, as their small group broke free of the crowd.

"I agree," Walter replied. "At least then we coulda' seen someone get the crap beat outta him . . ."

". . . instead of feeling like we got the crap beat out of *us*," Matthias added, laconically.

Two weeks later, Annika was awakened by the wailing of sirens. She had attended classes for almost seven straight hours, and following supper had spent a few more hours studying. By 2000 hours, she had reached the point where her mind simply refused to absorb any more material. Her eyes had begun to close, and though

58

she fought to stay awake, she fell into a deep sleep. It was only an hour, though, before she was awakened by the wailing of sirens. Normally, she could ignore them as they were common in the city, but this time they were accompanied by an incessant rattling of her window created by an unending convoy of heavy, emergency vehicles out on the street. Soon to follow was a staccato of footsteps clambering down the stairwell. Slowly, zombie-like, she dragged herself out of bed, wrapped a blanket around her shoulders, and entered the hallway.

"What's going on?" she asked, as Marie Kraus hurried past.

"The Reichstag's on fire," Marie answered, breathlessly. "You can see it in the distance . . . out the downstairs window." She continued running, beckoning Annika to follow, and together they descended two flights of stairs to the east-facing window. Pressing her face sideways against the glass, Annika could see a bright orange glow over the rooftops that was so intense, it illuminated a heavy, dark plume of smoke billowing from the flames. High above, the clouds flickered as if a strobe-light was announcing a theatrical performance.

Several of the girls went out onto the porch to get a better view. Not Annika. She had seen enough over the past few weeks, and needed sleep more than anything. She returned to her room, where she spent the next several hours tossing and turning in bed, never getting into a deep sleep.

Seven in the morning came much too early. She made her way to breakfast, where it seemed everyone was talking about the fire.

"They think it was deliberately set," claimed one.

"I heard it was the communists," said another.

"I don't know . . . That's not what the *Tageblatt* claimed."

"Yeah, well, everyone knows you can't trust that rag. What'd the firemen say?"

The table was buzzing with rumor. Everyone had a theory, but no one had the facts.

59

Democracy Abdicates

Nationalism is one of the effective ways in which the modern man escapes life's ethical problems.
Reinhold Niebuhr

<u>24 March, 1933</u>

Annika found herself confronting a looming reality: those opposed to the Nazis were shrinking, almost by the hour. There had been talk of an uprising, but so far it had failed to materialize. People had for so long assumed the Nazis could never win that now, with the Nazis having a plurality, the opposition was melting. She could actually see people switching allegiance, choosing to be with the mainstream where it felt safer. Membership in the Nazi party soared almost overnight, making the Fascists feel virtually untouchable; that they could do or say anything, no matter how discriminatory, how intimidating or brutal. Who was going to stop them?

Who, indeed? Annika thought, as she walked into the library. She found a vacant table, where she began to spread out her books and notepads. In front of her was the day's issue of the *Reichsgesetzblatt*, which someone had left behind. She picked it up with the intention of tossing it on the sofa behind her when something caught her eye. Unfurling the newspaper, she cringed. There on the front page was an announcement of new laws enabling the Nazis to arrest and incarcerate without trial persons thought to be enemies of the regime. Because of the Reichstag fire, Hitler had convinced the president that evil forces threatened to bring down all established order and that unusual measures were needed to combat the threat. The paper reported that Hindenburg agreed, and with the stroke of a pen, Germany had relinquished its rule of law. Henceforth, all political parties were banned, and detentions could now be made legally simply on suspicion of dissent.

The announcements took the wind right out of her. She looked out the window where she could see across campus. People were moving about normally, as if nothing had happened. But for Annika, the whole world had changed. Any thought of studying was inconceivable. Sitting over in a far corner of the library with his back to her was Jürgen, a student she had become friendly with through Doctor Bonhoeffer's class. She scooped up books and walked over to him, dropping the newspaper on the book in front of him.

"And a good morning to you, too," Jürgen said, with a bit of good-natured sarcasm. "To what do I owe this pleasure?"

Annika was in no humor for small talk. "Did you see this?" she asked, pointing to the paper.

"Of course, I have."

"And . . ." She was desperate to talk.

"*And* . . . I think we're screwed." He looked up at her, his face reddening slightly. "I apologize. Let me rephrase that. I think we're in grave trouble, Annika. Almost overnight we've become a police-state. Did you hear about the pardons?"

"No."

"You know . . . the five men who were sentenced for murdering the communist official." Annika nodded. "Yeah, well, Hitler's pardoned 'em. In fact, he's declared a general amnesty for all imprisoned Nazis. How's that for justice? Doesn't matter what they did. Meanwhile, his henchmen now have carte blanche to go around arresting whoever they want. No trials, nothing."

"So, Jürgen. Where's the resistance . . . the opposition?"

"Sitting right here in the library. Or out there in people's living rooms. Or in whispered conversations at the market. Everywhere but out on the streets. Annika, don't you realize? Everyone's scared. The Communists were the best chance for a challenge, but the leaders have disappeared, almost overnight. How can you legally resist when presidential candidates, like Thalmann, are arrested the day before the elections? It's a joke."

"It's true. I thought there were actually some students who shared my views, but it seems that so many of them are now siding with the goons."

"Of course, they are," said Jürgen. "No one wants to get their ass kicked, much less get arrested. I'm sure you've heard them talking about building prison camps."

"Yeah. I have. The KZ's."

"KZ?" Jürgen looked quizzical.

"Yeah, *konzentrationlagers*. The concentration camps." She seemed to wince at saying the words.

"Oh, right. Where they intend to dump all the protesters. So not surprising that a lot of people are feeling safer joining up with the Nazis rather than risking their lives by opposing them." Jürgen rubbed his forehead and sighed. "Unfortunately, that seems to be the way things are heading. We're losing our democracy.

"I just heard that most of the people taken into custody by the SA are being jailed in a camp on Friedrichstrasse. Can you believe that? There wasn't even a jail there. The SA is improvising prisons, even using houses as holding facilities."

Annika and Jürgen were overheard by another student, Hans Lichter, who turned in his chair to confront them. "Why do you whisper?" he asked in a loud voice so that anyone in the vicinity could hear his pseudo-patriotism. "You both sound like communists." Several heads turned in their direction.

Jürgen lowered his head and whispered, "Please, Hans. Keep your voice down."

But Hans simply straightened up like a bantam rooster and said, "Why keep our voices down? Are you afraid that people will hear you defend Jews?"

"Hans, get real. The SA are out there beating up innocent people. They're Germans, citizens of Germany – many of them even fought for Germany in the Great War."

"Innocent? Is that what you call it? People determined to keep our government dysfunctional simply to benefit themselves? To keep themselves fat and rich? That's the problem with you Jew-lovers. You're brainwashed by the damn Hymies."

"You're a bigot, Hans. Why don't you keep your thoughts to yourself? They certainly don't dignify you," Jürgen said.

"Whatsa matter, Jürgen? Am I hurting your feelings?" And then before Jürgen could respond, Hans said, "Wait, wait. I get it. You're a kike yourself, aren't you?"

Jürgen was not Jewish, but he had heard enough. Red-faced, he jumped to his feet, standing only inches away from his heckler's face, fists balled at his side. "I told you to shut the fuck up, Lichter!"

Hans took a step back, but looking around, he realized that almost everyone on the second floor was now aware of the commotion, and not wanting to appear weak, he persisted. "You may not like it, you and your little Fräulein here, but the people out there getting arrested are *enemies*, got it? They're not friends!"

At that moment, another student, large and broad-shouldered, someone unknown to Annika and Jürgen, sauntered over to the table. Standing next to Hans, he picked up where Hans had left off. "Lichter's right. The scum he's referring to . . ." he said, pointing to the window, "they've betrayed our fatherland. They *ought* to be rounded up." He used the palm of his hand to slick back a lock of thin, blond hair that had fallen into one eye. "I'll tell you what the truth is. One person gets beaten up and the newspapers rush in to glorify it as if we're all under some kinda dictatorship." Looking down at Annika, he said, "You guys are only freshmen. I'd say your ideas are sophomoric, but that would be an insult to the sophomores. Grow up and stop thinking like adolescents," he said with a laugh.

That was all Hans needed to feel further emboldened. "I see your biology books. Let me tell you something. Once you read *Principles of Human Heredity and Race Hygiene,* you'll realize that National Socialism is on the cutting edge of science. It'll teach you all about inferior races."

"Is that right? Well let me tell *you* something, Lichter. I have no interest in unscientific literature, so I wouldn't waste my time even looking at that degenerate horseshit," Jürgen replied.

"You hear that?" Hans said, turning to the students at other tables, his outstretched arm pointing directly at Jürgen. "Degenerate horseshit," he repeated, mockingly. "He's referring to Herr Professor Eugen Fischer, the man whom *der Führer* himself has nominated to be the new rector of our university." By this point, a few other students had gathered around the table, giving Hans even greater confidence. Throwing his head back, he declared with a voice dripping with condescension, "the more you young pups learn, the more you'll realize how simple and childish your leftist views are."

One of the other students slapped Hans on the back, then turned to Jürgen with a smile. "On your vacation in Oranienberg, smart-ass, you'll find out that you're the one full of horseshit." Then raising his right arm, he barked, "*Heil Hitler!*" Several other students quickly responded in kind.

Any further arguments were useless. Feeling outnumbered and humiliated, Annika and Jürgen gathered up their paraphernalia and headed towards the staircase. As they did, Hans belted out the first stanza of "The Song of Germany." Those around him chimed in.

> *Deutschland, Deutschland über alles,*
> *Über alles in der Welt . . .*

Annika and Jurgen wanted no parts of that. They disappeared through the stacks of books as a librarian rushed past in the opposite direction. They had not even gotten to the door when they heard the students upstairs breaking out into the Horst Wessel song, "*Die Fahne hoch.*" It was impossible not to recognize the tune. It was the Nazi party anthem adopted in 1930 after the assassination of Wessel, who at the time was the commander of the SA Brownshirts in Berlin. Now he lived on as a martyr.

That night, Annika wrote in her journal:

Fräulein

. . . Hindenburg is a fool. He gave in to the maniac, and now Germany is officially a police state. God help us... {24 March, 1933}

Scapegoats

Love, friendship and respect do not unite people as much as a common hatred for something.

Anton Chekhov

1 April, 1933

Annika left the dorm in search of a few toiletries downtown. She hadn't gotten more than a block or so before seeing a line of ten or twelve stormtroopers standing in front of Ehape, one of the more modern, low-priced department stores. It appeared that they were actually barricading the entrance, though there was no indication of why. Concerned, Annika continued on, eventually coming to Heitinger's, a higher-end clothier, where a similar scene was playing out. Not only were four uniformed SA men standing in the doorway, but scrawled in white paint on each of the store's four large windows was the word, *Jude!*, evidently signifying Jewish ownership. One of the guards was picketing the store with a placard reading, *"Deutsche. Wehrt Euch. Kauft nicht bei Juden!"* which translated means, "Germans. Defend yourselves. Do not buy from Jews!"

Annika spotted an older woman, probably in her sixties or so, standing a short distance away. She was facing the store. "What's going on?" Annika asked her.

The woman turned, her face wrinkled in bewilderment. "What's going on?" she asked, as if Annika's question must have been some kind of joke. "Fräulein, today's the one-day boycott of Jewish businesses."

Now it was Annika's turn to appear puzzled. It took a moment for this revelation to really sink in. "The one-day boycott?" Annika

66

looked back at the building and the soldiers. "Why are they boycotting?"

The woman looked at her first in disbelief, then with an air of suspicion. "What do you mean, '*Why?*'" she asked. "Why, in God's name, *not*? The Jews are enemies of the State. Not too hard to figure out. After all their cheating and conniving with Communists, they don't deserve to do business in Germany! They sold us out in the last war, and ever since, they've been trying to take over the world."

It struck Annika that the woman's statements were almost verbatim quotes from Goebbels. "Take over the world? How have they been doing that?" Annika couldn't restrain herself from challenging the elderly Frau.

The woman, though, twisted her face in a look of obvious disdain. Her eyes traced Annika's figure from her face down to her shoes and back again. Then squinting one eye, like a detective, she stared at Annika's face, her gaze shifting repeatedly from one eye to the other. After a slight pause, she asked, "You're not a Jew, are you?"

Annika was caught momentarily off-guard. To her, it sounded less like a question than an accusation. She had the unsettling feeling that she was being interrogated. "No, no. Of course not," she said, looking back at the woman, hoping not to appear uncomfortable.

The woman wasn't convinced. She lowered her eyebrows, cocked her head slightly to the side, but kept her eyes fixed on Annika, as if seeing through some kind of subterfuge. She then glanced over to the SA men, which suddenly made Annika feel that the woman was going to turn her over to the authorities. But that wasn't the case. Instead, the ill-suited dowager, after studying Annika for several more seconds, relaxed her posture and exhaled. Out of the corner of her mouth, she grunted, "Well, count your blessings," by which she meant not being Jewish, "because there's more in store for them, mark my words." And then, as if the encounter never happened, she turned dismissively and ambled away, slowly melting into the crowd of onlookers.

Annika was drained. The confrontation was so unexpected, and the woman's words – her tone, her overall manner – it all seemed so . . . sinister. Contemplating what had just transpired triggered a wave of panic. She realized that her heart was pounding, her breathing short and constricted. It was just like the time in her dorm room where she had felt light-headed, almost like she was going to pass out, maybe even vomit. She had to remind herself over and over that it was not she who was in danger. That helped, but only partially. It was impossible to remove herself from the reality of the discrimination against merchants with whom she was familiar, who were in every sense of the word neighbors.

It was clear that shopping today was no longer an option. She wanted to get back to campus where things would feel safe and secure. Maybe taking a different set of streets would avoid similar disturbances. Her hope was short-lived. There in front of F.W. Woolworth's 5&10 were more Brownshirts, jack-booted paramilitaries carrying signs just like she had witnessed a few blocks earlier. The scene here, though, tugged more fervently at her heartstrings, as this time there were not just curious bystanders, but smiling, joking spectators, some even jeering, joyous at the opportunity of venting deeply-held prejudices.

She made a wide berth of the melee. Walking briskly for about five minutes, she couldn't get back to her dorm soon enough. An ineffable reality was closing in on her. Up ahead, she could see the familiar spire of a Lutheran church, a sight that had always given her comfort, a steeple pointing to heaven symbolizing salvation through God's loving grace. For a fleeting moment, she relaxed. Out front was a sign boldly proclaiming Christ's resurrection while extending a welcome to all, newcomers included. *To all?* she wondered. *Would Jews be welcome? How about Negroes? Or Moslems?* Hypocrisy had never been clearer.

While walking home, it occurred to her that her denial of Jewishness to the old woman, while technically correct, was in some ways cowardly. It was a way to fit in, a way of avoiding conflict. And then she thought of Jesus, and how some of His disciples seemed to abandon Him during His time of need. She felt that even though not Jewish herself, she was somehow guilty for not having spoken up. Throughout the day, she could not stop thinking about her behavior.

Talking with Jürgen later that evening, Annika asked him, "Should I have stood up to her? Maybe debated her?"

"You would've been taking a big risk, Annika. You'd have definitely drawn a crowd, just like we did in the library, and you probably would've found yourself in the minority."

"What I really find confusing is the Church. Where are they in all of this?"

"You know as well as I do that the Lutheran Church is embracing Nazism. They put branches on the cross to create the swastika . . . you know, the 'hooked cross.' As Bonhoeffer told us, the German Christians are as antisemitic as the Nazis."

"How is that possible?" Annika asked, with all the innocence of a babe-in-the-woods. "It goes against everything I was brought up to believe."

"It's not unprecedented, Annika. Christian antisemitism goes way back. Remember, Martin Luther railed against Jews who wouldn't convert to Christianity. The difference is that Luther wasn't against Jews as a people. He simply encouraged them to convert. But the Nazis have made him out to have been one of history's foremost anti-Semites."

"Right, and German Lutherans are buying it – hook, line and sinker. This is crazy. People don't know what to believe. History is being openly reinterpreted . . . *with lies!* Don't you think we should be out there resisting this madness?"

"Think about it, Annika. Do you really want to be doing that at this point in your life? You're here working for a degree, pursuing a future. Expressing your beliefs on a street corner, or even here in what many think of as a liberal university, it could be the end of everything. The Nazis are in control, and there are just too many of them."

Jürgen was right. She knew of no organized resistance at this point, and besides, it would be political suicide to openly challenge the Nazis right now, especially on their home turf. As troubled as she was, she had to remain focused on her studies if she was to stay in school. German universities were among the most challenging in the world, doubly so for a woman. And that unsettling experience with Jürgen in the library taught Annika very quickly that if she expected to succeed, she needed to be much more circumspect with what she said in public.

Sleep didn't come easily that night. Her journal entry reflected her inner conflict.

I've never experienced anything like this. Up until now, my world has always felt reasonably safe and predictable. Revolutions and social unrest seemed to be things that happened to other people in other lands.

No more. It's going on all around me. I worry about the future or if I will even have a future. I see so muchnhypocrisy. Some of the very people who worship in my Church are the same ones out on the streets advocating for Hitler. Sometimes I feel like a hypocrite myself for simply being a bystander. {1 April, 1933}

Terror

The best political weapon is the weapon of terror. Cruelty commands respect. Men may hate us. But we don't ask for their love; only for their fear.

Heinrich Himmler

<u>18 September, 1935: Women's Dormitory, Berlin.</u>

"Tritzchler, you have a message." It was Frau Schindler, the dorm proctor.

"Oh . . . I hope I didn't forget a meeting," Annika replied. She had just returned from a full day of classes. Wednesdays were her favorite, the days she was scheduled to spend mostly in the science labs. This was a new academic year and promised to be her most exciting yet. She was now a junior with the distinction of being recognized as an upperclassman. Already projecting herself into the future, she was hoping to continue a family legacy in medicine. But that was still a long way off. Tonight, she looked forward to rest, starting with supper, a bit of socializing, and then settling into some quiet reading.

"*Vielen dank*," she said. Reaching for the paper in Schindler's hand, she lost her grip on one of the books cradled in her arms, and in making a quick effort to catch it, all the other books dropped to her feet. Fluttering along with them like a dying butterfly was the dorm proctor's message. The floor had been transformed into a smorgasbord of books and papers. "Great way to end the day . . ." Annika joked half-heartedly as she leaned over to begin retrieving her belongings. Other girls walked by, tittering at the mess Annika had created, and in her embarrassment, she almost forgot what had caused

71

the imbroglio in the first place. But then something caught her eye. It was the message.

Plopping her books on the counter in front of her, Annika read the crumpled memo. *"Your father has been hospitalized. He is at the Jüdischen Krankenhaus."* Annika's pulse quickened. The Jewish Hospital.

She ran up to her room, dropped off the load of books, and returned to the streets in the fading daylight. A short walk, and she was on the streetcar headed to the Wedding district, which she knew well. The fifteen-minute ride seemed to take forever. *What could be the matter with Papa?* She ran towards the hospital, yet in her haste stumbled on an uplifted part of the sidewalk and wound up with a skinned knee. "Lord, help me," she screamed, making no effort to disguise her exasperation. She wiped off the dirt and was back on her feet scurrying along the Iranischestrasse and up the steps of the old hospital. There in the dimly-lit lobby was her mother, whom Annika was not expecting so suddenly.

"Mutti!" she cried out. Her mother turned, and without even having recognized Annika, she was enveloped in a desperate embrace. "Mutti," Annika asked, "my God, what's going on? Where's Papa?"

"Oh, Annika. I'm so happy to see you. I'm so sorry to pull you away from your work . . ."

"Never mind my work," Annika said. "Why's Papa in the hospital?"

"Honey, your father's upstairs. He's OK, but he's been through quite an ordeal."

Annika was clutching her mother by the sleeves of her wool coat. "Well, tell me," she implored. "What happened?"

Eva's eyes welled-up with tears. "He was on his way to work this morning . . . a normal day . . . and was assaulted by a group of SA thugs. It was on the Alexanderplatz. They worked him over pretty well. He's upstairs in a ward. We're allowed to see him, but I need to prepare you, he's full of bruises and can hardly talk. I think his jaw is

72

broken."

Tears instantly filled Annika's eyes. "He can't talk?" She was dumbfounded.

"You'll see, dear. Let's go upstairs." With that, they were off, Annika literally pulling her mother to keep pace. Together they hurried through a maze of confusing corridors, up two flights of stairs, and down a hallway before entering a large ward with metal beds lined on both sides of the wall. The smell was a mixture of bandages, antiseptics and human waste – blood, feces, urine, and vomit – a bit overpowering for the uninitiated. Were it not for her mother's previous visit, Annika would have had difficulty locating her stepfather, and not simply because all the patients, covered as they were in white linens, resembled one another.

When they reached Otto's bed, Annika was not fully prepared for what she saw. His face was almost hidden under gauze, and his eyes were dark and swollen, the left one completely shut. His jaw appeared to be wired. "Oh my God. Papa," Annika muttered. She clutched his hand. She tried to appear stoical, but her eyes were awash in tears. "How could anyone do this?" On one side of the bed was a tray of bandages, scissors, and related implements. Next to him on the other side was a bottle of fluid suspended from a pole that was tethered to Otto's arm by a black rubber tube.

In spite of his discomfort, he managed a tiny smile, the best he could muster, upon seeing his daughter. "Hey there . . . *Pits'l*," he murmured, so softly she could barely hear him. The effort caused him to wince, but he continued. "How . . . are you?"

Her lips quivering, Annika sobbed, "Oh, Papa . . . how am I? Really. It's you we're worried about. I'm fine, but please, don't try to talk." She gently stroked his head with one hand, and wiped the drool from his lips with her other. "I am so, so sorry," she sobbed. She wanted to hug him, but his right arm was suspended from a frame over his head.

"The doctor told me he has a partial fracture, honey. Better to not touch him," warned Eva.

Otto stared lovingly up to his stepdaughter. "I . . . I'm going to be fine, honey . . . I'll be up . . . and around . . . in no time."

The nurse came over and told Eva and Annika that Otto had just gotten an injection of morphine. "It's best to let him sleep now. He really needs to rest. It's not just his jaw. He has some internal injuries as well. Doctor Rosenstein suspects his spleen is ruptured. And he has cracked ribs. Fortunately, liver and kidney seem okay, but it's going to take time for him to heal."

Annika bent down and kissed his forehead. As she did, Otto closed his eyes and smiled. Eva followed suit, putting her hand gently on his head while whispering something into his ear. Whatever she said caused Otto himself to tear up. With that, they left him.

"Who did this?" Annika asked her mother. "And why?"

"We suspect it was Nazi sympathizers, Annika. But we don't have any real information."

"There must have been witnesses, Mutti. If it was on the Alexanderplatz . . . in broad daylight."

"I'm sure there were people around. Probably lots of people. But no one would give any information. Every person questioned by the police said they saw nothing . . ."

"Yeah, I'm sure. Everyone's too scared to stick their necks out," Annika opined.

"That . . . and . . . oh, I hate to even say it . . ." Eva started to cry.

"It's okay, Mutti." Annika hugged her mother. "You don't have to say anything."

"Well, honey, we can't keep our heads in the sand. Let's face it; there is so much hatred out there . . . mostly of Jews. These are people we've been around our whole lives, people we've done business with . . . people your Papa's treated, even bringing their babies into the world." She dabbed at her eyes, first one then the other. "A lot of them are only too happy to see a Jew getting beaten up, especially one like your Papa who appears well-to-do."

Annika felt her anger rising. "*Ja, Mutti*. And you think the police care? No! They just stand by while someone like Papa gets beaten to a pulp. Probably out of uniform they would do the same Goddamn thing."

"Annika!" Eva was shocked. She had never heard Annika utter an obscenity. "The Lord's name in vain?"

"In vain? Really, Mutti? Papa nearly killed while those who are paid to protect him do nothing? Then yes. God damn them to hell!" She stood facing her mother, her hands balled into fists at her side. Eva reached forward to hold her in a tight embrace. As their cheeks touched, they could each feel one another's tears.

Monsters. We're surrounded by monsters. Papa was almost killed. An old man, savagely beaten because he's Jewish.

He's lucky to be alive. I don't know how we can survive this horror. {18 September, 1935}

Autumn

Our friends show us what we can do; our enemies teach us what we must do.

Johann Wolfgang von Goethe

28 October, 1935

Herbst. The season between summer and winter when cooler weather turns leaves into a kaleidoscope of colors before coaxing them from their once-nourishing branches. Today, Saturday, had dawned unusually mild, and were it not for the colorful foliage sprinkled along the city streets, one may have mistaken it for just another summer day. For Annika today was to be a respite, an opportunity to forget about life for a while. Her mother had called earlier in the week to propose a weekend outing like they had done so often in the past. "Spend some time together while the weather's on our side," her mother had said. Family daytrips had become all but forgotten since Annika had moved into university housing, and that made this day unusually special. They were to meet at the Tiergarten, just the three of them.

Annika was eager for a break from her studies. Sure, the semester was still young, but this little breather was already well-deserved. With a sumptuous blue sky overhead, she found it more agreeable to walk rather than ride the tram, and doing so brought her face-to-face with people, young and old, couples and families, lazily window shopping, seated at park benches, or congregated around Parisian-like tables at the numerous sidewalk cafes dotting both sides of Unter den Linden. There was no mistaking that they were soaking up what had to be the last rays of an unusually long summer.

76

Nestled along the main thoroughfare were an assortment of beer gardens, Berlin's famous *kneipen*, and what a time for them. This was *Oktoberfest*, that two-week ritual dating back to 1810 when Ludwig, the Crown Prince of Bavaria, was wedded to his beloved Therese. Annika couldn't help sharing in the excitement as she walked past the outdoor pubs. Glancing at partygoers seated at heavy wooden tables or sashaying under gaily decorated tents, she was amused to think that probably few of them had any had idea of how the tradition originated, not that ignorance would interfere with merrymaking, especially with this year marking the festival's 125th anniversary.

"Come and join the fun, Fräulein," pitched a hawker on the sidewalk. Above him was his rathskeller's medieval-looking sign, *Die Schlange und die Jungfrau* ("The Serpent and the Virgin"), showing a large snake curled seductively around a damsel's nubile body.

"*Nein, danke*," Annika demurred, pausing just long enough to look beyond portals adorned with hop vines and colorful Bavarian flags. Men and women of all ages, many garbed in lederhosen and drindls, were engaged in spirited, if sodden, conversation, while couples waltzed to the brassy tunes of a backyard oom-pah band. It was quite a spectacle, intrinsically German, and one deserving of her attention, even if she thought it a good bet that not all of the twosomes were paired up with the same partner they had entered with.

"Ah, you like, yes?" the vendor asked, grinning. Annika turned from him back to the entertainment, where she noticed a braided blonde barmaid with heaving breasts spilling out of a lowcut blouse drawing unapologetic stares from a bevy of lecherous old men already deep in their cups. In each fist, the woman clutched heavy semicircles of frothy, amber mugs. Just as Annika turned to answer the man, a wobbly patron gave a bold pinch to the alewife's curvaceous backside, eliciting a high-pitched squeal and throaty laughter that could surely be heard around the block. The brazen act must have been on a dare from the guffawing menfolk.

"Keep it in your pants," commanded the waitress, tongue in

cheek, as foamy beer sloshed from the mugs. She seemed to take it all in stride.

"A little too risqué for my taste," Annika joked.

"*Nein, nein, Fräulein.* Just a lively den of good-natured immorality," he retorted with a wink.

Annika couldn't disagree. Couched against a colorful backdrop of blue and white streamers along with an aroma of barbequed wieners and sausages was the almost forgotten spirit of *Gemütlichkeit.* It was a warmth and friendliness of people enjoying themselves, having fun, putting aside their differences. And it wasn't just the tavern. Everywhere she strolled on this balmy afternoon rang forth in *gemeinschaft* – that tradition of community where people were as unified as the ingredients comprising their bubbly. Everything was in good fun. She left the street vendor with a kittenish wave and smile, walking westward to the sounds of Bavarian drinking songs and foam-covered steins clinking out toasts to a Teutonic legacy, real or imagined.

It wasn't far to the Tiergarten. She was to meet her parents at the Victory Column in the Königsplatz, a small commemorative section of the park which Annika knew well. Entering the park, munificent in its natural surroundings, Annika felt, perhaps for the first time in months, happily unburdened of her stress. It would be wonderful to visit with her parents. The tower shone like a beacon, high above the trees as she strolled along the old Siegesallee. Flitting from branch to branch in the lush trees high above were the colorful songbirds for which the Tiergarten was famous. Too late in the season for mating, the varied species were flocking for their annual sojourn to warmer climes. Underneath the canopy, people strolled contentedly by as if they hadn't a care in the world. Two young children chased past Annika in a lighthearted game of tag, reminding her of her own childhood.

Eventually, she spotted her parents, alone and in conversation on a secluded bench adjacent to one of the many statues. Surrounding them were an assortment of well-tended flowers and manicured bushes, the blazing reds and oranges betraying resplendent signs of the winter to come. But preparing for winter would have to wait. For now, the sight of her parents was the perfect complement to a morning of sunshine, radiant colors, and warmth.

They greeted each other with enthusiastic hugs and kisses, and for a moment, but only a moment, Annika was able to forget her stepfather's ordeal. His one eye remained partially swollen and there was a bandage over his left temple, where his hair had been shaved to treat an underlying laceration. Annika could see a dark colored stain, presumably an antiseptic, peeking out from both sides of the dressing. She also noticed he winced a couple of times when talking. The overall scene brought renewed tears to her eyes.

"Papa," she asked, "how are you feeling?"

"I'm okay," he answered. "Why don't we take a walk. We can talk." He got to his feet with Eva's help and supported himself with a cane, which he had never used in the past.

"Why walk?" Annika asked. "Let's just sit here and talk." She didn't want to burden her stepfather with any unneeded effort.

"No, honey," said her mother. "we really need to walk." Annika looked puzzled, making no effort to move. Eva continued, "With what happened to your father, we're feeling like we need a little privacy. Please."

Annika sensed urgency in her mother's voice, so together they began walking down one of the paths, eventually coming to a small grassy area surrounded by large deciduous trees. "This'll do. Why don't we sit over there, under the shade," Otto suggested, pointing to the base of a large tree. The grass was soft and inviting, and as Annika spread out a sheet, Eva opened her basket and began to distribute sandwiches she had prepared earlier. High above them, a raven broke the serenity. Annika and her parents looked up just as another raven, black as the ace of spades, landed on a limb a short distance away. Within a minute, the two blackbirds were joined by a third, then a fourth, each of them cawing to one another. Annika got up and waved at them, hoping to scare them away. One by one, they flew off with a racket.

Annika returned to her plot of grass, as Eva handed her a glass of lemonade. "Annika, we brought you here so we could talk freely. As you know, your father and I have been through a huge ordeal. It's caused us to do a lot of soul-searching."

She had Annika's full attention, when Otto chimed in, "People are being denounced to the Gestapo almost daily, *Pits'l*." Otto added, brushing away a honeybee, "My assault was . . . if you'll excuse the pun . . . a walk-in-the-park compared to what would happen to me if I got arrested by the Gestapo. We've heard some horror stories."

Annika shot a quick glance to her mother, then looked back at Otto. "I-I don't understand, Papa. Why would you run afoul of the Gestapo?" This was exactly what Annika had feared, but to now hear it acknowledged by her stepfather, himself, took her by surprise.

"Things are no longer safe here," Otto began. "You've been trying to warn us. Down deep, I knew that what you were saying was true, but I didn't want you to worry. The truth is, you've been right."

Eva jumped in, "Honey, people are being arrested for things as simple as laughing at an innocent joke. Nothing seems safe anymore now that the Nazis have taken over. So, what we're going to tell you needs to be said in privacy. It can't be repeated." Annika straightened up, not knowing what she was going to hear.

Otto grasped Annika's hands in his own, and, looking her straight in the eye, said, "It's time to go, Annika. We need to get out of Germany."

Eva put her hands over top of Annika's with Otto's hands beneath. She gave Annika a light squeeze, as if to reassure her that everything would work out fine. "Annika, honey, we want you to come with us."

Annika's mind was swirling. What started out as a beautiful day had suddenly turned into a nightmare. In the distance, the ravens had resumed their cackling. Annika didn't want to believe things had gone this far, even though down deep she had anticipated it long ago. She saw her whole world crashing in. "I don't understand," she said, as tears welled up in her deep blue eyes. "Where are you going?"

It was Otto's turn to respond. *"Pits'l,* it's like this. The climate here in Berlin has become too threatening for me. The stuff that we thought was just a passing fad, stuff that we thought would gradually fade away . . . well, it's turned into a wave of anti-Jewish legislation. My practice as a physician is already sharply curtailed, and there's every reason to expect that Jewish doctors will soon be stripped of their license to practice. It's not just doctors, though. The same is happening to professionals all over Germany."

"But Papa, you're head of the whole department. How can they get rid of you?" Annika asked.

"Oh, honey, believe me, they not only can, they have! It's all part of the race theory. Jews are inferior and shouldn't be mixing with so-called Aryans at all. Having a Jewish doctor treat an Aryan is now considered unhealthy. We might contaminate them."

"That doesn't even make sense," Annika protested. "You yourself have told me over the years of how many scientific advances have been made by Jewish doctors – way more, if I remember correctly, than Gentiles."

"Doesn't matter, Annika. The Nuremberg Laws have stripped Jews of citizenship. It's only a matter of time before Jewish doctors are purged."

Sensing her daughter's anguish, Eva quickly added, "So that's why we're concerned about getting out of the country while there's still time, honey."

"But you have a lot of friends," Annika protested.

"Friends don't mean so much anymore, I'm sorry to say," Otto said. He took off his hat to wipe his brow before filling his pipe. "Anti-Semites are coming out of the woodwork," he said, sucking the flame into the bowl. "Not many people are going to stand up for us. Friends, neighbors, colleagues – people who used to show us respect and friendship – it's like they've all disappeared. Whether they're under the spell of Hitler or just too scared to voice opposition, more and more people want nothing to do with us. So many of them, people you'd never have suspected, now seem to despise Jews." Smoke curled from his pipe before being swallowed up in the air. "I never realized how much hatred there is out there."

Annika leaned back against the tree trunk. She looked skyward, as if searching for answers hiding in the puffy clouds overhead. "So, what are you both planning to do?"

"Your mother and I are thinking that we can all go to Belgium. I have friends there who have offered to put us up while we get settled. There are opportunities for me to resume my practice in Brussels."

"Move to Belgium? Leave Berlin . . . for Brussels? Are you sure?" Annika was clearly not prepared for that. "You've been telling me all along that this is just a passing phase and that people will eventually rise up against Hitler. Couldn't we try to just ride it out?"

"If we wait much longer," Otto responded, "the Nazis may pull our passports. Right now, they're encouraging Jews to leave, but with all the talk about exterminating Jews, I'm not sure how much longer they'll be granting exit visas."

"Not to mention," Eva added, "that most of the western countries are setting strict quotas on emigrating Jews. It seems most of them don't want us . . ."

Annika sat rubbing her head, elbows on her knees. "This is all too much . . ." she said, shaking her head.

Eva added, "You've been in school, Dear, and haven't seen a lot of what your father's been exposed to. Not only was he beaten up, but . . ."

Otto cut her off. "My own colleagues are shunning me, Annika. I can't survive if I don't have work. But even worse, we've had people at the hospital simply disappear. And I don't mean they've simply been fired. Last month, the Gestapo came into the hospital and arrested Doctor Rosenstein. No apparent cause. Said he was 'needed downtown to answer some questions.'" Otto held up two fingers on each hand to signify quotation marks. "That was a month ago. No one has seen him since. Imagine, Rosenstein! He was a leading histologist." Otto looked directly into Annika's eyes. "And he's not alone. Doctors from other departments have disappeared, as well."

Annika was shaken. "I believe you, Papa. We've had some notable professors at the university whose posts have been vacated. I'm assuming not by their own choice."

For a minute or two, there was silence. The three of them sat huddled close together, no one knowing quite what to say. It was hard to deny a premonition of some unknown horror yet to come. Where there had once been a glimmer of disbelief – faith that somehow, at some point, they would wake up from this growing nightmare and all would return to normal – this discussion dispelled all of that. They sat for a few minutes, no one uttering a word. It was late afternoon, and above them came the call of a nightingale.

Otto was next to break the silence. "So, we have train tickets to Brussels, Annika. We're all . . . "

Annika was stunned. "Papa, I . . . I can't . . ." She looked to Otto, then Eva, then up to the sky, hardly able to say what she knew would change her life forever. She grabbed their hands, one in each of her own. "I can't go with you," she stammered. Otto and Eva looked at each other, then quickly back to Annika as she continued. "Folks, I'm in my final year at the university, not all that far from graduation, and Professor Schneider said I have a very good chance of getting into the medical school. I can't pass up that opportunity. I've come too far."

"But Annika, dear," her mother interjected. "It's become so dangerous here. We've done everything as a family. You can always continue your education in Br . . ."

Annika cut her off. "No, Mutti. You both have raised me to be independent. You've given me everything, most importantly your love. You've encouraged me to pursue my education, to continue a legacy in medicine. I'm so close to doing that. I can't risk starting over. I'm settled here, I have important projects that I'm collaborating on, and I wouldn't have the same opportunities in Belgium. I can't just up and leave."

"*Pits'l*, honey, we're worried about your safety," her stepfather added. "Something very malevolent is happening here. Unprecedented. No one knows where it'll end up."

By now, Annika was crying. "I can't go, Papa. My work is here. I need to stay."

It was no longer just Annika; Eva was also crying. Otto leaned towards them and put his free arm around Annika's shoulder, which led to a group hug.

"Mutti and Papa, listen. Much as I hate to admit it, I totally understand your need to leave. I have been worried sick about you ever since I left home. But I'm safe in Berlin. Realize, I am not Jewish and with blonde hair and blue eyes, I'm not identifiable as Jewish. My last name is Tritzchler, not Baumann, and my birth records show my father as an Aryan physician. From the Nazis' standpoint, I am neither a Jew nor a *Mischling*. I have nothing to worry about."

"We know that, *Pits'l*. And we thought you might want to stay." At this point, Eva was sobbing, her face buried in a handkerchief. "I'm sure you know that our greatest desire would be to have you come with us." Annika was nodding. "But we will respect your decision if you choose to stay."

Annika was moved by her stepfather's words. "I love you both so much! I don't know what I'm going to do without you nearby. But we can still send letters and, God willing, even talk on the telephone."

Otto tapped his pipe against the tree. Annika noticed him frown, and when he again looked in her direction, she could see his jaw muscles twitch. Taking a deep breath, he said, "Annika, if you stay, it won't be safe to send letters or to telephone us, at least not initially. We've got to figure that everything is bugged, so for your own safety, we're going to have to be out of touch for a while. Will you be able to handle that?"

It took a moment for Annika to ponder that thought. "That makes sense, Papa. I can deal with that. But, if I'm not mistaken, as a German, I should be able to travel freely. I can't see any reason why I wouldn't be able to come to Brussels for visits."

"I'd be worried what might happen on your return trip, Annika.

Let's give it some time to see what might be possible. Who knows," Otto said, "maybe things will blow over and we'll be able to return." Somehow, his words rang hollow. She doubted that even he believed them.

The family spent the next two hours on the park bench discussing their respective plans – how to stay connected, job prospects for Otto, where they might be living, how Annika would survive on her own, and all the other details that any family might negotiate before loved ones move away. They agreed to meet one last time at the Hotel Excelsior in downtown Berlin, where Otto had booked a room for the night prior to their departure.

"Honey, here's our plan. You come on Monday evening to the hotel. I'll meet you in the lobby. We can all spend several hours together . . . maybe go out for a walk, grab some dinner . . . just the three of us. Since the Gestapo seems to be everywhere, we figure it may be safest to use the tunnel connecting the hotel with the Anhalter Bahnhof. I think it would be best if your mother and I say goodbye to you that night at the hotel, and the next morning, she and I will walk through the tunnel over to the train station. I think doing it that way will help make everything inconspicuous. Hopefully, we won't have to worry about the Gestapo seeing us all together."

By this point, the sun was nearing the horizon, casting long shadows across the landscape. Otto suggested that it was probably time to call it a day. Slowly, deliberately, reluctantly, they rose, turned to each other and, forming a small circle, held hands. As she had done hundreds of times over the years with her family, Eva began to pray out loud. *"Our Father, who art in Heaven, hallowed be thy Name. Thy kingdom come, thy will be done . . ."*

There was enormous sadness. They hugged, kissed one another, and agreed to meet again in a few days. Then, slowly, as if each was having misgivings about their decisions, they departed in opposite directions. Turning back to watch her beloved parents, now silhouetted by street lamps in the distance, she couldn't escape the fear of never seeing them again. That night, she wrote,

Autumn, for me, has always meant beauty, a time when nature displays its radiance. The Tiergarten this morning, ignited under blue skies and dazzling sunshine, bejeweled in brightly accented leaves and flowers, was a painter's palette. That all changed, though, when Mutti and Papa made their announcement. The rich, dazzling colors of the morning faded into an afternoon of morose, black and white hues. Withering flowers seemed to symbolize Rolf's insensitive attempt at robbing me of my innocence. . . to deflower me; Rolf's insensitive effort on these very grounds to rob me of my innocence. Autumn now takes on an entirely different meaning – a time of decline, a portent of challenge, an ending. {28 October, 1935}

A few days later, true to plan, Annika showed up in the opulent lobby of the Hotel Excelsior, where her stepfather was seated in a lush armchair calmly surveying the comings and goings of guests. Their eyes met simultaneously, and Annika hurried towards Otto as if she hadn't seen him in years. Her wide smile was no match for her tears. They took the elevator to the second floor, where Eva was anxiously waiting. Rather than leaving anything to chance, they decided to have their farewell dinner right in the hotel room. Everyone tried to appear stoical. There were countless reassurances that all would work out, and that they would eventually be reunified at some point in the future. As best as they could amidst so much uncertainty, they formulated plans, mostly thinly disguised attempts at generating hope, that this occasion was not to be a "last supper."

As the evening wore on, they realized that it would be best to bring things to a close. Annika had to leave or she would miss the last streetcar, which might risk being locked out of her dorm, and Otto had already voiced concerns about Annika venturing back to campus alone, though she tried to assure him that she would be fine, and that being out this late, even alone, was not unfamiliar or especially anxiety-provoking for her. Eva asked them all to hold hands, and then began a lengthy prayer beseeching God's guidance and mercy. In their embrace, Otto came forth with sentiments that Annika had never heard from him. It was a true moment for her, in the sense that her stepfather was disclosing a part of himself that was very meaningful, yet one which he had kept hidden so as to not interfere with Eva's efforts of raising her daughter as a Christian. *"Pits'l,"* he began, "in Judaism there is a tradition in which prayers or readings from the *Torah* are concluded with a recitation of the *Hadran Alach*. With my parents, and certainly in the Ashkenazi community I grew up in, this was commonplace, even though I stopped doing it long ago. Saying 'goodbye' was avoided, because to Jews 'goodbye' implies never seeing someone again. Instead, we recite the *Alach*, which really means that we will each return to one another."

As he said this, Otto's eyes filled with tears. He clutched Annika's hands tighter than ever and said, "I remember my grandfather saying 'a goodbye is never final in our lifelong engagement with Torah.' And now, here we are, parting for what could be quite some time. I want you to know how much I love you and how much I will miss you." Annika's cheeks glistened with moisture as she traced her stepfather's face, blurred as it was through her tears. He continued, "So instead of goodbye, my beautiful daughter, I will simply say *'Leich l'shalom,'* which is my wish that over the next few years, you grow at school, you continue to learn, but more than anything, you be a witness to God's love. That's the path to spiritual perfection, and that's the most important thing." Eva sat beside them, nodding her approval, equally moved by her husband's compassion.

Annika stood to put on her jacket. "You both have given me so much. You've instilled in me a love of God, and I will always try to glorify His name and put His wishes above my own. I love you both more than life itself. I think you know that, and I'll do everything I can to make your sacrifices and the gifts you've given me worthwhile."

She spoke with a solemnity that evoked in Eva and Otto a mix of feelings. They knew that she was genuine, that her integrity was real and unmatched, and that as parents they had succeeded in raising a pious child, someone who would go out of her way to help others. Their pride, however, was mixed with unspoken apprehension, for they realized that in these turbulent times when right was wrong, when evil was good, integrity was dangerous; too much integrity could lead to one's demise.

They gave each other one final, lingering hug before Annika made her way to the door. Before leaving, she turned, took one last look at her sobbing parents, and now, head held high, exclaimed, '*Leich l'shalom.*'" With that, she disappeared down the hallway.

Part Two

Geneva

We choose not randomly each other. We meet only those who already exist in our subconscious.

Sigmund Freud

8 December, 1938: Geneva, Switzerland

This was the conference she had been looking forward to for months, a three-day symposium featuring Jean Piaget, the Swiss psychologist who was emerging as one of the most prodigious figures in the field of child development. Annika's practicum over the past few years in which she provided clinical services to children had led to a strong interest in child psychology, and now that she was considering a possible future in psychiatry, she was eager to hear fresh, seminal ideas as well as to meet like-minded practitioners from all over Europe.

"Excuse me, Fräulein. Is this seat taken?" Annika looked up to see a tall, nattily clad man of about thirty, briefcase in one hand, a tweed topcoat draped over the other arm. He had found one of the last available seats in the cavernous auditorium.

The man looked to Annika like he might be a college professor. She straightened up in her chair and replied, "No, no. By all means, please." She cleared her jacket and pocketbook and motioned for him to sit.

"*Ah, sehr gut,*" he said, situating himself in a wooden chair that seemed more for children than grown men. "*Vielen dank.*" His German was good, but his voice, deep and accented, hinted of eastern Europe, possibly Russia. He was smartly attired in a charcoal gray jacket, dark tie, and khaki-colored wool trousers, and as he bent to place his folded overcoat on the floor between them, she noticed he was wearing brightly polished, cordovan wingtips, the same type worn by her stepfather. He opened an elegant leather briefcase to access a notebook and placed it on the table in front of them, and then, leaning over to Annika, he whispered, "So, *guten morgen, Fräulein.* I'm Pavel . . . Pavel Kushelevsky." He gestured for her hand.

"*Sehr erfreut, Herr Kushelevsky.* Pleased to meet you," she said, offering her hand. "I'm Annika Tritzchler." His hand, strong and masculine, dwarfed her own, yet he grasped her fingers with gentleness and poise – *obviously someone raised in polite society*, she thought.

"The pleasure is all mine," he said without a trace of the condescension she had become so accustomed to in Germany. So many of the men in Berlin tended to be officious and dismissive, yet Kushelevsky projected the bearing of a colleague.

But something else caught her attention. It was a vanilla-like odor, subtle but commanding, a fragrance deeply imprinted from childhood and now flooding her with memories of her youth. She turned to Kushelevsky. There was no mistaking it; he was sporting *Vol de Nuit*, the same cologne used for many years by her stepfather. Her head filled with reminisces of her parents, making her feel unexpectedly alone. The last she had heard from them was through a letter sent by her mother almost four months earlier which implied that everything was copasetic, that she and Otto were safe and residing with her cousin's family in Brussels. For reasons of security, though, which Annika had understood perfectly, no return address was given. That had been one of the agreements before their departure.

Her reverie, intense though it was, was quickly broken when a man walked to the podium with an announcement.

"Ladies and gentlemen. We would like to welcome you all to beautiful Geneva, Switzerland. I know many of you have come a long way, and I would like to personally thank you for coming. Before our symposium gets underway, I'd like to say a few words about our

Fräulein

Annika had goosebumps. What she knew of Piaget was inspiring. By the age of fifteen, still a high school student, he had already published two articles in reputable biology journals, and that grew to twenty publications by the time he was only twenty-one. His writings were influenced by Freud, that she had known, but Piaget had gone much further, basing his concepts more on science than pure theory. She particularly resonated with his notion that intelligence was not simply innate, but affected by the environment – a view not so popular among Nazis who believed that genetics could account for everything.

The conference began with an overview of cognitive development, which Piaget went on to explain in terms of a predictable series of stages along an age-continuum. It was a totally new way of appreciating human differences, and before long Annika could see how this would play a major role in the design of her future treatment plans.

By noon, everyone was directed to the adjoining dining hall for lunch. To her surprise, Pavel turned to her and asked, "Would it be an inconvenience if I joined you?"

"Inconvenience me? No, not at all," she replied. Secretly, she was delighted. Not knowing anyone, it was comforting to have someone familiar accompany her to one of the round wooden tables situated under dimly-lit, crystal chandeliers. Within minutes, they were joined by several others, three men and a woman. Introductions were made around the table. Two of them had traveled together from Vienna, the others had made the trip alone, one from Bonn, the other Zurich.

When Pavel's turn came, he said, "Nice to make everyone's acquaintance. I am Pavel Kushelevsky. I teach at the Jagiellonian Medical College . . . in Poland."

The student from Bonn said, "Jagiellonian Medical College . . . Where is that? I'm not sure I've heard of that school." He was trying to be polite.

Pavel took no offense. "Jagiellonian's in Kraków. Better known as the University of Kraków. The oldest university in Poland. Most famous student was Copernicus, himself."

To Annika's surprise, the gentleman from Vienna, Dieter Kestenbach, instantly piped up. "Yes, quite. I'm familiar with Jagiellonian. In fact, I wonder if you might have known a professor from there . . . Leo Sternbach? If I remember correctly, he came from Krakow."

"Well, well," Pavel said, a warm smile bringing out what Annika thought were the cutest dimples on each side of his mouth. "Small world. Doctor Sternbach was a couple years ahead of me at the College, but yes, I knew him. He was an organic chemist. Brilliant."

"That's him," the man replied. "I met him in Vienna at a drug forum. He was doing research for one of the pharmaceutical foundations there."

Annika smiled and nodded her head, though in truth, she too had never heard of the Jagiellonian Medical College, nor was she acquainted with any chemists from Poland. Nevertheless, she was excited to be part of this dialogue, and took a certain delight in learning a bit more about this man sitting next to her. "So, Pavel, do you mind my asking if you are originally from Poland?"

"Of course not. I don't mind at all." He hesitated, looking around the room. "The truth is, my history is kind of complicated. I was actually born in Kursk, a town in western Russia, where my father had owned a small business in the food industry. We moved to Poland when I was about seventeen."

Before he could go any further, they were interrupted by waiters serving cappuccino and tea. Discussions around the table became light and friendly, while the servers came around with plates of poached sausages alongside steaming beds of assorted vegetables. The luncheon concluded with a choice of yoghurt or chocolate cake. As they washed it all down with water, Pavel suggested that they all might reconvene as a group following the day's presentation and participate in a tour of the downtown followed by dinner. "An excellent idea," one of the men said, which was met with enthusiasm.

At five o'clock, they set out as a group for the Vieille Ville, Geneva's enchanting 'Old Town.' Getting there was no mean feat as it was almost all uphill. They wandered along a maze of narrow, winding streets, occasionally stumbling on ancient cobblestones. Annika found the architecture breathtaking, especially the high steepled churches with gravestones and inscriptions dating back more than a millennium. A historical marker in front of a circular fountain indicated that the square they were passing through was the site of an early Roman marketplace.

They paused in spots to admire dimly lit, medieval facades, and worked their way through several of the annual Christmas markets, each festooned with brightly colored lights to attract pedestrians with a variety of holiday-related crafts, candies, and food products. The atmosphere around the markets was jaunty and festive. Their walk took them past the spectacular spire of St. Peters Cathedral, which, they discovered, stood on the ruins of a 4th century Roman temple. A marker in front of the cathedral indicated its construction in the thirteenth century and that by the sixteenth century, John Calvin preached Protestantism from its pulpit. Eventually, they reached the Beth Yaakov Synagogue, built in 1859 as the first public place of worship for Jews, which was of considerable interest.

"Prior to that," Pavel pointed out, "Jews had no civil rights, and worship was held secretly in private homes."

They passed row upon row of masonry facades, their windows aglow with faint orange hues from soft lighting inside. Footsteps and muted conversations could be heard from the occasional pedestrians walking about. Tucked away on one of the side-streets was a medieval stone building with a faded sign that hung from a fancy bracket of *fleur de lis* ironwork. It read, *Café de la Petite Maison*. The group, by now famished and thirsty, decided to enter. Pavel tugged at a large iron ring to open the heavy wooden door which slowly swung clear with a distinctive creak. Stepping inside, he had to duck slightly under the stone lintel to avoid hitting his head. The interior was pleasingly dark with low, hand-hewn beams, a welcoming fire, and a scattering of tables lit by candlelight. Above the fireplace was the head of a large boar whose toothy snarl was obviously silenced long ago. All in all, Annika thought this the perfect setting for a step back in time. A sharply dressed *maître d'hôtel* escorted them to a table ornamented with a bouquet of flowers flanked by candles on each side. "Madame," he said, holding the chair for Annika as she sat.

"My oh my," said Kestenbach, admiring the ambience. "Looks like a scene right out of the middle ages." The others seemed equally enchanted. "You can almost imagine Henry the Second holding court with his noblemen."

At that moment, a *garçon* appeared with a large décanter and overheard the comment. "*Ah, oui Monsieur,* very clever," said the waiter, speaking with a heavy French accent. A clean white towel dangled from his folded left arm as he poured water for everyone. "Actually, the café *has* been frequented for centuries by aristocrats from all over the region. Napoleon himself was a guest at the inn upstairs," he said, making no effort to conceal his pride. The group smiled and nodded in gratitude at learning this unique bit of history. The waiter finished pouring and asked, "And now, would anyone care for wine?"

Pavel looked around, and judging from the nodding heads placed the order. "*Oui, merci. Nous aimerions une bouteille de Sauvignon Blanc et une de Pinot Noir.*"

The waiter nodded, courteously. "*Tres bien, Monsieur.*"

Pavel turned to the group and said, "A bottle of white and one of red."

For a Russian, Pavel's fluency with Swiss German, a nuanced dialect similar to the *hochdeutsch* of the German highlands, had, for Annika, been unexpected, but now to hear him conversing in French left her awed. But there was more. Glancing at the menu, she was struck by the assortment of dishes. They all presented an international flair, which may not have been surprising with Switzerland sitting square in the middle of France, Germany, Austria, and Italy, yet with such rich and varied cuisines, she hadn't a clue what to order. Once again, Pavel was surprisingly helpful. He came across as the quintessential master of ceremonies, which made the dinner conversation lively and friendly, informative yet spontaneous. He shared a wealth of interesting topics and experiences without any pontification or boastfulness, and instead of monopolizing conversations, he made every effort to draw everyone out, much as a teacher or professor might.

As he held court, she found herself at moments staring at him, enchanted by his wit and composure. It was during one of those very interludes, when Annika had been conspicuous by her silence, that Pavel turned to her and asked, "So, Annika, what might you have done in that situation?"

The entire table looked to her for a reply. Unexpectedly put on the spot, Annika blushed. She could feel blood rushing to her face and ears, which simply added to her embarrassment. She had been so distracted by his features, his repartee, even his accent, that she had actually heard almost nothing except maybe the last few words. She felt like a child caught with her fingers in the cookie jar. She abruptly straightened up and could only think of deflecting the question. "Well," she stammered, ". . . let me think . . ." She was at a loss.

Pavel looked deeply into her eyes. *I bet he can see right through me,* she thought. For a moment, it felt like time stood still. She felt a wave go through her body, starting with her face and cascading all the way down to her toes. It was a visceral response, part embarrassment and – if she were honest with herself – part desire. Momentarily tongue-tied, she proffered a weak defense. "Actually, Pavel, I was kind of waiting for you to tell us what you would have done in that situation . . ." It was all she could think to say.

Pavel wasn't fooled; a psychiatrist, he was no stranger to people's emotions, least of all women, and this was a time to help her save face. "Well," he began with a friendly smile, ". . . I was thinking you would do a better job than I, but sure, let me hazard a guess . . ." There was something mischievous about his smile that told Annika he knew perfectly well she hadn't been listening, and nervously she wondered if he could sense what had caused her lapse of attention. Before continuing with his explanation, he gave Annika a quick wink, discreet and unnoticed by the others, a gesture that to her communicated volumes. *Was that a twinkle in his eyes,* she wondered? At that moment, she wanted nothing more than to be with him, alone.

...He is unbelievably intelligent and sophisticated. Nothing at all like the men in Germany; he doesn't make me feel inferior in any way. If he were living in Berlin, I would certainly want to get to know him better. {8 December, 1938}

The next morning, the alarm went off right on schedule: six-thirty A.M. Annika sat bolt upright. *Six-thirty, already?* From the long walk last night, not to mention two healthy glasses of wine, she slept like a baby. It would have been nice to stay in bed for another hour or so, she imagined, but the next thing to enter her mind was Pavel. She jumped out of bed and tended to her ablutions with uncommon zeal, taking greater care tending to her hair, applying make-up, and choosing her wardrobe. *Not too flamboyant,* she told herself, *just enough to appear . . .* she hesitated, almost not wanting to admit something, even to herself *. . . to appear, well, presentable.* There, that felt safe. Just the same, she squeezed the perfume bottle not once, as per usual, but twice.

She wasted no time in arriving early to the conference room, where she hoped she might have some free time with Pavel before the meeting began. That was not to happen. By the time Piaget returned to the podium, there was no sign of Pavel. Could he have possibly sat somewhere else? *God, what would that say,* she wondered. She monitored the doorways as attendees began arriving. Knowing the symposium was only minutes from starting, she looked from side to side, trying to be inconspicuous, even scanning the rows behind her. Her spirits sank, and even though the acclaimed Piaget was making his way to the podium, it was now Pavel who took center stage in her mind.

Forty-five minutes into the presentation, the side door opened and in came Pavel. Annika's breathing quickened. After the previous evening, she now saw him in a new light, not simply a fellow conference attendee, but – *crazy though it feels* – a man who has sparked in her an interest. Today, he donned a three-piece, pinstriped, gray suit, padded at the shoulders, with a burgundy club tie. *For all the world,* she thought, *he looks so distinguished, almost like a diplomat.* Every instinct was telling her to stand right up and signal for him to come over, but her better judgment kicked in, reminding her not to appear like a lovesick schoolgirl. And it was worthwhile to have hesitated, because as soon as their eyes met, Pavel was making his way through the row of guests toward the seat she had saved beside her.

"Entschuldigung, bitte," she could hear him repeating, excusing himself as he jostled among those already seated to her left. He had almost reached her when his coat brushed a man's face, dislodging his glasses. *"Tut mir leid,"* he apologized. Annika found it a bit comical, this large man trying to maneuver through the narrow row of seats. In a matter of seconds, though, he was wrapping his coat around the back of his chair and, as if to erase her earlier anxiety, he placed one hand very lightly on Annika's shoulder and gave a quick, but gentle, squeeze. She looked up at him and smiled. Once settled, he turned to her and whispered, "So, good morning. Sorry to be late. My taxi had a flat tire . . ."

The day's symposium followed a similar format as yesterday. And once again, it took some time for Annika to shift her focus away from the man seated next to her in order to attend to the lecture. She found Piaget to be every bit as worthwhile as she had hoped. The syllabus for this, the second day, was to focus on the parameters of consciousness and how that relates to the origins of intelligence in children. The insights he presented went far beyond anything covered in her classes, or even the books she had been reading. He presented new ideas gathered from his extensive work with children, and even suggested interventions that his team had found helpful in improving the lives of children with learning disorders. The work of Carl Jung and John Dewey were mentioned in the context of educational reforms and teacher training.

Over lunch, Annika was seated with Pavel and two others, whom she hadn't met the day before: Johannes Meier, a recent medical school graduate from the University of Basel and a bewhiskered Philippe Laurent, professor emeritus from the University of Montpellier in southern France. As lunch was being served, a light-hearted conversation began, mostly about the food and each of their respective travel challenges to attend the conference. Gradually, the discussion moved to some of Piaget's ideas from earlier in the morning, and what they insinuated about mental disorders.

"We hear a lot about . . . *ahem* . . . theories of mental illness promulgated in Germany," said Laurent, reaching for his pipe. "What, *s'il vous plait*, are they teaching you up there in medical school?" His French accent was as thick as his tone was condescending.

"Well, Herr Laurent, I would say that most of the professors are of the opinion, at least officially, that psychological problems are inherited, caused only by genes."

"So no 'nature versus nurture' debate?" Pavel asked, trying to keep the dialogue light.

"There doesn't seem to be much of a debate, at least not in Berlin, where I come from," Annika responded. "Much of the medical community there is of the opinion that culture doesn't have much, if anything, to do with determining social problems. Their view is that race explains everything. Purify the race and you eradicate inferior genes, which effectively eliminates criminality, retardation, mental illness . . . even physical handicaps."

Laurent made no effort to disguise a derisive snort. He sneered at

Annika with upturned lip, as if grilling her in an oral exam. "Yes, well, I find the Nazi . . . pardon me . . . the *National Socialist* views rather . . . *simple*, if you will excuse my speaking candidly," he remarked. He held his pipe to his mouth, and as he sucked on the stem, small puffs of smoke belched from the corner of his lips where gray facial hair had turned brown. "Frankly," he continued, "the views coming from your . . . dare I say . . . *intellectual* community remind me of what I used to expect from college sophomores, unsophisticated ones at that." He sat back, smoke curling from his pipe, looking as contented as a chess master who has just placed an opponent in checkmate.

Annika blushed. Before she could respond, Herr Meier commented, "I surmise from your tone, Fräulein, that you may have some differing thoughts. Coming from a Swiss university, I would appreciate hearing whether or not you support such views." He had a thin smile. It was hard for Annika to discern whether he was being similarly dismissive, or genuinely curious.

Looking somewhat nervous as she scanned those seated at the table, she said, "No, you're right, Johannes. I don't share those views. The work I've done with patients in the hospital, young and old, suggests that the prevailing ideas regarding genetics, and especially how those ideas are used to support the eugenics movement, which seems to be the craze now, both in Germany and across the Atlantic, are not supported by science." She looked over at some of the adjoining tables before continuing. "I got into medicine to help people, to treat pathology. In placing all the blame on genes, the racial theories imply that treatment is unnecessary if you can purify the gene pool."

"I see . . . Interesting," Johannes said, with an affected nod.

"Unfortunately," Annika continued, "it's not entirely safe to express such feelings in my homeland."

A bell signaled the end of the luncheon. Pavel said, "We have similar reservations in my homeland, Annika. And I'm guessing that none of us sitting here agree with the Nazis' racial theories. If we did, we probably wouldn't even be here." He looked to the others. "I can only hope you find a way to remain true to your beliefs as you move forward with your career. And that there are others like you."

"Many others . . ." commented Professor Laurent, rolling his eyes.

As the others began to rise, Johannes remained seated, peering at Annika much like a scientist might study a lab rat. She felt his stare and turned. His eyes, dark and piercing, were visible even through the *pince nez* glasses tucked securely at the end of his sharp nose. At the moment their eyes met, Johannes' razor-thin lips curled slightly into a smile, one that she did not return.

Pasha

To love is to suffer and there can be no love otherwise.
Fyodor Dostoevsky

10 December, 1938: Geneva, Switzerland

It had been the final day of the conference. Piaget had spent much of it discussing the child's evolving sense of morality, which struck Annika as an interesting choice, given how politics was affecting the professions. The day's event ended with a round of applause for Doctor Piaget followed by the clamor of private conversations and chairs scraping on the floor as people gathered up their belongings before heading to the exits.

"Would you like to join me for dinner, Annika?" It was Pavel.

"Oh, sure. I'd be delighted. Should we round up the others?

"No need. I talked to Kestenbach at the afternoon break. He and the others are staying for the banquet. I don't know when I'll ever get to Geneva again, so I was actually thinking of taking in a few more of the sights. But if you'd prefer to stay for the banquet . . ."

"No, no. I've done enough socializing for the day. I'd rather get out and do some walking."

"Great. How 'bout meeting back in the lobby in, say, fifteen minutes or so?" It was agreed.

When they reconvened, Annika asked, "So where were you thinking of going? Should we go back into the old city?"

"Actually, Annika, if you wouldn't mind, I would like to visit a small town just south of here. Carouge. Supposed to be full of French and Italian cafes. Places to walk along the river."

With no protest from Annika, they hopped aboard a bus for the ten-minute drive to the center of the town, marked by an old sign reading, "Le Vieux Carouge." There was a distinct Mediterranean influence on the historical architecture, and along cobbled streets, frosted with early snow, were countless boutiques featuring craft shops, art galleries, even lingerie. They hadn't walked for long before being seated in a charming Italian restaurant. They picked a table by the window, a candle flickering atop a red and white tablecloth.

"This is a lovely atmosphere, Pavel. Much different from Geneva. What made you think of Carouge?"

"Actually, Annika, some distant relatives from my mother's side trace their lineage here. I never knew much about them, but I thought it would be interesting to see the town they apparently once lived in." He hesitated before going on. "So, let me ask you. Do you know much about the history of Jews in Geneva?"

"No, I don't. Until we passed the synagogue last night, I wasn't even certain there *were* Jews in Geneva. Everything seems to have such a strong Christian influence. In fact, I read on one of the plaques that the University of Geneva itself was founded by John Calvin."

"Yes, I was aware of that. But I did a little research before coming to the conference. Geneva has a long history with the Jews, and – surprise, surprise – much of it isn't so pretty. Back in the thirteen-hundreds when the Black Plague broke out, the townspeople accused the Jews of having poisoned the wells. So, of course, they began slaughtering them and eventually ran them out of the city."

Annika's shoulders dropped. ". . . not much different from other cities throughout Europe, right?"

"True, and, for the record, not just European cities. Genocides against Jews have taken place all throughout Asia and the Middle East, as well. We've certainly had our share of persecutions in Poland. In fact, every place I've lived – Poland, Russia, the Ukraine – they've all had their own antisemitic past. And, sure, as we're sitting here, there're bound to be more."

"There already are. Look what's happening in Germany."

The waiter came by with a bottle of wine. "Specialty of the

house. *Vino Nobile di Montepulciano*, from Tuscany. Care for a glass?" he asked. Annika and Pavel nodded in unison. The waiter walked around each of them, Annika first, and poured red wine into Bordeaux glasses.

Pavel picked up the tall glass and swirled the red liquid several times around the broad bowl. Putting it to his nose, he sniffed it, then took a sip. Nodding to the waiter while tilting his glass, toast-like, he said. "*Grazie.*"

The waiter was nonplussed. "*Prego,*" he responded, turning to Annika. "Madame?" he asked.

Annika followed Pavel's lead, taking a sip followed by a smile of appreciation. The waiter nodded, and left. Annika continued the conversation. "So, what happened to the Jews here in Geneva?"

"Well, they did return, but intermittent massacres continued. It seems like just when Jews have ever begun to feel safe and content, the population rises up against them. They had restrictions on where to live: first outside the city, then relegated to a separate quarter."

"You seem to have a great deal of interest in Jewish history. Like when we passed the synagogue last night . . ."

"It's true. I find it interesting . . . maybe poignant's a better word . . . that it was only after they had been in Geneva for fifteen hundred years that they were allowed a place of worship."

"So how could they keep their religion alive if they had no place to gather as a group?" Annika was trying to imagine living like that.

Pavel answered quickly. "Easy. They worshipped privately, in one another's houses. Usually secretly. They had no choice. They were forced to keep to themselves, even to live in separate districts. Back in the seventeenth century, Carouge itself, where we are right now, was a Jewish ghetto. That's why I wanted to come here."

Annika shook her head, realizing how passionate Pavel was about this. "Pavel, you seem to know so much about Jewish history. How is it that you – studying medicine and psychiatry – have learned so much about the Jews?"

"It's very simple. I'm an ethnic Jew. I don't practice Judaism, but my family history has both Ashkenazi and Hasidic roots."

Annika was surprised. "Wow, I wouldn't have guessed that."

"Why?" he asked.

"Well, I don't know. You don't really appear Jewish."

Pavel leaned back in his chair. "Oh, is that right? We're all supposed to look the same. Isn't that what your Führer wants everyone to believe?"

Annika's command of French was not at Pavel's level, but she certainly knew the word *faux pas*. She shifted uneasily in her chair. "No, Pavel. Please. I'm sorry. I didn't mean it that way." She hesitated, almost unsure of what to say next. Pavel's response made her aware of her own tendency to stereotype. The thought was abhorrent. "The truth is," she began, "my own stepfather is Jewish."

"Your stepfather? Jewish?"

"Yes. In fact, he and my mother have fled Germany to escape the Nazis."

Now it was Pavel who was surprised. "Oh my word. Annika, I had no idea. No offense taken, whatsoever." Annika looked down, hiding her emotions. "If anyone needs to apologize, it's me." Annika looked up with a weak smile.

"Well," Pavel continued, "it seems that we may be kindred spirits, yes? I have to admit, I'm a bit sensitive about Jewish stereotypes. Even though I was brought up Eastern Orthodox, I have many relatives who, over the years, were murdered in anti-Jewish purges. Both my father's grandparents were killed in Odessa during the Russian Revolution, and we had relatives on my mother's side who were murdered in Volhynia." Pavel pulled a pack of cigarettes from his coat pocket. "Do you mind if I smoke?"

"No, of course not." Annika had been out with men before, and she had assumed this would be nothing more than a casual date – friendly conversation, light entertainment, maybe even dinner by candlelight, if she was lucky. But in a situation like this, being with a man she would probably never see beyond this one conference, she never expected any level of intimacy, even if it was just in conversation. That was changing, markedly. Annika knew of the Russian revolution and Otto had talked of anti-Semitic purges, but it was something very different to be sitting next to someone whose life had been directly affected. "But your immediate family . . ." She almost hesitated to ask. "Everyone survived?"

Pavel clicked open his lighter and held it to his cigarette. Taking a deep draw, the end burned orange for a full two seconds. He took a moment to exhale, looking up at the geyser of smoke as if he had tapped into a rich deposit of memories. "Yes, I guess you could say we all survived. At least for a while . . ." His lips tightened as he looked down. Annika didn't know what to expect. A couple of seconds passed before he lifted his head, looked into her eyes, and said, "My father took his life four years ago."

For a moment, Annika was speechless. Instinctively, she reached forward to place her hand on his knee. "Oh my word, Pavel," she said. "I am so sorry."

"Yes, well, thank you." For a few seconds, Pavel seemed absorbed in his own thoughts. Then, he said, "Maybe I should put that into some perspective. Would you . . ." He hesitated, almost unsure of himself. ". . . would you care to hear a bit of my background?"

Annika nodded, encouragingly. "Absolutely. I'd be flattered if you would. Please, go on."

"Well, my history is kind of complicated. I was actually born in Kursk, a town in western Russia, where my father had owned a small business in the food industry – small, but fairly profitable from what I've been told. Unfortunately, with the outbreak of the Russian Revolution in 1917, we were pretty much forced to leave."

"Why?" Annika asked.

"Well, I'm not sure how much any of you know about Russian history . . . Let's just say that Lenin's rise to power meant that anyone known, or even *suspected*, to have bourgeois roots was in grave danger. For that reason alone, we ended up moving to Kiev to live with my mother's relatives. That was fine for a while, but Kiev had never been a particularly stable place to reside. Throughout history, it was constantly changing hands, so people could never be totally sure of their future . . ." He sighed. ". . . or, for that matter, their safety. From what I've learned, the Great War had been very destabilizing, especially afterwards when the Bolsheviks came to power. My father's family, being Jewish, faced incredible discrimination, and it was only years later, well after the pogroms, that he had some success in business. Trouble was, emotionally he never recovered. And when you think of it, how could he? During the Russian Civil War, more than a hundred thousand Jews were murdered . . . My father knew many of the victims."

He took another drag from his cigarette, followed by a sip of wine. As he looked off into the distance, Annika stared at him, transfixed, hanging onto his every word. "How was your father able to survive?" she asked.

"Well, this is where things get a little confusing. Lenin was opposed to anything bourgeois, but he was pretty accommodating to the Jewish people. Even the slightest discrimination – like calling a Jew a 'Yid' – was punishable by up to a year in jail. I suppose I was fortunate to be growing up then. I'm not sure how it was in Russia, but in Kiev I was permitted to attend school, which my parents really pushed. They felt that the only path to advancement was through education. With their encouragement, I did quite well in the *gymnasium* and was planning to attend the university in Kiev, but after Lenin died, Stalin began imposing changes – his so-called 'reforms.' Religion in schools was banned, people were forced into collective farming, and kids were pressured to join the Komsomol." Annika looked perplexed. "The Komsomol is the Communist youth organization. It was basically developed to indoctrinate young minds to the Soviet system. My parents didn't want me getting involved in that, and they feared the changes taking place in the Ukraine. That's when we moved to Poland. Since my mother had family there, my father had access to employment, and I was able to continue my education. I've been in Krakow ever since."

"It sounds like education's always been important to you."

"My father used to quote Epictetus. 'Only the educated are free,' he would say. I can still hear him saying that. He drummed it into me."

"He was a smart man." She looked deeply into Pavel's eyes. "So, what actually caused your father's death?"

"Well, as I was saying, with Stalin's reforms, the situation in Kiev worsened significantly. Stalin expanded his effort to eliminate kulaks – 'enemies of the state,' he called them – people who owned land or property or even small businesses." He went on to describe the fears that spread through the community. Annika listened attentively. As Pavel talked of the adversities, she intermittently shook her head from side to side, sometimes closing her eyes as she imagined the challenges he spoke of.

"My father was desperate to leave the city. Once in Poland, my father became depressed. He had work, but everything familiar to him was gone, including friends and family. He started to drink every day, always vodka. There were times when he'd become very angry, taking out his aggressions on my mother. I only learned about that afterwards. Anyway, he apparently failed to come home from work one night, and the next thing we knew, the police were at our door asking my mother to come downtown. They needed her to identify my father at the city morgue. He had apparently shot himself in the local Jewish cemetery."

Annika was leaning across the table, Pavel's hands firmly clutched in her own. "Oh, Pavel. That is so sad. I am so sorry for you."

"Yes, thank you." He lifted his goblet and drained it of wine in one gulp as if it were a shot of whiskey. "You know," he said, putting the glass down while wiping his lips with the napkin, "through my father's death, I've done some research on suicide, and some of it shows suicide being more prevalent in Jewish communities. Have you ever heard that?" Annika shook her head. "Well, apparently, the data suggests it's true. So, of course, there are now some who believe suicide may be genetically unique to Jews."

Annika didn't know how to react. Maybe this was Pavel's way to distract himself from talking any further about his father. "You sure the researchers weren't Nazis?"

"I agree," Pavel said. "I'm more inclined to think that, for some, it's a response to centuries of abuse, something that happens to people when they simply feel that they can't take anymore. When you grow up expecting to be mistreated, it's easier to give up trying."

"I have seen that myself in Germany," Annika replied. "I even wonder how much of what we call schizophrenia is really related to abuse." She took another sip of wine before turning to the waiter, who had just appeared for their order. Taking a moment to scan the menu, she said, "I'd like to start with the Bruschetta with Pickled Okra." The waiter scribbled some notes. "And then . . . how about the 'Ossobuco alla Milanese?'"

"*Bene*," intoned the waiter, then turning to Pavel.

"And . . . I think I will have the Grilled Antipasto with the Garlicky Bean Dip. Maybe follow it up with a plate of polenta." The waiter jotted down a few additional notes and, with a respectful nod, was off to another table.

Pavel poured more wine. "You know, there was a psychiatry resident I met a few years ago at a conference in Vienna," he continued. "Viktor Frankl. He came from a Jewish family and was studying depression and suicide. Small wonder, right? A Jew interested in suicide. Anyway, he told me that during his graduate work, he had been aware of a disturbing suicide rate in high school students, so he and a colleague developed a program which they designed to prevent suicide in teenagers. Believe it or not, while he was there, suicide rates didn't just drop, they were virtually eliminated. Now think about it. Would that happen if it were genetic?"

"I wouldn't think so. I'd like to learn more about that intervention. Sounds like one we might want to experiment with in Berlin."

Pavel sipped more of his Montepulciano. "It seems that we have a great deal in common, doesn't it? Both of us pursuing medicine, both interested in developmental psychology, and maybe more significantly both of us having Jewish roots," Pavel said, as he lifted his glass for another splash of Lafite.

Annika was certainly feeling similarly. She felt more relaxed and more open with Pavel than she had ever felt with anyone, excepting perhaps her parents. She had a few male friends, but none with whom she had ever felt any sense of intimacy. Pavel was a man whom she felt to be more intelligent, more confident and worldly, and yet someone who seemed to value her thoughts.

Eventually the discussion got around to politics. "I think it's interesting, Pavel, that we come from different countries, but we're experiencing many of the same challenges. I worry so much about Germany under Hitler, and from what you tell me about Russia, there seems good reason to worry about Stalin as well."

Pavel lit another cigarette. "Absolutely," he said. "Just to clarify, anti-Semitism is officially illegal in the Soviet Union, but Stalin hates Trotsky, his biggest rival, and because Trotsky's a Jew, Stalin seems to be moving toward a hatred of all Jews."

"Well, it's curious that Hitler and Stalin have so many similarities. You'd think they'd form some kind of coalition. But maybe it's all for the best that they don't, now that I think of it."

"You know as well as I do, Annika, that they're both narcissists. Narcissists have no tolerance for adversaries. The very thought makes them paranoid."

"And God help anyone who stands in their way . . ."

"Sure," Pavel agreed. "Disagree and you wind up in a gulag."

"Or a KZ." Pavel looked quizzical. "A concentration camp," Annika explained.

The remainder of their evening was filled mostly with small talk. The waiter had been most generous in allowing the young couple to stay well beyond the normal closing time. They were the only diners left in what was now a room of empty tables. Taking the last bite of polenta, Pavel looked at his watch and quipped, "Well, if we stay much longer, they'll be serving us breakfast," at which point he pulled a wallet from his inside coat pocket.

The waiter came by with two glasses of grappa. "Compliments of the chef," he said, setting a glass in front of each of them. "I'll take the check when you're ready.

Annika reached across the table and took each of his hands into her own. She looked directly into his eyes, and said, "Tonight was very special, Pavel. I really enjoy your company. Thank you."

Pavel responded in kind, "The pleasure has been all mine, Annika, more than you can imagine. This was a special night for me too." His hands were warm. "I wonder if you could do me a favor."

Annika didn't know what to expect. "Sure, anything."

"Please call me 'Pasha.' That's what all my friends and family call me. 'Pavel' is, well, way too formal."

Annika beamed. "Pasha." She said the name as if trying to capture its essence in her mind. "That's a beautiful name. I'd be delighted." She squeezed his hands.

Suddenly 'Pasha' seemed to light up. "Annika, I just had an idea. I've heard about a cute little town north of here, Nyon; it's right on the lake about an hour or so by train. Just beyond it is a village up in the Jura mountain range called Saint Cergue. It's a small ski resort. I don't know if you have any flexibility in your itinerary, but I wanted to ask what you would think about joining me for the weekend up there? I think it would be a lot of fun.

Annika was taken aback. A trip with Pavel? To a Swiss village in the mountains? Her mind ran wild. "Well . . ." she sputtered, "I, uh, I don't know how to ski . . ."

"That makes two of us . . . which kind of makes it even more fun. We'll be spectators. See what all the excitement's about. But if you have to get back . . ."

"No. That sounds divine," she replied, cutting him off in mid-sentence. But then not wishing to appear overly anxious, she added, "of course, I do have airline reservations." She figured she could change them, but thought it a bit wiser, perhaps more ladylike, to appear somewhat reserved.

"I have some experience with the airlines, Annika. If you need any assistance with your reservations, I'd be happy to help."

With that, they gave each other's hands a squeeze before leaving the restaurant, only to discover they had missed the last tram. Rather than call for a taxi, they chose to walk back to the hotel. They had the sidewalks almost entirely to themselves, and under the cool moonlit skies, they made plans for the next day's excursion.

At the table tonight, there was something so radiant about him, something that was at once familiar, yet unfamiliar; it was hard to describe. I felt like I had known him forever. {10 December, 1938}

A Budding Romance

The heart has its reasons which reason knows nothing of...
Blaise Pascal

<u>11 December, 1938: Nyon, Switzerland</u>

"Top of the morning, Frau Tritzchler." It was Pasha. He stood in the
hotel lobby dressed in his tweed suit with an overcoat perched over
his left arm. He held his wide-brimmed hat in the opposite hand.

"And a good morning to you," responded Annika in a polite, if
slightly coquettish, tone. The bellhop trailed a respectable distance
with her luggage, depositing it next to the concierge desk where she
would be checking out. Annika exuded an innocent, but unmistakable
sensuality that began with penetrating blue eyes peeking behind dark,
fluttering eyelashes. Pasha could not take his eyes off her. Smooth,
tight skin accentuated her high cheekbones, and when she smiled, her
full lips were red and glistening. It was hard not to appreciate her
gleaming teeth and the subtle dimples that appeared on each side of
her mouth. Rakishly tilted over her right eye was a pale-green fedora
spliced by a large, quill-like feather, the perfect crown to shoulder-
length blonde hair looking something like a cross between Rita
Hayworth and Jean Harlow.

Her account settled, she and Pasha exited the hotel to a waiting
cab, and within a short drive, they were at Geneva's busy train
terminal. Pasha purchased round trip tickets for both of them, and as
Annika reached forward to hand the clerk her share, Pasha lightly
blocked her hand, saying, "Please, I insist."

"Can I help you and your wife with the luggage?" offered a
porter.

"Oh, we're not . . ." began Annika.

"*Ja, danke*," replied Pasha, while gently touching her arm and very subtly shaking his head. Annika relaxed and allowed the porter to lead them to their seats. *People think we're married*, she thought, actually enjoying the subterfuge. It felt so good to be with a man who treated her not just like a lady, but with respect, like a colleague.

The trip to Nyon was relatively short, yet quite scenic, hugging the coastline of Lake Geneva. Annika's enthusiasm brimmed over into an almost schoolgirl-like giddiness as she acknowledged the fast-moving array of dazzling landscapes rushing by her window. Sitting across from them was an older gentleman, probably in his sixties, and attired in a dark, pin-striped suit with a gold watchchain dangling from his vest. He wore a green felt Alpine hat with a large red feather and carried in his lap a leather briefcase.

In a deep and heavily accented voice, Pasha asked, "Are you by any chance from around here? It's our first time in this area."

"Why, yes indeed. I am Günther Rohrbach." He reached forward to shake Pasha's hand. "Pleased to make your acquaintance." He had the bearing of a museum curator.

"*Erfreut mich,* Herr Rohrbach," Pasha said, returning the handshake. "I am Pavel Kushelevsky, and . . ." turning to Annika, "this is my colleague, Doctor Tritzchler."

Annika extended her hand as Rohrbach leaned forward to grasp her fingers. "I live in Nyon," he said, "but do business in Geneva. I'm an accountant."

"*Sehr gut.* So maybe you can tell us a little bit about this community?" The train had slowed almost to a crawl treating them to magnificent vistas.

"Well," Rohrbach responded, "you may be interested in knowing that we are only now passing through the town where the Baron Maurice de Rothschild resides. Up there," he pointed, signifying a hill on the opposite side of the train car. "The Château de Pregny. You've heard of the Baron perhaps, no? He's our most prominent resident, not to mention the wealthiest man in Switzerland.

A Jewish banker. Rather a nice man, as well," he added, as if to imply an incongruity between richness and affability, maybe especially among Jews.

This was interesting to Annika, having heard the Rothschilds depicted so often in the German press as "filthy Jewish bankers," and "parasites" on hardworking Germans. "Is it possible to see his villa, perhaps tour it?" she asked.

"No, I'm afraid not, my dear. It's quite private . . . in fact, visible only by boat, which of course at this time of year is impossible. But if you've never been to Nyon, there are many sights of historical significance. If you have the time, I'm sure you will find the town much to your liking."

It was only minutes later that the train rolled into the old town of Nyon. Once it jerked to a halt, the trio fumbled for their luggage. Pavel picked up both suitcases and led Annika out to the street. Through the buildings, they could see Lake Geneva just a few blocks down from the train station. Sitting adjacent to such a large body of water, the December air hovered at five degrees Centigrade – cool, but quite tolerable. "Tomorrow, we'll be in the mountains," Pasha said, "and things will be a lot more winterlike. Perfect day to take advantage of some sightseeing."

They hailed a cab, and within minutes were checking into a modestly priced hotel on the Quai des Alpes, a bustling street on Nyon's picturesque waterfront. As planned, they secured separate rooms, each with beautiful views of Lake Geneva. Annika took a few minutes to gaze at the bright sun rippling off the water, beckoning to the jagged, snow-capped Alps rimming the horizon. Nyon was a small town of only a few thousand, but reminders of its two-thousand-year history were everywhere.

First, they went on a self-guided tour of the Château de Nyon, a magnificent castle dating back to the Renaissance perched high on a hillside where knights of old could see the approach of marauding tribes. From there they crisscrossed a network of streets to the ancient ruins of both a Roman amphitheater and a basilica thought to have been from the time of Julius Caesar. Before they knew it, the afternoon sun had been swallowed by the mountains; opportune, as they hadn't eaten since breakfast.

Following a rejuvenating meal, they walked along the lakeside boulevard where traffic at this hour was almost non-existent. On one side of the street, under tranquil, starlit skies, was a panorama of glittering lights with small plumes of smoke curling from the chimneys. Stretching out on the other side was Lake Geneva, dark, translucent, and bisected by a shimmering ribbon of moonlight cutting across the water. "Why don't we sit for a minute," Pavel suggested, pointing to a nearby bench, which faced a line of twinkling lights on the opposite shoreline. The wind was light, but they could hear small waves lapping against the sand.

"Very peaceful," Pasha said, looking up at the moon.

"Peace on earth, good will toward men . . ." Annika replied.

"Spoken in true Christmas spirit."

They sat side-by-side, appreciating the solitude. Slowly, a high thin cloud passed across the moon, hiding its radiance behind a thin veil. Looking up, Annika said, "Yin and yang.'

"Ah, Chinese wisdom . . . Why do you say that?"

"Oh, I was reflecting on the moon going from brilliance to darkness. It made me think of everything in life consisting of opposites. You know, like day turning to night, health turning to sickness."

"Sure. Not to mention, right versus wrong, and good juxtaposed with evil."

"Yeah, exactly. Thinking about the universe of opposites makes me think how quickly it all could change. You know, how peace could easily turn into war and chaos."

They were silent for a moment. Then Pasha said, ""It really makes you wonder if this is just human nature. That people can't be content with peace for too long. That there will always be competition and greed." Annika looked up to the stars twinkling overhead. "We take a lot for granted, don't we?" Pasha continued. "Maybe that's

117

when we let our guard down. I think you're right in suggesting that people live as if things will go on forever, not realizing that it all can change in a heartbeat."

"I guess from your experiences in Ukraine, you know that better than anyone," Annika said. They sat in solitude for several more minutes. She sensed that Pasha was reflecting on his past, maybe his family and whatever happened to them. It made her think of her own parents. That brought tears to her eyes. Very softly, as if not to awaken anyone's slumber, she said, "I know it sounds corny, but I've often fantasized that my parents and I could be looking at the same moon at the exact same moment. It's one of the few ways that I feel a connection to them."

Pasha took Annika's hand into his own. "Well, whether or not they're looking the same moon, I'm sure their thoughts are as focused on you as yours are on them, even at this very moment."

Annika was touched by Pasha's tenderness. "I appreciate that," she replied, and then leaned over to kiss him on the cheek. Something was clearly happening.

The next morning, following a continental breakfast, Annika and Pasha boarded a much smaller train than the one they had ridden in from Geneva. Saint Cergue was a small village in the foothills of the Jura mountain range bordering France and Switzerland. Small, yet enchanting in its own right, the train rumbled along narrow-gauge tracks through snow-covered forests and high alpine meadows. Within two hours, they were at the town's outskirts, twisting their way up low mountains framed against a deep blue sky. Eventually, they chugged into the small station, where Annika pointed to a distinctive rock peak rising high above the forest.

"That's La Dole," announced the conductor proudly. "Sixteen hundred meters, highest mountain in the Jura Range."

Pavel asked for directions to the "Hotel de Saint Cergue," where in Nyon he had been fairly assured rooms would be available. However, the concierge clerk had added that reservations were not taken; it was walk-in only. They gathered their luggage and walked the half-kilometer along sidewalks mostly bereft of pedestrians, but dotted with patches of snow and ice. The town was everything Pavel had described – small, quaint and provincial, the perfect location for a romantic getaway.

Pavel suggested they stop for lunch on the way. The town was small and modest, and the few cafés they saw were all closed. Eventually, they spotted a bakery and were able to order an espresso and a baguette filled with ham and cream cheese. The waitress informed them that on Sunday, most establishments are closed and the few that remained open normally shut down shortly after noon. Happy to have something to eat, they sat at a small round table in front of a foggy window obliterated by condensation.

Finishing their brunch, they walked the short distance to the hotel, apparently the only one open at this time of year. It turned out to be less of a hotel and more of a traditional guesthouse, catering at this time of year mostly to skiers. When they arrived, the small entryway was silent, and no one sat at the desk to greet them. After several minutes, Pasha rang the bell, which prompted a toilet to flush in the adjoining room. Eventually, the hand-painted Dutch-door squeaked open to reveal a stout woman, probably in her sixties, wearing a blue dress, stained white apron, and a mobcap covering her thin bluish hair- a dated picture of traditional Swiss femininity.

She gave them a quick glance while ambling to the counter. In a perfunctory tone, not particularly welcoming, she said *"Grüezi.* What can I do for you?"

"We'd like to spend the night," Pasha said.

"Name?" she asked, bending down to look at her guest register.

My Lord! thought Annika, struck by the woman's enormous breasts. Barely supported by a red, lace-up corset, they were pendulous reminders of halcyon youth and now, to Annika's amusement, seemed perilously close to overflowing the frilly white blouse that was at least two sizes too small. Annika and Pasha glanced at each other, trying to suppress a smile.

Pasha greeted her as the innkeeper scanned her book. Puzzled, she looked up to eye them suspiciously. "You have reservations?"

"*Nein*," Pavel replied, explaining the recent arrival.

The woman frowned, then thumbed through her scheduling book. She muttered to herself in Swiss German, assuming she wouldn't be understood. "*Mein Gott* . . . people coming in without reservations . . ." Eventually, she peered at the couple from over her spectacles. "Well, it looks like we are all booked up for tonight."

"Are you certain? Nothing? We've just come up from Geneva." Pasha placed five Swiss francs on the desk. "Could you check one more time. We really need a room." He pushed the money toward the woman.

She glanced at him through narrowed eyes, then tucked the bill into her cleavage. Flipping a couple of pages back and forth in her book, she said, "Well, now, what do you know. I didn't see this. It seems there *is* a room available . . ." Pasha and Annika looked at each other, suppressing a smile. ". . . but," she continued, "it's rather expensive . . ."

Pasha wasted no words. "We'll take it!"

She assigned the room and handed them a key. "It's on the third floor . . . at the end. We serve dinner at six o'clock. Just go through that door," she said, pointing to her left. "And you are free to use the sauna. It's down the hall and through the green door. There's a changing room next to it."

Pavel thanked the woman and carried their luggage to the stairwell. The stairs were covered with a faded brown runner and creaked with each step as they made their way up three flights to their room. As they passed each floor, it was obvious the building was well occupied. Muffled laughter could be heard down one hallway, and two couples passed them coming down the stairs, one wearing bathrobes, presumably headed for the sauna. Opening the door to their room, they were greeted by a faint musty smell as if it hadn't seen visitors for quite some time. Aside from that, it was pretty much as described: neat and clean with a frosty window affording stellar views across Lake Geneva to the Alps beyond. Cragged and snow-capped, Mt. Blanc was easily distinguishable on the horizon.

Annika was happy to have a room, but her eyes settled immediately on the bed, one bed for the two of them. And then, only a few meters away, was the bathroom. With its thin door, it was not quite the privacy she was expecting.

With it being a Sunday, no establishments were open, they asked the clerk at the front desk for suggestions on where in the town they might walk. She suggested that the weather was perfect to go up to the mountain, where they could take in some views and local scenery. "Just this year," she boasted, "La Dôle erected a lift to take skiers up the mountain. No other mountain in Switzerland had lifts before this year. Do either of you ski?"

"No, afraid not."

"Well, it would be worth seeing. Not much else to do. I might be able to arrange a taxi."

"Oh, that would be magnificent. Could you?" Pavel opened his wallet and put down another franc. The woman immediately picked up the phone and made some arrangements.

The ride was nothing short of splendid. The small houses scattered along the twenty-kilometer route were the prototypical Swiss chalets, each constructed of thick wood with low-pitched roofs projecting at the gable ends over handsome balconies embellished with carved railings. The roofs, weighted under a generous blanket of snow, were supported by a variety of carved ornamental brackets. The taxi made its way up a twisting, narrow road until it finally reached the base. The new T-bar was in full operation. Pasha handed the driver an assortment of coins with instructions for him to return in two hours.

He and Annika ventured through the snow towards a rustic chalet where smoke wafted invitingly from high above the stone chimney climbing the outside wall. They had to skirt a huge stack of neatly piled logs, most over a meter in length, and then worm through scores of long wooden skis and poles, all sticking haphazardly out of the snow like a petrified forest of stunted elders. Opening the cabin door brought welcome relief from the deafening whirr of the petrol-powered lift, but it was instantly replaced by measured chaos inside where laughter and chatter jockeyed with clanging plates and clinking beer mugs. It was a kaleidoscope of brightly colored sweaters and tight wool leggings with damp leather ski boots lining the massive stone hearth and roaring fire. Odors of wet wool mixed with curried knockwurst and juniper-flavored sauerkraut, and there was the occasional downdraft to momentarily choke the *bon vivant* in a haze of creosote. But no one objected; this was the ambience of the modern ski lodge.

They muscled their way to an empty table closest to the fire vacated by a group that, like most, had grabbed a quick bite before returning to the action out on the hillside. The gaiety was infectious. Pasha ordered two mugs of pilsner along with some bread and knockwurst. Over in the corner, a man started in with an accordion, and several people sitting nearby joined in song. Conversation was difficult amidst the noise, but as they ate and drank, they found it supremely entertaining to see people on their gangly wooden skis, many landing comically on their backsides.

After a while, Pasha said, "Maybe we should get out of here before someone breaks their leg. I don't want to be the only doctor on hand. How about if we start walking down the road . . . take in some fresh air before the taxi arrives?"

Annika was quick to agree. They began walking down the winding road, enjoying the views and buffeted from the wind by the towering pines. After a kilometer, give or take, they could see the car in the distance, snaking its way up the narrow road. Annika was shivering by the time it arrived, but nothing could dampen her enthusiasm. Back at the hotel, they had just enough time for supper before returning to their guestroom.

"I'm still frozen from the walk," Annika said, stepping into the room.

"Me, as well," Pavel replied. He reached for a sweater, slung over the chair. "I never warmed up in the dining room." Yanking the sweater over his broad shoulders, he said, "Hey, why don't we head down to the sauna. They said it's open until 8 P.M."

"That's a great idea," Annika exclaimed. She was actually hoping for something to do. The room seemed so sterile and they had at least a couple of hours before bedtime. As comfortable as they were feeling towards each other, sitting in a room with no distractions would present a new challenge. So, without any debate, they grabbed some towels and headed downstairs to their changing rooms. Both emerged, her in a terrycloth robe, him with towels around his waist and shoulders.

Annika looked bemusedly at Pasha. "Well, Herr Kushelevsky," she said, aiming at some humor, "my compliments on your outfit. Very spiffy."

"And yours, as well," Pasha said, smiling.

The sauna was already occupied by two other couples – a youthful-looking duo on one side and a middle-aged pair in the opposite corner. Annika took a seat in the middle, while Pasha paused to ladle some water onto the rocks, which set off a hissing plume of steam. Within only a minute, beads of perspiration formed on their foreheads.

Pasha sat down next to her and, leaning back, said, "A welcome contrast from the ski slope, don't you think?"

Annika leaned back as well. "Absolutely. This is sumptuous," she purred, squinting her eyes. She glanced over at the other couples, and with the exception of the man in the corner, she and Pavel were the only ones draped in towels.

Turning to Pasha, she whispered, "Would it make you uncomfortable if I removed my robe?"

He looked at her for a second or two without answering. "Of course not," he said, turning back nonchalantly to face the stove.

Smiling, she wriggled out of the terrycloth, dropping it behind her, then leaned back against the wall, closing her eyes to more fully appreciate the warmth enveloping her.

"A nice way to cap off the day, right?" Pasha asked, as he settled in beside her. Annika's look of contentment was her only response, but it was enough.

They reclined for quite a few minutes without speaking, almost as if they were laying on a beach under a hot sun. With moist heat invading their windpipes and working its way into their pores, they were each lulled into a state of sublime drowsiness. Pasha turned to look as one of the couples moved to the exit, but in doing so, his gaze was stopped short by Annika's figure stretched unashamedly beside him. Glistening under beads of perspiration, her nakedness left him momentarily breathless. She had the body of a dancer: young, sculpted, and nubile. Her upturned breasts, round and symmetrical, moved in cadence with her belly, gently undulating with each breath in what could only be described as a rhythm of tacit sensuality. Pasha was no voyeur, no studied connoisseur of the female body, but in this one moment, his were the eyes of an aesthete, a man moved by a magnificence that defied description. It was like an artist in the presence of a Renoir. He had to turn away lest his awe keep him transfixed in desire.

A half-hour later, they were back in their room, still bathed in sweat. "I need to rinse off," Annika said, peeking into the bathroom.

"Me, as well. Why don't you go first? I'll have a cigarette and a glass of wine. Take your time. Want me to pour you one?"

"Oh, that would be grand," she said, scooping up some clothing. She disappeared behind the closed door and began filling the old clawfoot tub. It was not long before Pasha heard her body squeaking against the porcelain. He smiled. It had been a remarkable weekend, one which would end tomorrow. He was immediately struck with how bittersweet this felt. It would be only 36 hours before they would each be returning to their homes. *What irony,* he thought, *to have finally met a woman who feels like a genuine soulmate only to have to leave her.*

Just as he began to contemplate their separation, he heard Annika's soft voice. "Pasha, can you come in?"

124

"Sure. I'll close my eyes. What do you need?" He figured she may want him to hand her a bar of soap, maybe get a washcloth. Instead, he opened the door to find the room drenched in soft candlelight. She was immersed in the water, her body wavering under the gentle ripples of bathwater. "Would you like to join me?" she asked.

The words struck Pasha with an intensity for which he was unprepared. Here was a woman of his dreams, someone who, in spite of their vast differences, he felt he had known all his life. He couldn't deny that he was falling in love with her, and it was she asking him to join her – *naked* – in a bathtub. He hesitated, fearful of breaking the spell by showing himself too eager, but he untied the terrycloth belt, nevertheless, and as he did, the bathrobe opened, exposing himself to Annika for the first time. With no reaction from her, he wrestled the robe from atop his shoulders, letting it fall in a heap at his feet. The candlelight cast an orange hue, highlighting his chiseled physique.

Annika sat up and moved forward in the tub so that Pavel could nestle in behind her. She was squeezed on each side by his large, muscular legs, and once situated, she leaned back and rested her head on his chest. At first, his hands bobbed aimlessly in the water, but with her relaxation came enough confidence to interlace his hands just above her belly. He delighted to the feel of her smooth back against his abdomen. In the ambient glow, words were spoken in whispers as their breathing began to ebb and flow in unison. Time stood still, theirs the only existence.

Pasha began to knead her shoulders, working his fingers into the recesses around her neck and between her shoulder blades.

A half-hour or so elapsed before they were ready to step out. To her surprise, Pasha began to gently dry her shoulders with his towel. She stood with her back to him, eyes closed, smiling. Before he could go any further, she turned to him, and with her own towel began patting his chest with it. They each smiled, then turned away to continue drying themselves. Hanging his towel on the rack, Pavel turned to Annika. She was bent at the waist drying her legs. Sensing no other movement, Annika stood and turned to him. For a brief moment, they simply looked at each other. Then, without moving, she allowed her towel to drop at her side, this time fully aware of his admiring gaze. Smiling, he reached for her hands. "You are magnificent, Annika – truly beautiful." He pulled her closer. "I want you to know how much I've enjoyed our time together."

Annika looked up to his face. The flame from the candle reflected in his eyes; a symbol, perhaps, of the passion burning deeply within her. Not saying a word, she wrapped her arms around his shoulders, her breasts pressing against his ribcage. She peered deeply into his eyes to convey both acceptance and desire. Pasha reacted by coaxing her head forward, brushing her lips with his own until, as if on cue, their mouths opened. Her tongue rolled against his, tasting and teasing, airways nurtured by each other's breath. With their embrace came a resurgence of sweat lending viscosity to their skin. Hip against hip, Annika could feel Pasha's desire grow, and deep inside of her, for the first time in her life, she ached to be joined with a man. He reached down, and in one quick motion scooped her up by the legs, carrying her into the bedroom, where he gently lowered her onto the bed.

Their lovemaking commenced slowly, with deliberateness and sensitivity. Recognizing that he was Annika's first, Pasha did everything he could to make her experience one of profound pleasure, and responding as she did was an intrinsic gratification unlike any he had ever known. The night stretched on like this for hours, touching and caressing, giving and receiving, all in a selfless interplay that conjoined them. It was a magical interlude of two selves merging physically and spiritually into a single, transcendent essence. When it was all over, only one flame continued to burn. Its faint light created a silhouette of two young lovers, arm in arm, face to face, drained yet enlivened. Managing one last kiss, they yielded to sleep as the candle's final flicker disappeared in a small puff of smoke.

Nazi Medicine

A man sees in the world what he carries in his heart.
Johann Wolfgang von Goethe

17 January, 1939

Annika walked down the Charité's main drive amidst a sea of returning students, all bundled in heavy coats and hats to ward against the biting wind and swirling snowflakes. Hurrying past genteel, ivy-covered brick buildings, she reached her destination: a neo-Gothic edifice adorned with gold lettering, *Psychiatrische u. Nervenklinik*. She struggled to open the door, which was pinned by a strong gust that whined like a wavering harmonica. As it circulated against the edifice, the vortex ballooned her skirt, frosting her legs with icy tendrils. Finally, inside, she clambered up the semi-circular staircase and down a familiar labyrinth of corridors.

Suddenly, a bright yellow poster caught her eye. It depicted a white-coated doctor standing behind a middle-aged patient, obviously deranged and handicapped, judging from his contorted posture and facial expression. The wording on the poster was bold and stark.

60,000 Reichsmark is what this person suffering
from a hereditary defect costs the
People's community during his lifetime.
Fellow citizen, that is your money too.
Read 'New People,' the monthly magazine
of the Bureau for Race Politics of the NSDAP.

Another endorsement for sterilization, she thought. She shook her head, remembering Professor Laurent, who at the conference had derided Nazi medicine as having "the sophistication of a college sophomore," or something to that effect. In some ways, Geneva seemed long ago, painfully so. Nevertheless, it was impossible to reflect on the conference without being inundated with thoughts of Pasha. In her mind, she could hear him encouraging her to stand up for her principles. *My God, how I miss him,* she thought. Her heart ached. She had to remind herself that they would be seeing each other again, that their separation was only temporary.

For the moment, Professor Karl Bonhoeffer was on the agenda. A physician and chair of the Department of Psychiatry, he was Dietrich's father and a man whose politics and values were similar. She had become acquainted with him through a course that he taught on sterilization law, and it had been reassuring to hear him disagree, at least in part, with the Nazi's call for compulsory sterilization of the handicapped and mentally disabled, who they argued to be a huge and unnecessary drain on society. She knocked on his door.

"Yes, come in," said Bonhoeffer, signaling for Annika to sit in the chair beside his desk. "You wanted to see me. What can I help you with?"

"Professor, on my way in, I noticed a poster in the hallway." Annika described what she had seen.

"Hmmm . . ." He seemed to groan. "I haven't seen it yet, but – God knows – I'm not surprised. Probably one of DeCrinis's students."

"Sir?" she asked, not quite understanding his allegation.

"Max DeCrinis. You've probably seen him around here. He's the middle-aged man who dresses in the SS uniform. I would doubt that you've had any classes with him. He was recently appointed to the faculty here at the Charité," he said, closing his eyes and shaking his head. "He has a rather . . . *unusual* . . . interpretation of medical ethics . . ."

"What, like sterilizing mental defectives?"

"Precisely. But not just mental defectives, Tritzchler. The eugenicists believe that all disorders, from retardation and epilepsy to prostitution, alcoholism, even criminality – they're all disturbances that get passed on from one generation to another. They say that by tolerating such conditions, society prevents the gene pool from weeding out misfits."

"People really believe that?"

"Oh, indeed they do. More so now than ever. In fact, DeCrinis's views have caught the ear of the Führer . . . to the point where, if I'm not mistaken, they figured in *Mein Kampf.* That's why you see Professor DeCrinis wandering about in uniform. He's quite high-ranking in the SS."

"So, anyone not considered beneficial to the Reich is not worthy of living? Is that the idea? she asked.

"Let's hope it's not that extreme . . ." was all the professor could say, but his tone made Annika think he himself had deeper concerns.

Annika didn't know what to say. This was a professor that Bonhoeffer was talking about, and even if he had concerns, Annika was not about to risk a breach of protocol by saying anything that could get her into trouble. "I can't imagine such debauchery in this day and age. I mean, how would other countries react to that?"

"One thing you need to realize," Bonhoeffer said, "is that the topic of eugenics is flourishing . . . and not just in Germany, but in the U.S., and Britain as well." Annika cocked her head and grimaced, as if in disbelief. "Oh yes. In fact," he went on, "some of the most compelling German research in the field of genetics, research that has supported the Nazis' policies on 'race hygiene,' has been sponsored by America's Rockefeller Foundation."

"I wasn't aware of that. I know there are ideas like that out there, but I've always avoided them. Never thought they'd gain any traction. I mean, with the Hippocratic oath and all. There's so much other stuff to study . . . I've never been interested in eugenics . . ."

"And I'm not suggesting you should have. But it's worth realizing that not only are people taking this seriously, but it's nothing

129

new. Some of this originated decades ago. About twenty years ago, there was a psychiatrist who lectured on overcrowding in psychiatric hospitals, and he went on to publish a book entitled *Permission for the Destruction of Life Unworthy of Life*. Think of that. And more recently, maybe five or six years ago, a book came out titled *The Eradication of the Less Valuable from Society*. Have you come across that?"

"No, I haven't heard of it." Annika was slightly embarrassed. A top student in her class, she wondered if she should have been more knowledgeable in this regard.

"Well, it advanced the argument by contending that euthanasia is not only a humane intervention, but a major cost-saving to society. Quite appealing to people in an age of financial hardship. I would have to say you're going to be graduating at just the right time, Tritzchler, because I think our curriculum at the medical college is going to undergo some changes – perhaps rather significant."

"Might I ask, what kind of changes?"

"If I had my way, none, but the way things are shaping up, I'm thinking that our time-honored foundation of medical ethics may undergo reformulation. Mandatory sterilizations? That could be just a start."

"That's a pretty big start, Professor. From your course on sterilization law, I thought those statutes were basically fixed . . . unchangeable."

"They have been, you're right, but you have to realize that, like anything, they're subject to override. And over the past five years, we've certainly witnessed a major erosion of our established norms. Why would it stop with euthanasia?"

Annika had heard these ideas – everybody had – but she regarded them as nothing more than rhetoric from the far-right – presumably a minority. But now, it was unnerving to hear the chairman of the psychiatry department discussing them, as if doing so bequeathed them with legitimacy. All she could say was, "So Herr Professor, I guess I'm a bit lost. In this scenario, who would determine which individuals are dispensable?" The whole idea was inconceivable.

"Frankly, Tritzchler, I'd rather not even entertain such discussions. It's so anathema to every moral principle we've grown up with. But I will say this. Things can change very quickly. There's no telling where things will end up." Annika stared straight ahead, blankly. "But let's move on. What brings you here. Why'd you arrange to see me?"

"Oh . . ." She blinked, as if coming back to reality. "Well . . . I wanted to talk about graduation . . . what I might be doing with my degree."

"Right, right. Of course. Do you have any ideas as to what you might like to be pursuing?"

"Actually, sir, I do. I've been attending the Berlin Psychoanalytic Institute most of the past year. I've really enjoyed psychotherapy with patients. We've been using techniques from Freud and Adler. I'm not sure what types of employment possibilities there might be in that regard . . ."

"I'm not personally acquainted with Matthias Göring, but I know that the Institute is frowned upon. I suspect it's only because of his cousin that the Institute's allowed to continue. But, be that as it may, what sort of issues do you find yourself dealing with there?"

"Most of the patients, Professor, present with anxiety neurosis or depression. Some are alcoholics, some come in with sexual issues. The thing I've found is that if you can establish trust with them, you find that they tend to be feeling overwhelmed adjusting to the new social challenges."

"Like . . ."

"Like financial challenges, for sure, but also . . ." She lowered her voice. ". . . also living in fear . . . seeing neighbors arrested, co-workers disappearing, virulent anti-Semitism – things like that."

Bonhoeffer frowned. Looking around the room, then back at Annika, he said, "I must warn you, Annika, that what you're describing is precisely why the government eyes your group with suspicion."

"I know that, Professor, thank you. Between you, your son, Dietrich, and Doctor Rittmeister, I realize that we're on tenuous footing."

"Who is Rittmeister?"

"He's a neurologist originally from Switzerland. He joined our group last year. He's quite a gifted psychoanalyst. I've learned a lot from him."

"Very well. All I can say is please be careful." Annika smiled. "So back to your graduation. You want to be working, of course." Annika nodded in agreement. "Much as I am loath to admit it, Annika, finding a job . . . for you, I mean . . . well, it will be challenging. There aren't many positions available, even with your outstanding scholarship . . . you know . . . you being a woman and all."

She wasn't quite prepared for that. The words stung. Here she was in her final year of medical school with a superior grade-point-average, but being one of only two women in the medical program, she had encountered discrimination at every turn.

"Sir, with all due respect, I feel that I have the competence of any student here. Even more than many. Are you suggesting I won't be able to work?"

"What I'm saying is that prejudice against women doctors is rampant. You *are* better qualified than many, but competence – not just in medicine, but in all professions – usually takes a back seat to gender."

"I . . . I don't know what to say . . ."

"Listen, Fräulein Tritzchler. Don't abandon hope. You're a fighter. I have contacts at several psychiatric hospitals. I'll write to a few of my colleagues. My brother speaks very highly of you, and your performance here certainly stands on its own. Between the two of us, we should be able to help you."

Annika's discussion with Doctor Bonhoeffer left little doubt in her mind that Nazi ideology was creeping inexorably into medicine.

Good was defined by anything that was beneficial to the Reich, regardless of the cost to any one individual.

She left his office weighted down with anxiety. Between classes, labs, and term-papers, academics alone had always been challenging, but now were the added worries of finding work in a milieu decidedly unkind to women. She thought bitterly of how promising things had been during the Weimar era, which at this point seemed a lifetime ago, even though it was only a few years.

Later that afternoon, she sat down in the dining hall for a cup of tea, and was joined by one of her classmates. She didn't know him very well, since Helmut was a fourth-year transfer student from the University of Würzburg.

They were sharing small talk – the weather, the food, sights around Berlin – but when they touched on lab work, Helmut said, "I'll be honest. You are much better equipped here in Berlin than we were in Würzburg."

"In what ways," Annika asked.

"At our school, we never had enough cadavers. Much of our study was simply viewing tissue in jars of formaldehyde."

"My word. How can you understand anatomy without bodies to dissect?" She slurped some tea, giving him a moment to answer.

"It was a real problem. We found ourselves in competition for cadavers with other medical schools. I studied for a short while at Tübingen. There it was even worse. That was a big part of my reason for transferring to Berlin."

"I didn't realize that. I could never have understood medicine without actual dissection. So, students from Bavaria are being awarded medical degrees without a solid grounding in anatomy?"

"That *had* been the case, but from what I've heard recently, they're not having as much of a problem anymore."

"How so?" Annika asked, taking a last hurried sip from her cup.

"A lot of cadavers are coming in now . . ." He could see that she was bewildered. "They're from Dachau, and I guess some of the other KZ's. You know . . . concentration camps."

"I-I'm not sure I'm following you." Annika brought the cup of tea to her lips, while staring intently at Helmut. She took a slow, measured sip as he paused to look around the room before answering.

"Prisoners, Annika. Dead prisoners."

Annika coughed, spitting the tea back into her cup, trying not to regurgitate on the table.

Now whispering, Helmut said, "From what my former colleagues tell me, the cadavers show signs of execution: bullet holes, ligature marks around the neck, lacerations, and abrasions that they say are all consistent with torture. Maybe worse, many died of exhaustion. I suspect they were simply worked to death."

Annika had heard enough. Between Bonhoeffer's news and now Helmut, any thoughts of studying were gone . . . *I won't be able to concentrate tonight. Maybe a glass of wine when I get back.*

She walked back to the dormitory, everything looking bleak, until there in the mail slot was an envelope. *Could it be . . .?* It was from Poland. She ran up the steps to her room where, once inside and too excited to sit down, she opened it. In elegant script, it read:

1 January, 1939

To my beautiful German soulmate.

Here I sit, New Years Day. Everyone around me seems to be celebrating the new year. But I am alone, physically and mentally, thinking, dreaming, of you.

I so cherish the time we had together. I think of you every hour of every day. You are my first thought in the morning, and the last before falling asleep at night.

My work in Krakow continues unabated, and Doctor Sukhareva and I hope to be publishing our findings at some point within the next six months.

I have applied for a travel permit to attend a conference inVienna in July. Hans Asperger will be speaking at the University on childhood abnormalities, which could assist Sukhareva and me in our work on autistic psychopathology. See if you can obtain a copy of Asperger's recent publication, Das "psychisch abnorme Kind."

Fräulein

I'm sure you would find the conference useful.

It would be so marvelous if you could attend. Please let me know if that might be possible. If so, I 'll be counting down the days until we meet again.

Keep looking up at the moon, and when you see it, know that not only your parents but I too will be looking.

I love you, Annika,, now and always.

Pasha

Tears streamed down her cheeks as she read and reread every word. She fondled the letter, then pressed it to her chest, imagining their reunion. *Seeing Pasha again! In June!* She was going, damn the cost.

Juden Sind Verboten!

We are not shooting enough professors.
Vladimir Lenin

May, 1939

"*Approbation Als Ärztin.*" Holding the parchment with trembling hands, Annika read the words almost as if they were alien. *An endorsement to practice medicine. Me! A doctor.* The certificate blurred through her tears. *I made it!* All those wearisome hours in classes, labs, clinics and libraries were now safely behind her.

It was impossible to be in this moment without thinking back to her childhood. She recalled discussions with her parents about people who were disabled and how much she wanted to help them. She remembered her parents' encouragement to follow in the footsteps of her father and stepfather. So much had happened in her short life – so many changes, so much upheaval. No longer was she the impressionable little girl filled with naïve images of a good and perfect world. No, this was far from the Kingdom of God she had been taught to believe in. But as a physician, she would at least have the opportunity to put her values into action: to ease suffering, aid in the restoration of health; to be, in short, the steward that she believed Christ intended of her.

"Annika!" She turned. It was Jürgen. "Let me take your picture." Annika smiled, posing for the camera. "I'll send you a copy," Jürgen promised, before rejoining his family. Annika waved, but too late for him to see. What a bittersweet day. She desperately missed her parents, now more than ever. They would be so proud. She had tried to contact them as her graduation date neared, but none of her recent letters had been answered. *Oh well,* she thought, trying to console herself, *it's better they're not here. I know they're safe. Hitler's not in Belgium.* And then, smiling, *I'll send them Jürgen's photo of me holding my certificate.*

But her parents weren't the only worry. Pasha was on her mind, constantly. The longer they were separated, the more of an obsession he became. She was worried about Pasha's collaboration with Grunya Sukhareva, the noted researcher in Moscow. From everything he had told her during their time in Geneva, she figured that his connection with a Soviet professor could bring Pasha himself under scrutiny by the Soviet secret police. He had said that ever since Kirov's assassination in 1934, Stalin had tightened his grip, and that fear – particularly among the intelligentsia – was widespread. Annika had seen footage from the highly publicized show trials, where diplomats from the Soviet Politburo – even former friends of Stalin – had been found guilty of treason, and executed.

That said, Pasha had assured Annika that living in Poland was basically free from Soviet dragnets. He assured her he was safe. So, rather than worry, she was thrilled to think that in just one month they would be seeing each other again. It would be like a honeymoon. Ever since receiving his letter, she had spent weeks reading everything she could find about Vienna. Austria brought forth images of romantic boat tours on the Danube, surrounded by hillsides dotted with medieval castles. Vienna was Shubert's birthplace, and a virtual playground for Mozart, Beethoven, and Haydn. *That's it,* she concluded, *the Viennese Philharmonic!* Her imagination ran away with itself. By return mail, she had excitedly mentioned all the things they could do in Vienna.

The conference was scheduled for early July, a perfect time to be in the old city. They would be staying at the luxurious Hotel Bristol on Vienna's Ringstrasse. And they were each traveling by train in order to view the pristine Austrian countryside. With her academic study behind her, Annika saw this trip as a celebration, an opportunity to get out of Berlin for a while and really unwind.

As it turned out, the excursion to Vienna did not begin as magically as she had hoped. It was not only much longer than she expected, but there were ongoing reminders of the social upheavals she had hoped to get away from. Somewhere between Dresden and Prague, as the train was slowing to approach a small town, Annika spotted a sign that gave her true pause. At first glance, she thought she had misread it, but turning her head for a second look, she read,

Juden betreten dieses Dorf
auf ihre eigene Gefahr!

"Jews enter this village at their own risk." Her heart sank. *I can't get away from it. It's become a virus . . . growing, spreading . . . If Germany's the host and if this disease isn't eradicated, it will end up killing us, like any malignancy.* That thought weighed heavily on her mind. She couldn't escape it. It was like a song that gets stuck in one's brain, maddeningly repeating itself, over and over again.

More than 12 hours had elapsed before the train finally rolled into Vienna's *Hauptbahnhof.* Wearily, yet excited to see Pasha, she collected her luggage and walked onto the platform, fully expecting to be greeted by her soulmate. But, looking around, he was nowhere to be seen. She walked a few steps, craning her neck in every direction, all her senses focused on finding him. So rapt was her attention that she stumbled on an upturned section of pavement, catching herself just in time to avoid falling into a puddle. Still no sign of him. The station was only weakly illuminated by the lights overhead, so she stood as conspicuously as possible under an overhead light.

Fifteen minutes passed, then twenty, and still no Pasha. She checked the "Arrival" board and saw that his train had come in on schedule several hours beforehand. As she waited, Annika was a bit taken aback by the preponderance of German soldiers; they seemed to be everywhere. Maybe, she wondered, this shouldn't be a surprise. It had only been a couple of months since Germany annexed Austria, and it now appeared that Vienna was awash in Nazism. Even in the train terminal, Nazi flags and swastikas were everywhere. *Oh, c'mon Pasha. Where are you?* It was now approaching 2100 hours. After an hour of waiting, she figured something had happened; maybe he was at the hotel.

Dog-tired, Annika collected her luggage and walked out to the street, where a taxi was idling at the curb. Approaching it, she turned just in time to spot yet another disturbing sign, this one in front of a café, stating "Jews are not welcome here." *How naïve I guess I was to think I'd be getting away from all the Jew-baiting and race-mongering at home.* She shook her head in disbelief as she struggled with the bags. An image popped into her mind. It was her stepfather, distinguished-looking in his long white coat, stethoscope wrapped around his neck. She could feel the rage boiling inside of her. *What arrogance! What makes them think any self-respecting Jew would even want to eat in such a dump!*

The long trip had clearly taken its toll. She felt drained to the point where it was an effort simply to raise her hand to hail the cab. The hotel was only a few kilometers from the station, but the military checkpoints necessitated a circuitous route before reaching the *Bristol*, which overlooked Vienna's famed Opera House. The inner lobby was opulent and inspiring, but her last ounce of energy evaporated on learning from the concierge that Doctor Kushelevsky had not yet arrived. *Not yet arrived? How could that be? He should have gotten here hours ago.* For a moment, she wondered if she was actually at the right hotel, and then began questioning if she had made some kind of mistake on the date or – God forbid – perhaps even the city.

Before heading up to her room, she asked the clerk, "Could you kindly check to see if the train originating in Moscow arrived this morning?"

"I'm terribly sorry, Fräulein, but we'll have to wait until the morning. There'll be no one at the station answering phones at this hour."

Discouraged, Annika thanked the man, promised to check with him in the morning, and took the elevator to her room. The night passed restlessly, with her tossing and turning, uncertain and worried as to the whereabouts of her lover. The next morning, after showered and dressed, she returned to the front desk, full of expectation, hoping for news.

The clerk checked his book. *"Nein, Fräulein, wir haben nichts von Doktor Kushelevsky gehört."*

No news. There was nothing else she could do but grab a taxi to the university. She wondered if Pasha might arrive at the conference late, like he did in Geneva. The ride to the campus was actually more disquieting than the previous night. Daylight brought signs of a heavy military presence. People and traffic seemed to move about normally, with streetcars, automobiles and neatly dressed pedestrians carrying out their everyday chores, but swastikas hung freely from buildings, and people seemed to greet each other with a perfunctory *"Heil Hitler"* instead of the more traditional *"Grüß Gott."* And as the taxi wound its way through urban blocks, she noticed many storefronts with crudely painted Stars of David identifying Jewish-owned businesses. But it was a large sign on the main thoroughfare, cars whizzing by in each direction, that was most shocking of all. Written in large red lettering against a white background, it read, "Judaism is criminal," and appeared next to a sloppy caricature of a Jewish man with an abnormally long nose.

It was a relief to reach the university, where she could feel surrounded by intellectuals, people who would recognize the absurdity of narrowmindedness and prejudice, a sanctum of sanity, she figured. She found the lecture hall without any difficulty and secured a chair near the entrance. As in Geneva, she saved a seat for Pasha. Every time the door opened, her heart leapt, but none of the tardy arrivals were the man she had traveled so far to see.

The first day of the conference opened with Hans Asperger discussing his notion of autism being a condition fundamentally different from schizophrenia. It was a novel idea and a major shift in assumptions about mental illness, especially as it related to child psychology. But she was disappointed that his views on eugenics and sterilization were not essentially different from Nazi race theories, and as the lecture went on, she found it difficult to disentangle his clinical beliefs from prevailing political ideas.

Late that afternoon as the symposium was adjourning for the day, she was the first in line to speak personally with the vaunted professor. "*Herr Doktor*," she began, "my name is Annika Tritzchler. From Berlin. I'm supposed to meet a colleague, Pavel Kushelevsky, and was wondering if you might know something of his whereabouts."

"Oh . . . why yes indeed. Pavel." Looking her up and down, it was clear that he recognized the name. "So, you are an acquaintance, Fräulein?"

"Yes, sir, and please, call me Annika," she responded, demurely.

"Yes, well . . ." He looked down at a list. "Doctor Kushelevsky did write to me. He indicated that he would be meeting a female colleague from Berlin. I take it you're that individual, yes?"

Annika felt relieved. "Yes, that's correct, Professor. We had made arrangements to meet at a hotel downtown, but he hasn't arrived. Nor have I heard anything from him. I was just wondering if you might have heard from him."

The professor frowned. There were a few others from the audience waiting politely to speak to him, so he took Annika by the elbow and pulled her out of earshot. "Actually, Fräulein, I noticed Pavel wasn't in the audience. I was hoping, myself, to meet with him. You say you've made plans, but haven't heard from him?" She nodded. Just then, two uniformed men from the SS appeared in the doorway. Seeing them, Asperger said, "I wish I could help, but I'm afraid I have no information."

Annika looked back to the entrance in time to see the two officers turn and leave. She looked back at Asperger. "Professor, Pavel seemed quite determined to be here. I can't think of anything that might have interfered with his plans. He mentioned having talked with you about collaborating with him and Doctor Sukhareva."

Asperger peeked over to the now empty doorway, then over Annika's shoulder at the line of people waiting to speak with him. Scratching his chin, he said, "Yes, you're quite right. He did intend to be here . . . Let me ask you. Would you happen to know if Pavel has recently traveled to Moscow . . . maybe went there to meet with Sukhareva?"

"I don't believe so . . . I would think he would have mentioned that. But now that I think of it . . . I-I don't know. It's been difficult corresponding with him. Why do you ask?"

Asperger looked around the room. In little more than a whisper, he said, "Well let me just say, I have colleagues in Moscow who have informed me that things there have gotten, well, a bit out of hand. You know, with Stalin and all."

Annika's breathing quickened. Stumbling for words, she said, "I . . . I'm not sure what you mean, Herr Professor. Could you tell me what you've heard? I mean . . . about things in Russia?"

"Yes, of course. The thing is, my dear, Joseph Stalin is apparently on a rant. It's crazy. Many have been arrested, particularly educators, bankers, lawyers . . . even *priests*. Anybody considered to have influence . . . they threaten him."

Annika gulped, her eyes moistening. "But Pavel shouldn't be in danger . . . not in Poland, should he? After all, he's a professor, a scientist. He's not political." It was as if she was already pleading Pasha's case.

"If Pavel is in Poland, no. I wouldn't think that the situation in Russia would be of any immediate consequence to him. Poland's a sovereign country, Fräulein, as you know. But then again . . ."

"Then again, *what*?" she asked. Annika was feeling irritated by his continued use of the word, "Fräulein." She found it pejorative, especially given that she was now a physician, just like him and almost everyone else in the room. Yet before she dared correct him, Asperger asked a question for which she was totally unprepared.

"If you don't mind my asking, is Doctor Kushelevsky . . ." He hesitated as if the words alone were too incendiary. "What I mean is . . . is it possible he may be . . . *Jewish?*"

Annika was alarmed. She stared at him, almost in disbelief. "I-I'm sorry. What on earth would that have to do with anything?"

"Well, it's only, you see . . . from what I *hear*, that is . . . Stalin is paranoid. He believes he's being conspired against. My colleagues in Moscow and St. Petersburg tell me that he considers the intelligentsia to be bourgeois, which as a Marxist, as I'm sure you can understand, he's opposed to."

"And what's that got to do with Pavel being Jewish?"

"Stalin perceives the bourgeoisie to be followers of Trotsky, and Trotsky, to those who know him, is a Jew." Annika was nonplussed. "Stalin hates Trotsky and all his Bolsheviks. They threaten his power. So, his purge, as I understand it, is aimed at getting rid of all opposition, which means Bolsheviks, Trotskyites and – by extension, of course – Jews."

Asperger uttered the words dispassionately, as if he were talking about nothing more important than the weather. Annika, on the other hand, was overwhelmed with worry, even anger. Was this not the height of hypocrisy? *Who is he to be criticizing political upheaval in Soviet universities when the same scenario has already been carried out right here in Vienna?* She had learned that within weeks of Hitler's annexation of Austria, two-thirds of the entire Vienna Medical School had been fired simply because they were Jewish, and just as bad, there had been virtually no protest from the remaining faculty. Asperger was one of them. She asked herself, *would he really be concerned about Pasha if he knew him to be Jewish?*

Asperger could tell that he had upset Annika. He put an arm around her shoulders in a superficial, if somewhat bony, hug. "I'm terribly sorry, Fräulein. I didn't mean to worry you."

"It's *Doctor*," Annika said.

"I beg your pardon?"

"Doctor. *Doctor* Tritzchler."

"Oh, yes, *natürlich* . . . my mistake, Doctor . . . *Tritzchler*, right?"

Annika stood impassively. "So, until we hear differently, let's just assume Pavel's train may have been delayed, or that for some reason, he was rerouted. And, of course, it's very possible he could be stuck in an area without telephone." As she turned to leave, Asperger said, "I'll let you know tomorrow if I've heard anything." She simply nodded, making no attempt to respond.

It was only 4 P.M., still plenty of daylight, and with so much anxiety, Annika decided to walk rather than take a taxi. Armed with a map of the city, she headed southwest toward Schönbrunn Castle, the imperial summer estate of Ferdinand II dating back to the mid-1600s. Her journey was anything but sanguine, despite the casualness of other pedestrians. She hadn't been on the sidewalks for more than ten minutes before the melodies from a brass band became audible in the distance. As it got closer, a line of spectators formed on the sidewalk. Craning her neck, Annika could see a long parade of what she surmised to be Hitler Youth marching up the street in unison – two by two – all wearing white shirts, ties, and shorts. Three boys at the head of the procession each carried a flag: one Austrian, one Nazi, and the other, to Annika's horror, a flag with a skull-and-bones insignia. The jubilant spectators cheered, and as the flags passed, they thrust out their right arms along with a crisp *"Heil Hitler!"*

Annika ducked into an alleyway which led to the opposite block. There was no getting away. A large poster was fastened to one of the buildings. It dripped in sycophancy, with the message, *"Wir danken Adolph."* As she hurried on, she thought, *this beautiful city . . . so much of its culture and richness coming from Jews . . . and here they are, "thanking Hitler." Unfathomable.* Stores on almost every street had been singled out as Jewish owned. She passed one with hand-painted lettering across the façade stating that the owner was "on vacation in Dachau." Next to that was a Star of David and crudely-sketched gallows showing a figure hanging from it. Dried paint had dripped freely from the lettering. Soldiers were everywhere, some in a jocular mood, others standing grimly in front of Jewish businesses, hoping by their very presence to dissuade shoppers from patronizing Jewish merchants.

Eventually Annika reached Schönbrunn Palace. Plainly visible through a wrought-iron fence, its regal, mazelike gardens blazed in assorted colors. Birds sang; viceroy butterflies flitted about; and the late afternoon sun lent a marmalade finish to the castle's lush, manicured lawns. The world around her seemed to be going about its business as usual. She approached the gate, thinking she had just enough time to tour the gardens. But then, another sign.

Juden
in der Eintritt den Schlosspark laut Erlass
des Polizeipräsidium vom 24.6.1938
Verboten!

Jews forbidden to enter the castle park? By order of the police? Coming up behind her was a well-dressed man and woman, arm in arm, approaching the entrance. As Annika stepped back, the couple paused to peruse the sign, then, without hesitation, the man muttered something to his companion and pulled her forward, away from the entrance. The woman's hand was at her face as they hurried along. *She was crying,* Annika realized, watching them disappear from view. She could only begin to imagine their fear and rejection. She thought of her own privileged status as an "Aryan" – *an Übermensch, isn't that what they call us, the pinnacle of human evolution?* But as quickly as the words came to her mind, they lost meaning. *It's all an illusion,* she told herself, *a monumental deception.* Once again came the feeling of being deeply ashamed to be German.

The next day started out like the day before. The ride to the university, the lecture, the questions – it was pretty much the same. And without Pasha, there was nothing stimulating about it. Thinking of him occupied her every thought. At the luncheon, she was seated with other physicians and psychologists. Discussions began with

Annika making an observation about the size of the audience: "I would have thought more people would have attended."

A young intern sitting across from her responded in a humorous tone, "Well, we would have had a much bigger audience if the symposium had been held a few months ago, right Dieter?" He elbowed the man next to him. Several people chuckled.

Annika did not catch the joke. "I'm not sure I understand."

"Oh, c'mon. You don't see any Shylocks around, do you?" More sniggering.

Annika's face reddened. At that moment, an older man at the far end of the table put down his fork and said with an air of authority, "Gentlemen, please. Let's maintain some decorum. We have a lady in our presence." The man had thinning gray hair and wore a stylish tweed suit. When he spoke, everyone seemed to straighten up. But then, looking directly at Annika, he asked, "Where are you coming from, my dear?" There was no mistaking his condescending tone.

"Berlin," she replied.

"Oh, *sehr gut*." Looking around the table, he said, "There now, you see, gentleman? The young lady has traveled a long way for this conference. Let's please make her feel welcome." Then to Annika, he asked, "And what is your name, Fräulein?"

Annika cut him off. "Doctor Tritzchler," she snapped, matching his gaze with an assertive stare of her own. That brought a gasp of mock horror from one of the junior doctors, followed by a smattering of fraternal snickers.

"Oh, quite . . . quite," sputtered the speaker, upbraided and now slightly annoyed. "Well, Doctor Tritzchler, pleased to make your acquaintance. I am August Hirt." He extended his hand, and as Annika reached forward, he took her hand and brought it to his lips with an affected kiss. "I direct the anatomy institute at the University of Greifswald, not far from you in Berlin. What I think our young colleagues are implying is that the authorities here – just like in *your* city – have . . . shall we say . . . *retired* all of the Jewish professors."

"*Auf wiedersehen, Juden!*" joked a young man beside her.

146

"*Ja*," intoned another. "*Gute reise*," he said, waving his hand. More laughter.

"Please, gentlemen," insisted the speaker, holding up his hand to stop them. He again turned to Annika. "What they are referring to, Doctor Tritzchler, is that the medical school here has been tasked with replacing over one hundred and fifty positions."

It was all beginning to make sense now. "So that's why Doctor Freud isn't here?" Annika asked. "I expected to see him either on the panel or at least in the audience."

"Sigmund Freud? You must mean Sigmund *Rascher*? He's the distinguished looking chap sitting right beside you." There were peals of laughter. Annika looked to her left as Rascher, his mouth full of schnitzel, glanced over, tipping two fingers to his forehead in a mimicked salute.

Doctor Hirt continued, "Sigmund Freud . . ." He paused, mulling over the words. "Well, I hear Doctor Freud is no longer in Vienna. Apparently, he and his daughter were detained . . . or, rather, put in *protective custody* by the authorities."

"You mean, Gestapo, don't you Doctor Hirt?" Annika asked.

"Apparently so. But my understanding is that he is, perhaps as we speak, en route to England, where I'm sure he will be quite happy."

"Good riddance," barked Fritz, one of the junior doctors. "Another 'island ape.' They can have him . . ."

". . . And his kike daughter," said another, referring to Anna Freud.

Fritz snorted. "England's full of perverts, anyway. I'm sure it stirs their juices reading about his wet dreams and his fantasies of having sex with his mother . . ." He turned to his friends, who were all laughing. Then turning to Annika, as if remembering he was in the presence of a woman, he said, "*Ah, tut mir Leid.* My apologies, Fräulein…"

One of the men added, "You know, Tritzchler, I have to hand it to your young people. The best thing the Berlin students ever did was burning all those Goddamned hymie books."

"*Civilization and Its Discontents*," mocked Rascher, as he chewed on a roll. Then looking directly at Annika, he said, "Our only 'discontent' is that for way too long we've had way too many Jews around. Time to cull the herd, if you ask me," which prompted everyone seated to begin knocking on the table to show their agreement. Annika stared straight ahead, avoiding anyone's eyes. If this was an attempt at humiliation, it was working.

Just then someone at the head table began clinking a knife against a water glass in an effort to get everyone's attention. "The meeting will reconvene in five minutes."

Annika got up without a word to her detractors. She sat by herself through the remainder of the symposium. It ended as unceremoniously as it began, and she exited without bidding anyone goodbye. Finally certain that Pasha would not be coming, she decided that this would be her final day in Vienna. It was unusually hot and humid as she stepped out into the street, and within minutes her clothing stuck to her skin. The sun, oppressive and opaque, hid behind huge dark clouds conspiring off in the distance to assault the city, maybe bringing welcome relief.

Having gone only a few blocks, she heard a loud clanging of bells. Curious, she wove her way through streets and alleyways, eventually glimpsing over the rooftops an enormous tower jutting hundreds of meters into the air. She came to a large square thronged by tourists, where in the center stood St. Stephen's Cathedral, a massive medieval church. She had to arch her neck to see the cathedral's steep roof. It was constructed of multicolored tiles depicting on one side double-headed eagles, and on the other was a huge coat-of-arms. It dated back centuries to the Habsburg Empire. Strolling around the massive cathedral, awed by statues and gargoyles, Annika came upon two huge Romanesque towers. In the center was a mammoth wooden door – dark and ancient. To her surprise, the door was open to the public.

If the crowds outside felt in any way festive, the inside of the cathedral was just the opposite – dark and somber. People spoke in hushed tones under vaulted ceilings of soaring beams and ornate stained-glass windows. Looking up, Annika felt humbled by her humanness, insignificant in this atmosphere brimming with history and transcendence.

There were eighteen altars lining the interior walls, but her eyes were drawn to the sanctuary where a lofty tabernacle was framed by patron saints of old. She approached it slowly and with reverence. Directly in front of her was Saint Mary gazing heavenward to Christ, who Himself was looking down awaiting St. Stephen, the first martyr. Annika was overwhelmed. Never before had she felt such Divine presence. Several people dotted the nave, deep in prayer and succorance. She fell to her knees, alone before God. Rows of figurines looked down from a lofty perch high above – bishops, martyrs, and kings – all supplicants from long ago.

Closing her eyes, Annika recited the invocation taught to her by her mother. *Our Father, who art in Heaven, hallowed be thy name. Thy kingdom come; thy will be done . . .* As she did, she felt her parent's presence. She prayed for their safety, and that the day would come when she would see them again. Very softly, the columns of brass organ pipes began to moan from on-high, enveloping the spotty congregants in a baleful blend of tenor and bass. Something happened. Pasha seemed to be with her. She bowed her head and devoted the next ten minutes beseeching God to watch over Pasha, to keep him safe and free from any torment.

Finished with her prayers, Annika started down the aisle. Unexpectedly, a painting caught her eye. Dark, ancient, hauntingly striking, the portrait was called the "Maria Pötsch Icon." It depicted the Madonna holding her baby son, Jesus. She stopped, unable to pry her eyes from it. The more she stared, the more alive it seemed. *Something about the Madonna's eyes. What is it?* she wondered. Annika blinked once, then quickly again, and when she refocused, the icon's eyes appeared to be... *filled with tears?*

Annika was visibly moved. The experience was powerful. Filled with emotion, she stepped out into the street just in time to hear a thunderclap. The sky had grown dark, the air noticeably cooler. Suddenly, a flash of lightening, and then another deafening rumble. She looked around. People were scurrying about like ants on a griddle as the saturated clouds now spewed large droplets of rain – first only a few, then a loud, spattering downpour. Still transfixed by her encounter, Annika stood motionless while people in every direction ran for cover. Unfazed, she looked to the sky, oblivious to the driving rain pelting her body, drenching her in its cold torrent. Her curls drooped as hair matted her face. The overpowering sense of presence was a reminder of her insignificance, her complete vulnerability. Soaked, lightening flashing all around, Annika stood alone on the sidewalk and lifted her voice in prayer.

"Heavenly Father, I pray that You guide me through this difficult time. Help me to remain true to Your Word . . . and help us as a people to recognize sin. Grant me the strength to stand up for the downtrodden, those whose voices are drowned out by hate. I pray for courage and understanding, in the name of Christ Jesus, my Lord and Savior. Amen."

Bernburg

You will not drown the truth in seas of blood.
Maxim Gorky

June, 1939

Annika returned to Berlin confused and crestfallen. She had hoped to find a letter from Pasha explaining his whereabouts, but . . . nothing. She waited a week or so, figuring that the foreign postal service may be slowed by the social unrest. When nothing arrived, she tried making a long-distance call to see if she could reach him at the university in Warsaw. Even with a Polish-speaking friend to help translate, they came up empty-handed. In a moment of self-doubt, she wondered, *maybe he just didn't want to continue our relationship. Maybe for him it was nothing more than a dalliance.*

Worrying about Pasha wasn't the only thing occupying her thoughts. Annika needed to begin a medical residency, which led her once again to Karl Bonhoeffer. To him, she was more than just a student; he wanted to help her in any way he could. It was suggested that she consider interning at the Anhalt Psychiatric Clinic in Bernburg. He knew the director, Doctor Willi Enke. The sanitorium was located a hundred and seventy-five kilometers southwest of Berlin with over a hundred beds. It offered Annika as rich an exposure to the field of psychiatry that she could hope to find anywhere, so it was agreed. Bonhoeffer would write the recommendation and make all necessary arrangements.

It was soon October, and Annika found the village of Bernburg much to her liking. Situated in the heartland, the people and the town's medieval architecture lent a provincialism that made her happy to be out from the hustle and bustle of Berlin. She was thrilled to have found a flat on one of the town's older streets, where her window looked out to a half-timbered, four-story structure dating back to the late 1500s. One of the town's treasures was a magnificent Renaissance castle that looked down on the Saale River, and within days, Annika discovered a meandering footpath on the opposite side, which had already become a refuge following stressful days at the hospital.

Work was much different from life as a student. Being a professional meant long hours, constant contact with patients, and supervision by senior physicians, all of whom were male and quite chauvinistic. There were no other women doctors, which led to Annika being frequently mistaken as a nurse. Even when her credentials *were* recognized, her formulations were subjected to rigorous challenge, and often denigrated summarily. Her gender alone repudiated what she had hoped would be equal footing with her male counterparts.

Despite that, she approached her work with enthusiasm and an eagerness to learn. That meant, first and foremost, getting beyond the pungency of urine, feces, and infections, which at times was so overpowering that even liberal use of ammonia did little more than further irritate nostrils and airways alike. Beyond that, her hours were long and sometimes tedious, including many grueling night shifts. The hospital's many rooms were earmarked according to function, some filled with beds, dormitory style, others serving as dayrooms where patients congregated with no activities to engage their minds. There sat the forgotten – men and women in various states of dress or undress, most having no hope of ever leaving the hospital and treated by staff as if their lives were meaningless, which in this environment was true. For them, days had turned into years – for some, decades. Their existence was circumscribed within the gray walls that confined them. The longest among the residents were distinguishable by hollow eyes and vacuous stares, any sense of purpose being limited to the most basic functions: eating, eliminating, and an occasional bath. *We treat them like vegetables,* Annika lamented. *Life has abandoned them.*

"Wouldn't it be helpful to get a phonograph in the dayroom . . . give the patients some music?" she asked Herta, one of the nurses.

"Oh boy, are *you* a newbie," came the response. "Nothin' gonna help these folks. We just try to make 'em compliant . . . keep 'em from actin' out."

Maintaining order, a key goal, was not easily accomplished. All patients, regardless of diagnosis, were herded together throughout the day, often making tempers flare. Annika remembered research that described infighting among rats confined to a small cage. Here at Bernberg, it seemed the same. Those who became agitated were dealt with in a variety of ways. Some were transferred upstairs where rows of bathtubs awaited them. Strapped inside, they could spend hours immersed in water up to their necks with just enough room for bites of food served by disinterested attendants. Others were placed in ice baths, the thinking being that the cold water would slow down metabolism, thereby relaxing them. Insulin and electricity were also used to induce convulsions, another means of tranquilizing the rowdy. But most common, especially among psychotic or combative patients, were the camisoles – canvas straightjackets that kept their arms securely fastened about their torso. Such patients were pariahs, deprived of touch and emotional contact, often soaked in their own excretions.

Annika empathized with these patients, yet there were so many that she didn't have time to bestow the humanness and sensitivity that was so much her nature. She quickly came to recognize a difference between the idealism taught in school versus the pragmatism of the hospital. Her impression of Bernburg was that differential diagnoses meant little in terms of how patients were treated. Instead, it was the loud, rambunctious, or hallucinating patient that tended to get most of the attention. *Blessed are the meek,* she recalled, yet it was precisely those who tended to go unnoticed by the overworked and undertrained staff.

Dealing with so many patients, she found herself, like most doctors, developing favorites. Elsie was one of them. She was a young waif-like girl, barely sixteen, who went out of her way to have no contact with others – staff or patients. She wasn't violent or in any way unruly, simply avoidant. As such, the staff had little to do with her, most not even knowing her name. Annika viewed her differently. Each time she approached the patient, Elsie hunched her shoulders, turned her head sideways, and tucked her chin into her chest. Annika would try to calm her by gently placing a hand on Elsie's shoulder, or sometimes stroking her hair; anything to be reassuring, but that usually triggered her to push backward even harder, as if she was being electrocuted. Annika was never put off by her reaction, and would instead persist by whispering consolingly in her ear.

"Why do you waste time on her, Doctor?" asked Jutta, the head nurse. "She's a whack-job."

"I'm not so sure, Jutta." Annika saw something in Elsie others didn't. She wasn't sure what, but somehow the diagnosis – *dementia praecox* – didn't seem to fit. "I think, down deep, Elsie's as sane as you and me."

Jutta rolled her eyes. "Really. I don't. She's paranoid. Sees things. If she was any loonier, we'd have her in a strait jacket."

"Well, that's exactly what we *shouldn't* do. She strikes me as incredibly frightened . . . like she's been traumatized . . ."

"Um hmmm," Jutta muttered dismissively, continuing with her notations.

"I think there's a very scared little girl inside her . . . and my guess is the asylum is just making her worse."

"You'll have a hard time convincing Doctor Enke of that." With that, Jutta turned on her heels and walked down the corridor.

Annika knew she was right. This was more of a warehouse than a treatment facility. And even though Annika's residency was intended as a training experience, Doctor Enke, the medical director, was not one to involve himself in any form of scholarly debate.

154

Intervention, as he saw it, was less about cures than administrative costs. Patients here were numbers, pure and simple. Annika knew that about him, and was determined to avoid becoming jaded. She recalled Pasha telling her about his friend, Viktor Frankl, who had ended that spate of suicides by persevering with a novel treatment approach. *Isn't that what we're trained for? Here, it seems that anyone who is frightened or oppositional is labelled "schizophrenic."*

The records showed that Elsie had been a patient for the past three years, dropped off by wealthy parents who were said to seem embarrassed by her. They reported her as "odd," even delusional. *"You simply can't believe anything she says"* was their description when signing the commitment papers. Based on the parent's assessment, the intake staff notated her as psychotic, which was sufficient for Elsie to be admitted indefinitely to the institution. Since that date, her parents had never come for a visit nor did they call to inquire about her welfare.

𝔗𝔥𝔢 𝔉𝔬𝔯𝔪𝔰

The way you see people is the way you treat them, and the way you treat them is what they become.

Johann Wolfgang von Goethe

<u>14 December, 1939</u>

I haven't heard from Pasha in so long. And now with Germany having invaded Poland, it seems unlikely that I will see him anytime soon. I can only hope that he is safe, and that someday, when all this craziness is behind us, Pasha and I might reconnect. But is that even realistic?

She put her pen down, and then closed her eyes in prayer. While saddened by her unrequited relationship, not everything was going badly. She had been working at Bernburg for only three months and had already lost some of the timidity that most young doctors feel when taking on their first professional position. The hazing that had come from being a female in a mostly male setting never fully ceased, yet despite this she was regarded by many as an asset, given the preponderance of female patients and their unique needs.

On a routine morning in late November, while reading an elderly woman's blood pressure, she noticed a formal entourage walking slowly down the corridor. It looked like a tour, maybe some kind of inspection, involving several Nazi officers in black uniforms resplendent with embroidery and medals. Led by Doctor Enke and accompanied by two physicians in long white coats, the group occasionally paused to look into a room, but with no sense of urgency. Annika noticed a red silk hankie sprouting from the breast pocket of

156

Enke's natty tweed suit. As they got closer, Annika noticed the notorious death's head embroidered on their hats. *An SS contingent.*

Trying to keep her voice down, Annika asked, "What's the occasion, Jutta?"

Jutta tried to look busy. She whispered, "I'm not sure why they're here. The registrar told me the officer is a colonel, somebody named Bouhler. The doctor next to Enke? He's Imfried Eberl, the head psychiatrist at Brandenburg."

Annika knew of Brandenburg and had seen Eberl's name countless times. Every time a patient went from one facility to the other, documents with his signature accompanied them. She had never seen Brandenburg, but knew it was a large psychiatric hospital about a hundred and forty kilometers to the east, kind of a sister asylum to Bernburg. Now seeing Eberl, there was little doubt that rumors of his being a Nazi were true. She had also heard of Colonel Bouhler. The *Völkischer Beobachter* described him as a high-ranking member of Hitler's administrative staff and a key associate of Himmler.

A month or so later, during a departmental meeting, Doctor Enke rose to make an announcement. "Effective immediately, all physicians are to begin administering new questionnaires on each patient. Please take a moment to look at them." He began passing them out. After a few minutes, he said, "As you can see, instead of recording simple demographic information, as we've always done, the new forms will specify which patients (a) suffer from chronic psychiatric or neurological disorders; (b) are not of German blood; (c) were committed on criminal grounds; and (d) have been institutionalized for more than five years." There was a shuffling of papers around the room.

Annika leaned to one of the senior physicians and whispered, "Why do we have to start doing this, Doctor Wertheim?"

Ulrich Wertheim had worked at Bernburg for as long as anyone could remember. A short, stout man in his sixties, gray at the temples and never seen without a monocle, he was bald but had a drooping gray mustache that was brown-tinged from incessant cigarette smoking. Responding to her question, he rolled his eyes and replied disgustedly, "Who the hell knows?" Scooping up an array of papers scattered before him, he snarled, "God-damned bureaucrats! As if we don't have enough paperwork already . . ."

"Oh, c'mon, Ulrich." It was one of Annika's tormentors, Günter Schumacher. He gave Wertheim a playful slap on the back and said, "You know the bean-counters . . . They gotta have a way to justify their mindless jobs." Smirking, he looked over at Annika and winked.

She was not taken in by his superficial attempt to be chummy. No matter what position she took on any topic, Schumacher invariably lodged a contrarian view; he was determined, she felt, to make her look bad. It was obvious that he resented working with a woman. He had been a member of the Nazi party for years and subscribed to the notion that a woman's place was nowhere but in the home. Not only that, but he strutted about with a supercilious air that was unambiguously condescending toward his charges, often mocking them openly without regard to the presence of other patients or doctors, sometimes even in the presence of family members. His arrogance could have cost him his job, were it not for his toadyism with Nazis at the highest level, especially former classmate, Karl Brandt, Hitler's personal physician. Schumaker's ambitions were obvious: vertical mobility in the NSDAP hierarchy.

Turning back to Wertheimer, he said, "I wouldn't get too worked up about these forms. How hard is it to fill 'em out? Half the patients here are schizos, right? You think they can hold down a job? Or the epileptics? I can see it now: a 'spaz' working on a machine and then having a fit?" Looking at Annika, he chortled, "Probably get his dick caught in a lathe." Smirking, he put a cigar in his mouth and reached for a match.

Annika's face reddened. She knew it was better to let him rant – he was her superior – but she couldn't remain silent. "I would like to think, Doctor Schumaker, that there are quite a few patients here who could be trained to work."

"Oh, now, do you really?" he said sarcastically. "Like training the imbeciles to clean the toilets, right?" Annika squirmed. "Oh, but wait . . . we've already tried that, and what happened? They made a bigger mess on the floor than what they already had in their pants." Another laugh. "C'mon, Doctor Tritzchler, I would think that after a year here, you would know better. Let's be reasonable."

"Herr Doctor, with all due respect, there are already patients here in the hospital who are carrying out tasks. We've been experimenting with Adolf Meyer's model of occupational therapy."

"Oh, have you now." He pulled the cigar from his mouth before nudging Wertheimer with his elbow. Turning back to Annika, he said, "You mean like that homo who sweeps the floor? You think other men would feel comfortable working with a faggot?" Contented, he then spit a tiny fleck of tobacco from the tip of his tongue. To everyone's surprise, it landed squarely on Doctor Wertheim's lapel.

For a second or two, there was silence. The elder supervisor first looked down, then slowly raised his head to peer directly into Schumaker's eyes. The stare was much like two boxers squaring off before a bout. It lasted several moments. "Sorry old man," Schumaker said, trying to keep things light.

Saying nothing, Wertheim pulled a handkerchief from his coat pocket and in two quick motions flicked the offending speck from his suit. There was no disguising his anger. His eyes were riveted on Schumaker even as he got up and walked away. Annika was transfixed. To her, Wertheim's stare symbolized the division in German society, and how it was playing out even in the sublime sector of medicine.

After only a few months, Doctor Enke had given Annika space to conduct psychotherapy sessions. It amounted to little more than a closet, but afforded her a few hours per week to see patients and work on honing her skills as a therapist. She was grateful to Enke and considered his accommodations a vote of confidence in her work and growth as a psychiatrist.

Elsie had been one of her patients. Annika's observations of Elsie suggested that there was more to her clinical status than what was initially reported. It had taken considerable time, with Annika sitting through many sessions of near silence, but gradually her patient's defenses broke down. It seemed that Elsie's "paranoia" was more about anxiety than psychosis. Being in a psychiatric ward was terrifying to her, which ironically reinforced and intensified the very behaviors that led to her admission. The staff had neither the time nor inclination to look beyond the initial reports, interpreting her behavior as simply an exacerbation of pre-morbid schizophrenia.

Annika worked with Elsie using psychoanalytic techniques from the much-maligned Freudian school. After many hours encouraging the patient to free-associate on the couch, the young patient began to trust Annika. She confided that her father had "been touching me . . . for as long as I can remember." Her earliest memory was being molested in her father's study. She remembered his having called her in from the sandbox where she had been playing, so she was clearly very young at the time. However, Annika surmised that the abuse had begun much earlier, possibly as far back as infancy. In her notes, she wrote:

The patient is not simply unwilling, but has been unable to talk about her life because victimization began, according to her, when she was a "little girl." Multiple interviews suggest paternal abuse occurred prior to the age of three (Piaget's "sensorimotor stage"), even though it continued well beyond that. As the patient reached puberty, father is said to have lost interest, but intimidated her to maintain silence. Mother had long suspected the abuse and resented Elsie for having captured her father's attentions. Mother's resentments were acted-out in beatings, verbal abuse, and isolation – patient often being locked in her bedroom for long periods, sometimes days, with only limited food and drink.

Annika felt deep compassion for Elsie. But Elsie was not the only one. Another patient was Max, a short, stocky man of 36 who had been institutionalized for years and was as well-liked by the staff. He was raised in an orphan's home and eventually institutionalized because of "feeblemindedness." Subsequent intelligence testing had revealed him to be functioning somewhere between an imbecile and a moron. For the most part, Max was friendly and approachable, though he had limited tolerance for frustration and, when exceeded, could result in him lashing out suddenly and unexpectedly. On those occasions, it would take several attendants to get him in restraints. His history showed him to have never had anyone resembling a mother-figure, and Annika became a transference figure, even though she did not engage him in psychotherapy. If Annika was around, her words alone could soothe him without any need for restraints.

Unlocking stories which so often explained a patient's mental illness gave Annika a deep sense of fulfillment. Even small improvements in functioning reinforced her belief in "talk therapy," despite the Nazis denigrating psychoanalysis as Jewish rubbish.

At today's psychotherapy meeting, Elsie was the first patient Annika assessed with the new form. It would show that Elsie suffered not from schizophrenia, but from depression and anxiety related to early trauma, which had affected her personality. Could she work? Certainly not immediately, Annika reasoned, but in time, productive employment was not only possible, but could be therapeutic. The problem was that diagnosing her with work capacity would terminate her hospitalization, and that, in turn, would keep Elsie from getting the treatment that could help her regain her life. So, she checked off the box indicating no work capacity. She did the same for all twenty patients that she personally oversaw.

In December, she returned to Berlin to visit a few of her friends during the Christmas holidays. The recent involvement of France and Britain in what was becoming a widening war did little to upset a normal ebb-and-flow in Berlin, which gave her the opportunity to visit Lutz Pfeiffer, a former classmate and devout Christian whom she had met through Dietrich Bonhoeffer's group. He was currently in residency at the Children's Clinic in Berlin.

They met at a crowded pub on the Torstrasse, one of their old haunts near the Charité. Lutz ordered a beer, Annika a glass of wine, which they nursed while catching up on life since medical school. What began as collegial dialogue suddenly took an unexpected turn.

"At Bernburg, we have these new forms that we're required to complete on each of our patients," Annika said. "It's strange. Not sure what they want with that information."

Lutz became uncharacteristically reserved. Looking around, he asked in a low voice, "Are they, by any chance, from the Reich's Health Department?"

"Yeah. Why, do you have similar ones where you are?" Annika was nonchalant about the whole thing.

"Let's go for a walk, Annika. We need to talk . . . privately." He tipped his glass back, draining it, and then stood up. He pulled a few coins from his pocket and dropped them on the table. Annika thought better than to argue. She took one more sip of wine before getting up and following him. They passed through a Christmas market lined in colorful tents and craft stands draped in seasonal ornaments. Even with a war on, the atmosphere was mostly festive, busy with shoppers and revelers alike. After a few blocks, Lutz urged her down a darkened side street, devoid of people.

"Where are we going?" Annika asked.

Lutz stopped next to a fountain, bereft of people and empty of water for the winter months. Looking around to be sure they were out of earshot, he said, "You mentioned the forms." Annika hadn't the slightest idea why he seemed so worked up. "The forms, Annika, from the Reich Ministry. We've had to do the same thing here in Berlin. Initially, nobody gave them too much thought, but at the *Kinderkrankenhäuser*, we were required to report infants having any type of deformity . . . microcephaly, hydrocephalus, polio . . . things like that." Annika nodded, not sure what he was getting at. "Well, they also wanted to know about any intellectual deficits, like idiocy or mongolism – even missing limbs."

"Okay . . . so is that a problem? I just figured the Health Department was compiling statistics. Collecting sociological data. Maybe . . . I don't know . . . as part of the census? Or for research purposes?"

"I wish it were that simple, Annika . . . or that benign. Officially, it falls under a new policy . . . the 'Requirement to Report Deformed Newborns.' But there's more to it than that." Lutz paused to look around. "It's all very secret, which I suspect is why you don't know anything about it. Annika, listen. I could be arrested for telling you this. I need you to swear to keep this secret. Can you?"

"*Ja, naturlich.* You're scaring me, Lutz. What is it?"

"Annika, I believe the State is making plans to begin euthanizing children; kids that are deformed, those who are considered a drain on society."

Annika was stunned. "I . . . I'm not following you. What do you mean?"

"I'm sure you saw the movie, *Victims of the Past: The Sin against Blood and Race.*"

"Yes, of course. Who hasn't?" she asked, sarcastically. "The Nazis made sure it was shown in every cinema in Germany."

"Right. Well, it's all part of their effort to sensitize the public into accepting euthanasia against people considered sub-human . . . Hitler's *Untermensch.*"

Annika was speechless. She angled her head in bewilderment, taking several seconds to process what he just said. It was as if her mind was unable to digest something so unimaginable, so repugnant.

"Yes, it's true, Annika. Hitler, himself, sent out letters authorizing what he called 'mercy deaths' for incurable patients. That's *why* these forms are required." He looked around once again, then put his face only inches from Annika. In a whisper, he said, "Our facility has already begun transferring children to Brandenburg. I have it on good authority that they've begun to carry out the killings. Right now, it's all very top secret."

"How do you know this?"

"I overheard my boss discussing it with a psychiatrist from Brandenburg. I was in a bathroom stall when they came in. At first, they didn't know I was there. You know how long those doors are for each toilet. I kept very still. That's when I heard one of 'em say something about 'the Führer's directive.' If I heard 'em correctly, they referred to it as *Aktion T4*. Unfortunately, the toilet seat squeaked, alerting them that someone was in one of the stalls."

"So, what happened?"

"They stopped talking . . . right away . . . and left."

"Do you know who they were?"

"Yeah. My clinical director, Ernst Wentzler, was one. The other man was a Doctor Eberl. I've never met him."

"*Imfried* Eberl?" Annika was suddenly alarmed, as if a light bulb turned on.

"You've heard of him?"

"Yes, unfortunately. He led an entourage at our hospital just a couple months ago. He was surrounded by Nazi brass. SS." Annika didn't want to believe it, but now everything was beginning to make sense. "What about work capacity, Lutz? That's one of the things we're now required to document . . ." Like a lightning bolt, things became instantly clear. "So, Lutz, are you suggesting that the same thing could be happening at Bernburg? That our patients are at risk of . . . of mercy killing?" She almost couldn't say the words.

"That's exactly what I'm suggesting."

Annika immediately thought of her own patients; people she cared about, people she wanted to help. But almost as quickly came the realization: *these are people I have certified as having no ability to work!* "Lutz, what you're telling me is that these patients, *because of me*, are going to be euthanized? Murdered?"

"Annika, nothing's because of you. Remember that. We're living under a rogue government. It's evil. But listen, and hear me good, please! You *have* to keep this a secret. Eberl waited for me to come out of the men's room that day. It was obvious he wanted to see who might have overheard his conversation. He never said a word, but he certainly got a good look at me. I'm sure he looked into my dossier, which means I'm on his radar. Probably at risk." Annika looked at him with wide eyes, not knowing what to say. "I would be turned over to Gestapo in a heartbeat if any word of this gets out. Several people in our hospital have simply disappeared. No one knows where they are, but it's clear they ran afoul of Gestapo. You've got to promise me that you will never speak a word of this."

Annika knew that this was no exaggeration. People were being sent to concentration camps for trivial offenses. Without a doubt, Lutz's life would be imperiled if it came out that he had revealed classified information. And now that he told her, Annika realized that she herself could be in danger. But what to do, especially now that she had reason to believe that Bernburg, itself, might be engaged in a similar operation.

Her mind was racing. *Killing human beings,* she thought, *who, through no fault of their own, are born with incurable handicaps . . . 'mercy killings' . . . Is it really possible that doctors could go along with such barbarity? What would they tell parents and family members? What's Lutz going to do? What do I do when I get back?* It was too much to digest.

Back in her hotel room, she opened her journal. It was always the one place she could be honest with her feelings. Now, pen in hand, Annika felt paralyzed, not knowing what was safe to write. She scribbled the only thing that came to mind.

Things are happening here that are wrong. I fear being put in a compromising position as not just a doctor, but a human being. I don't know what to do. God help me. {19 December, 1939}

Lives Unworthy of Living

The only thing necessary for the triumph of evil is for good men to do nothing.

Edmund Burke

September, 1940 – February, 1941

Nine months had elapsed. It was now a hot, muggy day in September; the humidity index was through the roof. Annika was sitting in Doctor Enke's office discussing a few patients as part of her weekly supervision. Enke sat disinterestedly behind a large mahogany desk strewn with papers and dossiers. They were both being watched, it appeared, by the scowling countenance of the Führer whose larger-than-life portrait dominated the wall behind Enke.

Annika was sweltering in the plush brown chair that enveloped her. It trapped her body heat, and perspiration made her clothing cling uncomfortably to her skin. She was just about to move closer to the window fan when there was a knock at the door.

Enke seemed relieved by the distraction. *"Kommt rein,"* he ordered, at which point his secretary walked in, slightly hunched and flanked by two German officers.

"Forgive me, Herr Doctor," she apologized, stepping aside to let the two men approach. "I didn't realize you were still in consultation."

Enke and Annika rose to their feet as the visitors snapped to attention with a customary Nazi salute and synchronized clicking of their heels. *"Heil Hitler!"* they each barked almost in unison. Annika and her supervisor returned the greeting.

"Allow me to introduce myself, Herr Director," one of the men

166

said. "We are from the KdF Central Office. I am *Obersturmbannführer* Viktor Brack and this is Inspector-Colonel Adolf Kaufmann." Standing erect, Kaufmann crisply nodded his head. "Let me apologize if we are interrupting you." He glanced over to Annika and back.

"*Nein, nein,*" responded Enke. "Not at all. No need to apologize, gentlemen. We were just finishing." Gesturing with his hand to Annika, he said, "This is Doctor Tritzchler. She is a second-year resident from Berlin . . . training in psychiatry. Works mostly with the female patients."

Brack turned with an imperious air to Annika, his chin jutting forward. He was not accustomed to women in professional roles. Looking down his nose, his beady eyes scanned her up and down. Though she tried not to, Annika blushed. She tugged at her blouse, which in the humid air clung in all the wrong places. As she extended her hand in greeting. Brack smiled, sensing her insecurity. He took her fingertips into his own and bowed slightly at the neck, all the while keeping his gaze fixed on her eyes. "Charmed," he said, in a voice that left her cold. Kaufmann looked on without comment, though privately he knew of Brack's licentiousness, as did many of his colleagues, and he considered it repugnant – a smear on the dignity of a high-ranking officer.

Brack turned back to Enke. "I wonder, Herr Doctor, if the Inspector and I might have a word with you . . ." His head pivoted to Annika and back. ". . . in private." It was less a question than a directive.

Annika was not privy to those discussions, but it wasn't long afterward that Kaufmann became a more frequent visitor at the facility. Along with his presence came an announcement that the housing for male patients was to be remodeled according to specifications from the Reich Ministry. The construction proceeded quite rapidly, though with no clear understanding from staff as to its purpose. A large garage was built "for buses," they were told, so it was assumed Bernburg would become a transit facility, a place where patients from other hospitals would be temporarily housed while awaiting transfer to a different hospital.

Kaufmann was not the only new presence. To her dismay, Doctor Eberl had made a reappearance. Scuttlebutt had it that he had been transferred from Brandenburg to be the administrator of a new housing unit at Bernburg. Prior to this, all buildings had been supervised by Doctor Enke, but now they would be functioning as two very distinct facilities, one ascribed to Eberl, the other to Enke.

Eberl's presence was disturbing for Annika, both because of what Lutz had told her and the veil of secrecy enshrouding his role. She thought that maybe Lutz could shed some light on this new development. She attempted to reach him by phone at the Children's Clinic, but was told, "Doctor Pfeiffer is no longer affiliated with the Clinic." Annika was stunned. She asked where she might reach him, that she was a colleague, but the operator cryptically replied, "I'm sorry. We have no further information," then promptly hung up. It sounded ominous.

By November, Doctor Eberl's facility was up-and-running. Buses began to come and go with regularity, and there was active recruitment for new staff. Already, Annika had noticed several new faces on campus. It wasn't more than a few weeks later that Annika was summoned to Eberl's office.

Seated behind his desk, he said, "Doctor Enke speaks very highly of you, which is why I have requested this meeting. You have undoubtedly been aware of the structural changes we have been making. By order of the Führer, we are engaged in very important work that is humanitarian in scope, while simultaneously benefiting the war effort. Accordingly, we are interviewing for new staff, and we currently have an opening for a physician, someone to oversee our work with women patients. This is a supervisory post, an upgrade over your current duties and one that would significantly broaden your career. You are the only physician working exclusively with women, and that fact alone puts you highest on our list of eligible candidates. And your performance reviews show consistently exemplary work. We would like to have you join us."

Annika was flattered, but coming from Eberl, she was equally circumspect. "What sort of responsibilities would be required of me, Herr Doctor?" she asked.

"Let me begin by asking you how much you know about eugenics."

"I understand eugenics as a spin-off of social Darwinism, a theory that basically says that the fittest societies are the ones that have the best chance of survival."

Eberl smiled. "Precisely. And the fittest societies are those that have the best and the brightest, would you agree?"

"Logically, I would assume that makes sense." Annika felt that she was being steered, but was not sure in what direction.

"Well, Doctor Tritzchler, here's the thing. As you know, we are now at war with not just Poland, but now England and France as well. We are currently losing many of our best and brightest young men, men who have put their lives on the line to defend the Fatherland. At the same time, we are maintaining hundreds of thousands, perhaps millions, of patients at facilities throughout Germany . . . people who can't take care of themselves, who live at the expense of every upstanding, working German citizen."

"Yes, Herr Director. That's our job, right?"

Eberl nodded. "Yes, of course." He took a sip of tea and lit a cigarette before continuing. "But now our jobs are being expanded. We have entered a time, whether we like it or not, where we psychiatrists have a crucial role, one more important than anything we have undertaken in the past." Annika sat quietly, feeling almost like she was being lectured to. "Doctor Tritzchler, as a society, we recognize the need to hunt certain species of wildlife – deer and hogs, for example – in order to sustain a healthy herd. If we did not cull the herd, the species would overpopulate and die-off due to starvation. Yes?" Annika nodded. "Well, right now, Germany is in a similar situation. Our society has limited resources, even fewer now during wartime, and much of what we have is being wasted on people that you and I both work with, people whose lives are essentially meaningless. Wouldn't you agree?"

The word "wasted" exploded in her ears like the clashing of symbols at a parade. She could understand the logic, having heard it many times in school and in political speeches, but she believed there was much more to it than simple math. She thought of Max. Diagnosed a moron, he was always there with a wide, ear-to-ear smile. Was it a waste to be caring for him? These were human beings he was referring to. She didn't want to argue with her superior, knowing that he could make or break her career in a heartbeat, but she couldn't let his assumptions go unchallenged.

"Doctor Eberl, I'm involved with many patients who seem truly happy, and, I have to say, patients who show great appreciation for the care we give them."

"Of course, of course. Let me clarify that not *all* patients are considered to have wasted lives . . . not at all. I'm quite certain that the work you do is very meaningful and I know that many of your patients are not only appreciative, as you say, but benefit from your involvement. We both realize, though, that there are patients whose illnesses are so profound – you know, those with dementia or schizophrenia, people with epilepsy or, well, think of the imbeciles and idiots. Patients that need round-the-clock care simply to survive."

"So, what would my role be?" she asked.

Just then, Eberl was buzzed. "Ah, that's my next appointment." He looked at his watch. "Damn. I've gotta run . . . Tell you what, Tritzchler. Why don't you come to my office tomorrow morning? Rather than talking any further, I'll show you around . . . introduce you to some of the other staff." He got up, shook hands with her and escorted her to the door.

The next morning, Annika walked through the campus to meet Doctor Eberl in his office promptly at 0600. Dawn had just broken on what was an otherwise dank, raw morning. Walking up the long driveway, she was passed by another of the many buses she had seen

170

recently. This one, like the others, had blackened windows; *I guess to preserve confidentiality,* she thought. Things were already abuzz by the time she reached Eberl's unit. Nurses were rousing patients from their slumber, accounting for loud voices, occasional screams and even crying. The air was pungent with excretions from the past ten hours, but nothing unfamiliar to Annika. A radio crackled in the background.

"Good morning, Doctor Tritzchler," rang Eberl's voice from behind her. He appeared light-hearted and chipper for the day. "Once you get squared away, you can accompany me on rounds . . . give you a chance to meet a few of the other doctors and see how we go about things here."

As they made their way to the staircase, they were met by a junior doctor, Heinrich Bunke, who, like Eberl, sported a mustache resembling the Führer. He was only a few years older than Annika and greeted her cheerfully. "*Nett Sie kennen zu lernen,*" he exclaimed, holding out his hand. Annika wasn't sure how nice it was to meet him, but his enthusiasm was disarming, so she reached out to accept his handshake. In his zeal, his grip tightened around her knuckles, causing her to immediately wince and pull back.

"My apologies," he offered. "How careless . . ." Annika wasn't convinced it was unintentional.

"Come on, you two. Let's get to our rounds," said Eberl, grinning, obviously amused by the transaction.

A faint din of agitated voices echoed in the stairwell, growing louder with each descending step as the trio made their way to the basement. Eberl unlocked the metal door, opening them to a group of nearly forty male patients who had just arrived by bus. Most were in white hospital dress, though several had wriggled out of part of their clothing, despite the winter chill. The scene reminded Annika of images she had seen of Bedlam – men bickering and shoving, while others regaled imaginary friends in monotones of animated self-talk and bursts of mindless laughter. A blessed few were docile, even trancelike, yet the majority were confused as to why the cheerful nurses were herding them down this long, cold corridor.

Eberl trailed quite a distance behind, leaving enough space between them and the patients that they could observe and talk without interruption.

Annika noticed that several of the patients displayed red "X's" on their backs. "What do the 'X's' represent?" she asked.

Bunke replied, "Those are patients with unique physical disabilities. They merit special attention." Annika wasn't sure what he meant. Bunke, recognizing her confusion, responded, "With so many patients, it's easy for the special needs patients to get lost in the crowd."

They passed through an underground maze of drafty corridors, Gothic-style archways and miles of bundled pipes running unobtrusively in the ceilings above them. On each side of the hallways were cavernous rooms with two-toned green and white walls as well as polished, tiled floors, checkerboard style. The group of patients was led into a large room. The three doctors paused at the doorway while the men inside undressed and handed over whatever belongings they had brought with them. "The patients are being prepared for a shower," Eberl told Annika. Some were already seated on benches that lined the room. Eventually the entire group, all naked, was led into the shower room, where rows of faucets hung overhead. Once all the men were inside, the nurses closed the doors.

Doctor Eberl looked at Annika and said somberly, "As you can tell, none of these patients are capable of caring for themselves . . ."

"All incurable," added Bunke. "It breaks my heart to see people suffering so . . ." He then shot a glance at Eberl, who simply nodded.

They began to walk down the aisle when Annika thought she could hear some muffled yells and thumping coming from the shower room they had just left. "What is that?" she asked.

"The patients are restless," Bunke explained. "They'll calm down in a minute . . ."

Eberl turned to Bunke, scowling. It was a look that a teacher might cast on a petulant child. Eberl was not one to mince words.

Pivoting to Annika, he said with unaffected professionalism, "Tritzchler, this is where those who are beyond treatment are mercifully euthanized."

Annika's heart literally skipped a beat. She felt momentarily paralyzed, unable to speak as the other two doctors proceeded forward. She followed meekly, robotically, her labored gait resembling someone learning to walk for the first time. They stopped at a small window embedded in thick cinderblock. On the other side was pandemonium, the sounds of muffled hollering and banging on the walls.

"We probably need to add more soundproofing," Eberl said to Bunke. Then, looking over to Annika, he said, as if to be reassuring, "It'll all be over in a few minutes." He approached the small window and surveyed the scene. Then, stepping back, he motioned to Bunke, who strode forward to peer through the opening. He remained glued to the glass much longer than Eberl, appearing fascinated with whatever was unfolding on the other side. With a thin smile, he turned sideways gesturing with outstretched arm for Annika to have a look.

Annika felt their eyes on her. For a moment, she felt paralyzed, not wanting to take in the obvious carnage just a short distance away. "Doctor?" Eberl chided, imploring her to take her turn. There was no escape. She felt dizzy, almost nauseous, like a green, seasick sailor on the deck of a bobbing ship for the first time. Blood drained from her head as she approached the window. The spectacle awaiting her was a horror unimaginable in her wildest nightmares. Naked, frenzied men ran in circles aimlessly clawing for dwindling pockets of life-sustaining air. The weakest lay gasping at their feet, chests heaving, eyes bugged. Seeing their heads looking upwards with mouths wide open, Annika's first thought was of baby birds in a nest waiting impatiently for food from their mother. The resemblance passed quickly with men slipping in their own incontinence as if the floor had turned into a skating rink. Before she could recoil from the window, a contorted face suddenly pressed against the glass, mere centimeters from Annika's spellbound gaze. The wretched man was trying desperately to holler, but the depletion of oxygen robbed him of voice. His bloodshot eyes appeared to be popping out of their sockets as he glared beseechingly at Annika. In that one brief instant, she imagined that she saw . . . *Jesus.* Her own eyes widened in a spasm of helplessness, instinctively wanting to save the man. She turned fleetingly to Eberl, then back again, but in that split-second, the man had disappeared. Across the room was another man pressed against the sealed door, begging and pleading, until his knees buckled. Breathlessly, he slid slowly to the floor, joining the limp, contorted orgy of the unwanted.

Annika had seen enough. She pushed back from the window, heart pounding in a cold sweat, unable to focus any longer. Reality had ceased to exist. She began to hyperventilate, feeling weak and dizzy as her stomach began to retch. By sheer instinct, she put her hand to her mouth to catch the putrid bile filling her throat. Doctor Eberl grabbed her arm and ushered her into an adjoining WC, where she vomited convulsively as grisly images flashed before her eyes. When the regurgitation finally subsided, she bent forward on a toilet seat, head between her legs, and began to sob.

It was at least fifteen minutes before she emerged, bent slightly forward, arms folded at her waist. The maniacal cries had ceased, leaving behind an eerie silence offset only by low voices down the hallway. The two doctors were conversing with several nurses while gasses were being exhausted before removing the bodies. They looked in Annika's direction and began walking towards her.

"Well, you look better," Eberl remarked. "Don't feel bad. Everybody experiences a little queasiness in the beginning. Even Heinrich, here," he said, elbowing the junior doctor. It was a weak attempt at reassurance, though it elicited an embarrassed chuckle from Bunke. "It's really not much different than witnessing a surgery for the first time. Just takes a little time to adjust. You'll be fine."

His encouragement fell flat. "Doctor Eberl, I don't think I can be part of this . . ." Annika said.

Eberl wasn't surprised by this reaction; he had heard it before and responded as if he knew his young protégés better than they knew themselves. This was all part of their training. "Doctor Tritzchler, I want you to think of the word, 'euthanasia.' It is derived from the Greek, and actually means 'good death.' Think of all the slobbering, drooling patients, those who sit by themselves haunted by hallucinations, injured by epileptic fits . . . the imbeciles whose capacity for thought and reason is on a par with animals, even less than many. Think of the money and resources that are spent to keep them alive, when the most merciful intervention is not providing food and lodging, but putting them out of their own hellish existence. I'm sure you've talked to people who have said, 'if I ever had a brain injury and became like them, I'd prefer to die.'" Annika was too traumatized to respond.

"And think that by performing this merciful task, we are at the same time saving our Fatherland valuable resources that can be spent on more righteous projects . . . not simply assuring food and medicine for all, but cultural and technological pursuits, investments that will advance us as a culture."

She wiped tears from her eyes. It was difficult enough being a woman, but to show emotions did nothing but reinforce male stereotypes about the "weaker sex."

"Once you become accustomed to this work, Tritzchler, I think you'll find it extremely rewarding. Your participation will advance your career, substantially. You'll no longer be a medical resident; you'll be the director of the women's program, seeing patients from all over Germany."

At that point, Bunke added his own sales pitch. "This work has given me the opportunity to learn a whole new dimension of psychiatry. There is very strong collegiality among the staff, not to mention the chance to do scientific research. I wouldn't have gotten this opportunity anywhere else."

Annika tried to compose herself. "What happens to them now?" she gestured to the "shower" facility.

"Most will be cremated immediately," Eberl explained. "Those marked with the 'X's' will be examined – for research purposes." He pointed to an adjoining room, where Annika could see a dissection table. In a tone thinly disguised to sound noble, he said, "Without realizing it, these unfortunate souls have given their lives for the benefit of mankind and the new society we're building."

Nodding in agreement, Bunke waxed philosophical. "It's ironic that in the end, their lives actually *do* have a purpose. Strange, isn't it? Only death gives meaning to their suffering."

"It's a shame they'll never know how much they've actually contributed," added Eberl, shaking his head as if saddened. "A real pity."

Annika slept fitfully, if at all. Her mind was haunted by the images she had seen earlier that day. Several times throughout the night, she sat bolt upright in bed, eyes ablaze, trembling and bathed in sweat. In one dream, she was the executioner, opening the gas valves that would asphyxiate the very patients she had been caring for. In another, she was one of them, a naked apparition clawing for air while slowly drowning in noxious fumes that burned her lungs with every breath.

She awoke much earlier than usual. Her breathing was labored, her chest ached, and she felt uncharacteristically anxious. Nothing felt the same. She reached for her Bible, hoping for comfort, maybe guidance, from her morning devotions. By 6 AM, unable to concentrate, she untangled herself from sheets damp with perspiration, and ambled over to the mirror. *I'm a mess.* Splashing some water on her face, she remembered her scheduled meeting with Eberl. She had two hours to get ready.

When she arrived at Eberl's office, she was instructed to wait, as he was in conference. She could hear talking and occasional laughter from inside his office. Eventually, the voices grew louder and suddenly the door opened. Eberl emerged with three other men, all, except Eberl, in Nazi uniforms.

"Ah, gentlemen," said the director. "Here is Doctor Tritzchler.

She's in charge of the women's unit." Annika stood up to exchange a half-hearted Nazi salute with the officers.

Turning to Annika, he said, "This is Doctor Karl Brandt." Annika bowed slightly. "Doctor Brandt is the Führer's personal physician, and he's overseeing the work of the 'Charitable Foundation' – what we're doing here and at a few other select institutions throughout Germany." Brandt stared at her, not saying a word.

Eberl turned to the other man, whom Annika had seen with Enke several months previously. "And this is *Obergruppenführer* Bouhler, also from the Interior Ministry."

Bouhler's uniform, weighted down in medals, was a testament to ego, yet he was more congenial than his counterpart. Taking Annika's hand, he said, with a courteous smile, "A pleasure, indeed."

"The men are just leaving, Doctor Tritzchler." Then turning to the officers, Eberl added, "It is indeed our honor that they've taken the time to visit us and assist us in implementing the important work of the Reich." Pleasantries exchanged, Eberl ushered the officers past Annika and toward the hallway, leaving her standing for several minutes as the director bid them farewell. Once reseated in his office, Eberl took a deep breath and smiled. He was ebullient, obviously pleased with the connection he had just made with his overlords. Annika felt nothing but disgust at Eberl's boot-licking sycophancy. Slowly turning to her, he asked, "Well then, how are we doing this morning, Tritzchler?" There was a decided shift in his attitude. With the Reich ministers no longer present, his tone changed from acquiescent and self-serving to supercilious and domineering.

Annika recognized a need to be cautious in her comments, but at the same time she didn't want to miscommunicate. "Doctor Eberl, to be honest, I hardly slept a wink last night."

Eberl sat back, as if to distance himself from something he didn't want to hear. "Oh, I'm sorry to hear that," he replied, feigning ignorance. "Anything I might be able to help you with?"

"Yes, Herr Director." She felt it easier to maintain distance by addressing him as an administrator, not a colleague. "All my life, I've wanted to help people. I pursued medicine because I believe in treatment, in improving life for people who are suffering. Ever since being here, I've had a hard time with the sterilization policy, but now with euthanasia . . . sir, that runs counter to . . ." She tried to choose her words carefully. ". . . to everything I stand for, and especially to my religion. Seeing what happened yesterday was . . ." She was about to say 'an abomination,' but thought better of it. ". . . well, very difficult."

"I see. . ." Eberl responded, but Annika didn't think he saw anything.

She had to come right out with it. "Herr Doctor, meaning no disrespect, I don't see myself being able to participate in this process at all."

Eberl's chin touched his chest as he pulled back in apparent disbelief. "You realize that the position being offered to you is an honor, do you not?"

"I do," she lied.

"And," he continued, "that accepting it comes with a promotion, which of course will benefit your career."

"Yes, and I appreciate your considering me for that promotion, Doctor Eberl."

"Well, Tritzchler, I guess I made a mistake. I saw you as having strength and leadership. We do not *require* anyone to join the team if they choose not to. Most join out of a love of country, a duty to the fatherland, as well as a desire to move forward in their careers." Annika gulped. Another insinuation of weakness. She could feel the pressure. He was implying that not only would her refusal interfere with career mobility, but that it could be construed as disloyalty to the regime. Nevertheless, she nodded, looking down at her feet. She was determined to keep from dissolving in tears. "And just to be clear, you are formally requesting that I remove you from any consideration of involvement with this service, correct?"

"Yes sir . . ." she said, softly.

"Speak up, Doctor!" he ordered.

"Sir, yes. I am asking, with all due respect, that I remain in my regular duties under the auspices of Doctor Enke." There was no mistaking her resolve.

"Very well, then. You're dismissed." She rose to her feet and turned, expecting to leave. "Oh, and one more thing, Doctor Tritzchler. As I believe you have already been informed, the euthanasia program is top secret . . . direct orders from the Führer. Any breach of that will be met with severe penalties. Do you understand?"

"*Jawohl, Herr Direktor*," she replied. With that, he snapped to attention with a crisp Nazi salute, leaving her with no questions as to his loyalties. Annika demurely returned the formality, and both said, "*Heil Hitler*." He watched her disappear down the hallway.

No longer were the comings and goings of "Department Doctor Eberl" left to the imagination. Busses came and went every day, sometimes looking as if Bernburg had become an ersatz bus depot. Annika tried to distract herself by staying focused on her patients, but it was impossible to ignore what was going on in that building.

It was a chilly morning in February. Annika was not scheduled to work until noon, though she would be covering the nightshift, part of a typical rotation. Once at work, she sorted through the charts, looking at nurses' reports from the previous day. She couldn't find the chart for Elsie; it was usually near the top. She thought maybe one of the nurses had taken it while checking up on her. This was not out of the ordinary, so Annika casually walked to the dorm, expecting chart and patient to be located together. Once there, however, she noticed immediately Elsie's empty bed, now stripped of sheets. More concerning, her belongings were gone as well.

There was a nurse attending to a patient a few beds away. "Excuse me, Herta. I'm looking for Elsie. I can't find her chart." Looking around, she added, "And where are her things?"

"Oh, hello, Doctor Tritzchler. I thought you knew. Last night,

179

several patients were relocated to other dorms."

"Other dorms? Where?"

"I'm not totally sure, but I think some were moved to Doctor Eberl's building. From what I've heard, patients are being re-categorized by diagnosis."

Annika flew into a panic. "What? This was done without my knowledge?"

"I don't know, Doctor Tritzchler. Speaking for myself, I'm happy to have a few less patients to deal with, even if it will only be for a few days."

Before the nurse could say another word, Annika spun around and began hurrying down the corridor, almost dropping the pile of charts she clutched to her chest. Passing the dayroom, one of the other nurses turned to ask her a question. Annika simply rushed by. *No. This can't be,* she thought. *Not Elsie!* She quickened her pace. Dropping the charts off on her desk, she rushed outside and ran the full length of the sidewalks to Eberl's building. Breathlessly, she climbed the stairs and darted headlong to his office. His door was closed.

"I'm sorry," said his secretary. "Director Eberl is in . . ." She didn't get the words out in time to prevent Annika from barging in unannounced. The secretary was on her feet. "Excuse me!" she insisted. "The doctor is busy!"

Annika was not to be deterred. She burst into the director's office with his secretary at her heels. "I need to know where my patients are!" she demanded.

Eberl was in the midst of a phone conversation. With a few quick words to the person on the other end, he hung up the receiver and barked, "What is the meaning of this? Stand at attention, Tritzchler, and explain to me the nature of this visit?" His face was beet red.

"Several of my patients have disappeared, Doctor Eberl – taken without my knowledge or consent. One of my nurses told me they had been transferred here. I need to know where they are."

"You need to know *nothing*, Doctor! You're a resident . . . not a director, not a supervisor, not even an attending – you're a *resident!* You follow orders. You were offered a position with us, one which came with a big promotion, and you turned it down. Your job now is to attend to the patients on your ward. Nothing more, nothing less. You show me some respect, or I'll have you cleaning toilets in the back wards. Do you understand me?"

"I apologize, Doctor Eberl. I would appreciate knowing where Elsie Kellermann is. I have been working with her for almost two years."

"I don't know who you're referring to. I manage hundreds of patients. I can't be expected to know everyone by name, or by circumstance."

The secretary piped up. "Doctor Eberl. I can get her chart, if you like."

"Go," Eberl ordered. He and Annika waited for several minutes in silence.

The secretary reappeared, handing him the chart.

Eberl took another minute or so to thumb through several pages. "The woman in question, Elsie Kellermann, has been transferred to the Hadamar facility, in Hessen."

"But if I might ask, Herr Director, why?"

"Once again, Tritzchler, this is not your concern, but I will go so far as to tell you that the patient in question, like many others, are being transferred to facilities best equipped to meet their needs. Your former patient will be getting individualized attention at Hadamar. That's all I can tell you."

Annika folded her arms across her chest. "Well, Doctor Eberl, she was my patient. Can I at least check on her progress, maybe be included in her treatment?"

"Negative. Once a patient leaves Bernburg, we have no way of monitoring them. Nor do we need to. Their care becomes a matter for the physicians in charge – not us." He looked her up and down before continuing. "Now, Doctor Tritzchler, I'm sure you have other things to do. If you have no further questions, I'd advise you getting back to your duties. I myself am busy."

"But Doctor . . ." Annika persisted before being abruptly cut off.

"That will be all, Tritzchler! Good day!" With that, the secretary took Annika by the arm and escorted her out of the office. The door closed behind them.

Annika realized that she had placed herself in an untenable position. No longer would her status as a physician protect her from scrutiny- or worse. Confused and distrustful, she converted her thoughts to poetry. That night, in her journal, she wrote:

Lebensunwertes Leben

On my way to work, I stopped to observe a small mushroom, one that I had never noticed on this well-trod, pine-covered path. Peeking out from the shelter of a damp, rotting stump, it stood alone, vulnerable yet thriving, once happy in its camouflaged surroundings. But no longer, for unbridled faith in the protective canopy above had become an illusion. Those withering leaves on which it had depended now yielded in surrender as the chill of autumn brought them fluttering lifelessly to the forest floor below. Through bared limbs, the gnarly toadstool, innocent and harmless, has been betrayed in an orange shaft of late-day sunlight, denounced to all who pass by as not a valued mushroom, but only a fungus- ugly and worthless – a life unworthy of living.

Arrest

We have to put a stop to the idea that it is a part of everybody's civil rights to say whatever he pleases.
Adolf Hitler

October–November, 1941

Summer had yielded its warm days and lush foliage to a climate as unsettled as her mind. The seasonal change was an ebb and flow that reminded Annika of Pasha and the night they ruminated about yin and yang. Today, the morning dew checkerboarded a translucent landscape – summer's fading greenery now colorful in variegated hues of autumn. The air was a bouquet of decomposition, sustenance for new sprouts the following spring. An inexorable cycle, peaceful and orderly. She saw God in everything: trees and birds, insects and plants, and was forever pausing to drink in His handiwork.

Annika's reverie was stopped cold. A blood-red Nazi flag hung limply from a storefront bustling with shoppers. Vanquished for the moment was any appreciation of nature. *The longer I live, the more I see us as a bastardization of nature, an abomination in God's eyes.* She could no longer pass innocent-looking people on the street without wondering what evil lurked in their minds. The Bernburg facility, once thought of as a sanctuary, a place of healing, was now seen as a collaborator to murder.

"Doctor Tritzchler, Doctor Tritzchler." Approaching from the far end of the corridor was a nurse. Annika was up to her ears in work. *What could they possibly want now?* "Doctor Tritzchler, I just received a call from Doctor Eberl's office. He would like to see you right away." It was Herta, the head nurse. She was friendly and

183

reliable – nobody that she could confide in, but unswerving in her duties. "His secretary said it's urgent."

Annika was stooped over a tub in the midst of supervising a bath for one of her patients. Only the patient's head was visible, peeking out of the canvas covering that held her securely in place. Even so, she was squirming, and Annika was doing her best to calm the woman. This was clearly not the best time to abandon her post. "Any idea what it's about?" she asked.

Herta was insistent. "I have no idea. But it sounds serious. You better go."

Annika said soothingly to her patient, "Everything'll be fine, Frau Edelmann. Just lay back. We'll bring you something to eat." She turned to the nurse. "Can you take over until I return?" As Herta rolled up her sleeves, Annika was drying off her arms, wet and soapy from the bathwater. In barely five minutes, she was on her way to Eberl's building.

When she arrived, Eberl's door was closed, as usual. His secretary was already on her feet, preparing for the possibility of another scene. This time, however, Annika followed propriety and dutifully accepted the seat shown to her. Seated to her right was a large man in the uniform of the SS. He had the face of a bulldog, large jowls and a square chin. He stared at her as she sat down and waited to be called. Taking a deep drag from his cigarette, he tilted his head back and exhausted a plume of smoke towards the ceiling, then once again looked over at Annika, tendrils of smoke funneling from his nostrils. Annika cleared her throat as her lungs rebelled against the second-hand smoke.

The wait seemed interminable, even more so because of the man seated next to her. She had so much work to do, so many more patients to see. This interruption would simply extend her day, probably into the evening. But as she sat there, Annika started to become nervous. What could Eberl want with her at this point? She had already declined his offer to be part of the euthanasia program. What else was there?

184

The door opened, and Eberl gestured for her with a wave of his arm. To her surprise, the SS man stubbed out his second cigarette, got up, and walked in behind her. They were met in the office by another man dressed in suit and tie. A full-length leather coat was draped over the back of his chair. With everyone standing, Doctor Eberl, looking squarely at Annika, pointed to the man in civilian clothes. "This gentleman is from Berlin. He has some questions for you."

"Questions? I'm afraid I don't understand." Annika was confused. Had something gone wrong with one of her patients?

"Fräulein Tritzchler?"

"I am *Doctor* Tritzchler."

"Yes, well, I am Inspector Schmeling from the Bernburg Kriminalabteilung," he said, displaying a bronze disc while giving her a quick, once-over glance. The disc was instantly recognizable. "*Staatliche Kriminalpolizei,*" it read, with the number "872" stamped underneath.

KriPo. He's a detective with the local criminal division. Now she was thoroughly confused. "What could you possibly want with me?" Annika asked.

"You're under arrest. Orders from Gestapo. We are here to take you to Berlin for questioning."

"Under arrest? For what?" Startled, her heart was beating like a jackhammer, she almost couldn't hear herself think.

"I have no information as to the nature of any charges. We are commissioned only to transport you." He nodded to the SS man, who came from behind with a pair of handcuffs.

Annika's head swiveled from the Inspector to the broad-shouldered officer approaching her. She turned to Eberl. "Herr Director," she pleaded, "this has to be some sort of mistake. Please!" She could feel dry, burly fingers attaching to handcuffs to her wrists.

Eberl responded with his usual condescension. "I hope for your sake, Doctor Tritzchler, and for all of us, that this *is* a mistake. But for right now, it's out of my hands." He nodded to the officers, whereupon she was turned, hands manacled in front, and escorted out, an officer on each side.

The transport to Berlin was as humiliating as it was long and harrowing. With her hands cuffed in front, Annika felt the stares of passers-by as the trio walked to the platform awaiting their train. A few openly laughed; occasionally someone would point, but many watched in fear, probably imagining what their own arrest might feel like. It took several hours before the trio arrived at Berlin's Anhalter Bahnhof, the main concourse. Annika was hungry and in need of toilet facilities. Descending the steps, they were met curbside by a waiting police vehicle. For Annika it was a relief simply to get away from the relentless scrutiny of the hapless public. No sirens, no fanfare, just a short ride through a maze of streets before turning onto Prinz Albrecht Strasse.

Looming up before her was an imposing, five-story Gothic style stone building. A line of vehicles, many marked *Polizei*, were parked out front, and despite the hour, people were coming and going. Annika's heart was in her throat. Clambering out of the vehicle, she stepped to the sidewalk and paused for a moment to look up and take in the structure's immensity. "Welcome to Gestapo headquarters," said the Inspector. The greeting was not without irony. The two men placed a hand under each of Annika's shoulders whisking her up the steps and into the building. Once inside, an alliteration of footsteps and garbled voices echoed throughout the vast chambers that once housed a world-class art museum.

The *KriPo* man made a few comments to a uniformed clerk, who scrutinized them disinterestedly, jotted down some notes and waved them forward. She was marched downstairs to the basement, where several men, all sporting SS insignia, sat around a table, smoking and playing cards. One of the men looked over, clearly annoyed at the interruption, but got up, exchanged a few words with her captors, then took over custody of Annika. She was led by the guard down a dimly lit corridor to a small room where she was instructed to sit in straight-backed wooden chair. The room was stark, barren of pictures, with only the back end of a typewriter sitting on the small wooden desk in front of her. She sat for about forty minutes, not knowing what to expect. Eventually, two SS men entered, one taking a seat on the opposite side of the desk. He barked out a few demographic questions, primarily name, address and occupation.

"I'm a doctor," Annika said. "I work at Bernburg Sanitarium."

"Oh, a doctor," he said, sneering. "Well, you've come to the right place. We've got a lot of people here who could use some medical attention." He winked at the guard, who spit a stream of tobacco juice on the floor and laughed.

"So, tell me, *Frau Doktor*," he said sarcastically. "Who are your parents and where are they residing?"

Her heart skipped a beat. She hadn't anticipated her parents being brought into the conversation, so not wanting to implicate them, she stretched the truth. "My father died when I was two." It wasn't a lie, just not the full truth.

"*Und deine Mutter?*" He used informal German, not willing to show her any respect.

"My mother is living in Belgium."

"But you communicate with her, yes? What's her address?"

Blood rushed to her head. "I . . . I don't know," she lied. "Since the war began, I haven't heard from her. I have no idea where she is living."

The man stopped typing to look up at her. He studied her face, leaned back in his chair and lit another cigarette. Annika stared back, trying to appear confident. Taking a long drag, eyes fixed on Annika, he gradually turned back to the typewriter, giving her hope that she had succeeded in hiding her parents' location. After a few more keystrokes, the guard turned to the other officer, who was standing at the doorway also smoking a cigarette. "I'm done with the prisoner," he said.

Prisoner. The word was jarring. "May I ask, Officer, why I'm here, and when I can leave . . ."

His answer was even more disquieting. "You can ask *nothing*. We ask the questions here. You can rest assured that whatever

187

questions you have will be answered in due course." Then, turning to the other man, he said, "Take her away." The guard stubbed out his butt on the floor, took Annika brusquely under her arm and led her down a series of corridors. They passed cells on each side, and Annika's blood ran cold as she heard muffled groans resonating from inside. Before she had time to think, the guard opened a metal door, pushed her inside, and slammed the door shut.

Annika stood for several minutes, staring, not sure if this was real or a nightmare. The cell was small and filthy, maybe six feet by ten feet with a metal cot taking up much of the floor space. There was no sink or toilet, only a bucket in the corner. Once her mind settled down enough to process what was happening, she was repulsed by a foul odor. The only thing she could liken it to was a decomposing animal, something at the side of a road that you'd give wide berth to. She looked at the yellow wall, faded and heavily scratched with the markings of previous occupants. She saw something move. It was a roach making its way towards the ceiling. She rushed over and squashed it in what she would quickly discover to be a futile effort at purging her new quarters of insects. Like most people, she had heard of Gestapo prisons and their interrogations, but never figured that she, a well-heeled physician, could ever wind up in one. *This is crazy. It's got to be a huge misunderstanding.* She tried to console herself to keep from panicking. *There's no way they're going to keep me. Once they realize their mistake, I'm sure I'll be released, probably in the morning.*

Her stomach ached with hunger, yet her thirst was even worse. All she could think of was water, but she was too frightened to call out. She spent that first night seated on her cot, knees pulled to her chest, playing out scores of scenarios in an effort to figure why she had been arrested. Hunger, thirst, and fatigue played into her fears, and before long she was wondering if someone had set her up, maybe fabricated something to get rid of her. No matter how much she tried to downplay that possibility, it kept popping up in her mind.

It was in that small, dimly lit, grimy cell that she spent the next few days. Food and water were eventually brought in, which became a twice daily occurrence. The portions, however, were not only meager, but almost undigestible – a watery gruel with a few pieces of sour-tasting meat, the occasional, soggy vegetable, and a crusty piece of brown bread. A lightbulb high above her windowless cell burned day and night, making it difficult to guess at the time, much less sleep. A prisoner came by each morning to empty the chamber pot, yet that simple act did little to improve the air, which hung unmoved in her cell like a putrid fog from which there was no escape.

Nighttime was the most chilling, and easily recognized by bloodcurdling mayhem emanating from distant corridors. It usually commenced sometime after midnight, when prisoners were psychically at their most vulnerable, and continued on until dawn. She sat wide-eyed, frozen in fear, wondering if bearing witness to obvious torture, even if only from hearing it, was worse than being the actual victim. Her cot was a breeding ground for bedbugs and fleas, and it wasn't long before her torso was dotted with bites, some quite red and inflamed. And perhaps worse than anything was being isolated by herself, hour after hour, day after day, with no distractions – no books, no writing material, and no one to talk to.

As near as she could figure, at least a week elapsed before her door clanged open with two guards silhouetted in the doorway. "Get up," one of them ordered.

Annika was slow to rise. She was horribly disheveled and, without soap or water, reeked of body odor. "Where are we going?" she asked, tremulously. "Am I being released?"

He ignored her questions, placing her instead in handcuffs. He then led her through clammy passageways to the stairwell. Annika blinked as bright daylight greeted them on the first floor. Ascending the broad staircase, they were passed by an entourage of high-ranking SS officers, each with high-peaked officers' hats and long, black leather coats. In the center, Annika recognized Heinrich Himmler, whom, from State-run news reports, she knew to be one of Hitler's closest associates. Passing in both directions were prisoners escorted by SS guards. Some were bloodied and barely able to walk. Once they reached the third floor, *Abteilung II*, she was paraded down another long corridor to a small waiting area. The door to the adjoining office was closed, but the nameplate read, *Heinrich Müller, Chef der Deutschen Polizei, Amt IV.*

The chief of police, thought Annika. *Well, I'm going straight to the top.* Outside the office, perched rigidly behind a desk, sat a young, but stern-looking SS officer. He nodded to Annika's sentry before picking up the phone to announce their arrival. He then stood up, motioned to the guards and opened the door. Attired in a crisp, black SS uniform, Müller was seated behind a large, mahogany desk. He was studying a file, ignoring Annika and the guard for several minutes, leaving them standing, waiting. Eventually, after making a few notations, he raised his head. "Name," he demanded, as if he had been through the same routine countless times before. It was less of a question than a starting point. His narrow blue eyes, flashing and penetrating, bore into her almost like a syringe plunged deep into a muscle. A chill ran up and down her spine. As a psychiatrist, she was trained to judge character, and this man had all the earmarks of someone with a character disorder. When Annika replied, he gestured to the chair in front of his desk and, in an equally uncompromising voice, said simply, "Sit."

What began as routine questions of the sort posed several days earlier – name, birthdate, occupation, residence and the like – they quickly turned colder, more ominous and accusatory. "What do you know of *Aktion T4?*" he asked. Annika explained her exposure to the program, her offer of a position, and her decision to respectfully decline the post.

"And who have you discussed this information with?"

Annika was unprepared for this question. It was suddenly beginning to make sense why she was being detained. "I . . . I'm not sure I understand, Herr Inspector," she stammered.

Abruptly standing, both fists clenched on his desk, he leaned forward and said, "Oh, I think you understand perfectly well." His tone was crisp and unambiguous. "I repeat, *who* did you share this information with?"

"Inspector, I don't recall sharing that information with anyone."

"No?" he bellowed. "Well how about the name Lutz Pfeiffer? Ever heard of him?"

Lutz, she thought. *So that's what this is all about.* "Yes, I know Lutz. We were in medical school together."

"You were both in a lot more than medical school!" He was now sounding like a prosecutor. "We know exactly what you did with him. You met him in Berlin two years ago, didn't you?"

Annika had to think. It had been so long. "Yes, as I recall, we had dinner together." She was clearly becoming rattled. Lutz had disappeared and now this. *He must've been arrested, probably tortured,* she reasoned.

"Look at me!" Müller demanded. "And what did you talk about . . . *at dinner*?" he asked sarcastically.

"Sir, I . . . I don't recall. That was . . ."

He cut her off. "You don't recall? Well, fortunately he does! He says you told him all about the Reich's top secret *T4* program." Annika was trembling. She tried to keep from weeping. "Is it coming back to you, Doctor Tritzchler?"

"Sir, it was so long ago. We spent the evening together. We talked about so many things . . ."

"I'm not asking if you fucked him,'" he screamed. "I'm asking about your discussion of the euthanasia program. Do I have to spell it out to you?"

Annika was at a loss to recall the extent of her meeting with Lutz. "Herr Inspector, we only talked about the new forms that were required at our respective facilities. We may have speculated about the reasons for them, but sir, please understand, I knew nothing at the time about any euthanasia going on at Bernberg. We were colleagues, former students . . . comparing notes."

"Aha, innocently comparing notes. I see," he said sarcastically. "But certainly, one of you must have brought up the topic. It didn't just come up by itself, right? And let us suppose that you were 'just comparing notes,' as you say. What reason did you have for breaking the law by divulging any sort of classified information?"

"Sir, it was much later that I was told about the euthanasia program. Please. I am a doctor. I have been trained to save lives . . . to treat illnesses. Put yourself in my place. How can I, with the training I received in medical school, stand by in good conscience, much less participate, in the taking of life? It goes against . . ."

"I don't give a *damn* about your personal ethics! You think you're smarter than the Führer? People of far greater rank and intelligence than you have developed these policies and deemed them necessary and proper in promoting the ideals of the Fatherland. Where do you get off putting yourself above the law?" Annika realized that no amount of reason or any appeal to human charity would persuade Müller of the purity of her motives. She had no answer.

"And who else did you *'compare notes'* with?" Müller demanded.

"No one," Annika pleaded. "I went about my usual duties. What Doctor Eberl's group did from then on was none of my business." Annika was frightened. Knowing what she had heard about Gestapo tactics, like playing one person against another, or pressuring a prisoner under interrogation to incriminate a friend, worse yet a family member, she was determined to play down her knowledge and not tell them anything more than she surmised they already knew.

"Oh really?" Müller said. "Then why might Doctor Eberl have told us that you came storming into his office one day, unannounced, and demanded of him, your superior, *your boss,* that he tell you what happened to some of your patients? If what he did was 'his business,' as you put it, what right did you have to question him?"

Annika paused, trying to come up with a response that would satisfy him. "Answer me!" he demanded, pounding his fist on the desk. "You are a physician, educated at the State's expense, provided with a good job and paid good wages by the very government to whom you have an obligation. Am I correct?"

"Yes . . ." she answered, now whimpering.

"And am I not also correct that you were instructed that the program implemented at Bernburg by your director . . . and not simply *any* man, but a decorated physician committed to the glory and the future of the Third Reich . . . were you not told that that program is top secret?" His voice became louder, more impassioned, as he took on the tone of a state prosecutor. "And were you not under strict orders to never discuss it with anyone? Is that not correct?"

"Yes, but . . ."

"Don't 'but' me, Tritzchler." He wasn't allowing her any time to think. "Were you not also informed that betraying the confidential nature of this decree would be met with the strictest penalties?"

"I was told it was secret, yes. But the warning came *after* my discussion with Doctor Pfeiffer . . ."

"What are you, stupid? Does everything need to be spelled out for you?" Once again, Annika was in a situation of trying to hold back tears, but she was emotionally shaken, and Müller knew it. "So, let me tell you what's *not* secret, Tritzchler. You, with your big mouth, have betrayed the Reich. You're a perfect illustration of why the Führer proposes to keep women at home, where they belong, I might add . . . out of the professions. Unfortunately, you have relinquished your ability to even take up *that* role . . ."

"But, Herr Inspector, if you would give me a chance to . . ."

"Silence! I'm not giving you a chance to do anything. You've had your chance. For someone with your level of education, you have very poor judgment. That's why women shouldn't be in skilled occupations. If you were a man with these charges, I'd have you flogged, then put in front of a firing squad." He looked down at his file, shuffled through a few pages, then said, "You seem to like education. Well how 'bout this? I'm thinking that some post-graduate work at Oranienburg might teach you something . . . you know, enhance your resume."

Annika could only stare. Her knees trembled as she saw her

world crashing in on her. All her hopes, all those dreams. Müller looked up at her and relished the fear that was so evident in her face. She was no different from the hundreds of others he had bullied. Breaking down prisoners was his forte. "It's too late for tears, Tritzchler. You shoulda' thought about that before you blabbed. And let me warn you. If there's more to your story, rest assured that you'll be more than happy to tell us. We've had way tougher birds than you sing like canaries after their vacation in Oranienburg." He made a few brief notations, then stamped a form in two places. "Take her back," he commanded, waving to the guard.

Annika's mouth dropped. She wanted to speak, but no words would come. The guard didn't wait. He pulled her by the elbow, spun her around and escorted her out of the inspector's office and back to her cell, where she would spend another long, anxious night.

Sachsenhausen

Mostly it is loss which teaches us about the worth of things.
Arthur Schopenhauer

21 November, 1941

"C'mon, move!" the guard commanded, hustling Annika in handcuffs down the hallway, out of the building, and into a waiting police van. It was just after dawn and she was being moved from Gestapo HQ to the Sachsenhausen *Konzentrationslager* (KZ) in the small town of Oranienburg. While not that far from Berlin, the drive took almost two hours. All the while, she had an urge to urinate that grew more insistent with each bump and turn in the road. They finally came to an enormous facility spanning what looked to be hundreds of acres. It was surrounded by a gargantuan stone wall and imposing guard towers, and it didn't require binoculars to make out the barrels of fixed machine guns trained towards whatever lay inside those miles of barbed wire surrounding the lager. A chill ran up her spine, making her forget for a moment the ache in her bladder. The van stopped briefly at the entrance, long enough for two sentries, rifles slung over their shoulders, to hoist the gate. The van sputtered to a large white building distinguished by a cupola and clock at the peak. Emblazoned across the wide edifice was the word "*Schutzhaftlager.*"

She scoffed at the term. "Protective custody." It had become a familiar euphemism in Nazi Germany. The suggestion was that people confined inside were being mercifully protected from hostile elements outside. The rumors were far different, alleging that the prisoners (*Häftlinge*) would never encounter anything more cruel and depraved than the sadists who were selected to run these camps. She

195

was about to discover the veracity of those claims.

An SS sergeant sat behind a desk, with SS personnel walking about in every direction. The air was thick with cigarette smoke. Annika's escort handed him paperwork that had accompanied them from Berlin. The sergeant glanced at it briefly, then looked up to Annika.

"Name?" he asked.

"Annika Tritzchler," she replied, in a voice only slightly louder than a whisper.

"Speak louder," he commanded. "We know you can talk. That's why you're here, right? Your big mouth? Says here you were arrested for conspiracy and spreading lies?" He looked back down to the paperwork. "What's your occupation?"

"I'm a physician . . . a psychiatrist."

"Psychiatrist? So, you work with monkeys and rats? You'll feel right at home here, Fräulein Psychiatrist, cuz this place is filled with 'em. Monkeys and rats!" The escort smiled.

"*Sturmmann,* I provide treatment to patients with mental handicaps," Annika responded.

"Don't refer to me as *Sturmmann,* woman. You obviously know nothing about the military. My rank is *Scharführer,* and you will use that designation henceforth in addressing me." Annika's face reddened. "So, I'm gonna ask you again. Whatdya do with imbeciles? Try to make them feel good about themselves?"

"Sir, I try to assist them in becoming more productive with their lives."

"Productive? Fräulein, don't insult my intelligence telling me you treat people with mental illnesses. That's Jew-talk. I can't stand you rich bastards with all your highfalutin theories. You're totally out of touch with what's really going on in the world. Ya' know what? You'd win a prize if you could turn lazy, good-for-nothing idiots into productive citizens. But that's never gonna happen. Let me clue you in if you haven't found this out already. The people in asylums, babbling to themselves like hyenas, are either insane – and therefore worthless – or they're nothing more than work-shy Communists. No matter which category they fall into, they all should be exterminated. Like vermin."

Annika squirmed. She realized immediately that every Nazi idea every slogan that had always seemed to come from fringe elements would be the norm here and that it would be useless to respond.

The officer looked down at his paperwork. "Your parents' names?" he snarled.

Annika recoiled. She had never intended her parents to be brought into this.

"I *said,* what are your parents' names?"

Annika gulped. "Eva and Martin Tritzchler."

"Religion."

"Lutheran," she lied. Most of the Nazis, if they claimed any religion at all, were Lutheran. It sounded safest to say that.

"The reports that have accompanied you here indicate that you have been remanded to this camp as punishment for speaking openly about confidential information protected by the Reich's Ministry of the Interior." He looked up at her disdainfully. "Exactly the reason women shouldn't be put in positions of responsibility. Fucking gossip-mongers." Then shaking his head from side to side, he said, "Never met a woman who knows when to keep her mouth shut." He signed a form, stamped it with an official seal, then looked over to the guard. "Get an *aufseherin* in here. I'm done with her."

The guard turned, opened the door slightly, and motioned with his hand. A second or two later, a female guard entered. She looked to be about 30, maybe a little older, and was clad in a bland uniform consisting of a long, gray wool skirt with matching jacket and cap. She had broad shoulders, a deep, raspy voice, and short, scraggly blonde hair tied tightly to the back of her head. She had unmistakably large breasts, though they appeared to be bound – *maybe,* Annika thought, *to neutralize her femininity . . . make her more intimidating. If it weren't for that, she could easily pass for a man.* The woman immediately snapped to attention with a perfunctory salute. "*Heil*

197

Hitler, Scharführer."

The sergeant stamped the packet, and handed it to the woman guard. "Take this prisoner to the women's barracks. She's political. Doctor Mennecke will be seeing her today or tomorrow."

"*Ja! Sehr gut, Scharführer.*" Another stiff salute before grabbing Annika's left elbow.

As they turned to walk out, the sergeant's eyes trailed Annika's derriere. He looked over to the SS officer standing to the side and muttered, "A lot better looking than most of the cows they bring in here." The officer snorted in agreement.

Annika was marched double-time through the building to a door leading outside. They proceeded to a barricade manned by two sentries on each side of an iron gate. In the center of the metalwork were three cryptic words: *Arbeit Macht Frei.* Annika's heart quickened. "Work will set you free." They walked a short distance to a large sign, a dictum to all inmates.

Es gibt einen Weg in die Freiheit.
Seine Meilensteine heißen:
Gehorsam, Fleiß, Ehrlichkeit, Ordnung, Sauberkeit,
Nüchternheit, Wahrhaftigkeit, Opfersinn und Liebe zum
Vaterland.

The guard paused. "Read it," she commanded, as if this was some rite of passage. Annika read. *There is one way to freedom. Its milestones are: obedience, diligence, honesty, order, cleanliness, sobriety, truthfulness, sacrifice and love for the Fatherland.*

"Those, Fräulein, are the words of *Reichsführer* Heinrich Himmler. Ever heard of him?" Annika was too stupefied to respond. "No?" she asked, pushing her forward. "Well, look around. You'll be reminded of his words all throughout your vacation here." She pointed to the cluster of white buildings where, painted across each of their gable ends, was one of those nine adjectives, a different one on each building.

Fräulein

They passed thousands of prisoners, a veritable sea of men and women in striped clothing going about their duties in segregated groupings. Most were led by a fellow detainee; someone with the authority to not only bark out commands, but to use fists and clubs for ensuring compliance. Prisoners marched silently and submissively. A harsh regimentation prevailed throughout the camp. Annika was quick to notice that each time inmates passed an SS guard, they spontaneously snatched the cap from their head and lowered their eyes in an obsequious show of respect.

The complex was huge. The prisoners were tattered, forlorn and, above all, they looked scared. She and the *aufseherin* crossed a courtyard, where Annika saw four large posts, like telephone poles but with hooks at the top. "That's where we hang our laundry out to dry," the guard said. "Wrinkle-free, as long as you have a someone wearing it while it dries." Up ahead, an SS guard was supervising three men, all in a deep, squatting position, their arms fully outstretched, faces wincing in pain. "That's the 'Sachsenhausen salute,'" her escort joked. "Good for strengthening the quads." As they passed, one of the prisoners, an older man, rolled to his side, no longer able to maintain the squat. What followed was volley of loud, vulgar epithets. Annika looked back just in time to see the guard repeatedly kicking the man. "Bolsheviks." her escort said. "Can't follow simple directions."

She was then brought to another building where inside a crowd of women was being herded by overseers, prisoners themselves but flaunting armbands identifying them as "kapos." They dished out commands in loud, denigrating vulgarity and wielded clubs on the defenseless mob without any restraint. SS officers – all men – looked on from the periphery, smiling, sometimes shouting encouragement. Annika and the others, frightened and confused, did what they could to protect themselves. Once assembled, they were ordered to strip. Annika looked around, not sure if she had heard correctly. Turning to the woman next to her, she asked, "Take our clothes off? Right here?"

The other woman was significantly older, probably in her sixties.

Clad in a green, boiled wool jacket and matching ankle-length dress, she was undoubtedly a person of means. "I . . . I'm not sure," she responded, looking at the SS men, who were clearly entertained. "I can't imagine we're to undress in front of those men . . ."

They looked around, searching for cues from the roiling crowd when, out of nowhere, a stocky prisoner landed a club to the side of the older woman's neck, sending her sprawling to the floor. Annika jumped aside, startled. The kapo's assault was so unexpected, so vicious and unprovoked. Annika's mind swirled, thinking that the elderly woman had been no threat to anyone, and now she was being stampeded by a frenzied crowd whose shoes scraped against her face and kicked at her torso. The group of women were terrified and had no idea a person was squirming in the filth beneath them. Another kapo gave Annika a resounding shove, and hollered, "Get your goddamn clothes off! Now!" Her push was so intense that Annika stumbled over the ambushed victim at her feet. As quickly as she had appeared, the kapo melted into the crowd like a lioness stalking a herd of zebras. Shaken, Annika leaned down to help the woman up.

Everyone began to disrobe, as ordered. Writhing bodies of all shapes and ages tugged at clothing to remove it quickly to avoid further wrath from the roving mercenaries. Coats, bodices and undergarments dropped to the floor amid chortles and salacious comments from the SS. Was this the titillation of younger bodies or was it the power they lorded over their embarrassed captives? Annika wondered.

She joined a line of naked women not knowing what awaited, but not chancing any more questions. At the head of the line, a male prisoner was combing through women's hair. Those with lice were directed to his left where another prisoner cut off all the hair right down to the scalp. When Annika reached the front, he pulled her head towards his torso and began to roughly comb through her scalp. She was immediately repelled by his stench, but the greatest indignity was the insistent feel of his genitals against her. Even in such a macabre setting, Annika thought, one stripped of all humanity, here was a man still moved, still animated, by opportunity. She tried to pull away, but he held her fast, and she had already seen enough to recognize that screaming out would invite punishment from the guards.

It was only a minute or so before she was out of his clutches and shoved along with the others to the showers. Annika panicked, assuming that this had to be the end. She saw herself falling into oblivion, just like Elsie, Max, and so many of the patients she had known and worked with who had nevertheless been gassed at Bernburg. She couldn't help thinking that her parents would never see her again, that they would never know what became of her or where to find her grave. Swaying side to side on the cold, wet floor, the skin of countless women rubbing against her on every side, Annika began to pray. *The Lord is my shepherd, I shall not want . . .* Looking upwards as she recited the Psalm aloud, she tried to see beyond the faucets overhead, preparing for the transcendence of eternal life . . . *Yea, though I walk through the valley of the shadow of death, I will fear no evil for thou art with me . . .* Her recitations were interspersed with screams and wailing from the frenzied women surrounding her, but Annika heard none of it. Instead, a miraculous feeling of calm and resignation replaced the horror of the past day. There was no more fighting; she was ready to face her destiny . . . *And I will dwell in the house of the Lord forever.*

It was not to be. Her reverie was shattered by ice-cold water raining down from above. Despite the shock, it was nevertheless a chance to wash away dirt and grime from what for many had been weeks of confinement. "*Schnell*," the kapos screamed, demanding that the human assembly-line hurry into yet another room, where a guard began doling out clothing. Before Annika was ready, he threw a brown packet, hitting her squarely in the stomach. She coughed, dropping the packet to the floor. The guard repeated the same maneuver on each person and was amused anytime he succeeded in knocking the wind out of someone. Annika unfurled the foul-smelling packet to find an oversized one-piece smock. She eyed it with disgust. "*Sich anziehen!*" the guard yelled. Frightened, Annika pulled the scratchy clothing over her shoulders. It covered her like a potato sack. Everybody was in similar straits as none of the parcels had been distributed according to size. Then came the wooden clogs. No measurements; one size for all.

The last room of all featured two SS men seated behind desks. The first checked off names and announced designations to the second officer, who passed out individualized patches. Annika was handed a red triangle. Others were given different colored triangles: green, purple, blue, and black, though no one had any idea what they meant. Nevertheless, the triangles came with strict instructions that they be sewn onto the chest of one's clothing. The women were then hustled out of the building where they were greeted by screaming guards and baying Alsatian dogs. They were formed into a long line, five abreast, and marched through a parade ground, then down the main walkway, passing gallows followed by row-upon-row of long buildings to their new home, Barrack 43.

Annika and other newly-arrived inmates were told that during the first week of their confinement, they would be restricted to the barrack except for meals and roll-calls. That evening, they were instructed to line up with other inmates for chow.

"Go ahead. You're new. You can be first," said one of the more seasoned inmates to Annika. Others pushed her and the other new arrivals forward in line.

"Thank you," she said, nodding appreciatively, surprised by the collegial reception. It wasn't until much later that she would learn that the real sustenance to the soup, meat and vegetables, always settled to the bottom of the pot, meaning that those at the end of the line had the best chances for something to chew on. In contrast, her soup was watery and sour tasting. She soon realized that patience in the chow line gave meaning to a verse from the Book of Matthew: *". . . the last shall be first, and the first last . . ."*

The following morning, she was brusquely awakened by shouts and whistles. It was still dark out, but two kapos burst into the barracks wielding clubs and shouting obscenities to roust the women from their bunks. Startled, Annika jumped from the wooden bunk, but caught her dress on a splinter, causing her to stumble onto the floor.

"What the fuck are you doing, retard?" It was Gretl, the hyper-masculinized block leader. Annika cried out as Gretl delivered a kick to her backside. "Get your ass moving!" she demanded.

Annika had only been in camp less than twenty-four hours, and already she had captured the eye of the most feared kapo in Barrack 43. Gretl wore a green triangle. She was strong and well-fed with broad shoulders that gave her an ape-like profile. She had a blocky head, square jaw and arms splattered in jailhouse tattoos. Whenever she spoke, her upper lip curled into a sneer that accentuated a purplish scar running diagonally across her left cheek. It was only yesterday, during orientation, that Gretl herself had boasted of having been culled from a state prison by the SS precisely to take on this role. As *Blockführerin*, she had free rein to exercise brutality to maintain order in a barrack of over two hundred women. Annika jumped up and followed the others, fear overriding the pain in her hip. The women were allotted only minutes to use the latrines and straighten up their "beds" before hastily assembling outside for roll-call on the *Appelplatz*.

Annika's first roll-call was an ordeal lasting almost two hours – bad, but not as troubling as what followed. After all the prisoners had been counted and recounted, two women were called to the front of the vast crowd. The one woman was said to have been caught stealing food. The other was identified as her friend. Both were then led to a pole in front. A kapo, supervised by a phalanx of SS guards, forced one of the women onto a short stool, whereupon a rope was affixed to her neck. Both women were sobbing. The kapo pulled the rope just tight enough that there was no slack, and then instructed the friend to kick the stool from under the condemned woman's feet. Initially, the friend hesitated, but after two strong slaps to her face, she did, which sent her friend swinging and thrashing. The free woman put her arms over her head, unable to watch, much less grasp that she had contributed to the gruesome spectacle. Meanwhile, her friend danced on the rope in a wild effort to make contact with the ground only a few inches below, which only caused her to bounce up and down, prolonging the strangulation. What commenced in just a few minutes seemed to Annika like an eternity, yet eventually the victim stopped moving.

The prisoners were then required to file one-by-one past the gallows. "Everyone is to take a good long look," ordered the kapo, who had supervised the hanging. One woman, a newcomer like Annika and visibly shaken by what she had just witnessed, kept her head lowered as she ambled by, weeping. There was no sympathy. She was immediately plucked from the line and beaten by a kapo. Annika was forced to keep moving. She looked up at the lifeless body still twisting slowly on the rope. While horrified, she found herself astonished by the calm, peaceful look on the face of the dead woman. She had expected to see bulging eyes, protruding tongue, maybe even soiled clothing, but there was none of that. It seemed such a contrast from the chaos and gnashing of teeth only minutes before. *Maybe,* Annika thought, *she discovered in that final moment that death was liberation, deliverance from the evil of man.*

The Infirmary

The majority of men . . . are not capable of thinking, but only of believing, and . . . are not accessible to reason, but only to authority.
Arthur Schopenhauer

KZ Sachsenhausen, November, 1941- February, 1942

The new arrivals were still languishing in their barrack as part of their orientation. Everyone knew they would soon be assigned to work details, and the room was alive with anxious conversations as to what they might encounter in the coming days. It was all rumor, but nothing sounding auspicious.

"Tritzchler!" Gretl's voice thundered above the din. "Get your ass over here!" she demanded. Annika was terror-stricken, not knowing why she was being singled out. She walked to the front, stopping a mere meter from the *Blockführerin.* "You're to report to Doctor Mennecke at the *Revier,* immediately!"

The *Revier*? "We have an infirmary?" Annika asked.

"Of course, we have an infirmary. What're you, stupid? Follow her. Now!" Gretl signaled for another kapo, who escorted her to the building at the other end of camp.

Mennecke was seated behind a spacious wooden desk on which were stacks of papers and folders. Slightly off to the side was a half-eaten plate of pork and sauerkraut. Still chewing, he seemed agitated by the intrusion. He picked up a folder, opened it, and thumbed through a few pages before letting out a loud, juicy belch which he made no effort to disguise. "So, the information I have here states that you are . . . a physician?" He slowly looked up at her, rolling his eyes, appearing not at all impressed.

205

"*Ja, Herr Doktor.*"

"Specialty?"

"I was in my third year of post-doctoral training as a psychiatrist."

"Uh huh. Well, I'm a psychiatrist as well. Were you a party member?"

"*Nein.* I am not attached to any political party."

"No, of course not, which may help to explain why you're here . . . It says here you were arrested . . . hmmm . . . for activities that were considered compromising to the Reich?"

"Doctor, I'm not a traitor, nor am I a resister. I . . ."

He cut her off. "What do you mean you're not a resister? What explains the red triangle you're wearing. C'mon, Tritzchler, if you're a resister, stand up for what you believe in."

"Herr Director, I simply had a difference of opinion with the chief psychiatrist at Bernburg. And I mentioned my misgivings to a former classmate, which unfortunately is what got me in trouble."

"From what it says here, you furnished classified information to someone picked up for resistance activities." He looked at her for a full minute without saying anything. "You know, Tritzchler, you're lucky you weren't shot. That's a serious violation. So, what exactly was it that you apparently had a problem with?"

"Doctor Mennecke, sir, with all due respect, I have been severely warned to not talk with anyone – under any circumstances – about the work at Bernburg. If nothing else, my arrest, and certainly my confinement here . . ." she looked around the room, ". . . has taught me the seriousness of that policy."

"Well, I would assume you were told that while employed at Bernburg, were you not?" Annika nodded, and was about to speak when Mennecke continued. "And you took it upon yourself to make your own interpretations of institutional policy. I would suspect this means that you consider yourself as having greater insight than our Führer, right?" Annika squirmed. "Answer me!"

Annika felt that she was being tested. If there was any chance of getting out of Sachsenhausen, she needed to convince him of her allegiance. "Sir, I recognize my mistake. I committed a grievous error by discussing my sentiments with a colleague, which is what brought me to the attention of the authorities. I am young, apolitical, and reasonably inexperienced. I had no intention of undermining the institution . . . or the Reich, for that matter."

"Is that so?" Mennecke asked almost mockingly, drawing out his words. Through squinted eyes, he looked her up and down.

"Doctor Mennecke, I have no intention of making that mistake again."

"Well, you've been assigned to my supervision . . . not that I have any interest in working with a woman, much less one with the markings of a traitor. But orders are orders, which you're going to learn if you want to avoid consequences." Mennecke noticed Annika swallow. "I assume you have some knowledge as to how we deal with inmates who violate the rules, yes?"

"*Jawohl, Herr Doktor*!" She tried to sound convincing.

He smiled. "Good. Then listen, and hear me good. If you work under me, you'll do exactly as I say, nothing more, nothing less. You're no longer considered a doctor, and have no such privileges. In fact, most of your work will be limited to that of a nurse, sometimes even less, unless I direct otherwise. You'll only be responsible for prisoners *assigned* to you, and no one else. We *only* treat prisoners who are considered salvageable. Is that understood?"

"I beg your pardon, Doctor Mennecke. 'Salvageable' . . .? I'm not sure I understand."

"You leave that to me, Tritzchler. The inmates here have committed reprehensible acts against our Fatherland. They are enemies, and those who are able will be required to atone for their acts by working. That's how they pay off their debt. And this job is *your* opportunity to repay *your* debt. A last chance at salvation . . .."

Salvation, she thought. *What in the world would he know about salvation?*

Mennecke went on. "Our job is to maximize our workforce . . .

207

keep our workers healthy. We provide treatment to those who can *work* . . . no one else. Remember this. *Arbeit macht frei.* Work sets a man free! Do we understand ourselves?"

"*Jawohl, Doktor Mennecke.*" Annika was in no position to argue; she had already seen too much to realize that the deck was heavily stacked against her.

"And one last thing, Tritzchler. You are *not* to discuss this work with anyone. *Anyone.* Got it?"

Annika nodded. "*Ja, Herr Doktor. Ich verstehe.*"

Annika's work was far beneath what, as a physician, she had been trained for. She had to get used to performing such mundane tasks as changing bandages, emptying bedpans and monitoring vital signs, but she had no authority to diagnose illness. That was the job of the Nazi doctors. Instead, Annika was to keep meticulous notes and report her daily findings to Doctor Mennecke, who in turn made medical decisions regarding each patient's continuing treatment. She assumed that those with disease were transferred to separate wards, though she was not privy to their treatment once they left her sector.

One of her patients, who she knew only by number, was a middle-aged Polish man who had been admitted the previous afternoon with a hacking cough and very high fever. She greeted him with a smile.

"Can you tell me how I'm doing?" he asked in heavily accented German.

"*Ah, Sie sprechen Deutsch,*" she said, surprised. "*Wie heissen Sie?*"

"Juliusz," he stammered. "Juliusz Piatkowski."

"Well, Herr Piatkowski. Can you tell me what brought you here . . . to Sachsenhausen?"

"I came by boxcar . . . with many Polish people . . . all stuffed in the car. Like sardines." She stopped what she was doing to look at him. "Men, women, and children . . . Twelve died . . ."

"Don't talk for a few minutes. I'm going to take your

temperature." He opened his mouth to accept a thermometer. He had a very high fever, 40.7 Celsius. He said his head had been hot for almost a week and that he had severe body aches. It took Annika only minutes to detect swollen lymph nodes and a distinctive red rash in his mid-section that seemed to be spreading; classic signs, she thought, of typhus.

"I'll get you some water and see if we can't get a change of clothing for you."

The patient grabbed Annika's arm. "They told me not to come here," he said. "Told me that I'd never leave here alive."

Annika patted his hand and looked into his eyes. "We'll try to get you feeling better, Herr Piatkowski." He relaxed his grip, allowing Annika to leave. She documented her findings, careful not to diagnose, and submitted the daily summation to Mennecke.

The next morning, Piatkowski was gone. *They've taken him to the typhus wing*, she figured. She straightened up the bed in preparation for another patient. Scores of them were outside awaiting treatment. As she struggled with the sheets, Annika felt something under the mattress. It was a gold signet ring engraved with the letter "P." It obviously belonged to Piatkowski. Finding it presented a problem. Jewelry was strictly forbidden, and was to be turned over to camp authorities from the moment a detainee entered the camp. Piatkowski shouldn't have had it. The fact that he did suggested it was important enough to risk keeping it. Should she turn it over, Annika wondered. Maybe it was an heirloom, something from his parents. Maybe a wedding ring. She put it in her pocket.

Annika sought out her co-worker, Miranda, a "political" prisoner from Lauenburg with whom she had become friendly. They were not only bunkmates, but had formed a connection when Annika talked of her experiences at Lauenburg's medieval castle. From that point on, Miranda had treated Annika like someone she had grown up with, remarkable in a concentration camp where having a friend can actually get one into trouble, which everyone had witnessed at the gallows. Nevertheless, Annika pulled Miranda aside.

"That patient who was in this bed yesterday . . ." She pointed. "The man with the cough. I think his name was Piatkowski. He's been moved . . . Do you know where I'd I find him?"

Miranda looked like she had seen a ghost. The rule of thumb at Sachsenhausen was to keep to yourself, not ask questions. She could forgive Annika's carelessness, but nudged her to a remote corner where their conversation couldn't be overheard. "Why are you asking?"

"I found a ring stuffed under the mattress. I'm quite sure it belongs to him."

Miranda might as well have been told she had cancer. "Annika," she whispered, "listen to me. That's contraband, and if you're caught with it, you'll be sent to the bunker. Get rid of it!"

Miranda's admonition was no match for Annika's naivete. She responded, "He's a decent man. He's lost his family. The ring is all he's got left. If I could get to the typhus ward, I could slip it to him without anyone seeing me."

Continuing to scan the room for eavesdroppers, Miranda muttered a powerful rebuke. "Annika. Wake up. There *is* no typhus ward. Don't you see?"

Just then an SS guard strolled into the room. His hands were clasped behind him, clutching a riding crop. As he slowly swaggered down the aisle, he tapped the crop against his upper back, a symbol of his power. Intimidated, the two women looked down as he passed, knowing that to look at him directly was punishable.

When he seemed safely out of the room, Annika, clearly confused and anxious over what she had just been told, persisted. "What do you mean there's no typhus ward? Where do typhus patients go?"

Miranda stared at her with a look that communicated volumes. "You're like a babe-in-the-woods, Annika." She rubbed her eyes, red from lack of sleep. "Listen, prisoners who are of no use to the Nazis are sent to Station Z." Annika had no idea what she was talking about. "It's at the far end of the camp . . . and it's literally the end . . . where prisoners are murdered."

"Murdered?" Annika paused a few seconds, allowing this revelation to sink in. "How?"

"However the guards choose. Hanging, firing squads, gas . . ."

"*Gas?*" Annika was incredulous. *Déjà vu.* She didn't want to believe that here too the Nazis were using gas. Somehow, she had told herself that maybe Bernburg was an anomaly, that gassing psychiatric patients had only been an experiment, that Hitler's euthanasia program had ended. "How do you know this?" she asked.

"Annika, c'mon. You smell the smoke . . . we all do. It's from the crematorium. It's not just people dying from old age. Expendable prisoners are being murdered every day. Every person who comes in here with disease, unless they recover quickly, will end up at Station Z."

Annika's eyes, wide as saucers, glistened in the light. "How do you know this?"

"I'll tell you how, but you have to keep this strictly to yourself." She looked around while rearranging a bed, trying to look busy. "One of the crematorium workers let it slip what was going on, and it spread like wildfire. When Loritz, the camp commandant, got wind of it, he had the workers tortured until one of them confessed. After that, they all disappeared and were replaced." Annika looked stunned. Visions of euthanasia carried out at Bernburg played out in her mind – exactly what had landed her in Sachsenhausen. "A word of advice, Annika. Keep your head down and your mouth shut. It's all about survival, remember that."

Annika felt that she was running on nervous energy. Once again, she was burdened by the suspicion that she might have inadvertently contributed to the death of patients by documenting symptoms of disease. In the few weeks she had been stationed at the infirmary, many of her patients had disappeared.

Back in her bunk, she pulled the filthy blanket over her head and cried. Miranda leaned over, telling her not to worry, that it wasn't she who was guilty but the Nazi butchers who made the "selections." But Annika was facing an existential quandary: continue working in the infirmary where her reports would almost certainly lead to murder, or resign. Resignation would surely be considered political resistance, and there would be consequences, possibly severe. On the other hand, resigning would free her of complicity in murder. She thought of her past meetings with Professor Bonhoeffer, trying to imagine what he would advise.

She prayed long and hard for guidance, and that night, tossing and turning in tangled sheets damp with sweat, the answer came in a dream. She saw herself working beside Edith Cavell, the famous World War One nurse who had worked tirelessly to save the lives of wounded soldiers from both sides. Maybe it was Cavell's having been Belgian that Annika's parents appeared in the dream. They were laying side-by-side in a bed, helpless, unable to move. Nurse Cavell had extended a hand to Annika's father in a scene reminiscent of Michelangelo's depiction of God giving life to Adam. Just as her father touched Cavell's hand, expecting a miracle, German soldiers with faces like bulldogs burst through the room, guns in hand, and hauled them away.

Annika sat up in bed, her heart pounding. It was a nightmare, one which graphically reminded her just how precarious her parent's circumstances had become since Belgium surrendered to the Germans. Could they survive without help from fellow citizens? Probably not. Would anyone risk their neck for a Jew? It suddenly occurred to her that at the infirmary she was in a unique position to help.

It was nearly two months later that Annika was positioning a woman onto a bedpan when someone startled her from behind. "What's this?" bleated the kapo's raspy voice. He was holding her notes. Slapping the paper with the back of his hand, he barked, "I'm checkin' on Inmate *6023*. Your scribble here says that he has 'a cough,' nothing more. You say that he's improving each day. Who da fuck are you kidding? I just saw him coughing up blood. What is this bullshit?"

Annika straightened up. It was the block leader of the Jewish Barracks, a man the inmates called "the Vampire." His face was creased in a perpetual sneer and with his beady eyes and buckteeth, his nickname fit perfectly. People stayed out of his way, and with good reason. His real name, according to those who knew him in Lviv, was Jakub Gapinski, a staunch anti-Semite who had been raised in a devout Jewish family. He had spent most of his adolescence in and out of prison, and when the Nazis invaded Poland, he was arrested once again along with other Jews. Gapinsky, however, gained reprieve by volunteering as a ghetto policeman, and in that capacity, he flourished, developing notoriety for rounding up Jews with a ruthlessness that was said to have brought a shiver to even some of his SS overseers. Annika knew him as a man who relished authority and lorded it over the powerless like a cat toying with a trapped mouse.

"You tryin' to put one over on us?" Gapinsky demanded. "I seen enough tuberculosis to know that this lout got more'n a cough. I bet Doctor Mennecke will have different thoughts."

"*Aber, Herr Blockfuhrer . . .*"

"'But nothing! I know what I'm looking at."

Annika was caught. She had to think fast. Gapinski had uncovered a patient who was far sicker than the symptoms she had reported. It didn't matter that the patient suffered from typhus, not tuberculosis; either condition was a death sentence. She knew that the man could recover, but only with greater measures than allowed. Gapinsky was just about to leave with her paperwork.

Suddenly, Annika remembered the gold ring. Kapos may have authority, she thought, even power over life and death, but down deep they're not like the rest of us; they're "green triangle" criminals. She knew that Gapinsky had landed in Sachsenhausen after having been caught abusing his authority by fencing looted artwork on the black market. One of the Nazis he was in cahoots with ratted him out when it became apparent that Gapinsky wasn't giving him a fair shake.

Annika had no choice but to risk a bribe.

She first appealed to his need for respect. No kapo, she reasoned, wants to feel inferior to any prisoner, especially a woman, even if she is a nurse. *"Herr Blockfuhrer.* You're correct in noting how sick this patient is. You have good insight. However, he's not contagious, and he does not have tuberculosis, which means he *can* recover and will be able to work again."

Gapinsky wasn't buying. His face hardened to a sneer, his hands balled into fists at his side. Annika had to chance a bribe, knowing that if it failed, she'd face severe punishment. She stood up straight, looking him in the eye, "Herr Gapinsky, if you can see your way to overlook this matter. . . " She hesitated before going on. ". . . I- I can get you a gold ring." She did everything she could to keep her legs from shaking.

There was an almost instantaneous change in the kapo's expression. Was he outraged? Was he going to immediately grab her, march her to the commandant? She froze waiting for his response.

"A ring? Show it to me."

This was her moment of truth. She made a quick scan of the room to make sure they were not being watched, and proceeded over to a laundry bin. It was full of dirty linen that reeked of excrement – not a place where people would be nosing around, especially the SS, who were notoriously fearful of disease. She waded through the soiled sheets. Gapinsky wrinkled his face and kept his distance. Finally, Annika pulled out a blood-stained towel. Turning to the kapo, she discreetly unfolded it. There was the gold ring engraved with the letter "P." Gapinsky took the ring, rolling it between his thumb and forefingers. He looked up at Annika, staring deeply into her eyes. His face betrayed nothing. For a brief moment, she anticipated him turning on her. After all, bringing this to the SS would win him even greater privilege. Instead, Gapinsky put the ring in his pocket, nodded his approval and disappeared. Sweating, her heart pounding, Annika had read him correctly.

Several days following that incident, something happened during roll-call that terrorized Annika. It was early morning and she stood on the *Appellplatz* with nearly ten thousand prisoners for almost ninety grueling minutes while they were all counted. A mixture of drizzle and ice pellets had been falling the entire time, thoroughly soaking her striped, cotton pajamas. Most inmates were trembling, trying as best they could to fight off hypothermia, though no one dared to move, not even to fold their arms across their chests, lest they incur a beating. When an accurate count had finally been accomplished, the prisoners were preparing to break into their usual work groups when, instead, a wooden contraption was carried by two kapos to the front. There was murmuring in the ranks about punishments. Annika froze with fear. *Has Gapinsky turned me in?*

She watched as a prisoner was escorted to the front by two kapos. His crime – being caught with food on his person – was read aloud, and he was to pay for it with twenty-five strokes. *A starving man with a small amount of food in his shirt. What would they do to me if they found out what I've been doing to save people?* The man's shirt was removed, his emaciated rib cage in full display. His pants were pulled down to his knees, as he was strapped to the block. Doctor Mennecke made a brief, cursory examination of the prisoner, and then turned to Kommandant Loritz, declaring the man fit for punishment. Loritz issued the order, together with instructions that the victim was to count each blow, loud enough to be heard. At that point, a kapo administered the first thundering stroke with an ox-whip. It was loud enough to be heard by the entire hushed crowd.

"One," moaned the prisoner.

"I can't hear you, swine. Louder!" Another blow brought an ugly red welt across the man's back.

"Two," he screamed.

The flogging continued thusly throughout fifteen more strokes, each eliciting a weaker response from the prisoner. His backside had become a mass of hemorrhaging flesh. After another crack from the whip, there was silence. Mennecke walked over to check on the man and found him still alert. The doctor nodded, meaning the flogging could proceed.

"What number are we on?" bellowed the kapo, playing to the cortege of SS officers.

There was a pause, followed by a feeble, ". . . Seventeen."

"Don't lose count, or we start all over . . . from the beginning." Another loud snap.

". . . Eighteen . . ." His voice trailed off.

"Louder!" the guard screamed, delivering yet another.

Once again, there was silence. The victim had lost consciousness. Instead of discontinuing the torture, the kapo poured a bucketful iodine on the man's back, instantly rousing the condemned man. His legs, despite being tightly bound to the rack, moved a few inches up and down like a bicyclist as he tried to squeeze away some of the biting pain. The scene continued for another five minutes until the prisoner had completed his punishment.

Annika had sweated through the entire scene, wondering if she was the next to be dragged up. Instead, the call went out to reform into work groups.

An Unlikely Reunion

In general, there is always something exhilarating in another man's misfortune . . .

Fyodor Dostoyevsky

15 May, 1942

It was early evening, probably around six o'clock, when Annika thought she saw him.

She was among a small group returning to the barracks from the infirmary, where she had spent the past twelve hours. Her neck and back ached, and she hadn't had more than a few hours of uninterrupted sleep for as long as she could remember. Exhausted and famished, she was looking forward to the night rations, however meager and fetid it would undoubtedly be. Her group marched past rows of barracks, as they did every evening, and in one of the yards they approached was an SS officer barking out commands to a group of approximately twenty-five men.

It was the officer's voice that first caught her attention. Loud and high-pitched, it sounded almost like a bobcat in distress. *Where have I heard that voice before,* Annika wondered. She strained to look, but her group was moving fast, and she needed to maintain cadence to avoid attracting notice from her *aufseherin.* With the sun having already set, dusk was settling in, and the fading light made it difficult for her to distinguish facial features. She turned to take one last look. From seemingly out of nowhere came an excruciating blow to her shoulder. The pain was so intense that she lost her balance and fell to the ground.

"What do you think you're doing, bitch?" screamed the guard.

217

"You forget the rules?" She kicked Annika in the stomach, causing her to double-up into a fetal position. The woman struck her again with the truncheon. "Get up," she demanded. Awkwardly, Annika rose to her feet, at which point the woman pushed her forward. "Get moving, and this time keep your eyes straight ahead."

Two days later, that same *aufseherin* was nowhere to be seen. Most thought that she would resurface in a day or two, but It turned out that her disappearance was more than just temporary. Rumor had it that she had been sent on a transport to a new camp they were hearing about – Treblinka.

In that same week, as Annika was returning from latrine duty with two other women, she heard the voice again. She couldn't tell where it was coming from, as the pathway was crowded with *häftlinge* going about their tasks. But then she heard it again, this time more distinctly. "You women there. Halt!"

The three of them stopped. Swaggering towards them from an alleyway between two of the men's barracks came an SS officer. Annika's heart was in her throat. Inmates dreaded such encounters. If an SS officer deigned to speak to you, it usually had a bad outcome. Just last week one of them had stopped a man arbitrarily, whereupon he tore two buttons from the prisoner's shirt, threw them in the dirt, then berated him for being "out of uniform." The man was given fifteen minutes to report to his office with the buttons neatly sewn back. Somehow the prisoner showed up, buttons intact, at which point the enraged officer clubbed him and warned him against any similar infraction. And then there was the SS guard who ripped off a man's cap, tossed it into the high-voltage wires, and instructed the prisoner to retrieve it. One never knew what cruel trick an officer might pull.

"You two . . ." the officer said to the other women. "Get on with your duties!" He waved them off with his riding crop. Annika looked down, according to the rules. All she saw were his feet.

"Annika Tritzchler, so it really *is* you," he said. This was the voice she had heard just before the beating. Cautiously, she looked up, but only high enough to see his shoulder boards. He was an

Unterscharführer, a non-commissioned officer, someone who could make her life quite miserable if he so chose.

"Annika. It's me, Rolf." She looked up, almost disbelieving. "I saw you a few weeks back. And then, that, uh, beating you got from the *aufseherin* . . . I saw it. I thought it looked like you, but, well, I figured it couldn't be. 'What would Annika Tritzchler be doing at Sachsenhausen,' I asked myself."

Annika was speechless. Here was someone she had played with in childhood, but now someone who had the power of life and death over her. She had absolutely no idea how to greet him.

"Yesterday, I was reading the assignment lists and saw your name. I was dumbfounded. I thought it must be someone who simply has the same name, or maybe someone who stole your identity. I made it a point to locate you."

Annika was frightened, still not knowing whether it was safe to look him in the eye. He persisted. "You can relax, Annika. I'm not going to hurt you." She looked up at him. "So, what happened? What landed you in this place?"

Before she could answer, the siren blasted, signaling all prisoners to line up for roll-call. Annika responded like a trained dog. "I . . . I have to go."

Rolf understood. He looked at her, his eyes searching, as if for something lost, something perhaps he wanted to recapture. Then, waving his hand, he said simply, "Go."

Two weeks elapsed during which she neither saw nor heard from Rolf. Then, on May twentieth, as roll-call was just concluding, a gruff voice rang out. "Tritzchler." Before Annika could respond, the woman shouted a second time, "Tritzchler!"

Annika snapped to attention. *"Ja, Blockführerin."*

"Fall out!" she demanded. Annika muscled her way down the row of women and stood in front of the block leader.

"Follow me," came the command.

Annika followed dutifully. The pace was brisk, no words exchanged. They entered the administration complex and proceeded to an office complex where a sign announced, *Office of the Camp Commandant. Oberführer Hans Loritz.* When cued, she was escorted into his enclave. Seated to the right of his desk was another man, well-dressed in civilian attire. The man was clad in a three-piece, pin-striped double-breasted suit. A gold watch chain dangled conspicuously from his vest.

Annika was left to stand alone in front of Loritz, who took a drag from his cigarette while staring at her. He exhaled, then tapped his cigarette against the ashtray before speaking. "You've been at Sachsenhausen for six months now. You are being considered for release. I am not certain that you have learned your lesson. Let me ask you. Do you think you're ready for release?"

"*Ja, Herr Kommandant,*" she replied, trying not to appear too enthusiastic.

"And just what might you see yourself doing on the outside?" he asked.

"I would hope to continue in my profession, Herr *Oberführer.*"

"Your position at Bernburg is no longer available. Because of your arrest and confinement, no hospitals will hire you. I have discussed the matter with the *Reichsministerium,* and it has been decided that you will be assigned to the Jewish Hospital of Berlin, where at present there is a need for staff."

"But, Herr Commandant, with all due respect, my understanding is that Jewish doctors have been stripped of their licenses to practice. Is the Jewish Hospital even still functioning?"

"Yes. For reasons that are none of your concern, the hospital is fully occupied. Suffice it to say that the Jewish ghettos are breeding grounds for disease. One of the functions of the hospital is to provide treatment to Jewish vermin in an effort to prevent epidemics of typhus or tuberculosis that could otherwise spread throughout Berlin. Your work will be scrutinized by the *Reichssicherheitshauptamt.*" He looked at Annika. "*Verstanden?*"

"*Ja, Herr Kommandant. Ich verstehe.*"

Loritz began writing. After some hastily scrawled notes, he said,

"You are to report to the hospital's medical director, Doctor Walter Lustig, on Monday morning. He will be expecting you." He pulled a document from the corner of his desk, stamped it in two places, then handed it to Annika. "Give this to Lustig." Annika took it and nodded. Loritz rose from his chair, and in an imperious tone, said, "I trust we will not be seeing you again, Tritzchler. You're being given a second chance to work for your Führer. Don't take this opportunity lightly. If it were my choice, I'd keep you here where you belong."

Annika, already standing herself, said, *"Dankeschön, Herr Kommandant."* Her heart was beating a mile a minute.

He nodded at the guard. "Dismissed."

Violation

No one is more arrogant toward women, more aggressive or scornful, than the man who is anxious about his virility.
Simone de Beauvoir

<u>Berlin: 28 September, 1942</u>

Annika's work at the Jewish Hospital was exacting a toll. It hadn't taken long for her to figure out why a Jewish Hospital continued to operate, especially in Berlin. The answer proved none too complex. Most of the Aryan doctors had been sent to the front, creating a serious shortage in German cities. By necessity, the laws were amended to allow a small number of Jewish physicians to continue practicing, though initially only on Jewish patients. But there was another side to the story. To the dwindling numbers of Jews in Berlin, the Jewish Hospital had been made to look like a place of refuge, a safe haven where Jews took care of Jews. The truth was much different. Attached to the hospital was a *sammellager,* one of many temporary holding camps where Jews were collected and confined before being "resettled." No one knew where they were deported, but when they were never heard from again, rumors began to abound about death camps. Patients, and even Jewish staff, were being routinely selected for the *sammellager* by the SS, who paraded through the hospital at will.

Much like her experience at Bernburg, Annika again found herself in a quandary. Aside from the long shifts was the ethical conflict of feeling that she was an unwitting participant in treachery. She had to wonder if working at the hospital, knowing its ulterior function, made her guilty of collaborating with the Nazis. One thing

222

was clear: she didn't have the luxury of resigning. Sachsenhausen had clearly taught her the consequences of resistance. Instead, she settled on a two-pronged goal: treat her patients to the best of her ability as a physician, and to do whatever she could to shield people from selection, which usually meant diagnosing illness in patients who were actually quite healthy. The risks, of course, were enormous. At times, she chided herself for not having fled the country, like her parents. But it was too late for that. No one was getting out now, only soldiers.

On a cool evening in late September, somewhere near midnight, Annika returned home from a fourteen-hour shift famished and thoroughly exhausted. She hadn't had a day off in more than two weeks, and today, eating on the run, her only breaks came when she needed to use the bathroom. Now, late though it was, she couldn't wait to put something in her stomach and get at least a few hours of sleep before starting the grind all over again. Her ice-box was mostly bare, but she devoured some liverwurst and cheese hurriedly folded into a roll so hard and crusty that she almost broke a tooth biting into it. Crumbs spewed from it like snowflakes. Not waiting to finish, she changed out of her soiled white uniform, still chewing, and into a thin nightgown, her standard sleeping attire.

And then, inexplicably, came a knocking at the door. She froze. "Who on earth . . .?" she said to herself. Another knock. *Is that even my door?* She tiptoed closer, listening intently. Then came a more insistent rapping. No mistaking it; it was her door.

She pressed her ear close to the door. "Who is it?" she asked.

"Gestapo. Open up."

Gestapo? She was alarmed. *Why would the Gestapo be here?* Everyone knew that the Gestapo usually made arrests at night, but *why me?* She was nearly apoplectic with fear. She ran to the closet for a gown or housecoat, anything to cover up.

"Just a minute . . . just a minute," she gasped, throwing on a bathrobe. She fumbled with the drawstrings before opening the door a crack. Standing before her were not two or three Gestapo agents, but rather one lone figure. He was darkly silhouetted from the distant lightbulb at the top of the stairwell, but it was clear from his outline that this was no plainclothes agent. He was in uniform.

Emerging from the shadows, the man said, "Annika! Good evening." He pushed forward, compelling her to step back. The door swung wide open.

"Rolf! I'm shocked. What are *you* doing here?" A wave of terror shot through her on seeing the 'death's head' on his hat. For a moment, she was back in the camp.

Rolf noticed her glance. Removing his hat, he said, "Well, I had some business downtown. I was already in the area, so I thought I might stop by. Figured it'd be nice to catch up with you." From the stairwell, they heard a door close. Rolf turned. "Snoopy neighbors, eh?" he said, looking back at Annika. Smiling, he turned back to close the door, and when he did, Annika heard the metallic click of lock against doorframe.

"Rolf, what's going on? You don't need to lock my door."

He looked at her with feigned incredulity. "*Ach. Tut mir leid.* You had the door locked when I arrived, so I just re-latched it." He smiled at her. "Definitely not a bad idea, though . . . you know . . . with all the vermin on the streets, especially at night."

"Well, y-you scared me. You said you were Gestapo. I didn't know what to think . . ."

Rolf responded smugly. "Oh, my apologies, Anni. Just kidding around . . . like old times." Rolf looked around, dusting off his cap with his fingertips, then directly at Annika. "It's wonderful to see you. Especially in . . . well, different circumstances." He dropped his cap on a side table.

"How did you know where I live?" she asked.

"Not really much of a mystery. You didn't think you were anonymous, did you?" There was no question. He was slurring his words.

"I never really thought of it. It's just that—"

Rolf cut her off. "Don't forget. I'm an officer in the *Schutzstaffel*.

224

Your whereabouts are actually quite well-known, and not simply to me . . ." He let his voice trail off and smiled.

"Rolf, you're gonna have to leave. I've got to be up at the squawk of dawn for work."

"Don't be so hasty, Annika. Let's talk for a bit. You have any schnapps," he asked, walking toward the kitchen cabinet.

"No, I don't. C'mon, Rolf. You've got to go." Annika reached out to grab his arm, trying to redirect him back to the door.

He gently jerked his elbow from her grasp, and began opening cabinets in the kitchen.

"Please, Rolf. I'm asking you, please," she implored. She suddenly had a *déjà vu* of their encounter years before in the park and remembered how demanding and self-indulgent he was.

Rolf pulled a bottle down from a shelf above stove. "Well, well. Jägermeister." He fondled the bottle adoringly, then looked to Annika. "No schnapps, eh?"

"Rolf, c'mon. I forgot about that. It was a Christmas gift. Please put it back."

"Christmas cheer, eh? Jägermeister is meant to be shared with company." He began to open it. "Göring-Schnaps! That's what my men began calling this after Hermann Göring was appointed *Reichsjägermeister*. Good ol' Göring-Schnaps. *"*

Rummaging through the cabinet, he retrieved two tulip glasses and began filling them. He handed one to Annika, but stumbled, sloshing some of the brandy onto her robe. "Oh sorry, sorry," he said with affected contrition. He dabbed at her breast where the alcohol had spilled, then looked up, grinning.

Taking a step backwards, she pushed his hand away and took the glass to keep him from spilling any more. "Rolf, no. I don't want any. I don't have time. Please, let's meet some other day. Maybe for lunch. I have to be at work early in the morning. I need to sleep."

Rolf stubbed out his cigarette and rose to his feet. "No problem, Annika. Let's call it a night." He handed the empty glass to Annika. As she reached for it, he grabbed her wrist with his free hand and pulled her close. She dropped the glass, which shattered when it hit the floor. "How 'bout a goodnight kiss, hmmm? For old times' sake . . .?"

Annika panicked, instinctively muscling her hands up to her chest. She was encircled by both his arms, and the more she pushed against him, the tighter he gripped. The next thing she felt was a hand on her bottom.

"Rolf, no! Stop it." She tried to squirm out of his embrace.

"What, Annika? You said you need some sleep. I do too. Let's go to bed."

Still pushing against him, she pleaded, "No, damn you. Stop! If you cared anything about me, you'd leave right now, like I've asked. Please!"

Rolf was not taking "no" for an answer. Simply hearing her tell him what to do, as if she had the right to control his actions, made him angry. He had fantasized about Annika for years, and here was an opportunity he could only dream of. He yanked her off-balance and carried her, kicking and protesting, the few steps into her bedroom. Her cries did nothing but pique his drive. Dropping her on the bed, he fell on top, forcing his mouth onto hers. She bit his lip and shook her head violently from side to side, and then, feeling his hand on her breast, she began to scream. Rolf slapped the side of her head with one hand while pulling her hair backwards with the other. "*Keep your mouth shut*," he demanded, placing his hand over her mouth. Blood trickled from his lip. He jerked her robe open and tore at her negligee to partially expose her breasts.

As he reached down to unbutton his trousers, Annika rolled to the side, wriggled a hand free, and slapped him across the face, which freed her from his grasp. She leapt to her feet, veins popping from her neck, and screamed, "Leave me alone, Rolf! Get the hell out of here!"

Rolf lunged forward, striking her face with the palm of his hand, causing her to fall backwards into the wall. Her head struck with enough force to dislodge a framed picture of her parents. It hit the floor in an explosion of glass shards. Blood now ran from Annika's nostrils. Overcome by desire, Rolf shook her so hard that her head bobbed like a rag doll, taking much of the fight out of her. He pushed her back down on the bed, tugged at his belt, and once again dropped onto her. With one hand, he tore away the negligee, while planting the other securely over her face. Blood squirted through his fingers. All she could do was grunt and squirm, gasping for breath as he forced his way inside her. She was no longer able to resist, and as he indulged his lust, the headboard banged against the wall like a bass drum.

It ended almost as quickly as it began. He lay on top of her, spent and unmoving, crushing Annika under his weight. She pushed and squirmed, but to little avail. He had passed out. Suddenly, in the most unlikely reprieve, the door burst open and in rushed two city policemen, guns drawn. "What's going on here?"

Rolf didn't move, prompting one of the men to yank at his shoulder, rolling him off Annika. She arched her body away from Rolf and stood trembling before the officers, hugging her breasts, unaware of her own nakedness. Tears mixed with blood streaming from her nose, and everywhere about the small apartment were signs of a violent struggle.

"Are you OK, Fräulein?" one of the officer's asked. The other had his pistol trained on Rolf. Though she tried to speak, no words would come – only wracking sobs.

By now, Rolf had regained consciousness. Naked from the waist down, he muttered, "Calm down, men. Put your guns away. Nothing's going on here."

They weren't to be put off. "Do you need a doctor?" the officer asked Annika.

Rolf looked at her, then said to the agents, "She's fine. Let us alone. I'm with the SS."

Both policemen leveled their pistols at Rolf. "Get away from her," one said. "You're coming with us."

Rolf stumbled to his feet, obviously intoxicated. "You're not telling me where I'm going or what I'm doing. I'm *Unterscharführer*

Geiszler with the SS at Sachsenhausen. Get out of here this instant unless you want to find yourselves under my command in Oranienburg." Rolf may have been accustomed to giving orders, but his aura of authority was compromised as he fumbled with his pants. Hopping on one leg in a desperate attempt to pull them up, he stumbled and fell on the floor before finally getting a leg through. He stood up, glaring at the officers.

"Sir, you need to put your hands behind you!" demanded the one of them, all the while trying to maintain some respect for a man of the *Schutzstaffel.* The other policeman came around behind him with handcuffs, as if this was to be a routine arrest. Before he knew what hit him, Rolf had spun around with his fist, striking the man on the side of the head. He fell backwards, but the move bought him only a second or two as the other policeman – a large, burly man whose face was scarred from previous confrontations – lunged towards Rolf. In a flash, he knocked him down with the butt end of his luger. The other man took full advantage and twisted Rolf's right arm into a painful chicken-wing, while securing handcuffs to both wrists. They both pulled him to his feet by the cuffs. Rolf glared at the officer as a trickle of blood seeped down the side of his head.

"Do you need medical assistance, Fräulein," the officer asked, while maneuvering Rolf to the doorway. Annika simply looked at him with wide eyes, still unable to talk. Her lips were quivering. "?" the man asked again. This time, she shook her head. The men turned, one of them picking up Rolf's hat and coat, and left.

Denounced a Mischling

Once you label me, you negate me.
Søren Kierkegaard

Berlin: 29 September, 1942

Annika had already informed the hospital that she would not be coming in to work today. She was badly beaten up and needed the day to recuperate. The apartment looked like a cyclone had passed through. Furniture lay scattered about, while broken glass sparkled in the sunlight. An uncorked bottle of liqueur lay sideways on the floor with its contents soaking into the carpet; it felt sticky and spongy underfoot. Her body was a topographical map of swollen blood vessels radiating outwards in a spiderweb to blue, pulsating veins. She ached all over. Her nose was visibly off-center, probably broken, and she sported an ugly mouse under her left eye. She could feel a large lump on the back of her head, which throbbed with each beat of her heart, and standing in front of the mirror, she could plainly see the imprints of Rolf's fingers on her neck. As painful as those injuries were, none compared to the burning in her pelvis where blood trickled from her vagina, torn and bruised.

Annika's greatest injury, though, was less visible. It was the violation to her being – a defilement robbing her not simply of dignity and self-worth, but of naïve concepts regarding morality, dreams, and purpose. Predictability was an illusion, trust a mirage. The actions of the previous night assaulted her soul with a vigor that not even a lifetime could heal.

Over and over again, her mind replayed the incident. She began washing herself the moment Rolf was taken away, yet no amount of scrubbing could purge her of the filth she felt inside. In her gut circulated the seed of the SS, polluting her with an impermeable stain. She felt numb in a world which had become surreal. *What did I do to cause this?* The question echoed through her mind like a broken record. Reason told her that she had done nothing wrong, that she had been a victim, yet reason alone couldn't assuage her guilt.

She thought of Pasha, his smiling face, his gentle touch. She recalled quiet whispers as his lips brushed her ear. Her mind went back to their time in Geneva, how tender and caring he had been; the only man she had ever made love to; the only man, in fact, she had ever allowed to touch her. For years, she had secretly fantasized about his eventual return, and that gave celibacy profound meaning. He had been her soulmate, and she had never given that up. But thinking about him now, under these circumstances, brought an overpowering sense of shame. *How would I ever explain this to him? Would he ever want to kiss me again knowing that another man had been inside me? But could I even make love to a man again, any man?* She began to sob. Everything had been taken from her, her world turned upside down.

She moved slowly about the flat. The cup of ersatz coffee that usually began her day was too much of an effort. She felt weak, drained, and unmotivated. Just when it seemed that life could not get any more tenuous, the telephone rang. She hesitated, not wanting to talk to anyone, but the caller persisted. Her head throbbed with each ring making it impossible to ignore.

"Hello?" Her voice was weak and tentative. The receiver crackled. "*Nein. Ich bin krank,*" she said, trying to convince the caller she was ill. More crackling. Annika rubbed her forehead. "*Ja . . . Sehr gut . . .*" she muttered through clenched teeth. "*Natürlich. Ich werde mittags dort sein.*" It was *Kripo*. They needed to talk to her about last night. She agreed to report to their headquarters by noon.

Annika was ushered into the office of *SS-Obersturmbannführer* Werner Schneider. She walked stiffly, but respectfully. "Please, sit down," Schneider offered. "Thank you for reporting. I have a few

230

questions about the episode you were involved in last night. Our chief, *Gruppenführer* Nebe, has taken a bit of an interest in this situation." Somewhat nervously, Annika shifted her posture. "Judging by your face, Fräulein, it is obvious you have been through quite an ordeal." Annika looked at him without responding. "I have a report here," he continued, "outlining the events, which includes the arrest of an SS officer, *Unterscharführer* . . . let me see . . . ah, here it is, Geiszler, yes?"

"Yes, sir," Annika responded, somewhat timidly. She was unsure how to answer, knowing that being entangled with someone from the SS could have troublesome implications.

"Might I ask, are you having an affair with him?"

"No, sir. Not at all," she replied.

"So, tell me, why was he in your apartment last night?"

"Sir, he came over totally unannounced. I had only been home from work for maybe twenty minutes or so when I heard him knocking on the door. It was after midnight. I was already in my nightclothes."

"Is it correct that you and he knew each other in childhood?"

"Yes. Our mothers were friends. Herr Geiszler and I went our own separate ways when I entered the *gymnasium.*"

"But you saw each other more recently . . . at Sachsenhausen, correct?"

"Yes, sir."

"And did you approach him there?"

"No, Inspector. He approached me." Annika explained the circumstances of their reacquainting themselves at the KZ.

"Now he tells us that you are Jewish, yes?"

Annika was stunned. "What?" she exclaimed. "No sir. That's not true. My mother and father were Gentiles."

"But my dear," the Inspector continued, "he told us that your father . . . hmmm . . . Otto Baumann . . . was Jewish."

Annika could not believe this treachery. Rolf had lied to save himself. "Sir, my biological father was Hermann Tritzchler, a respected Gentile physician. He died when I was quite young of a brain tumor. Years later, my mother remarried another doctor, Otto Baumann. I am not related to him by blood."

"Ah, but Geiszler reports that you had told him of your mother's lengthy affair with Doctor Baumann, and that you were a product of that relationship." He pushed back in his chair to study Annika's reaction.

"Inspector, that is patently false!" Even through all the bruising, her face was turning beet red. "My mother was madly in love with my natural father and was devastated by his death. Doctor Baumann was a wonderful stepfather, but he came along later. He was definitely not my biological father."

"Yes, well, I must say, and please don't take this with any offense, but since Germany adopted the Nuremburg laws, I hear denials like yours pretty much every day. Not to say I disbelieve you. You sound quite sure of yourself, but let me ask . . . regarding our records from your registration at Sachsenhausen . . . could you please tell me why you never mentioned to the registrar the name of your, ah, 'stepfather'?" As he said the last word, he gesticulated with two fingers from each hand to symbolize quotation marks. "Your only statement was that your father had died and your mother was in Belgium."

"Herr Inspector, I don't recall that particular circumstance, but I would guess that, at the time, the registrar seemed only interested in the name of my biological parents. I know that race is important, so I would have furnished that information. I certainly would not lie, nor would I want to risk any confusion as to my racial identity." Annika hated to say this, but she knew that Rolf's accusation put her in a very serious situation.

"So, your answer was not to disguise your Jewishness, Fräulein?"

"Sir, I am not Jewish. There was no need for me to disguise anything."

"Well, you know, Fräulein, many people are often unaware of

their Jewish roots. But, anyway, thank you for coming in. We will need to refer this matter to the Office of Racial Policy. Geiszler has accused you of being a half-Jew, which, of course, will need to be investigated. I trust that what you are telling me is true. If not," he said, shaking his head, "well, that would be a rather serious matter, right?"

"Sir?" she asked, suddenly aware that things were sounding more ominous than earlier.

"Well," he explained, "if you are Jewish, that would mean that intimate relations between you and Geiszler violated the policy on *Rassenschande*. Race defilement, as I'm sure you know, is a very serious criminal offense."

"But sir, he is the one who . . .".

Schneider did not let her finish. "You may go, Fräulein. We'll be in touch." He buzzed the secretary and she was led out.

The following week, Annika received a call from Gestapo Headquarters. She was to report to the office of the *Kriminaldirektor* on Thursday, 15 October at 1100 hours. She arrived at 1045, announcing herself to the guard at the entrance, who pawed through several pages searching for her name. "Department B," he grunted, pointing to the stairway with a jerk of his thumb. "Office 4."

Department B was not on the same wing that she had been in before. *Maybe that's a good sign,* she told herself, trying to extinguish her anxiety. It didn't seem to help. Getting a full breath had become so difficult that she paused at the side of the corridor as uniformed officers passed in each direction, many escorting handcuffed prisoners. Halfway down the corridor, she came to *Office B4. Sturmbannführer Reusch.* She rifled through her pocketbook for the letter, presented it to the male receptionist, and took a seat alongside several other men and women. All were neatly attired, trying their best, it seemed, to look like upstanding German citizens. One man even sported a swastika pin on his collar. *Everyone looks as nervous as I feel. Head up . . . smile . . . be strong,* she told herself. *Nothing to be afraid of.* Deep down, she was scared to death.

Eventually the director's door opened and a couple, well up in their years, emerged. As neatly dressed as the two were, their faces told a different story. The woman was sniffling and dabbed at her eyes with a handkerchief. The man clutched her free hand, trying to comfort her while struggling to keep his own emotions in check. The small assemblage waiting their turn, including Annika, watched in stunned silence.

"Tritzchler!" barked the receptionist. Annika rose to her feet, forced a perfunctory smile and walked forward, whereupon she was led into the Inspector's office. It was a hot day and therefore not surprising that the man behind the desk, instead of wearing a suit jacket, was attired in a wrinkled white shirt with sleeves rolled above his elbows. His black tie hung several inches below his unbuttoned collar. The window behind his desk was open and a fan blowing from the corner, but neither did much to offset a sultry atmosphere tainted with an acrid combination of body odor and stale cigarette smoke. The investigator remained seated, offering no salutation nor even a gesture for her to be seated. His greasy dark hair, parted in the middle, reflected light from the window, and his ruddy face glistened with perspiration, almost as if massaged in Vaseline. If it wasn't for the distinctive graying of his Nazi style mustache, he bore a strong resemblance to the Führer, whose glowering countenance looked down on them from a framed portrait, just as it did in Eberl's office on that last fateful day at Bernburg.

Annika stood in silence while Reusch took his time reviewing her file. Still looking down, he said slowly, "We are aware of your recent encounter with *Unterscharfsführer* Geiszler." He then paused to glance up at her. "Judging from your face, Fräulein, I'd say you came out on the losing end." Annika's weight shifted from one foot to the other. "Says here you both engaged in a consensual relationship . . . one that perhaps went a bit too far. Maybe you like it rough, no?"

"Herr Director," Annika protested, "that's . . ."

"Silence!" he said, putting his hand up to stop her. "In my office, you will show me the courtesy of allowing me to finish. When I am ready for your response, I will ask for it, not before. Do we understand ourselves?"

Annika suppressed her anger in an apology. *"Ja, tut mir leid, Herr Direktor."*

"You were arrested in Bernburg in October of last year for sharing highly classified information. Following that, you were sentenced to Sachsenhausen for a period of six months and released in May, after it was assumed you had been rehabilitated. However, the report says that subsequent to your release, information was passed on that during your confinement you had been observed having private conversations with *Unterscharfsführer* Geiszler. As you had been instructed, such conversations were strictly forbidden. What was the nature of your discussions?"

"Sir, I did not know at the time of my incarceration that Herr Geiszler was stationed at Sachsenhausen. He somehow became aware of *my* presence and approached me. Our mothers were friendly during our childhoods, but we had not seen one another since the eighth grade, when I went to the *gymnasium*. I believe the *Unterscharfsführer* sought me out at Sachsenhausen simply to satisfy his curiosity."

"And following your release from the KZ you pursued a relationship with him?"

"Absolutely not, Herr Inspector! I never had any interest in Herr Geiszler. He came to my flat totally unexpectedly. It was after midnight, and I had to be at work early the next morning. I tried everything I could think of to get him to leave, but he was intoxicated . . . and refused. It was when I became more insistent that he assaulted me. My screams got the attention of the neighbors, and that's when the police came."

The examiner looked down, thumbing through a few documents. "As you know, Geiszler has filed a report denouncing you as Jewish."

"Herr Director, that is blatantly untrue. My parents . . . ."

"Your case" he said, in a voice that overpowered her own, "was

referred to the Office of Racial Policy in Berlin. Their report concludes that Geiszler's allegations are credible . . . that you were born out-of-wedlock to Eva Tritzchler and Otto Baumann. Despite retaining the surname 'Tritzchler,' you were raised by Doctor Baumann, a known Jew. He and your mother have wisely emigrated, and apparently their whereabouts are unknown. As a result, we have nothing that would substantiate your claims to be a full-blooded German. Unless, of course, you know your parents' whereabouts and can summon them to Berlin to vouch for you."

"Sir, I truly have no information as to their location. It's been several years since I've heard from them . . ."

"I'm sure," he interjected, sarcastically. "But just so you know, we *have* been in touch with the Reich Kinship Office, and they too lack birth or even baptismal certificates that would clarify your racial status. There is general acceptance that your birth mother was German. If it is determined that Otto Baumann is your biological father, then you are racially mixed and, for all intents and purposes, a *Mischling* of the first degree."

"But . . . but Herr Director. I have been a practicing Lutheran my entire life. I am not Jewish. You can even check with Professor Bonhoeffer at the uni . . ." Annika stopped suddenly, recognizing, too late, her slip of the tongue.

The Director smiled. "Bonhoeffer? Yes, indeed, I'm sure he would be a big help. For *all* of us." Annika felt trapped. "Once we catch up with him, he'll rot in prison – that is, if he's not hung first." He wrote something in the file, allowing a moment or two for that statement to sink in. "Either way, Fräulein, it appears that you're facing some very big problems."

"Sir, may I speak freely?"

"You already have. And just so you know, Jews who convert to Christianity don't change their racial status. From this date on, you are henceforth subject to all the rules and edicts pertaining to Jews." He looked at her sternly, like a schoolteacher about to admonish an unruly student. "Your identity card . . . give it to me."

"What?" Annika was bewildered.

"*Ihren Ausweis. Sofort!*" he demanded, holding out his hand.

She rummaged through her wallet and passed it to him, all the while fighting back tears. Glancing at it, the Inspector pulled a red stamp-pad from his drawer, tapped it a few times, and embossed Annika's card with a large red "*J*," now identifying her as Jewish.

The director continued. "You have the right to appeal to the Office of Racial Research for a change in status. Through legal representation, some people pronounced as *Mischlinge* have actually received the *Deutschblütigkeitserklärung*. It's the official German Blood Certificate, which certifies pure German ancestry. I would caution, however, that to qualify as *Deutschblütig*, the Office usually requires baptismal records dating as far back as 1750." He smiled. "I rather suspect this is unlikely in your situation."

Annika had always been proud of her stepfather, so to deny being Jewish felt in some ways like an extraordinary betrayal, even though technically it was correct. She also thought of Pasha and his family's persecution. Nevertheless, her experiences at Sachsenhausen told her this was no time to advocate for Jewish rights. "Is that the only option?" she asked, knowing that finding records going back that far would be nearly impossible.

He smirked. "Well, you could try the physiognomy route."

"I beg your pardon?"

"Skull measurements, distance between hairline and forehead, eye color, nose characteristics, that type of thing. I would think you'd know that from all the schooling we gave you." As he spoke, Reusch was staring at Annika's nose. "On the other hand, Tritzchler, I think with that 'schnoz' of yours, you might want to pass on physiognomy . . . *right*?" He snorted for emphasis.

She felt unexpectedly self-conscious. He then declared, "From here on out, you'll need to acquaint yourself – and I mean 'chapter and verse' – with the Nuremburg Laws, and follow them explicitly. Any deviations carry severe penalties, as I'm sure you know. If your classification as a *Mischling* stands, it means that whatever whoring around you did with Geiszler is a clear-cut case of *Rassenschande*."

Annika choked back tears.

"For now, Tritzchler, you're free to go. We'll let you know where things stand once our investigation has been concluded."

Annika felt light-headed. All she could do was stare. Her body ached all over.

"Oh, and one more thing. Until this all gets sorted out, you're no longer to use the title, 'Doctor.' You may still work at the hospital, but can only treat Jews, no Aryans. *Verstanden?*" She nodded, blankly. "*Sehr gut.* You may go."

Stunned, Annika turned and slowly walked to the door. The guard jerked it open in crisp, military fashion, and it was now Annika who ambled mechanically through the waiting room. All eyes followed her, searching her face for a hint as to their own fate.

<u>8 November, 1942</u>

Seated at her kitchen table, Annika dropped the folded newspaper on the floor. It was exasperating to read of glorious German victories in the push against Russia, while rumors abounded that the advance was actually going poorly and at great cost. She fingered her coffee cup, no longer hot, and began to mentally prepare for the day to come. A little more than a month had elapsed since her meeting with Inspector Schneider, yet still no word. She knew better than to think it had all been forgotten. Her face wrinkled as she slurped the last cool dregs of the turbid brew. Ersatz coffee tasted more like battery acid than the eye-openers everyone had enjoyed before the war.

Still blurry-eyed from broken sleep, she became aware of something out in the stairwell- footsteps coming up the stairs. She rarely had visitors, excepting the landlady, but it was much too early for her. Besides, the footsteps sounded heavy. Whoever was climbing the steps was big. She suddenly felt very awake, listening intently as the clomping came ever closer. Her mind was awash with threatening possibilities. Ever since the rape, she had determined to never again let herself be vulnerable; so, instinctively, she tiptoed to the drawer holding her utensils. Quietly opening it, she stared at the carving knife tucked between an assortment of serving implements. The polished steel winked at her under the glare from the lightbulb dangling overhead. Blade in hand, all she could do now was be still and listen, maybe offer up a quick prayer to calm her heart which was thumping against her chest. The footsteps had reached the corridor leading to her door, and they sounded ominously similar to Rolf's.

The person was now just outside her door. She could hear him fumbling with something. A skeleton key, a screwdriver . . .? Squeezing the knife, Annika reminded herself that she was resilient, that she had the wherewithal to defend herself. She flattened herself against the wall, ready.

Just then, the brass lid at the bottom of her door clanged and was followed by the faint sound of mail dropping to the floor. It couldn't be a postman. Since the outbreak of hostilities, mail was delivered to the post office two blocks away. Whoever it was, the man had begun descending the staircase. Annika's curiosity got the best of her; she cracked the door to peek out. The man heard her door squeak open and looked back just in time for their eyes to meet. He was an older man, bearded and neatly dressed. Somehow, he looked somehow familiar. As he rounded the landing, Annika noticed the *Judenstern,* the Star of David, sewn to the front of his topcoat, and then she remembered. He was the rabbi whom she had seen scrubbing the sidewalk amidst a jeering crowd. She wanted to call to him, ask what he wanted with her, but the man disappeared, his footsteps growing fainter by the second.

Quietly, she closed the door, and stood for a minute, her face against the wood panel. Very lightly, she banged her forehead several times against the wood. Her chest ached; her knees wobbled. Taking a deep breath, she ambled back to the kitchen and returned the knife to the drawer. For a second or two, she had forgotten all about the man's delivery. Looking back to the door, she saw the envelope laying beneath the mail-slot. Nervously, she walked over and bent down to retrieve it. The return address was more alarming than the footsteps in the stairwell.

Reichvereinigung der Juden
Kurfürstenstraße #115–116
Berlin

She gasped. *The "Reich Organization of Jews."* She held the envelope at arm's length as if it was a time-bomb ready to explode. It looked up at her, taunting, daring her to open it. Annika's muscles tightened, her breathing quickened, and her heartbeat could have doubled for a Gene Krupa drum solo.

There was no ignoring it. She had to open it. Her hands trembled as she ran a fingernail along the flap. The letter inside slipped through her fingers and fluttered teasingly back to the floor. Annika eyed it with foreboding, but stooped to retrieve it. Giving it a quick shake to straighten out the folds, she stared, stupefied. The header read "Berlin Jewish Organization," and although it read like a form letter – one mimeographed to hundreds, maybe thousands of Jews in and around the city – it was a formal announcement that she was to be "resettled" to a new region in the east; in other words, deported.

The instructions couldn't have been plainer. On December 15, 1942, she was to remove herself to the Jewish synagogue at Levetzowstraße, a designated collection point for Jews, where she and other "passengers" would be transported to Litzmannstadt. She had never heard of such a town. This was obviously a Nazi action, but the letter was written by the Jewish organization in Berlin, and signed by Jewish leaders. It assured the "evacuees" that all measures would be taken to ensure comfort and safety, though they would be limited to one bag consisting of underwear, warm clothing, bedding, and medicine. Birth certificates and passports were to be handed over to authorities, along with all cash, bank books and related financial documents, but they were guaranteed work, homes, and a new life. Of course, to make the process more orderly, the letter said, evacuees were required to have the *Judenstern* sewn onto their jackets for easy identification.

Annika read the letter with disbelief. She would be saying goodbye to everything she had known, everything she had worked for, everyone whose lives she had touched; in short, to everything that had made her life meaningful. Her mind swirled with uncertainty and sucked everything familiar into a deep, black vortex of the unknown. She felt paralyzed, muscles going from taut to flaccid, and as the letter pinwheeled to the floor, her own urine dampened her undergarments. She crumpled to the floor and, rocking back and forth, began sobbing inconsolably.

The Transport

*It is a quite special secret pleasure how the people around us
fail to realize what is really happening to them.*

Adolf Hitler

Berlin: December 15, 1942

There was a knock at the door. Annika knew who it was. She
unlatched the door and a middle-aged couple barged in, walking right
past Annika without so much as acknowledging her. They
immediately began looking around the apartment.

"Oh . . ." the woman said, obviously disappointed. "It's smaller
than I was expecting."

"Well, it'll have to do," responded the man, walking toward the
kitchen. "For now, anyway . . ."

"Excuse me!" Annika said, astonished at their boldness. It was
as if she didn't exist. "Would you two mind introducing yourselves?"

The couple looked at each other as if they had just been slapped.
The woman turned to Annika and said, "Why, I thought you knew.
We're the Krügers. Who'd you think we were?" Without waiting for
a response, she turned back to her husband and resumed poking
around. "Jeez!" she said. Her husband totally ignored the intrusion.

Annika had never encountered such rudeness. The woman
waddled, corpulent and disheveled, and in her wake, she left a
pungent trail of body odor, something resembling garlic, onions, and
rotten eggs. In contrast, her husband, dressed in the rumpled blue
fatigues of a municipal worker, was so thin he appeared almost sticklike. Neither had a vocabulary suggesting anything more than a sixth-
grade education, yet here they were, inspecting an apartment they

242

were being granted simply by virtue of their Aryan birthright.

As the man began unfolding a wooden ruler, his wife blurted out, "Oh ye gods, Baldour. Get a load of this couch. It's hideous." She stole a quick glance at Annika, then said to her husband, "You'd think Jews would have better taste."

"Let's see if this table will fit over there, Marlene," the man said. He and his wife began moving the heavy kitchen table, and in the jostling, one of Annika's brass candleholders fell on the floor, breaking the candle in half.

Annika was quickly losing her patience. "Please," she said. "I'd appreciate your waiting until I'm gone to begin moving furniture around."

The man spun around, malice in his eyes, and said, "Listen here, you. My brother was killed on the front lines . . . fighting Bolshevik Jews. Your people! You might as well get used to the fact that nothing here belongs to *you* anymore. This is German property. And we're moving in at the end of the month, so you can just go fuck yourself." He and his wife turned and went ahead moving the table, Annika simply looking on.

It was a dank, raw December morning when the Jewish families of the Wedding district began gathering at the large synagogue on Levetzowstraße. Many had been awakened unawares in the pre-dawn hours by an unexpected knock at their door, and then escorted to the collection point by police. Others, like Annika, deferred to the instructions received several weeks earlier and made their own way downtown with luggage weighing far less than their fear and uncertainty. Annika had packed some essential clothing, a small amount of food, and – with tears in her eyes – a few photos of her parents. She had also sewn her most valuable jewelry into the lining of her coat.

Jews were encouraged to accept the resettlement instructions with equanimity. The local rabbis had been persuaded by the Nazis to assist in keeping the whole operation as orderly as possible. The rabbinical council girded their congregations with admonitions that, in the end, God would provide. "Don't abandon your faith," Annika had heard one elder say. "Remember, God provided Joshua to lead the Israelites out of slavery and into the promised land."

Ambling to the synagogue, suitcase in hand, Annika's world had vanished. A moribund pallor hung over the streets as townsfolk stopped what they were doing to stare at the "chosen people." Bereft of hope, empty of spirit, they came from all directions. Without passports, escape had been virtually impossible, and very few Germans were willing to risk their necks to help. While most Jews wanted to believe that they were simply being resettled, others, a small minority, saw through the ruse. To them, this was the fulfillment of Nazi ideology: the extermination of European Jewry. So, it was not surprising that in the days leading up to the "evacuation," Annika had treated several patients who had failed in their efforts to commit suicide. The most common victims had ingested poison, while many jumped from windows or tried hanging themselves inside their own homes.

By 11 A.M., close to a thousand people had congregated at the synagogue, yet not even their body heat could keep the raw December air from penetrating Annika's bones. Soldiers, city policemen and Gestapo were all deployed to make this as orderly and methodical as possible. Initially, the guards appeared relaxed, even accommodating, which helped to calm the crowd. The message was that the people had nothing to worry about, simply a relocation. Accordingly, rolls were called, names checked off, and eventually all were directed to form tidy lines for their march to the Grunewald freight yards, a few kilometers away.

Along the way, city dwellers watched with expressions ranging from rapt silence to gaiety and even catcalls. Maybe more remarkable were the ones who went about their business like nothing out of the ordinary was taking place. As Annika shuffled along with the others, she looked up just in time to see a woman poke her head out of an upstairs window. In that brief instant, she saw the woman squint, shake her head from side to side, and disappear, leaving two sheer curtains waving silently in the breeze. The image seemed symbolic.

"Stay in line," ordered the soldier. Now that they were walking, the guards' earlier persona took on more disciplined tone. Sporting the black uniform of the SS and brandishing a bolt-action Mauser complete with bayonet, the young man, probably no older than nineteen, spoke with disdain and condescension. Annika thought it paradoxical that marching under his surveillance were hard-working Germans from every walk of life: farmers and factory workers intermingled with doctors, lawyers, professors, and engineers. Many had been soldiers themselves, having fought and bled for Germany during the Great War.

Glancing at a patch of snow brought forth the most intense reminiscence of the magical weekend that she had shared with Pasha. The sky back then had been a deep blue, much like today. She remembered the Château de Nyon overlooking the shimmering waters of Lake Geneva and the Alps beyond. How vividly she recalled those ornate Tyrolean façades with their distinctive shutters and carved wooden balconies. In her mind, she and Pasha were seated by a window in Saint Cergue dallying over cups of espresso as the sun began its slow ascent over the mountains. She remembered the buttery light it spread on a landscape still sparkling from the previous night's snowfall, and how the evergreens glistened with ice while snow sprinkled like talcum from branches groaning under its weight. She smiled as she recalled the luscious warmth of the sauna after their bone-chilling visit to the ski resort.

The daydream was short-lived as the crowd, hungry and thirsty, arrived at their destination – the Grunewald railyard. The mood changed abruptly as the awaiting cattle cars loomed into view. Any optimism evaporated with the realization of having been tricked. The once-congenial guards turned to intimidation and violence, forcing the weary pilgrims into the filthy carriages.

The only thing Annika could focus on at that moment was her bladder. She was determined to urinate before boarding the train.

Jostled and pushed, she made her way through the throngs to the station-house, where in the distance she caught a glimpse of a sign pointing to a "WC." She breathed a quick sigh of relief and made a bee-line for the toilets.

"*Halt*!" Ahead of her was a very serious looking, jack-booted soldier, his rifle leveled at her. At his side was an Alsatian police-dog pulling frantically at his leash, teeth bared, frothing at the mouth. Annika's sudden presence had triggered the animal to lunge forward into ear-splitting, savage barking. The soldier had to yell to be heard. "You there! Get back in line. *Now*, or this dog will tear you in half." It seemed to take every ounce of strength the soldier could muster to restrain the dog. There was no arguing. Her bladder would have to wait.

She retraced her steps to join a slow-moving queue, when suddenly she received a painful blow to the small of her back. In a heavy Berlin accent, a soldier bellowed, "Keep moving." The wallop from his rifle butt was so intense and unexpected that her thin body buckled as if cut in half. She lurched sharply forward into the man ahead of her, dislodging his glasses while dropping her own luggage. Her suitcase snapped open, spilling everything – clothing, food, and keepsakes – onto the jammed platform. Somehow, the old man's spectacles kept from smashing as they fell to the pavement, but as he bent forward to retrieve them, the same guard kicked him forward with the heel of his boot, yelling "*Schnell*." Annika scooped up her belongings, but the elderly man's efforts were too slow, and his eyepiece was crushed under a torrent of feet.

"Don't worry about them," the guard bellowed. "You're not gonna need 'em. You can get a new pair in Litzmannstadt . . ."

It looked to Annika like seventy or more people were being squeezed like sardines into each train car. In the confused clamor, she heard a blood-curdling scream as a soldier pushed a young mother into a cattle car without her child. For a minute or two, the young head bobbed up and down over the shoulders of the crowd, but was gradually swept away, lost like a swimmer caught up in a riptide. The mother's final shrieks were stifled behind the carriage door, as it was slammed shut and bolted.

Eventually, Annika herself was inside one of the wagons. It was dark with only a shaft of flickering light coming from the small window crisscrossed in barbed wire. The cries, the stench, the sight of so much humanity crammed into such a confined space where moving one's limbs was nearly impossible. The only toilet was a bucket in the far corner. *I've got to go so badly,* she thought, *but . . .* She scanned the faces of men and women, jammed so tightly that for some sitting was not even possible. Aside from self-consciousness, just getting over to the bucket would be a challenge. It didn't take more than a few minutes before the smell of human excretions began to waft through the air. Some had begun to relieve themselves right where they sat; women in dresses, men in suits and ties, all of them herded like swine to a slaughterhouse.

"Why are they doing this to us?" a woman cried out.

"Because we're Jews. Why do you think?" someone responded angrily. *And I'm not even Jewish,* Annika thought.

People squirmed inside for hours before the train came to life with a violent jerk, causing some of those standing, mostly men, to fall onto those at their feet. Was it merciful that the train was finally rolling? No one could say as anxious talk of extermination camps no longer seemed far-fetched. As the carriage began rocking back and forth, people's bodies swayed in rhythm. Cold, penetrating air blew in through cracks, and whatever good fortune Annika had to be seated was outweighed by her inability to stretch her legs. It wasn't long before they began to cramp. It was hard to tell which was worse: choking fumes from the locomotive or ripe odors from the waste bucket. Walled-in by people on all sides, she felt astonishingly alone, especially as tempers began to flare. Sleep came only in fragments.

Having been relieved of wristwatches, time was measured by daylight. Minutes had turned into hours, hours into a full day, but at long last the train squeaked to a stop. People were freezing, famished, and near-crazy with thirst. Already one passenger in Annika's wagon had died, an elderly woman in her late seventies. There were many in ill-health, and if this journey didn't end soon, Annika realized, there would be many more deaths. The sinister hiss from the locomotive was followed by a loud clang at the door, steel-on-steel, as it was unbolted and rolled open. SS troops shouldering rifles and machine guns lined the platform. The foul-smelling corpse, stained in bodily fluids and stripped of warm clothing, lay at the doorway. The soldiers greeted the cadaver with nonchalance. Almost mechanically, they motioned to the man and woman standing closest and barked out some orders. The couple pushed the body onto the tarmac, where it fell with a thud, and then leapt out to drag the woman to the side of the tracks. Peering out, Annika could see similar procedures up and down the line. By her count, fourteen corpses were piled at the wayside.

"Food for the wolves," joked one of the guards.

"*Ja* . . . if they don't puke on it first," responded another.

The train sat inexplicably for almost two full days which, with the exception of three thirty-minute respites outside, was tortuous. A water bucket and ladle was brought to Annika's group each morning, but the limited quantity required strict rationing, and in such crowded quarters, many people spilled their allotment. Food was equally meager – a few loaves of black bread, well below subsistence, to be divided amongst the crowd. And coping with the latrine bucket, always close to overflowing, was an unmatched challenge, especially for those sitting closest. It was easily spotted by the plume of steam wafting above it. The fetid odor was so vile that many became nauseous; some, including Annika, even vomited. However, unbeknownst to anyone else, she sensed that her nausea was not from the odors. She was pregnant.

Outside the car, Annika could hear one of the soldiers talking to another. "So, what's the hold up?" he asked.

"We're headed to Łódź, but there's a derailment about 20 kilometers from here. Fucking partisans blew up the tracks. Cocksuckers didn't realize it was a military transport they derailed."

"Casualties?"

"*Ja*. We lost a couple men, from what I heard. Several injured, but we hung twenty Polacks, ten for each of ours. Left 'em swingin' on the side of the tracks. Give the cocksuckers something to think about before pulling that shit again."

"Something to think about? Polacks actually think? Don't count on it. Those people are so fucking stupid. We oughta kill every last one of 'em."

The guard nodded. "We will." Looking up the track, he said, "Unfortunately, we can't get to Łódź anytime soon. Rail lines to Chelmno and Majdanek are completely blocked. Who the hell knows where we're going now."

Those inside Annika's carriage heard the entire conversation. So Łódź had been the destination, not Litzmannstadt. That answered one question. But now came another. Where were they headed . . . *if anywhere*? The nightmarish boxcar, their world for the past several days, was a depiction of hell worthy of a modern-day Hieronymus Bosch. Prolonged exposure to their toxic environment would have been unhealthy, if not lethal, even to the livestock the cattle-cars had been designed for. Everyone was miserable. Modesty was gone. Even the most genteel among them was forced to squat over a latrine bucket, in full view of everyone.

Late in the afternoon, two men rose from the center and began speaking to the group. One introduced himself as Levi. "Listen, people," he began, "we need to get serious. If we're to survive, we have to get much more disciplined with our food and water. Everybody should be afforded the same amount: no more, no less. It doesn't matter how bad you feel. We're *all* hungry and thirsty. We all feel like shit. I don't care how rich or important anybody is, *or was*. We're all in this together. If we can share, equitably, we all have a better chance of making it."

"He's right. My name is Jakob Messing. I'm a doctor." Annika recognized the name from the Jewish Hospital, though she had never met him. "I'd like to add that people can die just as easily from blood clots as from hunger and thirst. It would be really worthwhile to move around. Too many are sitting, all crunched up. I am recommending that we take turns standing and sitting, maybe see if we can orchestrate some group movement. We need to keep our blood circulating."

"Good advice," Levi added. "One more thing. The slop bucket should be used only for defecating. If you have to pee, use the cracks in the floor. We can't let the bucket get so full that it overflows."

These ideas gave the crowd something concrete to focus on. But hearing muffled cries, even shrieks, emanating from the wagons scattered up and down the track, it was difficult to think of survival. And then came gunshots.

"*Mein Gott*, they're shooting people," one woman screamed. She looked to those around her, as if pleading for verification. "You hear that?" Another gun shot.

"Monsters!" roared a man, as he peered through a crack in the wall.

"They're going to kill us all," said an older man, disconsolately.

The shooting subsided, yet death was becoming more real by the moment. In Annika's carriage, the journey claimed three more victims, each carried to the door where they were stacked one atop the other. Banging on the walls to have them removed was ignored. Their only salvation, if it be called that, was the cold air, which slowed the bodies' decomposition.

After what seemed like an eternity, the train lurched. "We're moving. Thank God," said someone. Few cared where they were going as long as they went somewhere, anywhere. But then, another agonizing delay. It wouldn't be until three hours later that the transport shuddered back to life. This time, they were genuinely underway, enabling people to settle back with the belief that their destination might not be far off.

Recognizing that the sun was directly in front of them, a woman observed that the train was heading west – directly opposite their original direction. "Maybe we're going back to Berlin," one of the men ventured. But a few hours later, it became obvious that they had taken on a northwesterly bearing, not towards Berlin. It was late in the evening, most of them sleeping, when a blast from the train whistle roused them to attention. The transport was slowing, approaching a station. A man stood on his toes to see out the window. "Fürstenberg!" he announced. Most recognized the name. They had made a long circle. Fürstenberg was approximately 75 kilometers north of Berlin. "What could we be doing way up here?" a woman asked to no one in particular. Her question would be answered soon enough.

Brakes screeched as the train jerked to a halt, followed by a loud belch of steam. Voices from the guards were heard outside the cars, and with a loud thump of metal-on-metal, the heavy door to Annika's carriage slid open. Awaiting them were heavily armed guards and baying dogs thirsty for a taste of human flesh.

"Raus! Raus!" soldiers screamed in an effort to hurry the frightened occupants out of the carriages. Thoroughly exhausted, people tumbled meekly out of the wagons, men still in suitcoats, women in long dresses and wool overcoats. Some were yanked forcefully from doorways causing them to fall face-first onto the ground. A putrid stench began to envelope the platform as the wagons disgorged the human cargo – living and dead. With zombie-like imprecision, they formed into lines alongside the train, swaying confusedly in their heavily soiled garments. From a distance, it resembled a city stockyard of squealing animals headed to nearby slaughterhouses.

Ravensbrück

I'll put an end to the idea that a woman's body belongs to her.
Adolf Hitler

Late December, 1943

Annika was in a long line of naked women, all newly arrived and beginning their indoctrination at this massive KZ. The women moved like an assembly line under the watchful eyes of male guards, who, just like at Sachsenhausen, leered and chortled from a distance. The women did their best to cover themselves with their hands and arms, but that made the scene even more entertaining to the men. Almost out of nowhere, a prisoner grasped her head and began parting her hair in a roughshod search for lice. Once her grip released, Annika was set upon by second woman, this one armed with scissors. She stood helplessly as every lock of hair fluttered to the floor, thick with large wispy clumps in every conceivable shade and texture.

The line moved forward bringing Annika to yet another prisoner, this one short and stocky, clippers in hand. "Squat!" the woman ordered. Annika knew better than argue with her. Before she knew what was happening, the woman was hacking away at her pubic area, gruffly extracting every kinky remnant she could see. The dull instruments did more ripping than shaving, leaving Annika's skin raw and weeping blood. Tears streamed down her cheeks as her identity disappeared in this painful defoliation. She looked around, humiliated and violated. The mass of naked women surrounding her were all the same. No longer was it possible to differentiate friends from strangers. Shorn of hair, denuded of clothing, all appeared remarkably alike – their identities lost in the fluffy piles on the concrete beneath

252

them. From there, the women were marched to another section of building and told to wait for a medical checkup. Naked bodies huddled together for warmth. Penetrating cold from the concrete floor created an impromptu chorus-line of hopping feet and gyrating legs – an unchoreographed dance step to keep from becoming numb. The wait felt interminable.

After more than two hours, a middle-aged man in a white gown appeared. Introduced as "Doctor Rosenthal," he was said to be a gynecologist dispatched to examine the women for "venereal disease." Everyone was to submit, including young children and the elderly. Any protest was out of the question. One by one, they underwent vaginal and rectal exams without the doctor pausing to wash fingers or instruments between patients. The procedures amounted to little more than unsterilized cavity searches for hidden valuables. Rings, bracelets, gold, or diamonds – anything that the patient had hoped to trade for food or other privileges – were routinely extracted. Those guilty of concealment were taken away.

No such objects were found on Annika's person, as her valuables had been relinquished undetected when she turned in her clothing. However, Doctor Rosenthal did discover something else. Without any emotion, he looked over to his nurse, Gerda Quernheim, and simply said, "Pregnant." The nurse nodded and smiled. She immediately went into action, leading Annika to another room and onto a cold ceramic table, where she waited for another hour while the doctor completed the cavity searches. Annika couldn't have known it at the time, but pregnancies among *häftlinge* were not permitted at Ravensbrück. They were *untermenschen,* genetically inferior, and official policy was that to reduce their population quickly and efficiently. Annika's fate had been sealed the moment Rosenthal made his observation.

The abortion was a grisly procedure, almost too awful for words. Annika had resisted with every ounce of energy she could muster. Prisoner orderlies were instructed to place her in physical restraints, but no anesthetics were given. Whatever implements they used were unnoticed through the pain. Annika tried to watch, wanting to be emotionally present during such an existentially significant event, but as the catheter scratched its way through her cervix, every muscle in her body tightened, including her eyelids, which remained squeezed shut. This may have been a blessing as it kept her mind from visually recording such a devastating event. With no anesthesia, Annika briefly lost consciousness the moment the fetus was pulled from her cervix. When, seconds later, she opened her eyes to catch a glimpse of the nurse scurrying off holding something to her chest. Annika tried to scream, but her voice was quickly muffled by searing pain in her abdomen. The only remaining evidence of her pregnancy was warm, bloody placenta dripping from her legs and belly onto the floor.

She languished in the infirmary for a full day, overwrought with pain – physical and emotional. Her insides throbbed. She was given no painkillers, not even aspirin, yet the ache she felt internally was not nearly as excruciating as the tortured thoughts racing through her mind. She ruminated on how she herself may have been responsible for her suffering – her decisions at Bernburg, the rape, her imprisonments . . . even her failed relationship with Pasha. And now to have a living being wrested from her womb . . . after having prepared herself to deliver the child. Having been raped, she thought, was no fault of the child. She had even allowed herself to think of what the child might grow to become. But now, everything meaningful was gone, lost forever. *If this is God's penance, what have I done to deserve it all?* She didn't need to be told that she was sinking into a deep depression.

The morning following the abortion, Annika, still quite sore, was abruptly awakened by a female kapo. "Get up," instructed the woman. "You're meeting the *Oberaufseherin*," the camp's senior supervisor. "*Schnell!*"

Annika rose to her feet, probably faster than she should have. She doubled over from a sharp pain in her abdomen. It was a momentary stabbing, but blood continued to seep from her vagina, and every movement triggered a bolt of electricity throughout her pelvis. The kapo gave her a few minutes to collect herself and then marched her out onto the *Lagerstraße*, the main walkway in the center of the camp, where they passed row-upon-row of long, gray barracks and hundreds, maybe thousands, of women in a variety of activities, most supervised by kapos with cudgels. Bent slightly at the waist, Annika shuffled forward, clutching her stomach with both arms. Those who dared stole a quick glance at Annika, but most walked by like robots, eyes fixed forward, trancelike.

They couldn't have reached the administration building soon enough. Annika's insides were on fire as she hobbled up the steps. The supervisor's office was identified by a small nameplate reading, *Chef Oberaufseherin Anna Klein*. The door was already open, and a woman dressed in gray uniform could be seen seated behind a desk. The guard gave two quick raps on the door.

"*Kommt rein! Schnell. Ich habe es eilig*," came the sharp response, beckoning them in while giving the impression that she was being interrupted from something far more important.

Annika's escort snapped to attention. "*Heil Hitler, Frau Oberaufseherin. Ich habe Sie den jüdischen Gefangenen gebracht. Nummer 7204, Fräulein Tritzchler*," said the guard. Annika was accustomed to being introduced as Doctor, but here, she was simply a female Jewish prisoner, one of thousands.

The chief supervisor got right to the point. "Prisoner number 7204, I have a telex from Berlin. Apparently, you appealed your designation as a *mischling*." Annika wasn't expecting this. Suddenly her ears perked up. "The Interior Ministry followed up and has informed us that your status is to be changed from *Mischling* to *Politisch*." She pushed forward the documents laying on the desk in front of her and leaned back, looking Annika squarely in the eye. "Let me congratulate you. Had we not learned of this upon your arrival, you would have already been on the next transport out of here, not one you would have wanted to be on. On the other hand, you wouldn't have had to undergo surgery . . . so I guess there's a silver lining to either option."

"May I be permitted to ask a question, *Frau Oberaufseherin*?" Annika had learned not to take anything for granted.

"Proceed."

"Thank you for that information. Does this mean I will be released?"

"You are implying that a mistake has been made. The government doesn't make mistakes, Tritzchler. It merely reclassified you. As a *mischling*, you'd be on your way to Oświęcim in Poland. We don't keep Jews here. But you're a political prisoner and will be treated as such. Do I make myself clear?"

Annika was confused as to why, with her reclassification, she was still to remain in a concentration camp. Just the same, she knew better than to press the point with a woman who seemed to have the power of life and death. "*Ja . . . Ich verstehe.*"

"*Gut.* Then we understand ourselves." She leaned forward, signed and stamped a document, and handed it to the guard. The block leader will give you a red triangle. Dismissed."

Annika's heart was almost beating out of her chest. If she wasn't a Jew, she couldn't have been guilty of race-defiling, which, after all, was why she was imprisoned in the first place. The guard snapped a quick salute, turned, grabbed Annika under her armpits, and escorted her out of the office. Annika looked back over her shoulder, not wanting to lose her chance to discuss it further, but the guard dug her thumb into Annika's tricep.

"You're a lucky bitch, you know that?" the guard said.

"I'm not sure I follow you," Annika responded, holding her belly.

"The *Oberaufseherin* could have let you continue on with that transport . . . to Oświęcim."

"Wasn't it headed to Litzmannstadt?" Annika asked.

"Litzmannstadt?" The guard laughed. "What the fuck is Litzmannstadt?"

"That's where we were told we were being resettled . . . when we left Berlin."

"That's a buncha horseshit. Ain't no such place. Them people's headed to Oświęcim . . . in Poland."

"Why?"

"You ask too many stupid questions. You sound like a fucking Polack. Ever heard of Auschwitz?"

Auschwitz. The word cut through her like a knife. So many rumors – reports of extermination, torture, starvation . . . stories that sounded, well, just too implausible. There couldn't be such a place. Annika stopped and looked at the woman. "Auschwitz?" she asked, as if there was deniability in simply saying such an awful word.

"*Ja, das stimmt* . . . that's where all the Jews go." She looked at Annika and smirked. ". . . the end of the line."

The following morning, Annika was awakened abruptly. The siren was still blaring when two kapos entered the barracks, screaming at everyone to get up. *It can't be any later than 0400,* Annika thought. She lined up with a sea of other women jockeying to use one of the three toilets. They had twenty minutes to wash up and make beds before roll call. In some ways, she felt fortunate to have been at Sachsenhausen, because the routine was familiar. As she hustled to the *Appellplatz,* she could feel blood seeping from her vagina, and her insides felt like they had been subjected to sandpaper. Standing for the two-hour roll call, her arms at her sides, was a torture of its own. But she was not alone.

A woman in front of her, much older judging from her slouch and wrinkles, must have lost the battle to use the toilet. As numbers were being called out, a puddle began to form at the woman's feet. It went unnoticed for so long that Annika thought she might get away with it, but just before the final roll was tallied, a kapo swaggered in their direction. Annika prayed that the overseer would veer off, but it wasn't to be.

"What are you doing, pissing on my parade ground?" she screamed, swinging a club at the the woman's head. The woman fell to the ground, at which point the kapo delivered another blow. "Get up!" she screamed. The woman struggled to her feet. "After *Appell,* you will remain standing. I'll teach you how to respect the parade ground by scrubbing this area until it shines."

Annika, like the others, stood and watched while their stomachs churned.

At the end of roll call, ten women's names were called, Annika's being one. All the other women were dismissed to their duties. Annika's group was ordered back into the barrack, followed by three SS officers and Margit, the broad-shouldered block-leader. The officer in charge, a tall Hauptsturmführer of about forty, began. "You women are new here and haven't yet been assigned to duties. You've been chosen to offer a service to the camp which can earn you light duty and release in six months. Those who are interested will be housed in our new camp bordello, where you will have increased rations, clean clothes, and comfortable housing. Your task will be to provide comfort to model prisoners, men whose exemplary work earns them the privilege of physical contact with women. Those selected will have daily access to hygiene and will be afforded protection from abuse by camp guards." The women shuffled in their line, looking to each other in astonishment at this unexpected, bizarre offer.

"Involvement, of course, is entirely voluntary. Those unwilling to participate will be reassigned to manual labor, like the rest of the camp." Looking directly at Annika, he said, "I can assure you. The work I am offering will be much easier than the alternative." Annika could not believe what she was hearing. Privileges and the promise of early release in exchange for prostitution. The women, all young, searched each other's faces for clues to help them decide.

"Those who are interested, fall out." No one stirred, each waiting for someone else to make the first move. "Ladies?" The officer's arms were folded across his chest, one hand holding his riding crop. "Am I to assume all of you wish to rejoin work platoons?" Four of the women stepped forward. He stood for a few more seconds. "Anyone else?" One more woman, wiping tears from her eyes, joined the line, leaving Annika and four others standing. Turning to the *kapo*, the officer said, "Take those women," pointing to Annika and the others who declined, "back to their *Blockovas*." Then turning to the recruits, "You others, follow me."

"Move!" commanded the kapo, giving one woman a shove. Annika's group was marched double-time across the parade ground and quickly detailed to the road-building crew, the hardest labor of all. It almost seemed like they were being punished for their refusal to participate. There she became part of a detachment assigned to shovel and haul gravel, spread it with rakes, and pack it down with an enormous concrete roller. The road being built led to the Siemens sub-camp, half a kilometer away, which had been constructed the previous year in order to profit from the Ravensbrück's slave labor. Annika was given a rake with instructions to spread gravel as it was deposited by a procession of women pushing wheelbarrows. It was back-breaking work.

On this, her very first day with the road crew, Annika noticed the arrival of an *SS aufseherin*. "Look sharp," muttered the woman next to her. "It's Binz." It was an ominous warning, and one which Annika was quick to appreciate. The guard swaggered from crew to crew, sizing up prisoners like a tiger stalking its prey. She wore a blueish-gray wool jacket with matching below-the-knee skirt and black leather jackboots. Her military cap was pulled jauntily to one side, partially covering her tight blond curls, and a Luger was strapped conspicuously at her waist. In one hand was a curled whip, in the other a leather lead joining her to a large Alsatian dog. She was a poster child of Nazism, if ever there was one.

Accompanying Binz was young guard, probably in her late teens, but dressed in similar garb – jackboots and all. It appeared to be a training exercise. "You can't take your eyes off these lazy bitches for a second," Binz bellowed. "None of 'em know the definition of real work. They've grown fat and lazy living off hard-working Germans." Her apprentice nodded without smiling. "Your job," Binz continued, "is to make sure they work . . . and I mean work *hard*! Teach 'em that this isn't no country club. You do whatever you have to – *anything* – to keep 'em working. *"*

She then turned to one of the prisoners, a woman probably in her early sixties who was struggling to move a heavy wheelbarrow. "You there!" she barked. "Fill that fucking cart to the top. You hear me? I said to the top!" The forlorn prisoner looked over to Binz with a certain disbelief, as the cart was already laden with so much dirt that even a strong man might strain under its weight. Her hesitation was to cost her. "You want to challenge me?" she screamed.

The woman made a quick attempt at placating the officer. *"Nein, Frau Aufseherin."*

Not to be appeased, Binz grit her teeth and swung the butt-end of her riding crop across the woman's face, knocking her to the ground. As the inmate slowly struggled to right herself, Binz kicked her squarely on the shoulder, toppling the wretch into a small ditch.

"Get up, you old cow. On your feet! *Schnell."* The prisoner, now covered with snow and dirt, managed to get to her feet. "Now fill that wheelbarrow!"

Exhausted and in pain, the woman picked up her shovel. Three small scoops was all it took before the barrow was overflowing.

"That's more like it," Binz gloated. She turned to her companion and winked. "Now, move it."

The prisoner reached down and with all her might lifted the handles. The wheelbarrow groaned and rolled forward a few feet before the front wheel lodged against a small rock. The woman steadied it as best she could.

"Move!" shouted Binz, unfurling her whip.

Now everyone's eyes were on the prisoner. The wheelbarrow, weighing more than the woman, wavered precariously as she tried to back it up. She then pushed with all her might in an effort to ram it forward over the stone, but it was too heavy and began to tip to one side. She struggled desperately to balance it, but the momentum exceeded her strength, and the whole cart toppled, spilling its contents directly at the *aufseherin's* feet.

"You dare to get that shit all over my boots?" Binz was livid. Her lash rained down on the defenseless woman followed by two well-aimed kicks to her side. Writhing on the ground, arms outstretched to ward off the blows, the *haftling* was no match against the overseer's fury. Just when it appeared that the victim couldn't take anymore, Binz turned loose the frenzied guard-dog. Ninety pounds of unrestrained fury launched forward with the savagery of a wild boar, knocking the flailing woman backwards. In a split-second, it was on top of her, tearing wildly at her clothing, shredding sleeves and skirt into ragged pieces amidst screams of helplessness. She rolled in the dirt, covering her head, her torso, anywhere the dog was biting, but the animal was simply too fast and much too strong. The more she resisted, the more insane the animal became. Its jaws tore into flesh, ripping it from her body by viciously shaking its head. It was only minutes before the old woman became listless as the canine tossed her around like a bloody ragdoll.

The prisoners looked on, horrified, not wanting to believe what their eyes were communicating. Satisfied, Binz pulled the animal back. She then turned to the bystanders. "Everyone back to work! Fun's over." She then turned to her apprentice. "These people are like 'kindeygardners.' The only thing they understand is brute force. You slacken up the tiniest bit, and they'll take advantage of you at every opportunity." Looking over to the crew leader, Binz said, "Put her in that wheelbarrow and get her outta here."

Siemens

He is sometimes slave who should be master; and sometimes master who should be slave.

Marcus Tullius Cicero

Ravensbrück: August, 1944

Annika had just entered the washroom. The stench was overpowering. Slumped in front of her was a motionless, solitary figure whose nakedness exposed the ravages of indescribable torment. Barely discernible was an outline of depleted breasts – lifeless nipples all but hidden in crumpled, misshapen areolas. It was a woman. White stubble dotted her scalp like tiny seedlings sprouting from a barren patch of earth. A thin layer of pallid skin clung to the woman's bones in a disorganized geometry of obtuse angles, and her scrawny legs had long since jettisoned any muscle. Across her back was a crisscross pattern of faded brown stripes, the all-too-familiar markings of past floggings. Her age was anybody's guess – common in a *KZ* where chronic brutality, starvation, and overwork played havoc with biology, where genes could no longer foretell the length of one's life. By appearance, she was in her sixties, though Annika figured she could have been much younger. Regardless, she lacked strength to reach the toilet and was now sitting in a putrid pool of her own excrement, one of the many victims of dysentery sweeping the camp. A hideous caricature of humanness, this woman was a living, breathing embodiment of Hieronymus Bosch's twisted imagination. She would almost certainly not live to see the next day. And there was nothing Annika could do for her.

It was no secret that the women were being pushed to their limit,

262

and that many would die because of it. With every German male of military age fighting on different fronts, there was a serious shortage of workers to keep up with the ever-growing demand for war *matériel*. The remedy was to conscript slaves from the vast network of concentration camps throughout Europe and sell their labor to major corporations at ridiculously low prices. This was the strategy to meet the demands for armaments while simultaneously boosting corporate profits. Prisoners were entirely expendable and easily replaced by the ongoing flood of new arrivals.

Annika sensed that she, herself, was slowly succumbing. It had been only a few days ago that she saw her reflection in a window, and was disheartened by the skeleton that looked back at her. Her face was pale and drawn, her clothing hung without form; even her teeth were brown and, from the pain in her mouth, probably full of cavities. But she still had strength, and was more focused on those around her than on herself.

"You've lost a lot of weight," Annika whispered to Elsa one night, as they lay side-by-side in the crowded bunk. Elsa was fast becoming like the woman in the washroom. Originally from Berlin, her husband had been active in the Communist party and arrested shortly after *Kristallnacht.* Elsa's arrest had come less than a year later.

"How 'bout you, Annika. You're skin and bones. Do you even get your period anymore?"

"No . . . not for months. When did yours end?"

"I haven't had a period for at least two years. Probably never will again. They sterilized me shortly after I arrived."

"Oh, Elsa, I'm sorry. I didn't know that."

"Yeah, well," she said, weakly, "it's the least of my worries anymore. I feel like I'm wasting away," Elsa replied. "I don't have any energy . . . Not sure I can keep going."

Annika wasn't surprised. Elsa had been at Ravensbrück longer than most. Annika reached into her clothing and handed her bunkmate a crust of bread. "Here . . . eat this. You've got to keep pushing. The only way we survive is to prove that we can keep working."

"No," she said, shaking her head. "Thank you, but save it. You need it as much as I do."

"You can't give up, Elsa. You've come this far . . ."

"I don't know if I can, Annika. The only way I'm ever gonna survive is to escape."

"Not possible, honey. C'mon. You know what they say . . . The only escape is through the chimney."

"Um hmm. And maybe that's where I'll end up. I don't know." A few moments of silence. "I guess anything's worth a try. It's just that . . . I don't know if I even care at this point. I think we're all gonna die anyway. What's the use?"

Two weeks later, Elsa was apprehended in the back of a lorry where she had stowed herself in a barrel intent on escaping. She was immediately sent to the "bunker," the camp's punishment block, but after a few days, word came out that she had been shot. Annika was crestfallen, as Elsa's place in the bunk was immediately filled by another woman. Annika felt her own resiliency waning.

But then, an unexpected opportunity to get out of hard labor presented itself one morning on the *Appellplatz*. As she stood with rows of other women, a small entourage, which included Fritz Suhren (the camp commandant) and a *Meister* from one of the local factories, walked slowly up and down the lines inspecting women as they would cattle at auction. Occasionally, at the direction of the factory boss, Suhren would stop and with his riding crop push a woman's head from one side, sometimes demanding to see her teeth. Others were instructed to hold out their hands to be examined for any signs of arthritis or disability. It was well known that companies like Bosch, Daimler-Benz, BMW, and Volkswagen were among Ravensbrück's many customers. Today, it was Siemens' turn.

A group of names was called out; Annika's was one. They were then assembled for transport to the nearby factory. With most of the German men having already been conscripted into the military,

Siemens' survival depended on labor, lots of it, and the Ravensbrück women were well-suited to assemble electrical equipment and field phones for the military. Having slaved outside performing hard labor, often in the bitter cold without adequate clothing, Annika was one of hundreds eager for indoor work. With so many volunteers, Siemens could afford to be selective as to whom they let in. Workers had to be in good physical shape and have basic intellectual skills suited for benchwork.

It began with an IQ test, the applicant having to demonstrate an ability to twist copper wires into a variety of configurations. It was followed by a task requiring paper to be folded into specified designs.

"What are you doing?" barked the plant director, Otto Grade, clearly annoyed. He slapped his palm down with such ferocity that everything on the table jumped an inch or so in the air. Startled, Annika quickly refocused. "Concentrate, or go back to the camp!" he threatened. He placed another design in front of her, and Annika's nimble fingers, expertly honed during her surgery practicum, went to work, quickly processing the engineer's design. She completed it perfectly. He gave her another, which she finished instantly. The director was quick to identify hand-eye coordination, and despite her easily passing his test, Grade gave her several more tasks, each of greater complexity to better gauge her usefulness. It didn't take long to convince him that this was a woman of unusual talent, maybe someone with leadership potential.

"Enough," he commanded, then turned with a wave to the foreman. Looking back to Annika, he said, "Go with him."

Annika was put to work with a crew of sixty or so others winding copper wire around wooden spools. This was not easy work; even with pliers the wire easily cut through skin. And the warm air she had welcomed as a relief from working outside was not for the comfort of the laborers, but rather to make the stiff wire more pliable. Nothing at Siemens was intended for the comfort or well-being of its prisoner workforce. Instead, everything was geared for one thing only – production – and whatever it took to meet their quotas – beatings, torture, starvation, exposure to toxic chemicals – was all quite open and acceptable to management.

Every morning following the dreaded morning roll call, a couple hundred dirty, tired, foul-smelling women would assemble on the *Lagerstraße* in rows of five. The factory was less than a mile from the camp, but marching there on an empty stomach wearing only wooden clogs made the journey seem endless. It didn't help that they were compelled to pass the gas chamber and crematorium, which always loomed as consequence of being fired.

Annika had seen more than her share of abuse in her time at the KZ, but one incident of cruelty would remain etched in her mind forever. The women had already put in their morning shift and, dog-tired, marched the considerable distance back to the camp for their mid-day ration. Unfortunately, upon their arrival, they found that someone had miscalculated; no soup had been prepared for them. The kapos responded by allowing the women just enough time to use the latrines, after which they were again mustered for the dismal march back to Siemens. By then, it was raining, so when they arrived at the factory, the laborers were soaked to the bone, nearly exhausted and above all famished. Nevertheless, a shrill blast from the factory whistle signaled a return to the production line. It took every ounce of reserve to continue working, even more to concentrate to avoid mistakes. Not everyone could muster that reserve.

A Polish woman in front of Annika had fallen behind in her quota. Her wet clothing clung so tightly that her backbone stuck out like a knotty branch on a leafless tree. Annika had noticed her pausing frequently to rub her hands in a futile effort to stimulate circulation. Out of the blue, a civilian production manager appeared. Seeing her meager output, he slapped the back of her head, ranting a string of obscenities. The commotion attracted a kapo. It was like chum thrown to a shark. As the manager walked away, the kapo slammed the worker's head against the machine she was working on. Her face bloodied, she fell to the floor crying for mercy. The manager looked back to see his overseer stomping the woman, but did nothing to stop it. Worse, Annika herself was powerless to intervene. *It feels worse to watch it than to have it done to me.*

Plant superintendents, dressed in their usual business attire, took a blind eye to such abuse. The prevailing attitude was that production was essential to the war effort and any worker falling behind was considered a saboteur, an enemy. But for the executives, it was less about winning the war than it was about profits. It would only be years later that the world would learn of the unimaginable wealth that industrialists from Siemens, BMW, Mercedes, I.G. Farben, Opel, Bosch, Bayer, Porsche, Volkswagen and others had accumulated on the backs of forced laborers.

Liberation

The mystery of human existence lies not in just staying alive, but in finding something to live for.

Fyodor Dostoevsky

KZ Ravensbrück: Spring, 1945

There was a flurry of disorganized activity in the camp unlike anything Annika had ever witnessed. Yelling out orders, waving batons and rifles, guards were hustling women into makeshift groups, but this was no work detail. Explosions that had been heard in the distance for several days were now much closer. The Russians were closing in. Annika took advantage of the confusion to slip unnoticed into her barrack where she found Gisele, a woman from her crew, gathering up items from the shelf.

"What's going on?" Annika asked.

"I think the stooges are getting ready to evacuate. Russians got 'em on the run."

Annika peered out the window. Guards were indeed running around the camp gathering supplies, pushing women, making ready, it appeared, for some type of exit. "Whatdya think they're going to do with us?"

Before Gisele could answer, the barrack's door flew open. "They're shooting people out there!" It was Ursula, one of Annika's trusted friends. She was wild-eyed, hysterical, and out of breath. "They're going to kill us! We've gotta hide!"

"*Who*?" Annika demanded. "Who is shooting people?" Ursula tried to talk, but no words would come. She looked behind herself, startled, as if expecting someone to break through the door after her.

Annika grabbed her by her shoulders and shook her. "Ursula, c'mon! What'd you see?"

Ursula began blubbering. "I saw . . . I saw Pflaum shooting women . . . out on the *Lagerstraße*. It was like anyone who . . . who couldn't . . . run fast enough . . ."

Hans Pflaum. Fat and ruthless, he was the labor director of the camp. He had total control over the women, and dealt with them strictly and ruthlessly in terms of their ability to work. His morning ritual had always been to ride his bicycle through the rows of women lined up on the *Appellplatz* and, using his whip, make selections for the daily work details. Once someone's work capacity faltered, they were summarily selected for execution. It was always very orderly, very mechanical.

"Anyone . . ." Ursula continued, ". . . anyone who looked weak . . . he was shooting. I saw him murder Oksana, the Russian seamstress. We were both running. Oksana tripped and before she could get up . . ." She rubbed at her eyes as if trying to erase an image too painful to visualize. Her chest was heaving, her voice cracking with emotion. ". . . before Oksana could get up, he put his gun to her head." Ursula looked up at her two friends, terrified. Tears streaked across her cheeks. "He blew her brains out. Right there on the path. I saw it." More gunfire crackled outside. "They're going to kill us all."

Annika flattened herself against the wall and stole a quick glance out the window taking every precaution to avoid being seen. Boisterous guards equipped with Alsatian dogs were herding throngs of prisoners along the *Lagerstraße*. In the background, smoke not only belched from the crematoria, but a grayish-black plume began to waft high above the administration building.

"They're gettin' ready to make a run for it . . ." scowled Gisele. "Fucking cowards. The Russians'll hang 'em by their balls if they get here first, and those bastards know it." More explosions thundered in the distance, the sound of heavy artillery.

"Looks like the *Lagerkommandant's* building is on fire," Annika speculated.

"Probably burning documents," Gisele offered. Annika turned to her with raised eyebrows. "Sure. It's the Prussian way. Right down to the last detail. Leave no trace of any crimes." The moment she said that, there was a resounding blast from the far end of camp. The building shook and they all jumped.

"Good Lord," Annika exclaimed. "What was that?"

It was Ursula who now ran to the window. "It's the goddamn gas chamber! My Lord. Did I ever think I'd see the day? They're blowing it up."

Any joy was momentary and quickly supplanted by fear. Annika began to pace, wringing her hands. She had every reason to be frightened. Everyone was. This was the day the inmates had long been worried about. Despite praying for liberation, there were rumors that the SS planned to murder every last prisoner before the Nazis vacated the KZ. "Dead men tell no tales," they had boasted, taunting the terrified women. One of the SS guards had laughed, "*Arbeit macht frei* . . . freedom through work, right? Try to remember that," he teased, "on your way to the crematorium. That's where you'll find the ultimate liberation."

More gunshots rang out as thousands of women coalesced at the gate. "Form into rows of five," the guards screamed, lashing out at anybody in their path. Just outside their window, a young woman, jostled in the chaos, fell to the ground. Annika noticed her leg. It was horribly misshapen with a long scar running almost from the knee to her ankle. It looked like most of her calf had been removed. She struggled to get up, reaching out for assistance, but before anyone could help, an SS officer pushed his way through and dispatched her with a round from his Luger.

"Fucking bastard!" said Gisele, looking back at Annika through gritted teeth.

"It was one of the 'rabbits,'" Annika said, her hands balled into fists. "Goddamned animals. I hope they burn in hell." It was unlike her to show such anger, but here she was seething. The "rabbits" were women who'd been subjected to cruel medical experiments. The

270

doctors had intentionally created surgical injuries that were then infected with bacteria to simulate war wounds. The few who survived the painful experiments became mascots to the prisoners.

The guard who shot her turned to the crowd and screamed, "We're all marching out of here. Anyone who can't keep up will be shot."

"Quick. Before the guards come around. Let's see if we can make it to the infirmary," Annika suggested. "It'll be safer there than here."

"Unless they murder everyone who can't walk," Gisele said.

"We don't have much choice. We gotta take the risk."

They were in Barrack Four, not far from the camp's entrance and easily noticeable if they went directly to the *Revier,* which itself was directly adjacent to the gate where the crowd had formed. Instead, they slid out a side window and ran in the opposite direction, flitting from one barrack to another – Annika first, then Gisele, then Ursula. Fortunately for them, the guard posts had only recently been abandoned, making it easier to slip along the perimeter. One by one, they made it to the *Revier's* rear door.

A prisoner nurse appeared almost instantly. "You can't stay here. You have to go."

"If we leave here, we're dead," Ursula said.

"If you try to hide out here, you jeopardize everybody . . ."

Hearing the nurse, Doctor Nikiforova came in. "Annika," he said. "What's going on." The doctor, a Russian POW, knew Annika from several prisoners she had brought to the infirmary over the past year, people seriously compromised, near death. He also knew she was a trained physician.

"We need to hide, Doctor Nikiforova. It's our only chance."

With no hesitation, the doctor turned to his nurse. "Leila. Take them to the east wing. Now!"

The nurse escorted them to the far end of the infirmary. "There's a bed there. One of you can use it. You need to look sick. The others can hide in the supply closet." She then turned and left them.

Annika peeked out the window. The sight was disturbing: long lines of ill-equipped women, tens of thousands of them, clad only in flimsy prison garb with nothing more than wooden clogs on their feet. Was this to be the massacre everyone feared? It was obvious that there were no provisions for bivouacking outside, and from what she could see, nowhere near enough food and water to meet the needs of this itinerant city. It looked like a human disaster in the making, and when the order was given to march, they filed out like a team of lemmings headed to oblivion.

Anxious hours passed for those inside the *Revier*. The only sounds were scattered moans from patients, yet even without medicines and anesthetics, most attended this change in rapt silence. Outside were intermittent rumblings from distant artillery, glimmers on the horizon. Some of the blasts came close enough to light up the sky overhead, outlining silhouettes of the camp's buildings and making the ground tremble as if an earthquake was underfoot. In between the explosions, the camp itself took on an eerie, blackened silence. The usual regimentation of whistles, sirens, shouts, and screams – the movement of vehicles, gunshots and barking dogs – it had all disappeared like the vanquishing of sound when a swimmer submerges in the water. The transformation was surreal. None of those who remained knew what to expect, which generated an apprehension almost worse than the everyday reality. Would execution squads be detailed back to the camp? Was an SS contingent still holed up in their now darkened quarters? Of the nearly three thousand left behind, no one dared to venture out. Instead, they waited.

Annika was watching. "I think they're gone," she said. "There don't seem to be guards anywhere." Her observation brought confused murmurs from the beds. With so much loss, so much suffering, so many letdowns, few dared to be hopeful. But circumstances were definitely changing, as one brave soul after another ventured cautiously out the doors. Not being met by guards, they became increasingly emboldened to circulate freely throughout

272

the camp so that before long, women who could walk emerged from buildings carrying clearly marked Red Cross parcels of sugar, flour, dried milk, bread, soap, and cigarettes – all supplies that had been intended for the prisoners, but expropriated by the SS.

By the next day, it was clear to Annika that she was free to leave the camp. It was a dream come true. She had prayed many times for just such a day, never fully believing that she'd ever get out. But now that the day was finally upon her, she couldn't bring herself to simply pack up and leave. All around her were patients, living skeletons. They needed her. She couldn't simply abandon them. It was like opening the door to a bird cage only to have the bird stay put. Without assistance, some of the patients would have only days – in some cases, only hours – to live. She offered her services to Doctor Nikiforova, who eagerly agreed.

A month elapsed with mixed results. The food left by the SS had seemed auspicious, but dwindled rapidly, and inmates continued to eat well below subsistence level. Many prisoners took immediate advantage of the newfound freedom and walked through the gates in search of better rations. Patients in the *Revier* continued to die on a daily basis, but many rallied, patients who would have been selected for gassing if the SS had still been around.

April thirtieth marked the long-anticipated arrival of the Red Army. It was a small advance unit that came first in motorcycles followed by mechanized vehicles. They broke through the gates with guns poised, not knowing what lay beyond the imposing walls. Anticipating resistance, they were met instead by something totally unexpected, something that in all their battles, they had never seen: defenseless, emaciated, tortured women – throngs of them, all clad in dirty striped clothing. Recognizing the soldiers as Russians, some of the women cheered, while some slunk away not knowing friend from foe. Others sat unfazed, a few nearly naked, next to piles of rotting corpses, oblivious to everything around them. Ignoring them for the moment, squadrons of men filtered cautiously through the camp, conducting building-to-building searches. It wasn't long before three soldiers burst into the infirmary, automatic rifles at the ready.

They were met by a woman wearing a long white coat. Underneath were striped prison fatigues. Speaking in Russian, she said, "I am Doctor Antonina Nikiforova. I'm in charge of the camp infirmary."

The soldier looked past the doctor to the rows of patients. With a look of what could only be described as repulsion, he said, "I am Captain Boris Makarow of the 49th Soviet army."

"Captain, we are pleased to see you. The SS left weeks ago with tens of thousands of our women. We have no idea where they were headed. We expected a massacre, but I suspect they didn't feel they had the time, so we were left behind. As you can see, most of the women here are near death. Typhus, dysentery, tuberculosis, lacerations, infections, starvation – we have it all. Many die every day."

Scanning the room from side to side, the captain replied, "Doctor, I-I have no words for what I am seeing. I am appalled."

"I am happy to know there are people who still feel. Most of the people here are traumatized beyond any capacity to feel. They've been horribly tortured, physically and emotionally."

"I can see that." He slowly shook his head. "I've been in countless battles, Doctor, have come here all the way from Stalingrad . . . I've seen more killing than you can shake a stick at. . . families uprooted . . . pretty much the worst war has to offer . . ." He paused, as if to understand the purgatory surrounding him. ". . . but I've never witnessed anything like this. You have my deepest sympathy. I can assure you that we are here to liberate your camp. How can we help?"

"Sir, the infirmary's a breeding ground for lice, bedbugs, maggots and scabies. They all bring typhus. We need disinfectants and medicine . . . not just to treat these patients, but to prevent an epidemic. But more than anything, we need food. Short of that, liberation, I'm afraid, will mean very little."

"I can see that. The main army will be here in another day or two. We will do everything we can to provide what you need. I can't make any promises other than to say that things should improve from what you've got here."

"I appreciate that, Captain. As you can tell, it can't get much worse."

While they were conversing, Annika noticed the other two soldiers had put their hands to their faces. One produced a rag from his pocket and covered his nose. It registered with her that they were feeling repulsed by the stench, something that she was all but desensitized from. Observing their response made her look around to see things from their perspective. Hundreds of patients stacked in bunks, sunken faces peeking helplessly from darkened compartments, a floor cluttered with women barely clinging to life, some gasping for oxygen, others comatose, their death rattles playing out like dueling snare drums. And not quite beyond the Russians' sight lay naked lifeless bodies stacked like cordwood, their eyes open and unblinking as if searching for angels to welcome their spirit. Nauseated by the pungent odor of urine, diarrhea, pustulent sores, and body odor, one of the soldiers began to convulse with dry heaves. At that point, the captain apologized, turned with his men, and all but tripped over one another in their haste to get out.

As the day wore on, more Red Army troops entered the camp. Always smiling, they offered tidings of "*Lyudi, vy svobodny!*" Only the Russian prisoners knew what this meant, but the translation quickly spread, and before long, prisoners of all nationalities were hugging each other and exclaiming, each in their native tongues, "We're free . . . We're free!" The celebration was short-lived. By late afternoon, soldiers were coming in from nearby Fürstenberg armed with bottles of liquor confiscated from the locals. Many were already quite drunk. Any sense of order seen earlier in the day had now devolved into chaotic singing and shouting marked by loud, derisive insults about "Nazi scum."

With the electricity having been cut off by the SS at their departure, darkness descended over the camp, the only light sources being kerosene, battery power, and crackling campfires. Dark objects moved about outside, detectable only from flashlight beams strafing the air like ray-guns out of a science fiction novel. As the hours – and drinking – progressed, the revelry took on high-pitched shrieks, obviously female. Annika looked out from a darkened window, where she distinctly heard one of the men scream something about "Nazi bitches." It sent a chill up her spine. Rumors of the Red Army raping women had preceded their arrival, but no one would have imagined any such debauchery amongst the sick and diseased. Her hope had been that the soldiers would regard the prisoners as victims, not Nazis sympathizers. After all, the men had greeted the women earlier in the day as "sisters."

Apparently, things had changed. The door to the infirmary crashed open, only this time it was not well-heeled soldiers, but drunken recruits looking for women. They pushed their way in, searching by flashlight. "Fräuleins," one demanded. It was obvious he couldn't speak German, but now it appeared that they all knew the word for "women."

One of the nurses came running to the door. "*Nein,*" she screamed. "These women are sick! You must leave. Now!"

A soldier put his arms around her, muttering something in Russian. He pushed her towards a bed. She yelled at him, trying desperately to get him to leave. "*Nein. Raus hier. Geh weg!*" Her screams were muffled by one man's hand over her mouth while the other tore at her clothing. She kicked at them, wriggled side-to-side in a vain effort to break free. It was too little.

Her screams brought in more men. It didn't matter how sick or infirm the patient might be, just that their quarry was young. One of the teenagers laid low with dysentery shrieked as her bedsheets were pulled back. She huddled in a fetal position, knees encircled by arms, a look of terror on her face. "All OK, sister. Just fun," laughed one of the men, as he fumbled with his belt. A male orderly, Erich, himself a prisoner compromised by malnutrition, tried desperately to intervene, but he was no match for the troops. His efforts were met with a barrage of punches and kicks along with derisive laughter as he crawled away.

Annika could hear the commotion from the opposite wing where she and her friends had been assisting with patient care. Her initial thought was that the captain or other officers would be alerted to the melee and come by to restore order before things got out of hand. That was not to happen. Apparently, judging from the growing chorus of male voices, word had gotten out that the infirmary was the place to be. Groups of soldiers swarmed inside like bees to a hive, singing, laughing and hollering inanities amidst shrieks from terrified women.

"We need to go help," Annika said

"We can't, Annika. Listen to them. There's not a damn thing we can do," Ursula stammered. She was terrified. They all were.

Heavy footsteps clumped down the corridor. "They're coming back here," Gisele said.

"Go hide!" Annika told them in a loud whisper. "The closet. Quick!"

The two looked at her. "Are you coming?"

"Go!" Annika replied. The two women ran down the hallway to a closet, closing the door behind them. Gisele, the smaller of the two, hid in a tiny compartment built into the wall. Ursula crouched behind mops and brooms standing behind a coat rack with several white medical cloaks. Annika remained in the center of the room, surrounded by patients, all panic-stricken as the footsteps came closer.

"Fräulein!" It was a short man in battle fatigues, a rifle over his shoulder, a bottle of schnapps in the other. He was trailed by three more men, all dressed similarly and each equally intoxicated. They were all babbling in Russian, but their intentions were none too disguised.

"Please, men, you have to leave," Annika said in German. If the men didn't understand the language, they certainly understood her affect.

"*Nemetskaya suka,*" said one.

His comrade laughed. He turned to Annika. "German bitch, *ja?*" He pushed her onto a mattress and began clawing at her dress. Annika screamed, which only seemed to heighten their excitement. She struggled with all her strength until the taller of the two got hold of her wrists, pinning her arms above her head. In less than a minute, the shorter man penetrated her and began thrusting wildly. When he finished and the soldiers attempted to switch roles, Annika rolled in an effort to flee. They grabbed her again, this time twisting her arm painfully. The harder she fought, the more brutal they became. When the taller of the two backhanded her across the face, resistance drained from her body like a burst balloon, supplanted instead by helpless sobbing as the second soldier had his way with her. Once he rolled off, Annika fled like a frightened cat to the far end of the room, cowering between two beds. She caught a quick glimpse of a third soldier, laughing and spouting vulgarities, astride an older, squirming patient just a few beds away. It was a pathetic sight, the woman's frail hands balled into small fists beating against the man's back in a futile effort to free herself. Annika could only sit; there was no longer anything she could do to halt the carnage.

More soldiers entered the room, drunk and hollering, until it seemed like the entire Red Army had declared open-season on the defenseless patients. It would have been bad enough if these were strong, healthy women, but in their uniformly debilitated state, they may well have been mannequins or grotesque sex dolls, yet to officers and non-coms, alike; it didn't matter. To them, it was a free-for-all, a brothel of women there for the taking. The younger ones were the first to be selected, most of whom were gang-raped, repeatedly. As the night wore on, soldiers became less discriminating, sometimes forcing themselves on patients old enough to be their grandmothers, as well as prisoners so emaciated, they looked like corpses. Repulsive skin conditions, communicable diseases, none of that made a difference; in the fog of alcohol, everyone became fair game.

To the Red Army, these were the spoils of war, and after years of fighting and horrific exposure to Nazi atrocities, they felt fully entitled and were not to be denied. Amidst the screams, she heard one of the soldiers loudly proclaim, "We save you . . . Nazis *kaput*." It was as if they were expecting the women to show appreciation, reminding Annika of what Rolf had done several years before.

The nightmare seemed to go on forever. A few of the soldiers stumbled back to where Annika sat crouched behind a bedside table covered in sheets. She sat motionless, praying that they wouldn't see her. Somehow, they passed by, leaving her weeping silently while listening to cries from the very women who, for the past month, she had cared for. Violated and broken, she could do nothing but leave them to their own fate.

By dawn, the rampaging soldiers had vacated the infirmary, leaving behind a twilight zone of shock and numbness. It had been a raid that tore at every stitch of one's moral and emotional fabric. Patients lay wide-eyed and staring. Others lay trembling in pain and disbelief. In many cases, those who had escaped physical defilement were even more traumatized at having witnessed the victimization of women they regarded as "sisters." Annika pulled herself together, ignoring her own injuries to minister to the others. What she couldn't do for them physically, she tried to accomplish emotionally. New patients were brought in throughout the morning – all rape victims bearing labial tears, lacerated rectums, broken teeth, torn nipples, widespread contusions, and life-threatening head trauma. Some had even been stabbed. The injuries made it clear that rape in wartime was as much about power and conquest as it was about sexual gratification. Comments made by the rapists revealed a clear intent to humiliate their male combatants as unable to protect their own women. It was a direct assault on the concept of Hitler's "master race," the hyper-masculinized *Ubermensch*.

While Annika did what she could, new squadrons of Red Army rolled into the camp. The *Lagerstraße* was transformed into a staging ground of tanks, motorcycles, horses, and foot-soldiers. No more drunken celebrations: the grounds were now structured and orderly with officers waving their arms to direct men and matériel. Shortly after noon, a small contingent of soldiers entered the infirmary, where they were regaled with screams from terrified women. The men were taken aback, until Doctor Nikiforova explained the events of the previous night. To the doctor's surprise, the officer in charge was angered and apologetic, assuring him that henceforth no such behavior would be tolerated. And he went beyond even that. Food, *real food*, and basic medicines were delivered later that day.

Inmates fell all over themselves trying to gobble up as much as they could before it might disappear. Annika tried her best to discourage them from overeating, but her warnings were universally disregarded. After all, this was the first genuine sustenance many had eaten in months; for a few of the survivors, it had been years. They crammed victuals into their mouths as if it was to be their last meal on earth. And, unfortunately, for many it was. Shrunken stomachs and digestive tracts long accustomed to starvation rations were simply unprepared for such indulgence. Within hours, many prisoners became violently ill, and over the next few days, the infirmary saw a spike in mortality simply from overeating. Even the medicines proved for many too little, too late.

An aide came up to Annika while she sat for a breather between patients. "How are *you,* Tritzchler?"

"Fine," she replied.

"If you don't mind my saying it, you don't look fine."

"Just a little tired. I'm fine." Annika was as traumatized as anyone, but had long since passed the point of acknowledging her own needs. As a doctor, she felt a deep obligation to assist the injured, which, in survival mode, she felt was a useful distraction. Processing her own violations would again have to wait.

March to Uncertainty

How do you expect the Germans to revolt when they don't even dare walk on the grass?

Joseph Stalin

Northern Germany: May, 1945

"We need to go, Annika. Now. Before it's too late. If we stay here, we have no idea what the Russians'll do to us." Ursula was adamant.

"I'm not so sure . . . The patients . . ."

"Annika, you're being naïve. We're German, remember? When they discover what the SS did to their POWs, there'll be hell to pay. Doesn't matter that we're prisoners also. The Russians'll want vengeance . . . against *all* Germans."

"But where, Ursula? Where in God's name can we go?" Annika felt trapped. Life had been a living hell at Ravensbrück, but she had been there so long that she knew every day what to expect. Leaving camp was entering the unknown.

Ursula was a more recent prisoner and wasn't as worn down as Annika. "Listen, honey. You're resourceful. You're strong. Together, we have a chance to survive. Staying here is to invite disaster."

Annika realized she was right. Russians and Germans were sworn enemies, and from what she had heard from prisoners, the Wehrmacht had committed heinous atrocities against the Russian people. Retribution was sure to follow. She realized that Ursula spoke from the heart. But one question burned in her mind. "Who's going to care for the patients, Ursula? We can't just leave 'em here."

"The Reds have brought in food and medicine . . . even blood for transfusions. Doctor Nikiforova's in charge. Think of it. He's in no danger . . . he's Russian. I talked to him. He agreed that once things settle down here, you and me and all the other Germans will probably be taken prisoner by the Russians. He encouraged us to go."

"So, you and I are going alone?"

"No, we'd be in just as much trouble out there alone. There's a group of women going, most of them Poles and Slovaks . . . several who can speak Russian. As a group, we'll be safer."

"Alright." She thought for a second. "I just . . . I . . . I need time to make final rounds . . . to say some goodbyes."

"Okay. Do what you need to do, but the group's leaving in two hours. I'm going with or without you. Are you coming?"

Annika looked at her. Ursula was a true friend. "Yeah. I'll be ready."

Annika and Ursula departed Ravensbrück with thirty-seven malnourished women in the breaking dawn of early May. Adorned in tattered, lice-infested clothing, the entourage presented a drab spectacle, a testament to untold suffering. While most wore wooden clogs, a few had only rags around their feet. They carried small knapsacks hastily woven of faded cloth culled from corpses awaiting burial. With muted optimism, they bent forward into headwinds of uncertainty, knowing they could trust no one – Nazis, partisans, locals . . . not even the Russian "liberators." The Allies were their only hope.

The journey began auspiciously under a blue sky in an early spring morning. Feeling apprehensive, many expecting the worst, the women hadn't walked more than an hour before countless months of sensory deprivation gave way to a scene both different and unexpected. An array of vegetation had come to life in shades of pink, white, yellow, and purple with bees and butterflies, even an occasional hummingbird, flitting disconcertedly from one blossom to the next. The morning dampness, thick with fragrances of lilac and lilies, brought forth songbirds whistling falsetto to the downbeat of a woodpecker as it harmonized to the sound of quivering beech leaves. Cradled in the thicket was a pheasant bobbing its head as if in time to this magical orchestra where each stanza ended with the resounding caw of a raven. The women stood in stark contrast to this extraordinary lullaby.

"Listen to it," said one woman, as she strained to hear every note in the performance. Her eyes filled with tears. Hard as she tried, words to describe such beauty had all but disappeared in a brain too long fogged by ugliness.

Annika chimed in, "Frauen. Look around you. We survived Ravensbrück. We made it!" Everyone stopped to behold the opus. Squirrels darted about, chasing one another and leaping like trapeze artists from limb to limb amid the towering oaks. The Schwedtsee, the region's iconic lake, stretched out on the horizon as a large, blue basin that shimmered enticingly in the early morning light. Sunlight reflected on wavetops like tiny mirrors, glittering all the way to the opposite shoreline. It was a dazzling foreground to the half-timbered houses that lay beyond. Early May, this was *Frühling*, the season of rebirth – a time for passion . . . and dreams. The day was bursting with possibility.

Not for everyone. Katya stumbled along, too depleted to think. None of this was registering in her mind. Annika noticed and flung her arms around her. "Katya, dear. You made it! We're out. Free! You have your life back. We have a future!"

"Freedom . . . beauty . . . a future." Though she said the words aloud, they somehow felt hollow. Annika repeated them, over and over again, trying to feel what rolled off her tongue as sound without meaning. For too long, she had lived in the grimmest of circumstances where visceral responses to everyday cruelty faded into emotional disconnect, robbing her of humanness in the process. As words lost adequacy in grasping those horrors, the language center of her brain began to atrophy. Annika had resilience, she was alive, but inside she was numb, a child without language, passively manipulating the environment with one goal in mind: survival.

Slowly, the group trudged down the roads looking a bit like mountaineers starved of oxygen, mustering every last ounce of strength to simply place one foot in front of the other. Within an hour, they reached Fürstenberg, a town of about ten thousand, the one that from the camp they had looked over to, fantasizing well-fed villagers going about their business while they themselves suffered under hard labor. They recognized the train station, where each had been transported, packed like sardines in excrement-filled cattle cars. The town was eerily quiet now, not at all like their arrival years before when they were marched under heavy guard from the railyards to the camp as villagers taunted them with epithets and children pelted them with stones and rotten vegetables. That scene had played itself out for years, and though they would later deny it, the townsfolk knew exactly what was going on across the lake. And now, descending on the town came some of the victims: Russians, Poles, Czechs, and Romanians – Jews and Christians alike – women of ashen skin, close-cropped hair, and filthy striped uniforms. Propagandized as *untermenschen,* these were the survivors: intrepid, tenacious women who had endured incomprehensible deprivations and atrocities – women whose wrath the villagers had good reason to fear.

But as it turned out, the Red Army had already laid waste to the village. Signs of destruction were everywhere, and conspicuously absent were menfolk. Women split into raiding parties in search of provisions for the long walk ahead. Annika herself, accompanied by two others, barged into a modest-looking home off the main street. There, cowering in the corner of a living room, was a middle-aged woman and a young girl in her early adolescence. They were clutching each other, looking terrified by the intruders.

"Please," cried out the older woman. "We've been through enough. Please, leave us." They held each other tightly.

Annika responded in German, "We're not here to hurt you. We simply need food and water, maybe some extra clothing." Annika's confederates split off to rummage through the small house, while Annika stayed with the residents. The girl's dress was ripped, and one eye blackened, while the older woman's hair was stringy and matted. Annika surmised they too had been raped. She came in thinking of them as the enemy, yet couldn't look at them without feeling some compassion. Instinctively, she reached out to comfort them. Their reaction was telling. Recoiling backwards, they flattened against the wall as far from her grasp as possible.

"What on earth happened to you?" she inquired. They remained mute. "It's okay," Annika said soothingly, "you can talk to me. We've had our own hardships, as I'm sure you can tell."

The women looked at each other before the older one spoke. "The R-Russians . . ." she stammered, ". . . they came through two days ago . . . rampaged through the town. Most of our men were rounded up. They shot the old men." Her lips quavered. "They beat people . . . stole everything of value."

"Go on," Annika encouraged.

The woman opened up to Annika, one German to another. "We hid here in the house, but they busted open the door and found us. At first . . . w-we tried to bribe them, but they ransacked our house and took our valuables. We begged them . . . pleaded with them . . . but the more we begged, the more abusive they became. Then, the soldiers . . ." She hesitated, unable to finish the sentence. "It wasn't our fault . . . We pleaded with them . . ." She squeezed her eyes, forcing tears to stream down her cheeks. "They *raped* us . . . repeatedly. Me and my daughter." She wrapped her arms around the girl, who sobbed at her mother's side. "I had to watch my own daughter . . . with those disgusting savages!" Annika nodded knowingly. "There was nothing we could do. The soldiers marauded through the town . . . did the same to most of the women. Some were even killed."

Annika and her two friends had been through far too much themselves to be shocked by the story. Nothing surprised them. Annika turned and grasped the girl's hand, saying, "I'm a doctor, hon'. Nobody's here to hurt you. We're from the concentration camp. When the Russians came into our compound, they did the same to us, even to the Russian women." She stroked the younger one's hair. "I have no medicine, but if you have any wounds that you'd like me to look at, I could at least help clean them."

The women shook their heads, still distrustful. "If we need to, we can go to the Fürstenberg Palace up the road. It's been converted to a hospital . . . if it's still there," she added. "God only knows what they might've done to it." The mother pleaded. "We're afraid they'll come back. What can we do?"

Annika found it ironic that she, a woman labelled an "enemy of the State," was now being asked by her persecutors for help. Nevertheless, she warned them. "You're right, there may be more Russians on the way. I don't know your town, so I have no idea where you can hide, but you need to find refuge. Things could get even worse if they come back." Annika's two companions had just reentered the room after having rummaged through the house for supplies. Annika turned once again to the mother and daughter.

"Listen, you're both welcome to join our group, if you want. We're in search of the Allies. Doesn't matter to us whether they're British or American, just so long as they're not Nazis or Russians. We're looking for shelter and protection, just like you."

The mother wailed, "This is our home . . . our life. Where are we supposed to go? This is all we know. We can't leave."

"Then I wish you luck," Annika said, as she and the others turned to rejoin the group.

The Ravensbrück contingent trudged on, but days of marching, especially without adequate footwear, proved too much for some. Katya, a Polish woman in her fifties, had developed ugly, bleeding ulcers on both feet. "The pain in my feet is unbearable," she cried, sitting down on the roadside. Rubbing her feet, she waved her friends forward. "You all go on. Just leave me. I can't go any further"

"You *can*, Katya. Try! Once we find some water, I'll take care of your feet. For the time being, let's just wrap them . . ." Annika bent down to assist. "You've got to keep going. You can't stay here," encouraged Annika.

With rags serving as bandages, she got up and tried once again, but after a hundred meters or so, she stopped. "Go on. All of you.

Please. I can't do it." It was no use. Her spark was gone. To stay with her or to seek refuge for her put the entire group in jeopardy. For miles, they had shuffled past decomposing bodies, some from the death march of the previous month (most with a bullet hole to the head), others simple townsfolk who, for whatever reason, had run afoul of the Wehrmacht.

"We need to keep going," someone said. Everyone knew she was right, yet leaving behind a "sister," someone who had shared in the camp's merciless suffering, was beyond poignant. Hugs and heartfelt words of encouragement fell on deaf ears, for Katya, like the others, realized this was her end. Having endured so many losses, she didn't anguish or express any recriminations, but instead accepted her fate with equanimity and composure. Katya would be the first, though others would follow.

The group journeyed on, often detouring through remote countryside to dodge Nazi patrols, at this point more imagined than real. Very few villages along the way had escaped Allied bombing, and while the dilapidated housing offered some refuge from the elements, there was very little to be scavenged. Hungry and tired, the women sensed they were in the crosshairs of two global forces, the Allied and Axis powers – armies which to Annika represented good and evil. *I feel like we're walking into Armageddon.*

But that wasn't to be. The soldiers they encountered scurrying through towns and fields looked unkempt, some partially out of uniform and carrying no weapons. "They're deserters," Irma said. "Running for their lives." Though the women gave them wide berth, the soldiers showed no interest in bringing further harm to these defenseless women. In towns and hamlets, people seemed scared and confused, but the consensus was that capture by the Americans was preferable to Russians bent on revenge and fast on their heels. So, the group persevered. They eventually came to a road sign indicating they were on the outskirts of Lübz, a small town known for its brewery. By this point, they had walked over one hundred kilometers, averaging eight kilometers per day. Walking down the center of the road, the women found themselves blocking the American 87th Cavalry Reconnaissance Squadron.

"We need to get through here," announced a young private. In one hand, he carried an M-14 rifle, in the other a cigarette. Chewing on a wad of gum, he commanded, "C'mon. Clear out!" Nobody moved. Annika knew what he was saying, but contacting the Americans was exactly what they had been waiting for. Their only chance. "Who are you, anyway?" the soldier drawled. He had never seen anything to rival this rag-draped mass now blocking his unit's mechanized advance. Haggard and sticklike, they looked like they were from another world. They were.

Several women mumbled to him in their native tongues, but speaking only English, he shook his head and frowned, having no idea what they were saying. With his unit stopped dead in its tracks, a jeep drove up hurriedly from the rear. An officer jumped out, the stub of a foul-smelling cigar clutched between his teeth, and walked over to the women. "I'm Captain Knowlton. What's going on here?"

Annika muscled her way through the group. She had studied English in the gymnasium and had read many American and British medical journals. "We're prisoners . . . from the concentration camp at Ravensbrück . . ."

"The what? I don't know what you're talking about."

"We were imprisoned for several years in a work camp east of here. Ravensbrück. There were probably thirty thousand women in forced labor. The SS forced all but a few thousand of us on a death march just before the Red Army came in. They acted as liberators but within hours began raping the women. We fled the camp and now we're caught between the Nazis and the Russians."

"You shouldn't have anything to worry about at this point." He tried to be reassuring. "We're moving east to meet the Red Army. It's advancing in our direction. The British are closing in from the north, not more than a few kilometers away. We've got the Nazis on the run. Yesterday, the Third Panzer Army surrendered to us."

These details were lost on Annika. She'd been confined for too long. Her only outside contacts were prisoners transported from other camps. Now it was simply a question of survival. "Captain, as you can see, we're starving. The Nazis kept us locked up for years. We've been on the run for over two weeks with almost no provisions. Can you help us? Please. Several of us can't go on. We've already been forced to leave several of our group by the roadside . . . probably to die."

The captain was initially irritated. His orders were to move forward, posthaste, yet there was something about the women that softened him. He turned to his radio operator. "Dixon, call Field HQ and see if we can arrange for these ladies to be transported to the nearest DP center."

Ladies? Am I losing my mind? Ladies. She repeated the word as if trying to force her mind to recognize it. She looked quizzically at the American officer, dashing, she thought, in his tight-fitting uniform. Then she looked back at the squalidness of her companions. The contrast was striking.

A few minutes elapsed before the radioman gave a "thumbs up" to the captain. "Two hours," he yelled. Turning back to Annika, the captain said, "We'll have trucks here later this afternoon. They'll get you to shelter. Meanwhile, ma'am, *if you don't mind*, we've got to push on." He looked at her for a few seconds. "Two weeks you been out here? Amazing. Listen, I'll leave your group with some food and water while you wait." And with that, he walked off, barking instructions and waving his arms, several times pointing back to the women. Annika watched him retreat, smitten by his courteousness and solicitude. *Ladies,* she thought. *Indeed . . .*

Two young recruits came forward with a case of C-rations and jugs of water. "We only have a few spoons and cups to spare, so you'll have to make do with these." The women didn't need to understand English to recognize generosity. They crowded forward with a deference that spoke a language all its own. Two of the refugees fell to their knees, hugging the legs of the recruits. They, in turn, were all smiles as the women were reminders of mothers and grandmothers back home.

"You probably ain't had any of these for a while," said the corporal, as he handed out American-made chocolate. Most had never seen a Hershey bar. Annika had. The candy bars brought forth a memory of a time back in Berlin where she and her father had sampled some of the imported chocolate. She remembered him contrasting it with Swiss chocolate. He had called Hershey's, "poor man's chocolate," but to the women, Annika included, it was nothing less than scrumptious.

"*Mein Gott,*" one crooned through lips stained in melted chocolate. "*Das schmeckt so gut!*" purred another. In fact, it was too good; one bar simply wasn't enough. Having had no sugar for years, the women devoured the candy to the delight of the soldiers, who continued to feed it to them until the box was empty. By then, Annika had eaten three.

"Careful, now," warned the corporal. "You don't wanna get sick . . ."

As Annika chomped on the remainder of the candy bar, she looked over at the others. It was a scene that she would never forget. Women who looked like they had been to hell and back – ragged and gaunt, smelly and exhausted – now clamored with the excitement of children, faces and hands smeared in brown. A sugar high. Things were looking up.

Bergen-Belsen DP Camp

Freedom comes from seeing the ignorance of your critics and discovering the emptiness of their virtue.

Ayn Rand

Northwest Germany: July, 1945

"C'mon there, lassies. Step lively, now. Up onto the lorries." It was a British sergeant. He was waving his arms in circles, encouraging the line of women to board several military trucks that were idling nearby.

The war was over, but widespread chaos had only begun. Shortly after their rescue by the Americans, Annika and her fellow marchers had been turned over to the British, who occupied Germany's northern zone. They were among the lucky, for hundreds of thousands of former prisoners and forced laborers were streaming aimlessly throughout towns and villages, all competing for basic subsistence. A human tragedy was in the making: starving refugees hundreds of miles from their native homelands, yet with railyards and roads suffering heavy bomb damage, there was no transportation to repatriate them. Even worse, though few knew it at the time, was that for those who did find a way back home, a majority would discover their houses either destroyed or inhabited by strangers determined to keep their ill-gotten gain.

"Where are we going?" Annika asked the sergeant. She was frightened. Even though these were British, the scene reenacted memories of arrest and deportation.

"Nothing to worry about, Mum. You're going to a DP camp . . . not far from here. Better facilities. Room and board. Now, c'mon.

291

Let's move it."

He didn't really answer her question, which made her even more nervous. "What's a DP camp?"

"D-P. You know. Displaced persons. There are millions o' blokes wandering all over Europe . . . no place to go, no homes to return to. In the cities, they're livin' in bombed-out buildings. No plumbing or electricity. People livin' in rooms without walls. But fact is, mum, they're better off'n people out'n the country. A lotta dem are sleepin' in the open, freezin' their arses off . . . starvin' to boot."

"Who's responsible for them?"

"Mum?" he said, not really understanding her question.

"The DP camps. Who's setting them up . . . managing them? Where's the money coming from? I can't imagine the Germans . . ."

"No, no, no. Not them bastards. The camps I'm familiar with'r run through the United Nations."

"So, where's the one you're taking us to?" she asked again.

"Oh, 'bout fifty kilometers south of here, I'd say. Couple hours. No more than that. Camp's called *Hohne*." His eyes met hers for just a moment before he looked away.

Another camp? Where we'll be treated well? Is this just another lie, another forced labor transport? Annika didn't know what to believe. *If the Brit's idea of liberation is what we experienced with the Russians, we might as well have stayed at Ravensbrück. After all,* she reasoned, *I'm a German – sworn enemy of the Allies. Even my own countrymen will turn their back on me when they learn that I was a prisoner of the Reich.* She eyed the rifle strapped over the man's shoulder, and then looked across to the other soldiers, some joking as they watched, *just like the SS.* But, once again, there were no options.

The women boarded the trucks. Three hours later, they were bumping down a long driveway leading to an abandoned SS checkpoint. It was now manned by well-armed British troops. They waved the vehicles through the gates and into a massive complex of brick buildings surrounded by walls and barbed wire. Thousands of people milled about, many walking skeletons, some in civilian clothing, but most wearing striped pajamas. Annika's heart sank. It looked just like Sachsenhausen and Ravensbrück.

"Another damn trick," screamed one of the women. "This is no relief shelter." Panic spread through the trucks, as women sensed their worst fears being realized. They were convinced the Brits had transported them to another forced labor camp.

Annika felt betrayed. Seething with anger, she did something she would never have done in a Nazi camp. *They can beat me, or even kill me. I don't care. I can't take any more.* She broke ranks, hurrying over to an officer who seemed to be in charge. He fingered his holster, not quite sure whether she represented a threat. "What is this?" she demanded. "We were told we were going to a United Nations camp! This is a goddamned KZ."

"Calm down, Mum. Bloody hell. No need bangin' on me," he responded. "I don't know what a KZ is, but this is a DP camp. For people what ain't got no homes."

"We've spent years in Nazi concentration camps doing hard labor. None of us are criminals, or ever have been. We were arrested for resisting the Nazis. Every last one of us has been starved, whipped, beaten . . . forced to work sunup to sundown in the worst weather, without adequate clothing. Thousands just like us were killed – every day! We can't do this anymore! You might as well kill us now . . . get it over with."

"Whoa, whoa . . . you got yer knickers all in a twist, Mum," he said, putting both hands up to stop her. "We ain't gonna kill any o' ya lassies. Them Nazi plonkers ain't got no bollocks. Every kraut we captured'll be in Her Majesty's Pleasure before they know what hit 'em. This here is the Bergen-Hohne DP camp . . . temporary quarters 'til we can send ye back to where ye come from."

Annika couldn't understand everything he was saying, so she got right to the point. "Bergen-Hohne? Who're you trying to kid? I saw a road sign for Belsen a few kilometers back. I'm no idiot. This has to be the Bergen-Belsen concentration camp. We were lied to!" By now, the atrocities committed by the Nazis at Bergen-Belsen had been widely reported by the wire services and were well-known, even among former prisoners.

"No, Mum. Wrong. You weren't lied to. This *is* the former site of Bergen-Belsen, but we liberated it. It's now a DP camp . . . not a bloody prison camp. We give it a new name: Bergen-Hohne." Someone called to him. "'Scuse me a second." He shouted instructions to two of his men, who were struggling with a few of the frenzied women.

Annika gasped. "Please! Let them go. Don't hurt them!"

"They'll be fine. Nobody's tearin' the piss outtn' 'em. We fancy our lassies. The sergeant there's just tryin' to get them outt'n way o' the lorries." The captain whistled to a jeep, making a circling motion with his arms. Turning back to Annika, he said, "Sorry, Mum. Where were we?"

"You were starting to tell me . . ."

". . . Oh, yeah, right . . . So, in fact, we've moved our camp a short distance away from the original camp for health reasons. See over there?" He pointed to rows of charred debris, where, judging from concrete rectangular foundations, buildings once stood. "Those were prisoner barracks. When we arrived, they were oozing . . . if you'll pardon the French . . . oozing in shit and piss and dead bodies. They stank to all get-out." Annika had no difficulty picturing this. "All the prisoners were covered in lice and rashes . . . you name it, they had it. We burned the prisoner buildings to prevent the spread of disease."

"Sounds like Typhus. We had it at Ravensbrück," Annika said, knowingly.

"Well, there was that and a lot of other stuff. I'm no doctor, but there's been a lot of disease here. Goddamned Krauts. It's wonky. Makin' people wallow in their own shit. Krauts ain't 'uman. No bollocks, none of 'em. Ne'er seen nothin' like."

"But Captain, there's still the smell of decomposing bodies in the air. That's something you can't hide."

"Mum, even just a fortnight ago, there was fifteen thousand

stiffs. Piles of 'em, rows of 'em. Bodies rotting in rail cars. They were all over the goddamned place. Prisoners sittin' next to 'em . . . even leanin against 'em, like they lost their marbles. We found starkers layin' in 'er bunks drenched in diarrhea, stiffs layin' right next to 'em."

"Fifteen thousand . . . dead?" Annika looked around, trying to imagine such a large number.

"No exaggeration, mum. This was a killing center. Everywhere . . . rotting, stinking corpses. We forced the camp guards and officers to bury them, but after a while, 'at was useless. So many bodies, we needed bulldozers to push 'em all into a pit. So, no, mum, this ain't no concentration camp. We're here to save lives, not kill people."

Looking around, Annika said, "But, Captain, if you'll excuse my openness, the majority of these people look wretched, like they're dying."

"You're right. Many are dying. About five hundred a day, at this point. The goddamned Nazis starved 'em and beat 'em so badly that I'm afraid no amount of food or medicine'll save 'em. What we really need are more doctors and nurses."

"I'm a doctor. Maybe I could help."

"You're a doctor?" He looked her up and down, as if in disbelief. "Did you say you're a doctor?" Annika nodded. "Well, Doctor, you've come to the right place. Follow me. I'll take you to the clinic. Introduce you to the medical staff." He paused for a second. "By the way, Mum. What's your name?"

"Tritzchler. Annika Tritzchler."

The Pianist

To live is to suffer, to survive is to find some meaning in the suffering.

Friedrich Nietzsche

Bergen-Belsen DP Camp: July, 1945

Annika had only been at the DP camp for a week, but already she had found the hospital sorely lacking in essential supplies. She was encouraged by a British lieutenant to make an inventory of her needs and requisition them through the garrison's command. She eagerly complied and took the completed forms across the campus for authorization. As she approached the adjutant's office, she heard faint sounds of a piano drifting from an open window above. She stopped for a moment to listen. It was Chopin, she felt sure, and with her love of classical music, she couldn't resist finding out who was at the keyboard.

She wound her way up the staircase to a small antechamber where she tiptoed to the doorway. By this time, the pianist, a nattily-dressed woman with her back to Annika, had begun with another composition, this one more ethereal. The performer was unmistakably a former prisoner, judging from her gaunt frame, yet any atrophy in her body had not found its way to her fingers, which glided along the ivories with the confidence and grace of a concert pianist. The slow, tepid arrangement was haunting and played with deep emotion. It lifted Annika high above the ugliness of a death-camp, creating, if only for a moment, a transcendence beyond words. She closed her eyes, basking in a journey produced by every heartfelt chord. When it was over, there was total silence, the pianist in a reverie all her own.

Annika waited almost a full minute before whispering, "That was beautiful."

The woman, who had been unaware of Annika's presence, remained motionless. As if to herself, she said, "Albioni."

"Yes," replied Annika, softly. "The Adagio, in G minor."

The pianist slowly opened her eyes as if something inside her had awakened. She turned with a smile, studying her admirer. Without saying anything, she patted the bench as if to acknowledge a kindred spirit. Annika sat beside her, and after arranging herself on the bench, she placed her own fingers on the keys. "Would you mind?" she asked.

"Not at all," the older woman replied with a distinctly Polish accent.

Annika hadn't been in front of a piano for years, maybe longer. It wasn't a question of remembering *how* to play; it was what all those years had done to her spirit. Could she elicit even a semblance of the life-force that had always animated her performance? Plinking out a few halting notes, her eyes quickly filled with tears, blocking her from being able to see the keys. She had to stop. Unrattled, the other pianist sat patiently, almost knowingly. Minutes passed in silence. Then the woman said, "Please . . . continue."

Something in her voice suggested that she understood. Wiping tears from her cheeks, Annika looked back to the keyboard and tapped out a few tentative chords. Something connected in her brain, and her fingers took over from there, creating a somber, almost haunting rendition of "Moonlight Sonata." The person beside her listened as if spellbound. Her eyes closed, a thin smile crossed her face.

When Annika had finished, it was clear that there was no longer one, but two pianists. The woman looked at Annika in the way a doting mother looks at her child. "I am Martyna," she said, extending her hand. "Martyna Raskiewicz."

"Annika Tritzchler. A pleasure. I was moved by your playing.

Would it be too forward to ask where you acquired such skill?"

"You are much too kind," Raskiewicz responded. "But let me say that if I have any skill, and many would find that debatable, I would give all credit to my instructors at the Conservatory of Music . . . in Warsaw."

Tilting her head, eyebrows raised, Annika said, "The Warsaw Conservatory? Where Chopin studied?"

"Yes. I studied there for a short time. I might have continued, but it became quite clear I didn't have the talent to achieve my aspirations, so . . . I enrolled in medical school." Her voice trailed off. Sounding melancholy, she said, as if an afterthought, "That was long ago . . . in better times."

Annika perked up. "You're a physician?"

"Yes. I'm a surgeon. And you?"

"I'm a physician as well, though undoubtedly quite rusty. Hard labor at Ravensbrück doesn't really keep one up-to-date with the medical world," Annika said.

Martyna grimaced. "So, you've been assigned to the infirmary?"

"Yes. I've only been here a week. Not sure yet how I'm gonna be able to help. The situation seems overwhelming here. I was actually on my way to requisition supplies when I heard you playing."

"I'm so glad to meet you. We *are* overwhelmed and, yes, supplies are stretched . . . in some cases non-existent. But we really need the help of trained doctors to reduce the mortality rate. I think we'll work well together."

As the weeks passed, hundreds of former prisoners died – victims of torture, exhaustion and starvation. But, gradually, the medical staff was able to contain typhus and tuberculosis, and the number of deaths per day began to drop. Annika's work was taxing, at times almost unforgiving, but she found great solace and energy from her collegiality with Martyna. She viewed Martyna's competence as unsurpassed, though sadly belied by her appearance. Only fifty years of age, the surgeon was already stooped and walked with a slow, deliberate gait, more like someone in their seventies. Her graying hair was so thin that no amount of coiffing could hide the faded, beige scalp underneath, and her arms and neck, wrinkled and lifeless, were pocked in dry, scaly patches, the remnants of boils and scabies that had been the scourge of prisoners throughout concentration camps. Perhaps more striking was the large gap in her mouth caused by two missing teeth.

Everyone at Belsen had a story, all of them tragic, yet few were more poignant than that of Doctor Raskiewicz. Annika learned that Martyna, who was Jewish, had initially escaped deportation after discovering that her mother and father had been sent to Treblinka, presumably murdered. She went into hiding, only to be captured six months later in Kielce, where she was making her way to the Slovakian border. A brutal interrogation by the Gestapo led to her missing teeth. In the end, having extracted no meaningful information, they deported her to Auschwitz-Birkenau where she narrowly escaped the gas chamber when it was learned she was a physician, someone who could be useful to the war effort. The I.G. Farben conglomerate had constructed a large factory at Auschwitz to produce buna, a synthetic rubber much needed for military vehicles, and medical personnel were needed to preserve the labor force. It was only when the Red Army neared the facility that she joined thousands of others in a brutal death-march, which took a further toll on her body.

The Austrian Patient

Each betrayal begins with trust.
Martin Luther

23 July, 1945

The first patient to be checked on as part of her morning rounds was a ruddy-faced, pleasant man in his early forties who appeared well-nourished and in reasonably good health, not the typical visage of a camp inmate. He had been admitted to hospital earlier in the week with nausea and severe stomach pains consistent with appendicitis. An emergency appendectomy was performed, which the patient tolerated unremarkably.

"How are you feeling today, Herr Van de Velde," Annika inquired, placing her stethoscope on the patient's chest.

"Much better than when I came in. My stomach's sore, but not like it was a few days ago."

Inspecting the incision, Annika replied, "Well, you're a lucky man. Your appendix was quite inflamed. I'd say you got in here just in time." She dabbed some ointment on the scar. "Everything's looking good. Sutures are secure . . . no signs of infection." Annika felt somehow uplifted to be back doing clinical work. It was her first glimmer that the war was ending, that maybe she had truly survived.

"I appreciate that." Lifting his head a few inches from the pillow to look Annika in the eyes, he asked, "So how long do you expect I will be here?"

"Why? You in a rush to get somewhere? Maybe a train to catch?" Annika asked, attempting a bit of levity.

"Oh, I'm just eager to get back home. I plan to leave here as soon

300

as this heals."

Annika thought this odd. Europe was a disaster zone with limited to non-existent transportation due to bomb damage. In addition, the cities were in chaos, controlled by British, French, American, and Russian forces, each having their own rules and regulations. Most people considered the DP camps to be the safest refuges, so it seemed strange, or maybe just ignorant, for her patient to be thinking of leaving so soon. "Well, you'll be here for at least a few more days. No rush. You're still catheterized. Once we remove the catheter and you can pee on your own, we'll transfer you back to your barracks." She placed the stethoscope on his chest. "So, tell me, Herr Van de Velde, what brings . . ."

The patient cut her off. "Oh, please, Doctor. Call me Jens."

"Oh . . . okay, *Jens*." She moved the stethoscope across his chest. "So, what I was going to ask you is what brings you to Belsen?"

"Trying to make my way back to Austria . . . to my people."

"Ah . . . and where are you coming from?" Annika asked, as she leaned down to close his gown and pull up the sheets.

"I was in Belgium," he casually replied.

Annika stopped what she was doing to look directly at him. "Belgium? Where?"

"Oh, a little town outside of Antwerp." He seemed vague. "Nice area . . . until the Nazis came in, that is."

"If you don't mind my asking, why were you in Belgium? You know . . . if you're from Austria."

"*Ach*, the *Anschluss*," he replied, without missing a beat. "When the tanks rolled into Austria, I got out while it was still possible. I had relatives there, and I thought Belgium would be safe. Never figured the Nazis would be invading every country in Europe."

"But why you would want to get out of Austria. I thought the Austrians welcomed the *Anschluss*."

He eyed her cautiously. "Don't know if you heard, Doctor, but the *Anschluss* wasn't so good for the Jews."

"You're Jewish?"

"Last time I looked . . ." He lifted the sheet and made a gesture of looking down to his midsection – a feeble attempt at levity, knowing that Annika was aware he had been circumcised. She smiled. "So, how 'bout you?" he continued. "Why are you in a DP camp?"

Annika thought this an abrupt shift, like he wanted to change the topic. But maybe not so unusual. After all, people had learned over the years to keep things to themselves. One never knew who it was safe to share information with, or where it might lead. On the other hand, with him coming from Belgium, he might be able to shed some light on the fate of her parents.

"I was employed at a facility that had begun euthanizing patients that were considered mentally defective," Annika began. "I refused to participate, which resulted in me being sent to Sachsenhausen, a concentration camp outside of Berlin. Maybe you've heard of it." Van de Welde frowned. "Well, eventually, I was released, but not long afterwards was denounced by a neighbor and got mislabeled a *Mischling* . . ."

"What does that mean, 'mislabeled?'"

"I was raised in a German Christian family, but after my father died . . . I was only two . . . my mother remarried a Jewish man. The neighbor . . . well, let's just say he was . . . vindictive. He informed the authorities that I had Jewish blood . . ."

"And they didn't send you to Auschwitz?"

"It's a long story. Not something I want to go into. Too much heartache."

"So, you'll be going home now? To Berlin?"

"I don't have a home there. Not anymore. My parents . . ." She looked away. ". . . they also emigrated to Belgium." Jens tucked in his chin and stared, wide-eyed, at Annika. "When Hitler came to power in '33, my parents saw how dangerous things were becoming. They figured it was only a matter of time before my stepfather would be arrested. I encouraged them to leave. It was, well, very hard, as you can imagine. But my stepfather had acquaintances in Belgium, which made it easier. They left in 1935. I haven't heard from them in almost three years, and have no idea where they are . . . or even if they're still alive." Her voice faltered.

"Have you checked with the UNRRA?"

"I . . . I'm not following you."

"Oh, sorry. The United Nations Relief and Rehabilitation Administration. You could try them. They're compiling lists of both casualties and displaced persons . . . trying to reunite families. They might have some information . . ."

"Really?" She raised her eyebrows and straightened up. "I haven't heard of that organization. Good steer. I'll definitely look into it." She pulled up a stool and sat by his bedside. In a low voice, she said, "Listen, before I contact them, let me ask you. You're coming from Belgium. Could you tell me what things were like there . . . you know, for Jewish residents? I've heard rumors . . ."

He cut her off. "Doctor Tritzchler, don't trouble yourself with rumors. Most of them are unfounded."

"Sure, but what I mean is . . . people have said that Belgian Jews were deported . . . you know, to the camps. They say that tens of thousands were murdered . . . at places like . . . Auschwitz." Annika could hardly say the word, but she stared at him, pleadingly, hoping he might have a clue to her parent's whereabouts.

Instead, the big man squirmed in his bed. "Listen. Everything was fine for Jews until 1940. That's when the anti-Jewish legislation went into effect. I don't know if your parents were there then, but that's around the time Jewish businesses were closed down." Sweat beaded above his lip. "Could you hand me a towel?" he asked.

As he wiped his forehead, Annika asked, "Is that when they began the deportations?"

"Resettlements," he said, correcting her. "They were resettlements, Doctor Tritzchler, not deportations." He rolled to his side, becoming entangled in his bedsheets. She reached down to help straighten them. There was something about his demeanor that made Annika think he was uncomfortable with the conversation.

"'Deportation' sounds terribly ominous, wouldn't you agree . . ." It was clear to her that he was somehow uncomfortable with the conversation. Hoisting himself into an upright position, he asked, "Could you pass me that water, please? I'm parched." She handed him the glass, which he took with a slight tremble, causing him to spill a few drops onto his belly. As he gulped down the water, Annika waited, which added to his tension. After a minute or so, he continued. "So, where were we . . .? Oh, yes . . . yes. You see, Doctor, many people *were* resettled, that's true, but not just Jews. They resettled Gentiles too, most of whom, I might add, were ordinary Belgian citizens."

"You say 'resettled,' Herr Van de Velde. It sounds like you don't believe they were murdered. Is that true?" Not feeling completely at ease with her patient, Annika reverted to his surname.

"Listen. I know you're worried about your family, and I would be too if I was in your shoes, but if it eases your mind a little, most of those who were resettled, at least as far as I know, were sent to work in German factories." Annika looked perplexed. "Think of it this way, Doctor. The Nazis weren't stupid. They weren't going to kill people who could work for them. Right?"

"And what about those who weren't capable of work? You're not suggesting that the Nazis would just let them be, are you?"

"My dear, The Germans would keep them alive to preserve the family. After all, a happy worker, or at least someone who's not anguishing over lost family members, is going to be more productive, and isn't that what the Nazis needed more than anything? Maximum output. They did anything they could to achieve that goal."

Annika didn't know what to make of this man. Sure, she wanted to believe in the possibility of her parents still being alive, and sure, both she and Martyna alike had been used by the Nazis to keep able-bodied workers alive to bolster the production of war materiel, but after all she had seen and been through, the man seemed to be leaving out the bigger part of the story. *Is it possible he could be so unaware?* she wondered. She didn't know what to make of his rationalizations.

She didn't want to prejudge him, but *he almost sounds like an apologist for the Nazis.* "You're trying to be optimistic, Herr Van de Welde, to give me hope, and I appreciate that . . ."

"Not at all, Doctor Tritzchler. Trust me, there's a lot of mistruth out there. People just don't know. And I'm not convinced we'll ever know the whole truth." He reached out to take Annika's hand, holding it gently while trying to sound reassuring. "What I'm trying to say is, there's certainly a chance that your parents are still alive."

Annika forced a smile. "Well . . . that would certainly be nice." She looked away, not at all convinced. "But for now, you need to rest. Maybe we can talk more later."

She had encouraged Van de Welde, who had been bedridden for almost two weeks, to get his blood circulating by walking up and down the aisles of the clinic. It was on one of these forays that Annika heard a loud disturbance break out down the corridor. Annika turned just in time to see a woman, who was screaming at the top of her lungs, push a patient backwards into a bedside table, dislodging the contents onto the floor in a thunderous crash of metal and shattering glass. Annika ran down the hallway while the perpetrator, a malnourished woman with scraggly dark hair, stood over Van de Velde hollering, "You goddamned collaborator! You fucking scum." With all the force the woman could muster, she kicked him repeatedly in his side, causing Van de Velde to let out a piercing shriek. "You're a fucking traitor," she screamed, this time delivering a forceful kick to his head. As he writhed on the floor, she dropped down to pummel him with her fist, pounding his head like a blacksmith forging a piece of iron. Attendants were on her in seconds, but by then Van de Welde, who was clutching his side in a fetal position, was only barely conscious. The woman was dragged away screaming profanity-laced accusations of Van de Velde "murdering his own people."

Annika couldn't get there fast enough. Taking one look at her patient, she kneeled down to examine him. Blood was already pooling on the outside of his robe. "Try to stay still," she said, opening his gown to check on the incision. Through the blood and gore, she could tell that only a few of the sutures remained in place. It was almost a certainty that he had internal injuries. "We need to get you to the operating room – *fast*." She waved for help.

Gritting his teeth, Jens muttered, "Th-that . . . woman. Make her stop . . ." He wasn't convinced the beating had stopped. He squeezed his eyes in pain, while Annika cradled his head. Three orderlies reached down to maneuver him onto a stretcher.

"Take him to the O.R.," Annika directed. "I'll call Doctor Raskiewicz."

A Collaborator

The greatest braggarts are usually the biggest cowards.
Jean-Jacques Rousseau

<u>24 July, 1945</u>

Annika met Martyna in the dining hall later that evening. She carried a tray to the table, where the surgeon was already seated with a bowl of goulash and bread. Chomping on a piece of bread, she looked unusually fatigued, but brightened when she saw her friend.

Annika pulled out a chair and sat opposite her. "How did things go . . . with Van de Velde," Annika asked, spreading marmalade on her bread.

"Quite an undertaking. We had to go in and re-stitch the abdominal wall. It was an absolute mess. Spleen and liver are both bruised and edematous. We've got to make sure the swelling doesn't cause abdominal compartment syndrome." Annika sipped her tea. "At the moment, though, things are stable. No indication of peritonitis, but that could change depending on the hematomas. It'll be touch-and-go, I suppose, for the next few days. He's concussed, as well, as I'm sure you figured." She paused to take a bite of her own food.

"That's probably the least of his problems," Annika said, through a mouthful of goulash.

"What on earth triggered the attack?"

Annika put down her spoon. "I talked with the woman who had the outburst, Estelle Janssen. She was still pretty hysterical, even though they had sedated her. I have to say, Martyna, if her allegations are true, I feel like a complete fool."

Martyna looked at Annika through raised eyebrows as she lit a cigarette. "And . . ."

"First off, Frau Janssen alleges that our Jens Van de Velde is not at all who he says he is. His real name, according to her, is Gustav Bergmann . . ."

Martyna interrupted, "I don't understand. Why would he give us a false name?"

Annika held up her hand to stop the surgeon. "Well, wait. Let me finish. It gets better. He's not just Gustav Bergmann. He's *Rabbi* Gustav Bergmann."

"*What?* He's a rabbi?" Martyna waved away smoke from her cigarette. Annika had her full attention.

"Yeah. From what she says, this man, Bergmann, is a collaborator. He grew up in a Jewish family which immigrated to Belgium when he was in his teens. He became well-educated and established himself as a rabbi in Brussels, where he officiated at weddings, funerals, bar mitzvahs and the like. She says he was quite well-known. Anyway, when the Nazis came in, they formed a *Judenrat*. You know what that is, right?"

"Yes, of course. We had one in Warsaw."

"Yeah, well, in Brussels it was called 'The Association of Jews in Belgium.' Most people referred to it simply as the 'AJB.' The Nazis needed men who could convince their parishioners they had nothing to fear, that by going along with Nazi policies, everything would work out fine. From what I've learned, Bergmann was just that man. They knew of his social standing and figured he was in the best position to influence the Jewish community. He spoke with an air of authority, the type who could convince people that they were simply being resettled to a new town, one that was for Jews only, a place where they'd have work and a new life."

"And, of course, they swallowed it – hook, line and sinker . . ."

"For the most part, yes. What else did they have to hang on to? And with all the persecution, many welcomed resettlements. Truth is, they were tricked."

Martyna closed her eyes and slowly shook her head side-to-side. "And how can you blame them? The Jews trusted their leaders. They walked to the trains like sheep, with the Nazis undoubtedly snickering in the background. Same way they organized the ghettos in Warsaw and Łódź."

"Not to mention a hundred or so other towns all over Europe. That's what I've been told," Annika replied."

"Should I be surprised? Wasn't that their *modus operandi?*"

"Yeah, well, according to Frau Jansenn, our Rabbi Bergmann went above and beyond what was required of him. He took it upon himself to amass the names of all the Jews in Belgium, which he did, in part, by getting membership lists from every synagogue in the country. He also used the powers given him by the SS to compel people to inform on friends and neighbors, sometimes even family members. She says he compiled massive lists, which the Nazis relied on to organize the deportations."

"And let me guess," Martyna asked, ". . . what was in it for him? Did she say?"

"It certainly doesn't take a genius to figure that out. He was given all sorts of perks. Lived high on the hog."

"By betraying his own people . . ." She took a long drag on her cigarette. "And what made it so personal for Jannsen?"

"She said that her parents didn't trust the AJB and went into hiding. Months later, Bergmann had used his influence to find out where they were, at which point Jannsen immediately went to him pleading that he not betray her parents. He promised her she had nothing to worry about. She left that meeting feeling reassured. Next thing she knew, though, Bergmann had turned the information over to *SiPo.*"

Martyna looked at her quizzically. "Sipo?"

"You know . . . the security police." Martyna nodded in recognition. "So, as a result, her parents were found and taken to Breendonk, a concentration camp halfway between Antwerp and Brussels. She said she was told by an eyewitness that they were horrifically interrogated . . ." Her voice quavered. ". . . before being hung."

"How did Janssen get that information. Wasn't she also rounded up?"

"Yes, but not until after her parents were caught. In fact, she says, it was almost immediately after their execution that the Flemish police came for her. But there's more. From what she heard in prison, she believes her own arrest was orchestrated by Bergmann, as well. He knew of her whereabouts and passed it along to the authorities."

"To save his own ass . . . Wow, that's a lot to digest. Do you think her story is credible?" asked Martyna, tilting her head back to finish her water.

"I wondered the same thing, but Frau Janssen anticipated that and encouraged me to consult a woman in one of the adjoining barracks – woman by the name of Renate Bouwmeester. Said she could verify Bergmann's identity."

"Did you meet with her?" Martyna asked.

"Yes, I talked with her just before coming here. She didn't know Janssen personally, but having worked for the rabbi as a secretary, she recognized her name. Eventually, she herself was arrested, along with most of the others affiliated with Rabbi Bergmann."

Martyna stroked her chin. Annika had known her to be basically unflappable, but now her shoulders were hunched, she was breathing with her chest – which Annika had learned to associate with stress – and tears glistened in her eyes. She lit another cigarette. "You want one?"

"No thanks," Annika replied, slurping the last of her tea. "So anyway, the rabbi himself was never arrested."

"No, of course not," Martyna snapped. "He had protected status with the SS, I'm sure. Once they purged all the Jews in his *shtetl*, he would be useful somewhere else." She lit another cigarette. "So how was it that this Frau Bouwmeester made her way to Belsen?"

"She was deported from Belgium in early 1944. She said they were destined to Auschwitz, though for some reason the transport never made it past Buchenwald. It was supposed to have been only a transit stop. As it turned out, she was there for a week or so before being transferred to a sub-camp in Magdeburg – I think she said the Polte factory. Regardless, she said it was a huge ammunitions plant and was run almost entirely by slave labor . . ."

"Nothing surprising there."

"No, not at all. Anyway, to make a long story short, she was liberated by U.S. forces in April, 1945, and eventually made her way here. Not sure exactly how."

"Interesting. So, do you think she can identify him . . . the rabbi?"

"No question. She said she'd be more than happy to."

"All right. Why don't we finish up here and take her to see Van de Velde . . . or Bergmann . . . whoever the hell he is." Martyna exhaled a plume of smoke before carefully stubbing out the cigarette, saving the half-finished butt for later. "Oh boy, are they good. American tobacco. I had almost forgotten how good it tastes," she said, pushing her chair away from the table.

They located Frau Bouwmeester in the latrine where she spent much of her time burdened with dysentery. They gave her ten minutes or so to compose herself. Annika introduced Martyna, who immediately offered to see her later in the day for some medication to help with diarrhea. "I would appreciate that," she replied, adding "Back in Buchenwald, I woulda been killed if had been in a top bunk." Martyna and Annika gave each other a wry smile, knowing that those in lower bunks were frequently defecated on by patients above who were too weakened to get to the latrine.

The three of them walked to the infirmary, where the alleged rabbi was sleeping. Surrounded by rows of patients, all covered in sheets, the rabbi's prodigious belly jutted out like a snowcapped volcano in a land of undulating foothills. He was under sedation and unaware of their approach. His face was a patchwork of contusions. One eye was black and swollen shut, while his lower lip was lacerated and held together by a few stitches. A tangle of tubes projected from his body like serpents feasting on his insides. A catheter snaking from his groin filled a crimson bag hanging at the bedside, and his left arm was tethered to a bottle dripping from above. "As you can see, he was quite severely injured. He needed a blood transfusion," Martyna explained.

Annika nodded, and turning to Bouwmeester, asked, "Can you see through his injuries? Do you recognize him?"

Her response was quick and unequivocal. "No amount of injuries could hide that ugly puss," she said, staring at this man who had held such power over his brethren. "It's definitely Bergmann, no doubt about it. I only worked for him a short while before I was deported, but it was long enough to verify his connivance with the SS. It was disgusting. Everyone knew he was a bootlicker. The worst part about him was his hypocrisy. In the mid-thirties, he was sermonizing about the evil of anti-Semitism. Telling people that Hitler was a travesty, someone who'd quickly disappear, who'd amount to nothing more than a footnote in the annals of history. But that all changed when the Nazis moved into Belgium. Oh, yeah, then he fawned all over them."

Annika looked over to Martyna, who wrinkled her face in a look that conveyed both understanding and disgust. "I'm quite certain," Bouwmeester continued, "that I myself was added to the rolls by Bergmann . . . my own boss. Loyalty meant nothing to him. He'd sweet-talk you to your face, but if there was any threat to his own position – real or imagined – he'd do whatever needed to save his ass. Make you think everything was going to be okay, convince you to relax, but once you let your guard down, he'd betray you. He wouldn't think twice about stabbing his own mother in the back."

Just then, Bergmann opened one eye. He looked at each of the doctors, then at Bouwmeester. Squinting, he seemed to show recognition, raising an arm a few inches to point at her. Whatever he attempted to say was indecipherable, but the sound of his voice alone was enough. Suddenly and without any warning, she lurched forward and slapped his face so hard that his head twisted sideways. Annika and Martyna jumped forward to restrain her, but as they pulled her back, Bouwmeester unleashed a mouthful of spit that landed squarely on his face. As the doctors dragged her away, Bouwmeester, like Janssen before her, screamed a string of epithets. Bergmann, meanwhile, heavily sedated, rubbed his face, distributing the saliva across his mouth and into the lacerations. There was no mistaking Bouwmeester's recognition.

Once they had returned her to her barracks, Martyna took a deep breath and then, exhaling, shook her head from side-to-side. They walked across the courtyard back to the clinic. "So, what do you think?" she asked Annika.

"What do I think? I think we've got a problem." They continued to walk, both looking straight ahead. "We've got a collaborator in the clinic, and not just a small functionary, but someone who could be responsible for hundreds, maybe thousands, of innocent people sent to their deaths. Possibly my own parents."

"Any idea what we should do with him?"

"Well, we could turn him over to the British. Let them figure out what to do with him."

"Sure," Martyna said, "we could do that, but he's in no condition to be moved. Probably not for several weeks. I can tell you from experience, the British have no facilities for dealing with invalids. They'd undoubtedly keep him right here until he's able to be moved to a secure facility."

"Well, then, I think we're stuck with him, at least for the time being.

The Tin Goblet

The loneliest people are the kindest, the saddest people smile the brightest, and the most damaged people are the wisest. All because they don't wish to see others suffer the way they do.
                              -Anonymous

30 July, 1945

Annika was seated alongside the switchboard operator in an office that was being refurbished by the signal corps. It was the only place she could go for a long-distance call. She needed assistance from the operator, meaning there was minimal privacy, except for the pair of headphones covering her ears. Speaking into the mouthpiece, she said, "From Mechelen? Yes . . . Ok . . . But you can't be sure?" She listened with one hand on her forehead, rubbing it slowly. The woman seated next to her looked over just in time to see Annika wipe tears from one eye. "And you have no further information?" she said into the mouthpiece. Another pause. "I see . . . Yes, I understand. Thank you for your help." Looking straight ahead, she sat for a moment, alone in her thoughts, then slowly pulled off the headphones and stood up.

"Are you okay, Doctor?" asked the attendant.

"Yes, thank you. I'm fine," Annika replied, but it was clear to the operator that she had been rattled by the person on the other end. Smiling at the attendant, she got up and walked out. She felt drained and wanted nothing more at that moment than to retire to her quarters in solitude. That, however, would not be possible, as she had already taken time away from her rounds and needed to get back to the clinic.

Later that afternoon, after seeing at least a dozen patients, she came across Martyna, who was checking on someone transferred from the surgery ward. "Where have you been?" Martyna asked, good-naturedly. "I was looking for you."

Annika demurred. It wasn't the time or the place to talk about her personal issues. "I had a phone call to make," she said. "Maybe we can talk . . . later this evening?" It sounded like a request.

"Sure," Martyna responded. "How 'bout right now? Let's go to the canteen. We can grab something to eat and then walk over to the annex."

"Sounds good."

"And to sweeten the deal, I have a little surprise." She tapped her knapsack with one hand and smiled. "Doctor Rabinowitz gave me a bottle of French wine yesterday. Said he thought I needed it." She winked, grabbed Annika's hand, and they walked together across the courtyard to the mess hall.

Staring at the bratwurst and spätzle in front of her, Annika did little more than pick at the food. The egg noodles were overcooked and mushy, but that wasn't the issue; she had no appetite. In contrast, Martyna, famished from a full day's work without much of a break, dug into her meal like a starving dog with a rump roast. After a cup of tea, they retired to a nearby building formerly reserved solely for SS officers. It was empty, as they'd hoped.

Annika pulled up two metal chairs, facing them diagonally to each other, while Martyna rummaged through the cabinets for glasses. The most she could find were tin cups, but that didn't stop her from grinning a bit mischievously as she pulled a bottle of vintage French wine from her rucksack. Holding it to her face, she read, "*Mommesin Clos de Tart, 1940.*" Wide-eyed, she looked over to Annika. "Eh . . . *eh?*" she prodded, hoping for some enthusiasm from her partner. "*Oui, mademoiselle,*" replied the surgeon, adding a bit of flair as she filled the metal cups. They seemed curiously ill-suited to the occasion. "Only our best!" Handing one to Annika, Martyna raised the makeshift goblet to her nose, smiled and squinted gratefully as she studied the wine's bouquet. "A bit tinny, perhaps, but otherwise quite tempting, I'd say."

Annika looked at her mug, and then slowly, almost mechanically, began to swirl the liquid- around and around – encouraging the fermented wash to mix with air, as she had done so often in better times. An image of her stepfather appeared in her mind. "The machinations of the connoisseur," she remembered him saying, while modeling the technique. That was ages ago. Annika had learned it well and was careful to avoid over-spilling the rim. Her eyes followed the rhythm of the fluid encircling the container, and, within a minute, she felt drawn into a kind of existential self-awareness, almost as if she was in a trance. In those brief moments, she had fleeting images of experiences with her parents, which were followed by a poignant recollection of Pasha, smiling across from her at a romantic café in Geneva.

Martyna took a sip of wine, rolling it throughout her mouth while she closed her eyes in a genuine display of appreciation. "Ahhh . . . *Magnifique!*" she purred, lighting a cigarette. She looked over at Annika whose glass remained full.

Ignoring the wine, Annika pointed to the cigarettes. "Could I have one?" she asked.

Martyna reacted with bewilderment, as she had never known Annika to smoke. Sensing that something was on her friend's mind, she chose not to question her and instead leaned forward, handed her a cigarette and struck a match. She waited while Annika took a drag, then asked, "So what do you think?"

"Huh?" Annika muttered, lost in her own thoughts.

"About the wine." Martyna tilted her glass, as if toasting.

Annika was perturbed. Her friend's enthusiasm, normally appreciated, was – through no fault of her own – unsuited to the feelings bottled up inside of her. She responded with irritation, "What do you want me to say, Marty? Nice legs?" It was an expression her stepfather had taught her when observing wine adhering to the sides of a swirling glass. Expressed sarcastically, the tears in her eyes betrayed her.

Martyna put down her cigarette. She reached forward, placing one hand on Annika's. "Hey," she began, looking her friend directly in the eyes. "I know you've got something you want to share. That's obvious. And I want to hear it." She gave Annika's hand a mild squeeze. "I'm here for you. Whenever you're ready."

Annika brought the goblet to her lips, snapped her head back and gulped the entire contents. She paused to feel the liquid making its way down her throat. Minutes passed as Martyna waited. "M-my parents . . ." It was all she could get out before dissolving in tears. Martyna pulled her chair alongside and put an arm across her shoulders. Annika turned into her, welcoming the embrace. She tried to talk, but speech was indecipherable as wracking sobs brought a quiver to her lower lip while her to shoulders trembled in unison.

"Shhh," Martyna soothed, gently rocking her friend. "It's okay. You don't have to say anything . . ."

Eventually, Annika straightened up. Wiping her eyes, she began, "I contacted the UNRRA, as Jens – I mean *Bergmann* – recommended. They connected me to the Central Tracing Bureau. I asked if they could help me in locating my parents. It took forever. They patched me through to an agent. Not sure where he was located, but he took down my information and said to give them a couple of days to see if they could find anything.

"I was notified today to call back. This time, I spoke with a woman, who told me they had records of a Doctor Otto Baumann imprisoned at *KZ Breendonk* in September of 1941. There was no record of any Eva Tritzchler at Breendonk, but both names *did* appear on deportation rolls at the Mechelen transit camp." Martyna handed her a handkerchief. Annika wiped her eyes, then blew her nose. "It's believed that both my parents turned up voluntarily, along with thousands of other Jews, as ordered by the security police. I asked her why my mother – who wasn't Jewish – why she might have been deported, and the woman said that more often than not, people in mixed marriages refused to be separated, especially given the lies about their simply being resettled."

"And do you know where your parents went?" Martyna asked.

"Apparently, some came right here to Belsen, some went to Sobibor, but most traveled in freight cars to Auschwitz." Martyna tightened her embrace. "At this time, they don't have definitive information as to their fate. Even though the Russians liberated the camp, they've provided no records . . ."

"Maybe there aren't any," Martyna offered. "Probably burned." She immediately wished she hadn't used that word.

Once again, Annika broke down. Her eyes darted around the room. "Th-the . . . the man said . . . that my parents would have to be . . ." She paused, squeezing her eyes shut, as if doing so could block out something very painful. ". . . I guess . . . they're presumed . . ." Her chest heaved in rapid, shallow breaths and inconsolable crying. Martyna took one of Annika's hands into her own, and with the other hand pulled her friend's head to her cheek, gently stroking her lifeless hair.

For some thirty minutes, the two women stayed joined in a comforting embrace. Spilling from Annika were the tears of a child, a longing for nurturance from parents no longer there. Recollections of her biological father, long entombed in the deepest recesses of her mind, now sprang forth with unwelcome robustness. Martyna, herself a survivor of Auschwitz, was equally moved. Together they wept, holding and rocking each other until, at last, their tear ducts were empty.

"My parents are dead, Marty. They killed them."

"I know, hon," Martyna said, kissing her forehead. "I know."

Kaddish

I have learned to hate all traitors, and there is no disease that I spit on more than treachery.

Aeschylus

<u>2 August, 1945</u>

It was just before midnight when Annika was finishing her rounds. Lina, the night-shift nurse, was at the far end of the ward assisting with a bedpan. Rabbi Bergmann was Annika's last patient. He opened his eyes as she approached.

"You're up awfully late tonight, aren't you?" he asked, his voice hoarse and gravelly.

"This is what people do who take their oaths and obligations seriously."

"Oaths?" He watched her as she took his wrist to check pulse rate. "Not sure what you mean, Doctor Tritzchler."

Annika felt his forehead. "My oath, Herr Bergmann. As a physician. I'm sworn to take care of my patients." She fiddled with his saline drip.

"Well, I'm happy for that. But, listen, I'm in a lot of pain. I need some more *Eukodal.*"

Annika stopped what she was doing and looked him straight in the eyes. "A lot of pain? I don't think you know what true pain really is, Bergmann."

"*Eh?*" he said, befuddled by Annika's remark. "Now you call me by my last name?"

"What would you prefer? That I call you, Rabbi?" Bergmann frowned. "Well, let me ask you again, *Rabbi* . . ." she said the word

319

sarcastically, ". . . you think you know what true pain really is?"

"I don't know where you're going with this, Doctor Tritzchler."

"I'll tell you where I'm going with it. True pain. Like the pain of seeing your best friend beaten with a whip. Or seeing a family member hung by the neck in front of your eyes. Or seeing an old woman torn to shreds by an attack dog. You familiar with that kind of pain?"

Annika had bottled up her feelings for too long. "What I'm talking about, *Rabbi*, is the trauma of seeing a whole community herded like steers into a gas chamber. Then seeing them thrown into an open pit, some still alive, to have their bodies incinerated. You think you could handle that pain, Rabbi? I'm just wondering, Bergmann, how you can sleep at all, knowing of your complicity in the murders of your own people. Are you haunted by their deaths?"

"Let me tell you something, Tritzchler. The Jews walked to their deaths of their own volition. They knew what was happening. They had every opportunity to resist. Frankly, it's almost embarrassing to call myself a Jew. God gave me a brain, and I used it. That's how I survived."

"So, what you're saying is that the Jews, including my parents, were just too stupid to survive?" Annika was trembling with anger.

"I don't know what happened to your parents. And frankly their fate is of no concern to me. If they're dead, they're dead. You're not. Get over it. You've survived. Like me. Just be thankful for that."

"No, Bergmann! Not like you. I kept my integrity. I didn't murder innocent people, and I paid the price for resisting. At least I can go to my grave, knowing that I didn't betray people who depended on me."

"You know what? Right at the moment, I don't give a rat's ass about your integrity. You and your staff couldn't keep me safe from a crazy woman, and now I'm paying the price for your dereliction. I'm in a lot of pain. My intestines are on fire." He turned to look for another nurse. "If you aren't going to give me more painkiller, I'll call for someone else."

"No need to," Annika said. "We'll take care of your pain." She produced two *Eukodal* tablets. "Open your mouth," she instructed, placing the medication on his tongue. She put a water glass to his lips. He tilted it forward, dribbling water down his chin as he swallowed the pills. Annika took the glass, mixed some powder in the remaining water and stirred the solution. Handing it back to him, she said, "Here. This'll help you to sleep."

Bergmann took the glass and drank. "Eww," he said, wrinkling his nose. "Could you have made it any better!"

"It's Veronal. Between that and the pain pills, you should sleep like a baby. Someone'll be back in few hours to check on you."

"Before you leave, I need a bedpan." His request fell on deaf ears as Annika disappeared in the shadows.

Annika was awakened by a shaft of early morning sunlight settling across her eyelids. Blazing through the legs of an adjoining watchtower, it formed incandescent ribbons on her floor and the adjacent wall. She opened her eyes to a hot mist filtering through the open window as dampness from the previous night's shower burned off in a cauldron of steam. The air in her room was stifling, nearly gagging her in the humidity, and her nightgown clung to her as if she had just come in from the rain. She looked at her watch. It was 0830. She had slept longer than anticipated.

Splashing some water on her face, she walked over to the infirmary where, in the usual morning buzz of activity, things appeared to be copasetic. Nursing aides scurried about with breakfast trays, medications, bedpans, and mops. Once in the makeshift intensive care unit, she saw no sign of Bergmann. His bed was empty.

"Where is the male patient, Bergmann?" she asked one of the nurses, who responded with no recognition. "The rabbi," Annika persisted.

The nurse thumbed through her chart. "I'm not totally sure. I got in only 15 minutes ago. Are you talking about Van de Velde?"

"Yeah. That's him."

"Let me see . . . *hmmm* . . . Oh, yeah, here it is. Van de Velde. He died overnight. Says it right here," she said, pointing at the nursing note. ". . . complications from surgery. Looks like he had a heart attack."

Annika looked surprised. "He died?" Annika took the chart from her. Taking a moment to glance through the notes, she asked, "Where's the body?"

"Well, I don't know. Like I say, I just got in, but I would assume his remains are on the way to the crematorium." She spoke nonchalantly. Hundreds were still dying every day, and the protocol for reducing the risk of disease was to rapidly cremate the remains.

"No autopsy?" gasped Annika. In any other setting, it would have been a routine question.

"Autopsy?" The nurse was perplexed. "I-I don't see any note in the chart about an autopsy. Should one have been ordered?"

Annika recognized almost immediately the absurdity of her question. During the Nazi regime, autopsies had been limited to SS doctors as part of their obscene experiments. Here at the DP camp, post-mortems were pretty much out of the question. There was neither the time nor the manpower. She hurried down the corridor in search of Martyna, whom she found bent over a man whose leg she had amputated the previous day. She was busily debriding the wound.

"Martyna!" she said.

The surgeon raised her hand without looking up. "Just a minute, Annika," Martyna whispered. She looked haggard. Annika waited while her friend bandaged the stump. After a few minutes, Martyna straightened up to scrutinize her work, then turned to her nurse. "You can finish, Johanna. I'll check back later on." She wiped her hands and walked over to Annika.

"Sorry to intrude like that, Martyna," Annika offered.

The surgeon merely smiled. "No harm done . . . How are you?"

"Well, fine, I guess. I just learned that Bergmann is dead. Do you know what happened?"

"Well . . . I'm thinking he may have become septic and then

suffered a heart attack. We knew there was a risk of infection, but, you know, with no antibiotics, there was only so much we could do. When I went home last evening, he seemed to be stable. Evidently took a turn for the worse. I saw your note in the chart from last night. Anything remarkable?"

"Not particularly."

"Well, when they came around to check on him this morning, he was gone. Not much anybody could do."

Annika stared at her. "I-I don't know what to say . . ."

Martyna looked at her with compassion. "You don't have to say anything, dear. He died. Like thousands of others." She looked her friend in the eye. "You know as well as I that stuff like this happens. Here today, gone tomorrow. Truth is, Annika, I'm not sure he deserved our sympathy, even though we did everything we could to treat his illness." Annika nodded.

"Oh, and by the way . . ." Martyna added, ". . . something you might want to know. Sarah, the young Jewish nurse, told me that Bergmann had pulled her aside the day before yesterday. She had kept it to herself until this morning, but said that Bergmann had asked her to hear him recite the *Viduy* . . . Are you familiar with it?" Annika, looking puzzled, shook her head. "It's the Jewish prayer of confession . . . traditionally said before someone dies."

"I don't know it. W-what did he say?"

"Well, according to Sarah, he quoted the prayer almost verbatim, acknowledging his sins and transgressions. It was like a confession, as if he sensed he was going to die. She said that he wanted to atone in the presence of another Jew, someone who hadn't known him."

Annika was speechless. So, the rabbi actually had a conscience. She didn't know what to feel. It was all so complicated.

"Hey, c'mon." Martyna tightened her embrace. "Let it go. We've got a lot of work to do." They walked down the corridor, arm-in-arm.

Part Three

Immigration

For most of history, anonymous was a woman.
Virginia Woolf

<u>4 August, 1950: New York City</u>

This was Annika's third week in New York City. A refugee, she was one of the lucky ones. It had taken three years, but her immigration to America had been approved. She had wanted nothing more than to leave her homeland, the source of so much heartache. She processed through Ellis Island, was given temporary housing through the Hebrew Immigrant Aid Society (HIAS) in Manhattan, and assigned a social worker, Sarah Lieberman – a demure, middle-aged woman whose job was to make sure her basic needs were attended to. Employment being a key priority, the social worker looked into getting Annika credentialed in medicine. What she found was that the process was fraught with obstacles. First was proving Annika's completion of medical school, which, given the massive bombing and continued disarray in Berlin, would be difficult. Second, her training would have to show itself commensurate with rigorous American standards, and only then would she qualify not for direct licensure, but simply to sit for the difficult exams. But perhaps most formidable challenge would be prejudice, especially with what came out about the depravity of German doctors under the Third Reich. The entire process was certain to be daunting.

"Don't be discouraged," Sarah enthused. "We can do it. I know several physicians who I'm sure would be willing to help. We even have a psychiatrist on our Board."

"You think it's possible . . . with me being German?"

"Of course, Annika. You were not one of *them*. You resisted. That's what landed you in prison."

Annika pursed her lips. "I know that . . . you know that, but how many others do you think will believe it? Especially with my accent. I mean, listen to me, Sarah. Do I sound American?"

"You know what they say . . . 'Rome wasn't built in a day.' I can easily get you into a language class that will help with your diction. I can also try to arrange some tutoring to prepare you for the exams."

"Sarah, please. I need to be honest with you. I really appreciate your help. I do. But . . . I don't really want to be a doctor anymore."

Sarah was taken aback. "Don't want to be a doctor? You're not serious . . . Why on earth not?"

"Every time I think of it . . . I don't know . . . I-I start to panic."

"Panic? Why would you panic? You're a doctor . . . trained, experienced."

"It's just . . . I don't how to put it . . . I've just seen too much. You've no idea . . . I don't really want to talk about it, Sarah. Can we just leave it at that?" Her lips began to tremble.

Sarah saw it and switched the conversation. "Okay . . . I understand. Why don't you just rest. I'll look into some other possibilities." She put her arm around Annika. "I'll see you in a few days." Knowing that her client's only transferrable skills were in medical settings, Sarah couldn't understand Annika's reluctance. Maybe just a lack of confidence, she thought. So only a week later, she burst into the flat with news of a job vacancy at nearby Mount Sinai Hospital, located in Manhattan's upper east side.

"Isn't that a psychiatric hospital?" Annika asked.

"Yes, they do have a psychiatric ward, but that's not what we're looking at. There's an opening for a nursing assistant . . . in the general hospital. Basic responsibilities . . . bathing, feeding, cleaning up . . . that kind of thing, but easily stuff you can do."

Annika was quiet. Sarah looked at her with raised eyebrows, waiting for a reaction.

"Nursing . . ." Annika said it slowly, deliberately, as if she needed to get used to the word rolling off her tongue.

"I know . . . I know. It's a step down for you, Annika, but think of it. It's a permanent position, *with benefits*. After you get your feet on the ground, get to know people, who knows? Maybe you'll want to get back into medicine . . . what you were trained for." Annika gave her a blank stare. "Listen. You need money. For right now, that's the number-one priority, and unless you want to work in a laundromat, or maybe be a waitress, this offers some promise."

Annika was reserved. Nevertheless, she followed up with an interview and four days later was working on the second floor. Sarah may have thought Annika's job a fall from grace, but privately, to her surprise, Annika felt contentment in what she called "the bedpan brigade." Having been drenched in waste from overflowing slop buckets in the cattle cars, or awakened in camp by diarrhea seeping from the bunks of dysentery patients above, her new responsibilities were easy and predictable, uncomplicated.

As I sit and ruminate, it almost feels as if I need to be doing things that others consider degrading. Wiping down a patient, cleaning them of feces, urine, blood and pus. It feels somehow comfortable. I can't describe it. It takes me away. {4 August, 1950}

4 February, 1951

Six months had already elapsed at Mount Sinai. It was cold and gray outside. Inside felt no different, though the coldness had less to do with temperature than the gloominess of her routine. It was just before lunch when she was instructed to look after a young woman, Ellen, in the maternity ward. She had just given birth to a stillborn. From what Annika was told, Ellen's baby had been whisked away immediately following delivery as the despondent mother, nearly hysterical, was wheeled back to her room. She had no relatives, no friends, and no visitors. Her former boyfriend, the biological father, had abandoned her months ago, his whereabouts unknown. Ellen was all alone.

When Annika entered the room, Ellen was propped against a pillow, a vacuous gaze framing tear-stained cheeks and scraggly hair.

"Can I get you anything?" Annika asked. This was outside the purview of her responsibilities.

"My baby's dead," the mother repeated to no one in particular. Obviously sedated, she stared blankly at the wall. "My baby . . . I killed him . . ."

Annika stood motionless, unexpectedly overcome. The woman's words were a trigger. Looking at her laying there, empty, in pain, emotionally torn, Annika had a sudden flashback of her own abortion. Standing to the side of Ellen were Doctor Rosenthal and Gerda Quernheim, fetal tissue dripping from their stainless-steel instruments. The blood drained from her head while her heart pounded against her chest.

Just then, a woman poked her head in the doorway. "C'mon, Fräulein. We need these patients cleaned." It was Annika's supervisor. "Fräulein." She used that nickname whenever she wanted to get a rise out of Annika.

Annika's eyes glazed over. "*Ja, Aufseherin. Sofort!*"

The supervisor, whose intention had been only a brief check, instead stood quizzically at the door. "What? Are you speaking German?"

Annika blinked. This was her supervisor, not an SS overseer. She quickly corrected herself, "Oh, I'm sorry, Mrs. Russo. I'll take care of it."

"I don't know who you think you're talking to . . ." She looked over at the patient, then back at Annika. "C'mon, we've got new patients coming in." She studied Annika for a second, then disappeared down the corridor.

"Can you get out of the bed so I can change your sheets? I can help you over to the chair?"

The dazed woman narrowed her eyes, fixing her attention onto

Annika. "They took my baby. All I wanted to do was hold it. Just once . . ." she wailed. "*Just once*. Is that too much to ask? Can you get my baby for me?" The mother was sobbing, disconsolate and delusional.

Annika touched her arm. "I'm not sure that's possible at this point." Annika saw herself in this mother. She could feel what the woman was going through. She knew it was unlikely that such a request would be granted, especially at this point, but she needed to say something. "I'm just a nurse, honey, but . . ."

Tearfully, Ellen begged, "*Please*, I need to see her, to hold her!"

Very lightly, she squeezed the woman's arm. "I'll go check for you. See what I can do." Annika hurried off, took to the stairs and located the baby in the morgue, where a pathologist was hunched over a stainless-steel dissection table conducting a routine autopsy. He turned to Annika, which afforded her a full view of the child. The skull and torso were already incised. There would be no returning to Ellen with her baby.

"Can I help you?" It was Doctor Levine. She had met him several times. Outside of work, he could be quite congenial, but in his practice, he was not one who liked interruptions.

"Doctor Levine, I just came from the second floor. The baby's mother, Ellen Fiedler, is quite ill-disposed, grieving . . . She's asking to hold her baby. I was just wondering if, while there's still time, we might be able to get a lock of the child's hair. Something for her to remember him by."

He looked at her. "Is this really your responsibility? Shouldn't social services take care of this?"

"Yes, Doctor. Absolutely, but I knew time was of the essence, so . . ."

"So . . . what?"

"Well, it's just that the patient . . . Miss Fiedler . . . she's really suffering. She has no family, and I just thought . . ."

The doctor stopped what he was doing and turned to her. "You want a lock of hair?"

"Yes, that would be wonderful. I think it might help her to move on."

Levine didn't waste any time. He picked up a pair of scissors and snipped off a few lockets of very fine, dark hair. He then placed it on sterile gauze before handing it to Annika. "You'll have to rinse it," he advised, as the hair still had traces of blood.

Annika smiled. She took the tiny token to the sink and used a small, cup-shaped strainer to very carefully let the water run over it. Tenderly, she dabbed at the hair. She took the utmost care that not one precious strand would get washed away. The entire lock was a treasure, a keepsake which Annika herself never had and was determined to preserve for her patient.

The pathologist watched her. Sensitivity afforded lifeless tissue was not part of his usual routine, so it was with curiosity that he watched the child's blood trickle through her fingers into the white, ceramic sink. Never had he stopped to consider that along with the blood disappearing down the drain were the hopes, dreams, and the unrequited love of a forlorn mother.

"Nice work," the doctor said. "You have great dexterity . . . Impressive." Annika turned to him and smiled. "I hear people call you 'Fräulein.' Do you mind my asking your name?"

"I'm Annika Tritzchler."

"Well, Mrs. Tritzchler, I'm pleased to meet you. I'd shake your hand, but I'm afraid . . ." He looked at his gloved hands.

"I understand. I'm pleased to meet you. And . . . well . . . it's *Miss* Tritzchler."

"Ah, I see. Well, anyway, Miss Tritzchler, you show great sensitivity. I'm sure this isn't part of your normal duties."

"No, sir. It's just that the mother . . . well, the woman who lost her baby, is quite upset. I believe maybe slightly delusional. She expressed that she feels responsible for its death."

"Well, that's not the case, at all. The post-mortem revealed that the lungs had not developed."

"Pediatric pulmonary hypoplasia?" Annika asked.

The pathologist looked stunned. "Well . . . yes. *Exactly*."

Annika turned back to the locket of hair, not wanting the doctor to see the tears welling up in her eyes. She carefully slid the remains into an envelope. "Thank you, Doctor Levine. I'm sure the patient will appreciate it. Ellen Fiedler, I believe, is her name."

As she walked to the doorway, Doctor Levine called out, "Wait." Annika turned, thinking she had left something behind. "I want you – " he began, but then hesitated. Whatever airs he carried as a doctor gave way to something else. "Please let her know that it was a beautiful baby . . . and that . . . that she did everything right."

Annika nodded. "Thank you, Doctor." With a certain reverence, she brought the priceless tribute to the grieving mother, handing it to her much like a priest offering Communion bread to parishioners. For a split-second, she silently intoned the words, "Body of Christ . . ." It was the first time in as long as she could remember that she had had any thought of religion. Ellen held the envelope, gently pulled out the ringlet of hair, and clutched it to her breast, sobbing. Annika sat down on the bed next to her, put her arms around her and gently pulled her close while whispering words of comfort. Together they both cried. When Annika stood to leave, her blouse was wet with tears.

Panic

And if thou gaze long into an abyss, the abyss will also gaze into thee.

Friedrich Nietzsche

<u>5 February, 1951</u>

Annika was getting ready to punch out when she was summoned to Mrs. Russo's office. "Thank you for coming in, Tritzchler. I'm afraid I have some unpleasant news. I've spoken with the Director of Human Resources, and, *ahem,* he agrees that we're going to let you go."

"What?" Annika was dumbfounded. "I don't understand."

"Well, it's really quite simple. You crossed a boundary yesterday. Your duties are quite specific, and they don't include intervening on a patient's behalf with doctors. That's the job of social services. The patient whose baby was *born dead . . .*" Annika winced at the words. ". . . she told us what you had done. She showed us *the hair . . .* You obviously don't understand your role."

"She . . . was upset with me?"

"I don't think you understand. We can't have our cleaning staff interrupting the doctors or running special favors for every Tom, Dick, and Harry that tugs at . . ."

Annika interrupted her. "Mrs. Russo, I may be mistaken, but I'm part of the *nursing* unit. No disrespect to anyone, but I'm not a member of the cleaning staff."

"Just the same, what you did yesterday was inappropriate. We can't have that."

"But . . ."

334

"Please, no 'buts.' I'm sorry, Tritzchler. You're done here. You can turn in your uniform and pick up your final paycheck next week. Or we can mail it . . ." Annika stood as if in a stupor. The supervisor could see it in her face. "Do you have any questions?"

Annika's mind was spinning. She was back in Germany. "*Nein, Chef Oberaufseherin.*"

Russo stood up, and leaning forward with both hands on her desk, said, "Are you being smart with me? I don't cotton to any of that Nazi talk." She assumed Annika was insulting her in German. But it wasn't sarcasm. In that moment, Annika saw before her not Mrs. Russo, but Anna Klein, the chief supervisor at Ravensbrück, a woman who could order a severe lashing or twenty days in the Bunker as dispassionately as she might have ordered her breakfast. At a loss for words, Annika stared, then slowly turned and, in a daze, walked out.

She was tired, bone-weary and emotionally overwhelmed. Instead of a ten-hour day, it felt more like twenty hours. She had eaten very little all day, but her appetite was gone. All she could do now was get to her apartment in Queens. She'd have to call Sarah, let her know what happened.

A little after five o'clock, the sidewalk was already teeming with people, bumping and jostling in their individual quests of getting home to cocktails, evening news, supper, and some limited family time. This was Midtown's rush hour, that incarnation of capitalism that tempts civilized people to suspend propriety in securing a coveted seat on the next commuter train as if lives depended on it. But Annika had herself become part of the same phenomenon. She joined the lemmings in a collective cadence that snaked through streets lined with cafes, laundromats, paint dispensaries and everything in between.

Along the boulevard, she coughed through exhaust fumes, triggering a flashback to Ravensbrück's *Lagerstraße*. It was the same choking sensation she used to have when downdraft from the chimneys filled the camp with the smoke of burning flesh. Now, with it once again in her lungs, her psyche took her from downtown Manhattan to the depraved hell outside of Furstenburg. She struggled to stay in the present, reminding herself: *This is New York . . . I'm on my way home.* But the interaction with her supervisor had been destabilizing. She couldn't think of Russo without conjuring an image of *Sturmbannführer* Reusch, her Gestapo inquisitor. Both had blindsided her with misinterpretations of things she had done with the best intentions. She knew she was losing her grip. *I've got to get home.* She walked faster, relying on exercise to control the anxiety which escalated by the minute.

It took less than twenty minutes before she was boarding the subway to Grand Central Station. The mob of commuters jamming the doorways prompted a flashback to Berlin's Hauptbahnhof. In an instant, she felt herself being forced into a cattle car for transport to Litzmannstadt. Once inside, it was standing-room only, faceless people packed like sardines. Annika grabbed the handhold for support, but as the train lurched forward, she felt the man behind her nonchalantly rubbing up against her backside. She spun around, staring directly into his eyes. It was Freidrich Brunner, a kapo from Sachsenhausen, one of the most reprehensible men she had ever met, and there had been many, too many. He grinned at her through beady little eyes. Behind him were two young soldiers, talking and laughing. *SS,* she thought. *They're leering at me.* Paralyzed with fear, she saw a group of women huddled a few meters in the opposite direction. One wore a striped suit, the others had long dark coats. *It's my work group.* She muscled her way over to them in a full-blown panic, watching the floor to avoid tripping over the slop bucket.

Grand Central was jammed. Her heart was beating so fast, she could hardly breathe. Bits of trash circulated like dirt devils, nipping her ankles as she walked to a second subway, this one taking her across the East River to her neighborhood in Long Island City. A loudspeaker blared as officers approached from the opposite direction. Instinctively, Annika, still disoriented, removed her hat and looked down, hoping they would pass without noticing her. Once their voices faded, she rushed to the staircase leading to her train and descended through stagnant layers of tobacco smoke, having to skirt the intermittent gobs of spit and chewing gum. The hum of the city with its montage of automobile horns gave way below ground to a din of voices drowned out by the intermittent whoosh of passing subway cars.

Walking shoulder to shoulder in this subterranean purgatory, acrid body odors competing with occasional whiffs of Chanel or Old Spice like water mixing with oil, Annika was unable to avoid a puddle of vomit. She paused briefly to inspect her shoe, but was bumped from behind and almost lost her balance. She continued walking, slowing only to drop a quarter into the open guitar case of a street musician. Homeless men were wrapped in dirty blankets underneath tiled walls thick with scum. A quick glance at them brought to mind the emaciated *muselmänner* of the camps, those who, with no more work capacity, were resigned to death. She wedged her way onto the last subway car and stood between a smartly dressed businessman and a scraggly beatnik with long stringy hair and a beard. Reeking of alcohol, he clutched a brown paper bag curled at the top.

The remainder of her journey was on foot through working-class neighborhoods contrasting sharply with those in upscale Manhattan. Something here was incongruous. These were the victors of the world war, the people who had fought for freedom and morality. But looking around, they seemed to treat the homeless and hungry no differently than they had in Warsaw, or Leningrad, or anywhere else throughout the fascist empires. There people went about their day-to-day business by stepping over bodies of fellow countrymen who had perished not from bombs or street-fighting, but from disease and starvation. Was this the reward to those who had suffered and died in their battles against fascism? Were these the spoils of victory? Was this even democracy? Her mind was back in Ravensbrück and Sachsenhausen. She walked past a construction site, but instead of dirt, she saw a pile of rotting corpses. Turning to her left was a woman perched on the stoop of a brownstone, but instead of a carefree apartment dweller, she saw a partially clothed young woman, dazed and immodest, on the steps to her barrack, her open legs caked with blood from unchecked menses . . . *one of the new arrivals,* Annika thought.

By the time she walked up the stairs, she was in a wash. Nothing looked familiar. She had long been an expert in comforting others, crying at the bedside of the dying, hiding women slated for the gas chamber, tenderly massaging ointments into the lacerations of flogging victims, even nurturing expectant mothers. She had done all that while repressing her own traumas. *Stay busy to keep from thinking* – that had been her mantra. But it wasn't working this evening. Her experience with Ellen had been unnerving in ways she hadn't expected. For the first time, she was having flashbacks: fetuses ripped from the wombs of screaming young women, tiny bodies floating in pails of bloody water, abortions performed at full-term, babies bludgeoned against train cars; it all came rushing back in a syncopating delirium of psychedelic malevolence. The more she struggled, the more insistent they became. She thought of the teenagers twisting from gallows; the "rabbits" undergoing excruciating medical experiments, ashen corpses stacked like firewood . . .

Not one to drink, she grabbed a bottle of schnapps, set aside for guests, and gulped down first one, then a second shot. Anything to calm the nerves, to stop the hallucinations. She recalled admonitions she had made to anxious patients. "Write it down," she would have instructed. "Externalize your feelings to gain control." She grabbed her notebook and commenced to scribbling, trying desperately to make sense out of fleeting cognitions, chaotic and disturbing. She wrote like a woman possessed, pages and pages of tear-stained thoughts, passages that began rationally, but which became increasingly disjointed with each passing hour.

. . . Living beings turned into defenseless zombies passively awaiting consignment, numb to serpent-like flames that tease the sky in flickering tongues of crimson. Mothers and fathers, aunts and

338

uncles, friends and neighbors; some lined up against a wall, others kneeling at the edge of a pit, all awaiting deliverance. Deemed sub-human, they are the unworthy, their existence to be erased from all eternity.

But what about morality? Is there such a thing? Or just a word, an invention of the powerful designed to sublimate man's most primitive impulses. Morality. The word sounds meaningless – an empty concept muscled out by the inexorable instincts of man's primordial bestiality.

Ideologies are temporal; they imprison us in chaos and debauchery . . . false prophecies aimed at deceit, tricking people into believing they are the fulfillment of evolution, the pinnacle of perfection. But there is no utopia, no Kingdom of God and no heaven on earth. No, this is a Darwinism bereft of all ethics. We are the alpha and the omega, the host and the parasite, and like all parasites, we kill ourselves through ignorance and self-interest. If God is in the firmament, He must be shaking His head and asking Himself, What hath I wrought?

Reason had given way to uncertainty, even contradiction. She was confused. Nothing seemed to make sense. Her writing became disjointed.

. . . What does it all mean? In fact, what does "meaning" even mean? Using one word to understand the same word . . . An arithmetic "mean" . . . a "mean" concept . . . "mean" feelings . . . "meaning" of life . . . Nothing is meaningful. Those naked cadavers of gray, sagging skin and upturned, lifeless eyes . . . what were they staring at? Something . . . or nothing? "Nothing," said Heidegger. But what is nothing? No-thing. "Nothingness," argued Sartre. And that's where we are, subsumed amidst a cauldron of nothingness . . . a delusion that would actually be funny if nothingness held any meaning. So, what do people want to live for, when their goals, their happiness, their very lives are nothing but fantasy? . . . Shakespeare

said, "to be or not to be." What does it mean "to be"? What is being? *Anything, or nothing but the sense our mind makes out of things we touch or see, the proverbial "categories" of Kantian apperception. But there must be something behind what we perceive, an essence, as it were, to being, or is even that essence pure delusion. Those people I saw hanging on the gallows, tortured in the "bunker or beaten before my eyes – a figment of my imagination? Meaningless . . . I can't know reality, then. It is limited by my finite mind. Reality, then, is . . . nothing but appearance- the way in which we, in our ignorance, make sense out of absurdity. In the end, life has been a meaningless illusion. Death is nothingness.*

It was almost dawn when Annika stopped writing. She had been awake for more than twenty-seven hours, and her mind was still racing, though with just enough self-awareness to realize she was losing her grasp. That alone made her want to scream, yet she couldn't. Instead, she sobbed. Unlike other situations in which crying had been cathartic, her tears this time failed to dampen the searing images threatening her sanity. She staggered through the small living room, bumping a table, knocking her phone and a pile of papers onto the floor. Splashing water on her face accomplished almost nothing, so she climbed into the shower, still in her pajamas. She closed her eyes to the water, but doing so immersed her in a blackness that simply intensified her claustrophobia.

Stumbling out of the shower-stall, she wiped the foggy mirror with her hand, trying to make out a likeness, but all she could see was a blurry image of hollow eyes and wet, tangled hair. As quickly as it appeared, it faded in the steam. *Is that me?* she asked herself, leaning forward. She swiped the glass with her towel, around and around, determined to see more clearly, but staring back at her was a wraithlike apparition with deep-set eyes ringed by heavy, dark circles. It was disarming. She blinked repeatedly as the image disappeared in the fog. Forcing a smile, needing to see something familiar, the mirror refused to smile back. Instead, as the steam dissipated, a face took shape, but not one that she expected. Scraggly wisps of thin gray hair sprouted from the sides of a once-bloated face where skin now hung in pallid folds. Annika rubbed her eyes and all at once beheld, in front of her eyes, an apparition, one she recognized immediately. It was Rabbi Bergmann.

Beside herself with irrepressible horror, she pounded the mirror like one possessed. Shards of bloodied glass fell resoundingly into the sink and onto the floor below as she buried her face in her arms, screaming at the phantom, "Go away, Bergmann! Leave me alone!" She reached down for a long, dagger-like sliver and, grasping it firmly, incised her fingers almost to the bone. The intense pain bought momentary relief, but seeing the blood dripping from her hand, she lost any remaining semblance of reality and, instead, sliced the sharp edge of the glass across her forearm, cutting deep into her muscle. Torrents of plasma extruded from her flesh like a broken water main. She dropped the glass and retreated to the living room where, exhausted, she slumped into a chair.

She hadn't been there more than twenty minutes before there was frenzied knocking at the door. With no response, the banging became more insistent until finally the door to her room burst open. It was Sarah.

Identity

The more a man can forget, the greater the number of metamorphoses which his life can undergo. The more he can remember, the more divine his life becomes.

Søren Kierkegaard

6 February, 1951: Bellevue Hospital

"Hey. Wake up, Miss Tritzchler." It was one of the floor nurses. She was straightening things around the bed. "How's your arm feel?"

Annika was mildly sedated, but alert. She looked down at her arm, which was heavily bandaged. "It feels . . . okay, I guess.

"Well, we've got to get you cleaned up. Do you have to make water?"

"What . . .?"

"Use the commode?" Annika shook her head. "Okay. So, let me ask. Do you know where you are?"

"I-I'm in the hospital . . . Mount Sinai, I assume."

"Close. You're at Bellevue. Downtown. You came in two days ago. Bleeding pretty bad, from what they say . . . You had to be sedated, but . . ." She looked at Annika's arm. ". . . it looks like they fixed you up okay. Are you feeling any better?"

Annika was still too sedated. "*Mein Gott.* I've been through a lot . . . I don't know. I guess so . . ."

"Well, I hope so. You have a visitor. Here, let me prop you up." She puffed up the pillows at the headboard, as Annika made an effort to sit up."

"A visitor. Who? Sarah?"

"No, it's just one of the doctors. Not sure who. I've never met

342

him, but . . ." She looked directly at Annika and winked. ". . . he's a handsome gent. Looks a bit like Cary Grant." She straightened the cover on the bed. "So, it'll be just a bit. I'll let him know you're ready," she said, walking out.

Minutes later, a man rapped briefly at the door before walking over to the bed, not waiting for an invitation. Annika looked up – at first without any recognition, but then . . .

"Doctor . . . *Levine?*"

"Yes. Good morning. It's Annika, right?"

"Y-yes. That's my name. Wh . . . what are . . ." She paused. "You work here too?"

"No. No. Only at Mount Sinai. I heard what happened . . . losing your job and everything. What your supervisor did was wrong, boneheaded actually, and I've addressed the situation with our vice-president. He's looked into the matter and basically assured me that you'll be reinstated . . . with no loss of pay."

"I'm . . . confused. How did you hear about it?"

"The woman . . . you know, the young mother who lost her child . . . well, your supervisor had apparently talked to her. The patient was concerned . . . found out what had happened and, I guess, lodged some sort of protest. The H.R. director came to me to get my version. Anyway, to make a long story short, I ended up talking to your social worker – Sarah, I think her name is, the woman who brought you to the hospital."

"Oh . . . right." She had only sketchy recall of her trip to the hospital.

"Well, Sarah shared some of your background with me. I have to say, I'm glad she did. Things made a little more sense to me."

"Like . . . ?"

"Like when you correctly identified the cause of the baby's death. Right then and there, I knew you were no ordinary nursing assistant. I figured you had had some sort of medical training . . . but I never would have guessed you were a physician."

Annika stared off in the distance. "That was quite some time ago."

"Uh huh. I gather. A lot's happened over the past ten years . . ."

"Even more over the past *twenty* years . . . enough to last a lifetime . . . literally."

The doctor pulled a chair alongside the bed. Leaning forward, he said, "I know you're convalescing, and I certainly don't want to be a burden. But . . . I wanted you to know that . . . well, I was moved by what you did for that young woman. It was touching. And I guess what I'd like to say is that having heard a little bit about your background, it would be a privilege if you might be willing to share with me a little more about yourself. That is . . ." he added quickly, "if you don't mind."

Annika studied him before responding. She probed his eyes, wondering if his concern was motivated by compassion . . . or was it something else? She responded guardedly, "What would you like to know, Doctor?"

"Well, first of all, if you would be so kind, I'm hoping we can dispense with formalities. We're both doctors. Please, call me Jerome."

Annika felt concussed. *We're both doctors . . . doctor . . .* The word, the sentiment; it was at once familiar, but unfamiliar. For so many years she had been known simply as "Fräulein," or "Nurse," or "you there," or – worse yet – "Number 7204." She lost sight of her identity long ago.

"That's very kind of you." She wasn't quite ready to call him by his first name. It sounded too . . . intimate. "So, what can I tell you?"

"Well, I guess first of all, I'm wondering how you became a physician. I didn't think Germany was too receptive to women in medicine."

"Nor in any of the other professions, once the Nazis came to power. Things were different, though, during the Weimar period, which is when I grew up." She shared with him a brief outline of her life: her upbringing, her father's death, mother's remarriage, and what life was like in pre-war Berlin. He listened attentively, making her

344

feel comfortable responding to his questions; he seemed sincere. He went on to ask about her medical training and her residency. He responded with some tidbits about his own life and what led him to pursue a career in medicine. Eventually, their dialogue became more pointed.

"If it wouldn't cause you too much distress, Annika, and please tell me if it does, can I ask why you were in a concentration camp?"

"I was actually in three camps. Not one. Sachsenhausen, Ravensbrück, and Bergen-Belsen." She explained the *T4* euthanasia carried out at Bernburg and how her refusal to participate led to confinement at Sachsenhausen.

"I see. So why, after being released from Sachsenhausen, were you re-arrested?"

"Well, my stepfather was Jewish. Not long after being expelled from the hospital, along with all the other Jewish physicians, he and my mother immigrated to Belgium. I stayed in Germany to continue my career. As things heated up in Berlin, I was denounced a Jew . . . by a neighbor."

"But you . . . you were not *born* Jewish, right? According to Nazi racial policy, shouldn't that have insulated you?"

She chose to equivocate rather than discuss the circumstance with Rolf. "Even though – yes, by their definition I was full-blooded German – despite that, my neighbor claimed I was born out-of-wedlock, and that my stepfather was actually my biological father. They believed him and labeled me a *Mischling*. As an 'enemy of the people,' I was sent to Ravensbrück."

Levine listened, waiting attentively for her to finish. "I can't begin to imagine what you've been through." Annika showed no expression. "I knew from your accent you were from Germany, but, well, I kept my distance, not knowing but what you might have been . . . *hmm* . . . I don't know, maybe a supporter of the regime." She stared at him, blankly.

Levine continued, "I should tell you, Annika, that my grandparents . . . they, too, disappeared in the holocaust."

"Your grandparents . . . I thought you might be Jewish," Annika said.

"Yes. In fact, my grandparents may have been among the earliest victims, I suspect. They were living in Luxembourg, which at the time had a small Jewish population. Just before Hitler marched in, most Jews escaped across the border . . . to Vichy, France. Not the best move. The Vichy government sent most of them to Theresienstadt, I believe. My grandparents, however, never left Luxembourg. They didn't want to abandon their beloved town. And it was a beautiful town. Growing up, I visited them twice with my parents." Annika smiled as she brushed a strand of hair from her eyes. "Anyway, we learned a few years ago that they were arrested by Nazi sympathizers, and instead of being deported . . ." he said, his voice never cracking, ". . . they were lined up against a government building and shot."

"Jerome. I am so sorry," Annika said.

"Thank you. Their end, I guess, was swift – probably nothing like the prolonged suffering it sounds like you've experienced."

They talked like this for the better part of two hours, each sharing bits of their lives as well as political and religious persuasions. Eventually, the discussion came around to Annika's hospitalization.

"I don't remember much of that night," she said. "Most of it's a blur . . . I think getting fired just – what's the expression? – pushed me over the edge?"

"Well, sure. And why not? With all you've gone through, it's hard to imagine how you maintain any sense of normalcy."

Annika confided, "I try to keep busy but, I suppose if I'm honest with myself, oftentimes I'm just going through the motions, not really aware of what I'm doing. Sometimes . . ." She paused to see how he was reacting. ". . . sometimes things I see – even simple, everyday things – they cause me to think back . . . like I'm reliving some event from my past." She rubbed her forehead, while pulling hair away from her eyes. "Usually, I can handle it, but . . ." She then glanced at her bandaged arm. ". . . well, I guess you can tell, when it reaches the point that it did this week, I guess it sometimes feels overwhelming.

It's never happened like this before. This week was definitely the worst."

"Annika, listen. I'd like to help you. I have a friend . . . well, actually a colleague; he's a psychiatrist." She closed her eyes, taking a deep breath. "No, hear me out. You have so much inside, so much buried . . . I can't imagine you're ever going to really gain control over your life until it comes out. Talking with a professional I think could really help. Why don't you let me see if I can arrange a visit with him. "

"I don't think so, Jerome. I appreciate your offer, but . . . a psychiatrist? Psychiatry is what led me down this path. I don't know if I could do that . . ."

"Annika, do you mind if I speak freely?" She looked at him and nodded, though more out of obligation than true interest. "It's not a question of whether you can do it; you *need* to do it! Think of it. You were trained to be a psychiatrist, but psychiatry wounded you; it victimized you. You carry its scars. Do you think you'll get better by avoiding that part of your life, keeping it all locked up deep in your mind? In some mental compartment where it only comes out when you least expect it, and where it takes you back to that hell each time it comes out? Seriously, how will you ever be able to move forward with your life if you don't confront your demons? If psychiatry created those demons, what could be better in resolving your problems than interacting with a psychiatrist?"

"I don't know. Seeing a psychiatrist is probably the last thing I would ever want to do . . ."

"Of course. It's a risk. Facing feelings that have been buried so long that they've grown roots. But you *can* do it. In fact, Doctor Tritzchler, you've already started. Both with me, but also with yourself – the other night. That, Annika, whether you realize it or not, was an important step . . . painful, but important."

Annika began to whimper. No one had ever confronted her like this. She thought for a few minutes before answering. "What you're saying . . . it . . . it all makes sense, Jerome. I know it does . . . it's probably what I would have told one of my own patients . . ." Jerome nodded in agreement. "Thinking about it, though," Annika continued, "it's just . . . so scary." She looked down and began to cry. Jerome took hold of her hand. Her full attention was on him as tears began streaming down her cheeks. She reached forward to place her arm around his neck. Without hesitating, Jerome returned the embrace, and for several minutes they sat locked in one another's arms. Annika's heart was beating rapidly, and as she warmed to his touch, a feeling came over her – a rapture almost, something to which words could never do justice – and for the first time in years, maybe longer, she felt peace.

A few minutes passed. Eventually, Jerome whispered, "So, Annika, what do you think? Can I contact Doctor Holmes?"

She leaned away from him, looked deeply into his eyes, not knowing for a moment how to respond. Then came the words that would set her life on a new course. "Okay. I'll try it."

Psychiatry

Happy is he who learns to bear what he cannot change.
Friedrich Schiller

7 February, 1951

The morning after Jerome's visit, one of the doctors came in to clean her wound. Gently peeling back the bandages, he said, "We'll just clean you up a bit before you go."

As he slowly removed the dressing, the full extent of her injury revealed itself for the first time. Annika recoiled at the discolored, roughly nine-centimeter scar running down her left forearm. "How many sutures?" she asked.

"Let's see . . . it looks like about eighteen, I'd say. You were lucky, though. No major arteries involved. Just muscle. That should heal nicely. Can you wiggle your fingers for me?" She did. "Very good. No nerve involvement." He debrided some dead tissue, applied some ointment, and rebandaged the arm. "Keep it dry for about two weeks. You'll want to follow up with your family doc. Other than that, I think you're all set."

Later that morning, Annika was visited by Bellevue's chief psychiatrist, Doctor Reinhart. He took a seat by her bedside where, thumbing through her chart, he began by asking her how she was feeling and, as best as she could recall, why she was in the hospital. He prefaced his question by explaining that he had already talked at length with Jerome, whom he knew only tangentially, but who had provided a good bit of instructive information regarding her background.

"Well, Doctor Tritzchler, from what I'm told, I know you have some training in psychiatry, so I won't mince words with you. You were admitted to Bellevue with a diagnosis of manic-depressive reaction and a reference to rule out schizophrenia. Maybe you could tell me how you feel about that?"

"*Ja*, well, I have no history of mania or depression, and I've certainly never had any episodes of psychosis prior to my hospitalization. Yes, I've had a lot of very disturbing experiences that occasionally trouble me, sometimes greatly, but I believe I have enough wherewithal to know that I do not suffer from schizophrenia or manic-depressive illness."

"Okay. I'm inclined to agree with you. Some of my colleagues felt differently and had scheduled you for a regimen of . . ." He looked at her closely, and thought better of being blunt. ". . . therapy."

"Are you suggesting *electro-shock therapy*?"

"Well, yes, as a matter of fact. We call it ECT, but yes. It can be very helpful with severe depression . . . and schizophrenia." Annika fidgeted in bed. Blood rushed to her face. Reinhart noticed it immediately. "Don't worry . . . please, calm down. We're not going to do that. Actually, I have downgraded your diagnosis to what here in the US we call 'neurotic-depressive reaction.' From my discussion with Doctor Levine, I think we can consider you suitable for discharge . . ." Annika exhaled. ". . . but it's with the understanding that you will follow up with Doctor Holmes on an outpatient basis. I've already spoken with your caseworker . . ."

"Sarah?"

"Yes, Sarah. She'll be picking you up in a couple of hours . . . get you settled-in at home. We've made arrangements for you to meet with me once or twice before returning to work . . . We don't want to throw you back into anything that might spark a relapse." Annika nodded. "So, anyway," he said, extending his hand, "I'm happy to make your acquaintance and I wish you all the best."

He shook hands with her, picked up his coat and hat and prepared to leave. At the door, he turned and said, "I must say, Doctor Levine had a lot of nice things to say about you."

Fräulein

After he left, Annika did something that she usually avoided, something that for most people would be easy, maybe even routine, but for her was too great a threat. She reflected on the past fifteen years, admitting to herself the horrifying memories that occasionally bubbled to the surface, mostly when least expected. She acknowledged the terrifying dreams that invaded her sleep: images of bodies, cattle cars, beatings, rape, hangings. She thought of the Nazi doctors, how coolly and methodically they went about their experiments, how unfeeling they were to their victims, dispatching them with a shot of phenol directly to the heart once their usefulness had ended. She was able to think it a testament to her resilience that, after all she had experienced, she could function at all. But functioning, she realized, was a two-edged sword. It kept her busy and distracted, on the one hand, but often was a trigger for painful flashbacks, which had proved its potency these past few days.

It had been more than a decade since she had felt any genuine stability. If anything, the world felt terribly alien. She desperately missed her parents, feeling pain beyond words to know that she would never see them again. And there was Pasha. Even after all these years, she anguished over their brief, but intense affair. Pasha was the only man with whom she had ever felt entirely safe. Their intimacy was more than corporeal; it was spiritual, a connection that Annika had been certain could never be replicated with anyone else. She had long since abandoned any notions about their eventual reunion and a life together. Those fantasies had died along with almost everything else.

Which always brought her to the related question: *Why did I survive when so many others didn't?* Guilt was a central theme, but not just in terms of her own survival. No, even more troubling was her perceived complicity in the rabbi's death. Whenever she thought of that night – not getting out of bed to see him – she ruminated that subconsciously she must have *wanted* him to die. She reasoned that having fallen back to sleep rather than getting out of bed and attending to him was the fulfillment of an unconscious wish. Her lack of action meant that she – Annika Tritzchler, compassionate psychiatrist, devout Christian – was in reality . . . a murderer, no better than the evil SS doctors. As such, she considered herself a disgrace to her parents, as well as an abomination in the eyes of God. She had never been able to share this with anyone. It was her secret, and it was eating her up inside.

Her first psychotherapy session was not entirely what she expected, nor did it seem to lay the groundwork for a needed breakthrough. Doctor Holmes was a man in his mid-fifties, much older than Annika, and trained, as most psychiatrists were in these days, in Freudian psychoanalysis. His walk-up office on Bleeker Street was in a Bohemian section of Greenwich Village, only a short distance from the historic White Horse Tavern, a magnet for *avant-garde* poets and writers. He met her in a quiet, softly lit waiting room with a greeting that sounded perfunctory and distant. Bearded and obese, hair graying at the temples, Holmes was attired in a rumpled, black suit appearing at least one size too large (*looks like a tent,* she thought) and adorned at the shoulders not with ostentatious epaulets of SS officers that she had been used to in the camps, but a dusting of dandruff that even he should have noticed. His office was outfitted in Victorian furniture with dreary, turn-of-the-century pictures on the walls with the exception of oversized, gaudy diplomas above a cluttered roll-top desk. As she stepped further into the enclave, smelling faintly of mildew, her eyes fell upon a dated chaise lounge covered by a thin dark blanket of oriental design. This, she surmised, was that drab, ubiquitous feature of the Freudian mystique, popularly known as "the couch." She felt that she had just stepped back into late nineteenth century Vienna.

"Please," he said, gesturing to the settee.

"Should I sit, or . . .?" She left the question hanging.

"Most people are more comfortable reclining . . ." It sounded like he had responded in the same way countless times in the past. She lay on the chaise, propping herself up at the shoulders. "So why don't you start by telling me about yourself," he began.

Everything about him sounded mechanistic and detached, not at all how she had interacted with patients during her brief foray into psychotherapy. Her insecurity was intensified by the way he had her positioned on the couch. She felt constrained to look away, while the doctor was free to gaze upon her from a few feet behind, his notepad straddling his lap. With all that she had been through in Germany, the setting reeked if not of voyeurism, then certainly of power imbalance.

"Perhaps you could tell me a little bit about yourself," said Holmes, as he reached for his pipe. Annika leaned back, as instructed, and began talking about her early childhood. It went on like this for about ten minutes, all the while Doctor Holmes swiveled back and forth in his leather-backed, wooden chair. It squeaked like a dying hyena, and became so annoying that at one point Annika stopped talking. *Does he not notice, or is he testing me?* she wondered. Holmes waited, puffing on his pipe with such resolve that it sounded like the bellows to a forge.

Eventually, he broke the impasse. "So that's all fine and good, Mrs. Tritzchler . . ." he said, as prodigious clouds of gray smoke wafted to the ceiling, ". . . but tell me what it is that has brought you here?"

There was a dismissiveness to his tone, which emboldened Annika to respond in kind. "Doctor Holmes, if it would not be too much of a burden, I'd appreciate it if you would address me as either Annika, which most of my friends call me, or Doctor Tritzchler. Please don't call me 'Mrs. Tritzchler.' I'm not married, after all."

"Ah! I beg your pardon," Holmes said, as he jotted something in his notebook. "A bit of a slip on my part, Mrs . . ." He abruptly stopped and shook his head. "Uh, there I go again. I mean, *Annika.* Pardon me."

Maybe it was tension created by the doctor's aloofness; maybe it was the impersonal, almost alien ambience of his office; whatever it was, Annika's mind suddenly was awash in disturbing flashbacks. The smoke from his pipe had enshrouded the overhead light bulb, and as she looked at it, Annika was reminded of a deep orange sun

353

obscured in the haze of Ravensbrück's chimney. Parading through her mind were images of faces, people she had known and cared for who had been relegated to the ovens, then sprinkled as ash onto nearby fields. She thought of Elsie, her young patient at Bernberg, euthanized while the doctors nodded approvingly to one another. And poor Max – retarded, yet happy and full of life. She imagined his cheerful smile as he walked unknowingly into the euthanasia chamber.

"So tell me, *Annika* . . ." Holmes' raspy voice snapped her back to reality. The flashbacks vanished as quickly as they had come. "Why, my dear – if you don't mind my asking, that is – why are you *not* married? You're certainly beyond the marrying age."

A simple question, none too complex, yet in an instant everything she had tried to forget came rushing back with a poignancy so deep, so intense, that for a moment she lost sight of where she was. Standing before her was Pasha, bright and vivid, his unmistakable grin galvanizing deeply set smile-lines to the sides of each eye. This was a moment, a reawakening to the beauty of a soulmate, whose warmth and unsurpassed sensitivity were more, so much more, than the bittersweet reminiscences forever etched in her subconscious. But her reverie was fleeting.

While Holmes awaited her response, his rocking resumed into the same relentless, irritating squeal of metal-on-metal. Annika's image of Pasha evaporated like the vapor from one's breath on a cold, damp morning. Replacing it was Rolf, looming over her, intent on fulfilling his needs. Suddenly, without warning, Doctor Holmes dropped his leather tobacco pouch. It landed on the floor with only a soft thud, but with her nerves already on edge, she was startled and gasped loudly enough for Holmes to take notice. Her heart pounded against her chest, and she had the dreadful feeling that she might have lost a few drops of urine. That not only added to her anxiety, but with her attention now focused on her bladder, she began to have horrifying imagery from the night Rolf brutally raped her. Years may have passed, but she could still feel him tearing into her vagina, could still smell his hot, fetid breath in her face while her body was pinned beneath him.

Annika squirmed on the couch under Holmes' watchful gaze as he puffed thoughtfully on his pipe. "Hmmm?" he asked, in a voice more akin to a sing-song.

Annika steeled herself. "The war years . . . t-they . . . too much happened." She couldn't bring herself to share anything of an intimate nature; it was too premature.

"Ah, of course. But the war's been over for almost four years now. No 'knights in shining armor' since then?"

Annika's emotions suddenly surfaced in subdued rage. *He has such a cavalier attitude*, she thought. *He knows nothing of war, even less about suffering.* "You know, Doctor Holmes, with all due respect, you people in America, if you don't mind my stereotyping, you're ignorant to what's going on in the world. Here, the war is over. A sense of normalcy returned in 1945. People have gotten married; everyone's having babies. If anything, your standard of living has increased; your cities are unscathed. You take everything for granted: running water, plenty of food, high employment, education, electricity, even indoor plumbing. Americans have no idea what life is like overseas."

"Pray tell, what's that got to do with you, now? We're not in Europe. We're not at war . . ."

"*You* are not at war, Doctor. But I relive the war every day! It was only a short time ago that I left my homeland. Bombed to the ground. It was like Armageddon." Holmes puffed contentedly. "The cities throughout Europe were turned to rubble . . . and most remain that way *to this day*. Most of us who survived lost friends and relatives. Some of us, me included, lost our entire family."

"I see . . ." said the psychiatrist, unmoved, yet wanting to encourage more free-association.

"I'm not sure that you see at all. Thousands of us who survived had been tortured, directly or indirectly, and all for what? Our religion, our politics, our ethnicity?" He looked at her over the rims of his spectacles, the stem of his pipe barely touching his lips. "You ask about 'knights in shining armor . . .'" Tears began to appear on her cheeks. ". . . like I can pick up and get on with life as if nothing happened."

"Please continue. I'm listening," Holmes said, crossing his legs.

Choking back tears, Annika continued, "Those who didn't qualify as 'Aryan' were expendable – 'enemies of the state.' We were herded from our homes, often in the dead of night, separated from our loved ones and thrown into cattle cars so crowded that most couldn't even sit . . . *for days* . . . no food, no water, not even toilet facilities. And where were we going? We didn't know. I wound up in Ravensbrück. Ever heard of it?" Holmes raised his eyes and shook his head. "It was a concentration camp for women, a work camp, yet one that killed thousands. But there were so many other camps, thousands of them, and a lot of them, as I think you know, were extermination sites: Treblinka, Buchenwald, Auschwitz, places where people went not to work, but to be murdered."

The squeaking stopped. Holmes tapped his pipe against the ashtray, where he then left it. He leaned forward in his chair, putting his elbows on his knees, and looked directly at Annika, who had risen to a sitting position, returning his stare.

"But you know what the biggest insult is . . . *Doctor*?"

"I would like to hear it."

"It's that the Germans, the people who perpetrated this unprecedented misery – genocide in its purest form – they lost the war, but what's their consequence? Nothing. Sure, many died, cities were destroyed, but who were the real victims? The citizens. The allies are plowing tons of money into rebuilding Germany, but the very people who arrested us, tortured and killed us, most of them have returned to normal lives. Doctors who subjected us to painful experiments, killing hundreds in the process, maybe more, have returned to clinical practices, claiming to defend the 'Hippocratic oath.' And then, the so-called 'leaders of industry,' some of the same people who produced not just armaments, but chemicals for the gas chambers, even instruments of torture, businessmen who *used slave labor to do it* . . . where are they now? I'll tell you. They're back in the very same companies that colluded with the Nazis . . . Mercedes, BMW, Siemens, Bosch . . . the list goes on and on. They're back making fortunes, while the pitiful few who survived the holocaust are in many cases still homeless, and very much still unwanted."

". . . and, if it wouldn't be too difficult, I wonder if you could tell me how you feel about all that?"

"How I feel? I feel goddamned frustrated . . . and angry. My life ended in 1939. I'm . . . I'm devastated."

"I'm sure you've thought about moving forward . . . you know, getting on with your life . . ."

"Right, right. Move beyond the past . . . forget about it. Is that what you're suggesting?"

"Maybe it's more about forgiving than forgetting. Do you think that's possible?"

"Let me tell you a couple of incidents that haunt me. While I was in Bergen-Belsen, I had a patient from Poland. She told me of how the Jewish policemen were paid to round up fellow Jews and root out those in hiding. Once found, they would all be forced into the town square, listening all night long to shots ring out in the distance. They knew their people were being executed . . . by the hundreds, and it was obvious to them that their group would be next. Curiously, individuals conversed with resignation, accepting the inevitable and consoling one another until, one by one, they too were taken off to the forest, stripped naked, and forced to lay down at the edge of a pit. The woman who told me this survived a gunshot that only grazed her skull, which enabled her to hide in the mass of bloody corpses. At some point during that massacre, she saw two young women, teenagers, apparently best of friends, who, rather than being led away separately, ran to the pit arm-in-arm, where they laid down beside each other and, joining hands, met their tragic fate together."

Doctor Holmes quietly shook his head. "I have to admit, Annika, you're the first survivor I've ever talked to. I-I don't know if I have the right words to express my . . . profound . . . well . . . *humph* . . .

sadness. That's quite a distressing story. Let's hope that was an isolated incident."

"It was no isolated incident, Doctor. Villages all throughout Europe were annihilated by *Einsatzgruppen,* special killing units that murdered entire towns, cleaning them of any resistance before the Wehrmacht came through. In some regions, they butchered everyone – indiscriminately – especially the *intelligentsia.* The Nazis figured that those with education would see through their vacuous ideology, and pose a significant threat, so they murdered indiscriminately."

"Mmmm," was the only thing Holmes could mutter.

"Think of it, Doctor Holmes. You, an educated person . . . if you were living in eastern Europe when the Nazis came through, you'd be dead by now. Didn't matter whether you were Jew or not. And part of the rationale for killing was to make way for German immigrants, the people who were going to 'Aryanize' Europe to create Hitler's fantasy of world domination." She accented the word 'Aryanize' with two fingers from each hand to simulate quotation marks. "German families simply moved into houses vacated by the murdered owners. And it wasn't just housing that was given to German settlers. They were even given the clothing, right down to the underwear, of Jews who had been murdered in the camps."

"That's quite astonishing," Holmes said, shaking his head.

"To you, and to most Americans, yes. Not to Europeans, who witnessed this sort of thing routinely, both during and after the war. Here's an example. Shortly after the war, I once overheard a man on the train proudly showing off to his friend a vicuna coat he was wearing. He called it 'a Jew coat.' I couldn't believe my ears. But it wasn't just coats. Shoes, jewelry, paintings, furniture – it was all redistributed from the killing grounds. The internal exams I witnessed in the camps – rectal and vaginal – were only performed to find jewelry that inmates might have secreted. That's why the Nazis made 'em strip before killing them."

"Annika, what you're telling me is horrific. I'm sincerely moved . . . I am. Please, lay back and, if you can, take a couple deep breaths.

Try to relax."." Annika lifted her legs back onto the couch, but was too worked up to feel capable of fully reclining. Holmes pressed on. "So, going back to my original question. Are you telling me all this to explain why you haven't been able to form a meaningful relationship . . . you know, since the end of the war? As I said, the war's over, and you're no longer a prisoner. I'm sure you thank God at having been liberated . . ."

Holmes had struck a nerve. Bolstered by her own monologue, Annika, for the first time, was getting things out, talking about experiences she had repressed, and it was empowering to see the psychiatrist come out of his shell and respond to it with what appeared to be genuine emotion. But so far, he knew only the tip of the iceberg. It would take weeks, months, maybe years to get it all out, and probably even longer to process it all.

"Let me just say, Doctor Holmes, that when the Soviets came through, everyone assumed they'd be liberators, that they would treat survivors, few though we were, with kindness. But that didn't happen." She looked again to the ceiling. "Not only did killings continue, but even more flagrant was their treatment of women."

"Oh? Please, explain," said Holmes.

"In every town the Russians conquered, women were raped, *en masse.* Old and young alike. Even children. What people don't realize is that ordinary civilians were caught in the crosshairs of both the Germans and the Russians. When the Russians took back lands that the Nazis had occupied, they, the Russians, became the oppressors. Anyone suspected of collaboration with the Nazis was murdered, and in fact, simply having survived the Nazi occupation was often cause for the Reds to consider you a collaborator. Innocent civilians were sent by the thousands to Russian work camps."

Holmes thought she was avoiding his question, and he wasn't going to let go. Tapping his pipe against the ashtray, he asked, "So, Annika, were you raped?"

"I'd rather not talk about that," she replied.

359

Jerome

What counts in making a happy marriage is not so much how compatible you are, but how you deal with incompatibility.
Leo Tolstoy

<u>20 April, 1951</u>

"Care for some company?" It was Jerome.

"Oh, my word. Of course, Doctor Levine," she sputtered. She had been back to work at Mount Sinai for two weeks already and was seated in the cafeteria by herself on a lunch break. She pulled food items towards her to make room for him on the opposite side.

"I thought we had dispensed with formalities, *Doctor Tritzchler*," Jerome said, emphasizing her title to make his point.

"Yes, of course. We did, thank you. Sorry, Jerome."

"Well, Annika. It's good to see you back. I'd been wondering. How have things been going?"

"I believe I'm making some good headway with your friend, Doctor Holmes. We got off to a bit of a rocky start, but . . . I think I'm gaining."

"What you talk to him about is confidential, of course, but I'm glad to hear that it may be working out. You told me you've got a lot bottled up inside, so it seems like a great opportunity to get it out." She nodded. "You know, to be honest, I think your experiences will define you . . ." Annika looked down. "No, listen, I mean define you in a very positive way. You're a survivor. You have tremendous resiliency. You've proved it, over and over again."

"Probably not the night I was brought in to Bellevue . . ."

"I think you probably needed to get to that point, Annika. You

360

were crying for help, but couldn't bring yourself to verbalize it. You've spent your life doing for others and haven't known how to ask for help when you, yourself, really need it. And don't we all have times when we need help?"

"Yeah, sure," she said, but it didn't take a psychiatrist, or even a pathologist, to suggest to Jerome that she was embarrassed by the events that led to her hospitalization.

Jerome put down his glass of water. Looking around the room, he said in a soft voice, "Annika, there's nothing to be ashamed of. What you did, and where you landed, was entirely natural, in some ways even predictable. Don't let that bother you. It'll only hold you back. Move forward. Remind yourself of your strengths, of all that you've accomplished . . ."

"Well, thank you for your encouragement. Not sure where I'm gonna go with all that. Certainly would've been better if it had never happened." She looked at him with affected joviality. "Who knows . . . I might've been a colleague, can you imagine . . .?"

Jerome took a bite from his sandwich. Washing it down with a gulp of water, he said, "Not only can I imagine that, I think you should get back into medicine. Better yet, psychiatry . . ." He said it so nonchalantly that it sounded sincere, even realistic.

". . . Oh, c'mon," she said, looking down, shaking her head. "I can't . . . it wouldn't . . ."

"Listen to you," he chuckled. "I can't . . . Of course, you can. It makes all the sense in the world. You're already trained. You even have experience. But, Annika, you have something much more, something few people in the profession possess, even Holmes. You have lived through profound adversity, inhumanity at its most obscene. You have suffered, and witnessed suffering. You, of all people, have something highly unique to offer, especially, *especially* . . ." he repeated for emphasis, ". . . to patients suffering loss and depression. You don't see it, Annika, but I do. It's there . . . for the taking, and I hope you take it."

"Oh, I don't know . . . It's nice of you to say that, but . . ."

"Not 'nice' at all. It's a fact. I don't mean to push you into anything you don't want, but I really hope you'll think about it. I hope you don't dismiss thinking you can't do it or that you have nothing to offer. You may not be ready now, but when, and if, you ever are ready, I'll do everything I can to help you." When Jerome got up to leave, Annika rose to join him. Together, elbows bumping each other, they exited the cafeteria.

As the weeks rolled by, Jerome too was becoming a bigger part of Annika's life. Shared lunches in the cafeteria evolved to include dinner invitations. Initially, it was simply to a local café for an after-work "bite to eat," but as the impromptu meals became more frequent, they were getting to know one another as more than just co-workers. He took an unusual interest in her psychological recovery.

"Jerome, I want you to know . . ." She faltered. "I'm not sure exactly how to word this . . . I-I appreciate your encouragement. It's been helpful, maybe more than you realize, but to be honest, my . . . my behavior . . . what led me to be hospitalized, that is . . . well, it's been really embarrassing for me to talk about."

Jerome was unfazed. "It shouldn't be embarrassing at all, Annika. Anybody who's gone through what you have . . . and especially then to be expected to reenter society – as if nothing ever happened? That's pretty unrealistic."

"But that's exactly how it is. And, yes, I'm glad you can see that. It's very hard." He reached forward, taking hold of her hand. She looked at him, her eyes beginning to float with tears. "So, how is it that you can be so understanding? In ways other people can't? I could never tell anyone else that I had been a patient in a mental hospital."

"Remember I told you that I had worked as a surgeon during the war." She nodded. "Well, one of my assignments was at a field hospital on the Cherbourg Peninsula . . . in France. It was during the summer of '44."

"Cherbourg?" she asked.

"Yeah. You'd probably know it as Normandy. We saw hundreds and hundreds of casualties. It made quite an impression on me. But you know what? The battle wounds were one thing, as I'm sure you can imagine. But just as striking were the soldiers who had reached a state of emotional collapse. 'Psychoneurosis' they called it. Men who had seen too much. 'Shell shock,' 'battle-weary' . . . whatever name you give it, it all means the same. The mind can only handle so much. Many of those who were valorous on the battlefield – heroes, in every sense of the word – well, some of those same men suffered a breakdown, but not until they got home . . . When you think about it, what is home but a place where it's safe to feel again. That's how I see things going with you."

Jerome's words were like morphine to pain, maybe sunshine on a rain-soaked field. She squeezed his hand, relishing his comfort and above all his acceptance. She could tell that he was attracted to her, and there was no denying her growing attraction to him. But giving in to her emotions wasn't as easy as either of them might have liked. She was finding it difficult to let her guard down. One night, following an elegant dinner at a quaint restaurant in downtown Manhattan, Jerome leaned forward to kiss her. It was a first, a symbol of his feelings towards her. For Annika, though, it set off an unexpected wave of anxiety. As his lips brushed up against hers, she froze, statue-like, unable to requite his gesture. Somewhat confused, he pulled away, fearing that he had acted prematurely.

"Is everything okay?" he asked.

It took a moment for her to respond. "Yes, of course. It's quite okay. It's just that . . ." Looking down at the table, she stopped. It was obvious that she was in conflict. They only thing not so obvious was why.

After a polite silence, Jerome said, "I didn't mean to . . ."

Annika put her hand up. "It's not you, Jerome." She looked into his eyes and, taking his hand into her own, said, "It's me. I like you, very much. The talks we've had, the meals we shared . . . it's all been very special. I'm just not sure . . ."

"Not sure you're ready?" He answered for her. "I understand, Annika. I'm not looking for any commitment. I can . . ."

"No, please. You don't have to do anything. I think we've reached a crossroads where . . . well, there's something I need to tell you . . . or at least something we need to talk about." She proceeded to tell him about Pasha, about their meeting, their tryst in Geneva, the letters they shared, their plans to meet in Vienna, and then the abruptness with which everything ended. "I've often thought of Pasha. Sometimes wondering if he might somehow return, maybe show up on my doorstep. I know that's foolish, but I've never known what happened to him . . . whether it was me, or whether he met someone else . . . or, worse, that, God forbid, something might have happened to him . . . because of the war."

"It's hard to let go of those feelings, I'm sure. Is that what you're saying?"

"I guess so. I think it's all part of my moving forward . . . being able to let go . . . of everything."

"Have you ever tried to locate him, or investigate as to his possible whereabouts . . .?" She shook her head. "I wouldn't want to intrude on something so special to you, but would it help if I tried to find out some information? I still have contacts in Europe."

"I haven't tried. I guess I've always been worried that I might find out something that would have been better not to know. But, yes, I think I need to know, if it's at all possible." She got up and took a step to him, hands outstretched. He grasped both of them as he, himself, stood. Then, spontaneously, they hugged. If at first a bit tentatively, they rapidly became enveloped in one another's arms – a true bear hug.

Annika's mind was whirling. *Who is this man?* she wondered. *Where did he come from?* There was something so different about him, something she couldn't put her finger on, but it was there from the first time they had met. For ten years, the only man she ever thought she could have a relationship with was her "soulmate," Pasha. And now, though she tried to resist them, some of the same feelings she had experienced with him were bubbling back to the surface, this time with Jerome.

It wasn't more than a week later that Jerome saw Annika in the hallway. He had been looking for her. "Hey, good morning. Let's meet in the lobby after work . . . say around five?"

"Oh, thanks, Jerome. I'm pretty exhausted. How about . . .?"

"I have some news, Annika. I think you'll want to hear it."

Jerome walked her through Central Park. Coming upon an empty park bench, he suggested they sit. "I've been doing some digging, Annika. I-I received some information about your friend, Pavel."

Annika's eyes opened wide. "What is it?" she asked, sitting on the edge of the bench, facing him. "Tell me."

"I took the liberty of making some contacts, trying to see if we might learn the whereabouts of Pasha."

"Why? Why would you go to that effort?"

"Annika, I know how much Pavel has meant to you. You and I have developed a very close relationship, but there's an impediment. You and I both know it. If there is any chance of Pavel being alive or coming back into your life, I want you to know that I will be the last person to stand in the way. So, I agree with your statement last week that we have reached a 'crossroads,' as you put it. Until you get clarity on Pavel, our relationship, valuable and intimate though it is, seems to have reached an impasse."

"What did you find out?"

"Well, I went through several channels, and finally made contact with a registrar at the University of Krakow, Blanka Woźniak. I mention her name because she's agreed to mail you some documentation, including a page from the *Special Prosecution Book - Poland*. You've probably never heard of it – I hadn't – but it was a list of scholars and activists the Nazis considered a threat to the regime. The name Pavel Kushalevsky appears with over sixty thousand other names. It was nothing short of an enemies list that had been compiled under the auspices of Reinhard Heydrich in Germany immediately prior to the invasion of Poland. No doubt you've heard of Heydrich." Annika grimaced. "Well, once they invaded, anyone on the list was subject to arrest. Mrs. Woźniak discovered that Pavel, along with hundreds of others at the university, was arrested in September, 1939 – part of what the SS called the *Intelligenzaktion*. Now comes the hard part." He took her hand into his own. "Are you ready?"

Annika sensed what was coming. "Yes. Please, go on."

"The Nazis committed massacres all throughout Poland. We knew that. Mrs. Woźniak was given access to some of the records recovered from the *Einsatzgruppen*, and found that your Pavel was executed in October following a brief imprisonment."

Annika looked away. "I might have guessed as much. Do they know how he died?"

"I'm not sure that's important, is it? Why don't we leave it at that . . .?"

She looked at him, imploringly. "It's important to me . . ."

Jerome eyed her, pausing for several seconds. "Well, she said that he was one of the first to die; probably, she thought, because of his Russian roots. How they might have known that is uncertain, but according to eyewitnesses she spoke with. . ." He hesitated, not wanting to go on.

Annika was wide-eyed, braced for the answers she had waited so long to hear. "Go on, Jerome."

"Apparently, Annika, he, along with several colleagues, was publicly hanged. His death was followed almost immediately by mass executions, mostly by firing squads. Tens of thousands were killed, even more sent to camps where most died."

She put her head down, her eyes closed, showing little outward sign of emotion. Jerome continued to hold her hand. Now it was his turn to wait. Eventually, she spoke, first to the floor, but then, raising her head, directly to Jerome. "Somehow, I knew it all along. None of this surprises me. Please don't take this the wrong way, Jerome, but what Pasha and I had . . ." She squinted her eyes. ". . . brief though it might have been, was sublime, that's the only way I can describe it. I felt very strongly that he would never have simply walked away from me. To have not heard anything from him for so many years . . . I *knew* he had to be dead. And, God have mercy, part of me, well, part of me actually *wanted* him to be dead. Isn't that awful?"

"Not awful, at all, Annika. I totally understand. It was the only way to make sense of his absence." Jerome wrapped his arms around her. At first, she sat stiffly, but as his words registered in her mind, she slowly turned into him, joining his embrace. The warmth and understanding she felt from Jerome in that moment was a catharsis. For the first time in years, Annika felt free, a liberation even greater than the day she departed Ravensbrück. She cried as Jerome held her, rocking her ever so slightly, back and forth, while whispering words of comfort.

With her head on his shoulder, tears streaming from both eyes, Annika said, "I appreciate what you've done, Jerome. It hurts . . . but . . . after all this time, I'm so relieved to know what happened. Maybe, maybe I can finally let go."

Unlocking a Secret

*Every advance in knowledge brings us face to face with the
mystery of our own being.*

Max Planck

April - September, 1951

Annika had continued her weekly visits with Doctor Holmes. If
nothing else, the sessions convinced her that while the demons were
still there, and maybe always would be, she was now facing them
head-on without avoidance or denial. Those who had told her that
time itself would diminish her torment had been wrong. This was
work, pure and simple. In early April, when her early sessions with
Holmes were at the most challenging, she had written in her journal
the following:

*It's maddening to think that back in the camps, I felt mentally
strong, able to persevere under unimaginable stress, yet here in
America, where I have a safety net of meaningful work, plenty of food
and even the promise of a future, my former resilience seems to be
failing me.*

Holmes reframed this not as weakness, but as genuine progress.
"Your resilience isn't failing you," he had said. "It's what is enabling
you to come to terms with your trauma. Without resilience, you might
have perished long ago. Talking about events that have been
suppressed will prove liberating in the long run, remember that."
Annika rubbed her mouth, thinking, digesting. "I wonder if you could
tell me about your dreams . . ."

"My dreams? The only dreams I remember are my nightmares."

"Okay. Let's start there."

Annika took a long time before responding. Holmes waited, patiently as usual. He sensed that she was deep in reflection, and from her sweat appearing on her forehead, he could tell that what she was imagining was disturbing. Finally, she spoke, "I've had a lot of nightmares. Some of the most disturbing are not about anything that can be put in words. In the dream, there is nothing, no time, no people, nothing sensory. It is as if . . . I don't know if I'm alive or dead . . . I just have awareness . . . but it is of . . . nothing. Nothingness. Like I'm dead, but aware . . . I-I can't describe it."

"Are there any you *can* describe . . . any that stand out?"

Annika thought for a moment. She looked down at her hands, then a few seconds later over to the wall, and finally back at Holmes before answering. "Well," she paused, ". . . now that you ask, yes. A lot of my dreams have – in one way or another – involved horses. I've never mentioned that to anyone. In fact, until now, never really thought about it." She took another minute or so, her eyes peering wistfully around the room as Holmes puffed patiently on his pipe. "Looking back, it seems that the worst times in my life were accompanied, maybe even preceded, by dreams – no, nightmares – involving horses . . ."

"Horses? Interesting. What do you make of that?" Holmes asked.

"I don't know . . . I think . . . maybe they have something to do with the Quadriga . . ."

She seemed deep in thought. Holmes gave her a few minutes to expound, but when she remained silent, he asked, "What is the Quadriga?"

"Have you ever been to Berlin?" Holmes shook his head. Well, the Quadriga . . . I guess you'd call it a statue . . . It's at the very top of the Brandenburg Gate. Growing up, I never really understood it, but somewhere in my adolescence my stepfather explained that it portrays the Roman goddess, Victoria. If I remember correctly, she's being pulled triumphantly in a chariot by four horses. Every time I've ever passed under it, I'd stop to look up – even as an adult – kind of mesmerized. It looked so . . . so regal, like, I don't know, *other-worldly*. I can't explain it, but whatever, it always had some kind of effect on me. I always just passed it off as an artifact of my youth." She looked at Holmes, who seemed to be listening intently. "Maybe," Annika continued, "maybe the dreams had something to do with that."

"Do you remember any of the content . . . like what happened in the dreams? It could be important."

"I do remember. The first one occurred just before my parents left for Belgium. It was really vivid. There was a man sitting bareback on a massive white horse. He was herding throngs of people to . . . I couldn't tell where . . . to prison, to their death . . . All I knew was that it felt bad. He was like an overseer, directing them. It was the same dream, over and over. I was in the crowd, separated from my parents. People were getting trampled by the horse. I tried to get to my parents in the dream, but then things would go blank. That's when I would have that feeling of nothingness. There was no reality. Everything sensible was gone.

"Then there was another one. It came years later. In that one, there was a warrior . . . I could never make out his face, but he was also riding a horse, the whole time wielding a sword . . . swinging it back and forth. He got really close to me. The horse wheeled around and reared up. I can still see that long mane blowing in the wind as the horse stood on its hindlegs. In that dream, I would always seem to wake up just as the horseman swung his sword at my head."

"That sounds frightening," Holmes said, rocking slowly in his chair. "Do you still have either of those dreams."

"No. But in Ravensbrück, I started having a different dream, another nightmare revolving around a horse. It was terrifying. I'll never forget the horse in those dreams. It was always the same . . . a black stallion. Behind it was . . . utter blackness. When I would look at the horse and the dark background against which it was silhouetted, everything . . . stopped. I don't know how to explain it. It was like a black sky without any stars . . . or anything. There is no way to describe the feeling that accompanied it. The only words that might make any sense would be . . . complete emptiness." She stopped, suddenly overcome. "I guess that's why it was so frightening. It was like being dead . . . but alive. I never could put my finger on it, but I would feel like I was being swallowed up by some alien force. I always woke up in a panic."

"You've had a lot of time to process those dreams. Do they have any meaning to you at this point?"

"I'm not sure. I've often wondered about . . . I don't know . . . whether they had any symbolism, something like that." She blew her nose. "They never suggested that I make any changes – you know, like to my plans, or what I was going to do that day, or anything like that. The only thing I can say is, they always seemed to come before something bad happened . . . as if they were some kind of omen. Maybe that's why they were so frightening . . ."

Holmes puffed on his pipe, nodding. He interpreted her dreams as reflections of the events around her, but more importantly, her innate insight. After explaining this, he said, "I'd like you to think about those dreams. Your inner voice speaks to you, often in mysterious ways. Sometimes it's direct and comes from easily interpretable dreams. Other times, its hidden in dreams we don't remember. Dreams that are more vivid are often disguised by symbols, like a poem, or an impressionistic artwork. But those symbols hold meaning and often require work to decode them. I can't tell you what it means, other than possibly give some hints. The true meaning comes from the perceiver, and that's you. I would encourage you to write them down, especially right after you have one, when it's fresh in your mind."

He went on to explain the flashbacks as happening now only because of her being in a safe place. "Back in the camps, traumatic events had to be suppressed in order to survive. Most people turn off their feelings in the face of shocking, highly disturbing events. They get buried, but they don't disappear. It's only when a person feels safe that the memories begin to come out. Now, Annika, you're free to explore; it's safe. The flashbacks are telling you they're not going away. Only by exploring those traumatic memories can you reduce their potency. Eventually, they'll extinguish all on their own."

To Annika, this all made sense. She grew to trust the doctor, despite the ambivalence with which she faced each session. As her confidence grew, she took the risk of telling him how distracting she found his squeaking chair. "It grates on my nerves . . . to the point I've actually thought of leaving. I can't believe you don't even notice it," she said. This was a watershed moment. The detestable noise had disappeared by her next session.

Doctor Holmes knew of her budding relationship with Jerome, enabling him to put aside his earlier concerns about "repressed homosexuality." But he also sensed that there were still things locked up inside her, issues needing to be identified and worked through. Finally, one day, in a moment of mute silence, Holmes said, "You know, Annika, you've been making remarkable progress. I think we both can agree on that. You've clearly come a long way. But let's be honest. I know there's more. Something's still bothering you." Annika fidgeted, suggesting to Holmes he had struck a nerve. "The thing is, until you acknowledge it, you're going to stay stuck."

Holmes hadn't expected his words to have such immediate impact. Annika's face reddened. *He's seen right through me*, she thought. Her hands began to tremble. Yet she remained quiet. "C'mon, Annika. I can see it. You're right there. You *want* to get it out, I know you do. Don't pass up this . . ."

"Okay! *Okay!*" she literally screamed. Her eyes looked as if they might pop out of her skull.

Holmes put down his pipe and sat erect, resolute, hands folded in his lap. He had never seen her so distressed, even during one of her flashbacks. This was different. There was no dissociation; she was fully present. "What do you want to tell me, Annika? I want to hear it."

"I . . . I'm responsible for the death of one of my patients . . .

372

Rabbi Bergmann." she blubbered.

Holmes clearly hadn't expected this, but if he was shocked, he didn't show it. Annika buried her face in her hands. She told him about the rabbi, his alleged complicity in the deaths of thousands, possibly including her own parents.

"Please, Annika. Go on."

"He was a monster. I killed him . . . in the course of my duties as a doctor. I never told anyone. Not even Martyna . . ." She buried her face in her hands and began sobbing. "I don't want to talk about it. I need to go."

"You do want to talk about it, Annika. You're right there. You've buried it for so long. It's eating you up. Let it out."

"I went in to check on him. I probably shouldn't have, but I told him he was responsible for the murders of the Jews in his community."

"Yes . . ."

"He got angry. Told me he didn't care, that they went to their deaths on their own accord. Called them weak . . . and stupid."

"And . . ."

". . . and he told me . . . he didn't care, not even about my parents. He said they were all responsible for their own fate."

"And that bothered you . . . deeply. Didn't it?"

"I mentioned integrity to him . . . told him that he had made a commitment to care for his congregants, and that he had betrayed them."

"And what did he say?"

"He said . . . and I remember his words distinctly . . . he said he didn't give a 'rat's ass' about my integrity . . ." Annika's face was awash in tears. She rubbed her nose with her sleeve. Holmes handed her several tissues, which she grabbed without looking at him. She dried her eyes and blew her nose. He handed her several more.

"How did you feel, Annika?"

"How did I feel?" She stared at him, her eyes wet and piercing. She swiped at a lock of hair that had fallen in her face. "I felt anger.

Intense anger. I tried to control it, but . . ."

"But what?"

"He changed the topic. Demanded pain medication. I gave it to him, but I was so emotional. I tried not to show it, but inside I was reeling. I felt like I had met the Devil. I lost sight of reason."

"So, what did you do?"

"I-I gave him his meds, but in a much larger dose than normal. He had also been on a sleep regimen, so I gave him . . ." Her voice quavered. ". . . a large dose of barbiturates."

"And what happened?" Holmes had already figured it out, but he needed Annika to say it.

"I left. The next morning . . . well, he had died. The records showed that he had died of a heart attack." As she said this, she could feel a wave of panic coursing through her body. Along with it came another hallucination of Bergmann. Annika put her hands to her temples and shook her head from side to side, weeping uncontrollably as she tried to chase away the vision.

Holmes could see what was happening, but was not ready to let her stop. "Is there more?" he asked.

"The next morning, Martyna told me that one of the aides had informed her that Bergmann had made a confession. Some kind of Jewish ritual when someone is about to die. He had confessed to the aide that he had felt guilty and wanted his death to be an atonement for his sins."

"He knew he was going to die?" Holmes asked.

"On some level, maybe. I don't know. But hearing about his confession just intensified my guilt."

"Annika, I want to ask you. Is it possible he set you up?"

"I don't know what you mean. What are you asking?"

"From your description, I can't help wondering if he tried to coerce you into killing him." Holmes had Annika's full attention. "What I'm questioning is whether he may have tried to manipulate you by saying all those incredibly insensitive things in the hope that perhaps you, or maybe someone else, would do what he himself couldn't – take his own life."

Annika leaned forward, her elbows on her knees. She looked down, weeping. She had no words to respond. Then Holmes did something uncharacteristic for him. He reached out for Annika's hands, which were cold as ice. He held them tenderly, warming them with his own while whispering, "It's okay, Annika. You've gotten it out. You're the one in control now . . . not him."

Holmes sat with her for an additional hour. This was the breakthrough he had been waiting for. There was no more need to prod. Annika's emotion spilled like water from an overflowing dam. She went on to tell him that her biggest impediment, bigger than even Bergmann's death, was having hidden it from Martyna. Admitting it would have been devastating, an acknowledgement of her failure as both a doctor and a human being.

"This secret . . . it's torn you up for years, I can tell," Holmes said, now handing Annika an entire box of tissues. "I'm guessing it's what accounts for your lack of desire to reenter medicine, right?" Wiping her eyes, she nodded in agreement. "Have you been able to share this with Jerome?" he asked.

"No. God no. He thinks too much of me. Like Martyna. I can't risk losing them."

"Not true, Annika. You *can* take that risk. You're a human being. Remember that. You're someone whose reality was shattered by inhumane circumstances – circumstances that lead people to do things they wouldn't normally do, especially in wartime."

Taking a minute to blow her nose, Annika replied, "What are you suggesting?"

"It's not up to me to suggest. I'm simply trying to help you come to terms with your demons. How you handle them will be up to you."

"You think I should tell Martyna . . . is that it?"

"That's something that only you can decide. All I can say is that secrets have a way of eating us alive, from the inside out. They're like a cancer. Listen, why don't we talk about it in a few days. Give you a chance to think about it."

Annika composed herself and, at his urging, assured Doctor Holmes she felt safe going home. When they met again three days later, she informed the psychiatrist that she had written to Martyna. "I told her everything. I-I acknowledged my role in Bergmann's death."

"Do you plan to tell Jerome?" he asked.

"No. Not yet. I need more time."

Six weeks elapsed, during which Annika reported more flashbacks than usual, and sleep that was punctuated by night terrors. She informed Holmes that it often took several minutes sitting bolt upright in bed drenched in sweat before she could distinguish reality from the hypnagogic hallucinations. He listened calmly, interpreting this as a predictable phenomenon, akin to fever spiking before one's recovery from illness. Responding to her request for sedatives, he cautioned against it, suggesting that it would interrupt her progress. "Let's ride it out," he urged.

A fateful day came in September. Annika took her position on the couch. Looking up to the ceiling, she watched as the smoke from his pipe curled upwards, gradually enshrouding the lightbulb as it had done in each and every session in the past. This time, however, to her surprise, she had no flashback. It was simply smoke swirling around a lightbulb. For the first time since being with Holmes, she felt relaxed.

"Everything okay?" Holmes asked, a bit mystified by the apparent change in mood.

Without answering, Annika pulled an envelope from her handbag. She flipped it open and began reading. The letter was written in German, which for Holmes she translated to English:

Fräulein

Martyna Raskiewicz
286 B Mostowa Street
Warsaw, Poland
15 August, 1951

To my very dearest friend, Annika.
It was so good to hear from you. To know that you are alive,
living in America, and best of all in the care of a psychiatrist. We all
could use that, Annika. We used to dream of survival, but survival by
itself, I find, is not enough. We have too many memories and too many
losses. Life will never again seem normal, but with any luck life can
take on new meaning with opportunity to once again find fulfillment
in our work and personal relationships.

I am in good health, and as you can see from my address, I have
located to a flat in downtown Warsaw. The city was devastated by the
Germans. Most of the Jews were killed. I am one of the few returning
physicians and am working at the Hospital of the Holy Spirit. It has
partnered with the old Wola Hospital, which lost a majority of its
medical staff to massacres by the Nazis in 1944. When the Soviets
came in, many of the survivors were arrested. Things have stabilized
somewhat, and there has been considerable rebuilding, but still a
long way to go with much of the population remaining quite
traumatized. Not much in the way of psychiatry here.

I appreciate your feelings about the circumstances surrounding
Bergmann's death, but instead of you apologizing for what you did
not tell me, it is really I who should make the apology. There were
things which at the time I felt uncomfortable discussing with you.
Bergmann had provoked me and others with the same kind of
outrageous statements that he did with you, It seemed that once his
true identity became known, he abandoned any pretense of self-
righteousness, trying instead to justify himself through empty
rationalizations. Word was getting out, though, that he had the blood
of thousands on his hands and feared retribution from the camp,
which I suspected was coming, whether from the inmates or the

377

military. Like other collaborators, he was a coward at heart.

Here's the truth, Annika. After his repeated taunts, I stopped providing medication to him. You must have seen my instructions on his chart. I determined that this man was destabilizing to the unit, and in my view as medical director, his disruptiveness abrogated his status as a top-priority patient. With our medications in precariously short supply, I triaged him as "non-urgent," even knowing that without drugs, he could easily become septic. I was prepared to let him die a natural death if it meant that the same drugs might save one or more others who, like us, had suffered because of people like him. When I came in on the morning of his death, I was not surprised and simply diagnosed his passing to cardiac arrest secondary to septic shock.

My decision regarding Bergmann would not have been made in normal times, but under the critical circumstances we faced at Belsen, where people of all stripes and nationalities were trying to coexist and survive, I could not in good conscience keep this man alive at the expense of other patients. In short, Annika dear, it was not you, but I who take responsibility for Bergmann's death. And even though I too reflect back on that situation, I have no regrets. To think that such a man might have returned to his homeland to once again "lead his people" while having been guilty of mass-murder on the grandest scale seemed to me unconscionable, as much then as it does now.

I have untold remorse for the guilt you have carried all this time. For that, I am truly sorry. I can only hope that my acknowledgement will now unburden you and allow you to get on with your life. You are a picture of strength and stoicism and have always impressed me as a caring, competent, and ethical physician, someone I am proud to call my friend. With all the harm done to our profession by the Nazis, the field of medicine is in dire need of doctors like you who can help us to reclaim the Hippocratic ideals that for millennia have earned us the respect and admiration of our communities. I pray that your therapy, and hopefully this letter, will help you to move forward with your life in the productive and meaningful way that God intended.

Fräulein

I love you with all my heart and soul, and look forward to the day we can again raise a real goblet of wine (not one made of tin) in a happy toast to our survival.

Be safe. Know that I am always thinking of you.

Martyna

Annika placed the letter in her lap. She bowed her head and quietly wept. Holmes sat in silence, giving her the space to process her feelings.

The Pale Horse

You are not judged by the height you have risen, but from the depth you have climbed.

Frederick Douglass

The letter Annika received from Martyna had been as great a liberation as that miraculous day in northern Germany when she and the Ravensbrück "ladies" eagerly devoured Hershey bars from the advancing Americans. Her words provided an emancipation from the enslavement of a crippling belief, the conviction that she had been complicit in a homicide. It gave her the opportunity to move beyond the past and look to the future.

Martyna's revelations breathed new life into Annika's relationship with Jerome, as well. To no longer think of herself as a closeted murderer was to jettison emotional ballast that had long threatened to sink her. In addition, learning of Pasha's fate, deeply upsetting though it was, freed her of any misconceptions regarding his possible return. He had been a soulmate, of that there was no question, but as time wore on, she was to discover a boundless capacity for love, which made more than one soulmate a distinct possibility. She had long been known for her eagerness to give, but with her recovery came something new: a willingness and a capability to receive. That had always been difficult and was only possible by rebuilding trust, something the Nazis had robbed her of, but her greatest challenge wasn't simply trusting others, it was learning to again trust in herself. Achieving that goal proved to be the foundation for true intimacy.

Jerome and Annika were married in June, 1952 at a private ceremony in the City Clerk's office just a few blocks from their two-

380

bedroom apartment on Manhattan's Upper East Side. Not long afterwards, Annika went on, with the support and encouragement of her new husband, to pursue her medical license. She was able to secure from Berlin transcripts of her medical education as well as records of her post-doctoral involvement at the Bernburg facility. Because of her lengthy absence from medicine, she was required to take refresher courses at Columbia, which she welcomed. Her day of reckoning came when she appeared before the licensure board. If there was any prejudice against this middle-aged woman with the strong German accent, it didn't prevent her from providing a poignant and convincing explanation of the events that landed her in two of Hitler's notorious camps, and she was granted state licensure by unanimous vote.

Although still young enough to conceive, Annika's abortion and sterilization at Ravensbrück prevented her from bearing any children. It was only then that she came to terms with the deep emotional scars left by Rosenthal and Quernheim. She and Jerome had considered adoption, but in the end decided against it due to the lack of predictability in their respective work schedules. The absence of children in her life was probably what led her to pursue a residency in child psychiatry at Cornell's Medical College, a short distance from home. There, she was able to recapture the gratification of working with patients like Max and Elsie, knowing that this time around, she was free to invest to her heart's content. Her reward was in being around long enough to witness her patients' growth, many of whom went on, in spite of their disability, to lead creative and fruitful lives.

With Jerome working only a short distance from Annika at Cornell, they enjoyed considerable time together, sometimes meeting for extended lunches, more often for dinners out after work. Annika's training in psychoanalysis propelled her to become active in the New York Psychoanalytic Society, which itself was close by and boasted not only a storied history, but ongoing meetings and seminars attended by some of the world's biggest names in psychoanalysis, including refugees from Europe, some of whom she had met years before the war at the conferences in Geneva and Vienna. If there had ever been any doubts as to Annika's future, her life since 1951 had laid them to rest.

Her many happy years with Jerome were to culminate on a cold day in early February, 1982. Annika was awakened that morning by a nightmare, the first in as long as she could remember. Instinctively, she reached over to feel for Jerome. His side of the bed was empty, and in her state of arousal she panicked, not realizing that he had already left for work. Pushing herself to a seated position against the headboard, her heart beating like a jackhammer, sweat seeping from her pores like thousands of tiny faucets, she felt the same sickening dread that had accompanied night-terrors in the past. This one had come out of nowhere and was so fresh in her mind that, even sitting there, she could almost see it unfolding before her eyes. It involved a man slowly cantering a pale horse, his back turned away from her. She couldn't identify him, but she could see that he was attired in what looked like a cloak of burlap, and it appeared that his entire body was covered in a thin, grayish film. The dream was as familiar as it was unsettling. She immediately got up and called the hospital.

"Oh, good morning." It was the charge nurse. She sounded cheerful. "Doctor Levine's in a meeting. I'll have him call you when they get out."

Annika was relieved. Everything seemed routine. Around 11:00 AM, the phone rang.

"Jerome! I'm so glad you called . . ."

The voice on the other end was a man's, but not Jerome's. "Doctor Tritzchler? This is Sam Weintraub . . . I'm the ER doc at Mount Sinai."

Annika recognized his name. She assumed she was being summoned for a psychiatric emergency. "Yes, good morning, Sam. What can I do for you?"

"Annika, I need you to come over to the hospital. It's . . . about Jerome."

Annika panicked. "Jerome? Is he okay?"

"I-I'm afraid not. Annika. Jerome's suffered an 'M.I.' . . . a pretty severe one."

"A heart attack? Jerome? Where is he now?"

"He's here, Annika. In the ER. Listen, I need to convey some very upsetting news." Annika was already in tears. "We performed CPR, got him intubated and prepared for surgery, but, well, it was to no avail. His heart gave out." He could hear her sobbing. "I'm terribly sorry, Annika. Jerome and I were very good friends."

Annika buried her beloved companion of nearly thirty years in a tightly-packed Jewish cemetery in Queens against a backdrop of skyscrapers and smokestacks. There, Jerome shared a large vault in a family mausoleum, which Annika visited every week. It was a place of solace and introspection, a place where she could reflect on life, embrace her losses and leave feeling energized.

She distinguished herself at Cornell for her compassion as well as leadership in advancing an understanding and acceptance of childhood autism. Her work continued until 1990, when she retired at the age of seventy-five. Jerome had always wanted to visit Germany with Annika, so that she could show him where the odyssey of her youth had played out. "Only when you're ready," he had said, which, during his lifetime, she never really was. That changed in 1996, when in her journal she wrote, *It's now or never . . .*

Annika flew out of JFK airport with a group of aged holocaust survivors destined for a tour of Berlin. They were met at Tegel airport by a small tour bus that was at their personal disposal. Annika was struck by how much of the city was unrecognizable due to the rebuilding necessitated by the extensive Allied bombing. The Soviet's long occupation had also left its mark, but with the fall of the Berlin wall, the group was free to travel anywhere it pleased. The group walked through the Tiergarten, triggering poignant memories of her parents' farewell. Driving under the Brandenburg Gate, Annika looked up to the Quadriga as she had done countless times throughout her childhood. Something had changed. No longer did those majestic horses radiate the splendor and wonderment that for so long had mesmerized her with mystery and intrigue.

From there, the bus rumbled down Potsdamer Platz, and when it took a left onto Niederkirchnerstraße, an almost-forgotten chill ran up her spine. This was the site of the former Gestapo headquarters, where she had been transported, handcuffed, and interrogated prior to her imprisonment. To her surprise, the huge, imposing building was gone, one of many architectural casualties, and even the street it had sat on, Prinz-Albrecht-Straße, had been renamed. *So strange to still have anxiety fifty years later*. The next day, at her request, the group traveled down to the Horseshoe Estate, where her family had moved during her early adolescence. Not only was it still there, but it had recently been accorded status as a German heritage site. She walked around the pond, uncannily bucolic in this otherwise urban setting, and recalled the innocence and contentment with which she came of age.

On her third day in Berlin, Annika chose to wander about by herself. She entered the Jewish Hospital, where she had been sent following her release from Sachsenhausen. The corridors echoed with voices from the past. She could almost hear Doctor Lustig cavorting with women, could see the Jews assembling in the adjoining *sammelager,* preparing for deportation. *So many ghosts . . .*

Once outside, she took a short walk over to Hochstädter Strasse, where she had rented an apartment at the time of her arrest. It was only a short distance from the flat where she and her parents had lived prior to the Horseshoe Estate. She found it to be a relaxing, tree-lined side street with newer apartment buildings on each side. The original buildings were gone, but she found it easy to reimagine her life back in the early 1940s. As she got closer to the location of her former residence, she noticed the sun glinting off several brass plates embedded into the cobblestones. Each plate measured approximately four-by-four inches and was inscribed with lettering. Suddenly, it dawned on her. These were the "stumbling stones" – what locals called *Stolpersteine*. They were small brass plaques memorializing those deported from their last known residence before being deported by the Nazis. One of them stood out, leaving her speechless.

Hier Wohnte
Annika Tritzchler
Ärztin
JG 1915
Verhaftet 1942
Gefängnis KZ Ravensbrück
1943- 45
USA Uberlebt

Translated, the marker read: *"Here lived Annika Tritzchler; Doctor; Birth Year 1915; Arrested 1942; Prison KZ Ravensbrück 1943-45; Survived USA."* At that moment, a flood of memories came rushing back: everything, from her home life to her schoolwork, her parents, her dreams and expectations, all of it. She felt momentarily weak and walked to a nearby chair outside a small cafe, where she sat for at least an hour, staring off into the distance, her eyes glazed over as memories supplanted her vision.

Rejoining her group, Annika asked the tour guide how the information for her stumbling stone had been acquired. He directed her to a nearby museum, which had long been collecting holocaust memorabilia. It was then that an even greater coincidence occurred. The curator was an elderly man with a snowy, white beard. A *yarmulka* covered the crown of his head. When he heard her name, he asked her to wait while he checked the records in the back. Fifteen minutes later, he emerged with a brown paper bag. "I have a feeling these might belong to you," he said, pulling from the bag three dogeared notebooks, each bearing the name "Annika Tritzchler / Berlin." As he pushed them toward her, Annika noticed the shriveled numbers of an old tattoo across his right forearm.

Annika looked at the books, not believing her eyes. They both stood for a minute in silence.

"You look a bit *verklempt, ja?*" the curator said.

"Where did you get these?" Annika asked.

"I'm not sure we could ever know the answer to that. It was so long ago. My guess is that they were found in the rubble during the clean-up. Someone must've paged through them and thought them possibly worthy of keeping."

Annika slowly thumbed through the pages, dumbstruck. "I-I simply can't believe this . . ."

"So, I take it, they're yours, *nicht wahr?*"

"*Ja . . . ja,*" she answered slowly. "I began keeping a journal when I was quite young. Wherever I moved, my journals went with me . . . until I was arrested . . ."

"Um hmm. *Ich verstehe,*" he replied, quietly. "Well, Fräulein, God apparently has preserved them for you. There must be a reason." Annika looked up at him, stupefied, not knowing how to respond. "They're obviously yours. Would you like to take them?"

Annika returned them to the bag, thanked the man, and then, feeling dazed, exited the building, clutching the bag to her bosom as if it was a long-lost child.

Revelations

Whoever lives among many evils just as I, how can dying not be a source of gain?

Sophocles

Bayshore Nursing Home: August 15, 2016

"Time to rise and shine, Doctor Tritzchler." Danisha gave a quick tug on the shade sending it hurtling to the upper sill, where it spun around several times in a thundering racket. "Sorry, sorry," she apologized. "Didn't mean to do that."

Annika was undisturbed. Instead, she took a moment to watch the aide going through her duties, and then said, "You know, Danisha, in all the time I've been here, you're one of the few staff members to call me by name... definitely the first to address me as 'doctor.'"

"No way!", the aide replied, though she knew Annika was correct.

"*Ja*, really. Throughout my life, I've been called 'Fräulein' or 'Missus;' sometimes just 'Tritzchler.' So much so that I grew to ignore it. It was only when I got back into medicine that my credentials begin to mean anything, and even then, I was often mistaken for a nurse...'

"Well, you told me you're a doctor. The way I was brought up, that's how we address doctors," Danisha said, as if such salutations were plain as day. "And actually, you're the first resident to call *me* by my name, as well. Most people, if they say anything at all, just say 'girl,' or 'aide, or 'you there.'

Annika frowned. "Well, I've always believed names are important," replied Annika. She thought back to Sachsenhausen and Ravensbrück where, instead of a name, she was a number. "And besides, your name, 'Danisha'... it's a lovely name..." As Annika said this, she closed her eyes. Suddenly, she felt very tired.

Danisha smiled. "Well, that's very kind of you," she replied, taking the notebook from Annika's lap and placing it with the others on the bedstand. "My mother would be delighted to hear that..." She picked up some dirty linens, threw them in the hamper and began sweeping the floor. "You're from Germany, right?"

"How would you know that?" Annika asked.

"I can tell by your accent. I'm a graduate student... at the New School... for Social Research. One of my professors there was German." The way she said it, Annika could tell she was very proud.

"Ah, very fine school," Annika remarked. She paused for a moment, as if lost in a daydream. "Years ago, I had friends there, in the psychology department. So, tell me. What are you studying?"

"Well, I had an undergraduate major in political science and women's studies at CCNY. I went on for a master's degree in sociology at the New School, and now I'm pursuing my doctorate. Focusing on political development in historical perspective." Annika nodded. "I've got a dissertation staring me in the face."

"What will you be researching?"

"Well, to be honest, I haven't quite settled on a topic yet. I've always been interested in World War Two, but not really sure how to turn that into a thesis."

"World War Two? Really. I wouldn't think many young people know much about that time period or, for that matter, that they have much interest. What makes you want to study it?"

Danisha lit up. "My grandfather was in the war. A pilot. One of the Tuskegee airmen. Have you ever heard of them?"

"Yes, of course. They were all African-Americans, right?"

"Yup. And very brave. My grandfather flew a fighter-bomber. Saw a lot of combat and, from what I'm told, had several kills. He was nominated for the Distinguished Flying Cross, but as the story goes, he never got it because of..." Danisha stopped what she was doing and looked out the window. "...well, I guess because of the politics at the time."

Annika didn't blink an eye. "I think you mean, the prejudices. If I remember my history, the Tuskegee airmen were very discriminated against."

"Yeah. Exactly. But not unlike most of the black soldiers who returned home after the war."

"Was that the way it was for your grandfather?"

"Unfortunately, Doctor Tritzchler, my Grampie... he didn't make it home. He was shot down over Italy."

Annika grimaced. She could tell that Danisha was at once both proud and sad. "I am sorry to hear that. The war was very cruel. But, you know, Danisha, that might be a good topic for a dissertation."

"Thanks for the suggestion. Actually, I already wrote a master's thesis on my grandfather's unit. The department wants me to do something different... "

"I see..."

"Do you mind my asking if you were in Germany during the war?"

Annika's eyes squinted. She paused a second before answering. "Yes... I was there. But not in a combat role... I- I... was a prisoner... of the Nazis."

Once again, Danisha stopped what she was doing, this time pulling up a chair to the bedside where she directed her full attention to Annika. "You were a prisoner? Why?" Annika grunted as she shifted her position in the bed. "I'm sorry, Doctor T. I didn't mean to be so blunt. I hope I didn't..."

"No, no. Please. You're fine. It's not a problem," Annika said, wincing. She seemed to be quite uncomfortable, and Danisha noticed that her breathing was labored.

"Here, let me get you some water."

Danisha put the glass to Annika's lips. Taking only a small sip, Annika turned to the side, shaking her head. "*Kein mehr... Das ist genug,*" she whispered.

Danisha pulled the glass away and stared at the old woman. "Doctor Tritzchler, you're speaking German."

Annika's eyes rolled to the back of her head. She waited for a moment before speaking. "I'm sorry... That's... that's enough. No more," she said in a hoarse voice. Her face appeared strained. Over the past few months, she had been heard lapsing into German, particularly when distressed. It was as if she had reverted to an earlier time in her life.

"Are you okay," Danisha asked, putting the glass on the tray. She leaned forward with her face only inches from Annika's.

"Danisha, over there," Annika said, pointing a bony, arthritic finger to the cabinet. "I have a stack of journals that I began keeping when I was about ten. They cover much of my life." Danisha looked over to the armoire. "I have no one to leave them to. I don't even know why I kept them. They all seem a bit meaningless now... Anyway, if you'd like, you can have them. They might tell you a little bit about what it was like to grow up in a democratic country that was turned fascist." She looked over to the window, then back to the aide. "You know," she mused, "it all came about so fast. . . so incredibly fast. Few people at the time believed it could ever happen."

Danisha listened attentively. "Really? You would give your journals. . . to *me*?"

"Yes, I will. Maybe... who knows? Maybe something you come across will help you with your dissertation. Or at least give you some ideas. If you end up not wanting them, just throw them away. Won't be any great loss."

"Doctor Tritzchler, my Lord, that would be so. . . so interesting. I'm honored. Truly." Her eyes appeared to be swimming.

Just then began a procession of wheelchairs being escorted down the corridor. "Sounds like the breakfast brigade," Danisha said. "I better get going. Are you okay? Do you need anything?" Danisha placed her hand on Annika's.

"No, no. I'm fine. You go. I'm not really hungry."

"You sure?" she asked, wondering if she could trust the dismissal. With Annika nodding, Danisha said, "Okay, but promise me you'll ring if you need anything."

Annika closed her eyes and smiled. "I will, hon. I will."

Fräulein

Danisha returned on schedule early the next morning. Annika was in bed, her eyes closed. The aide picked up a water glass, emptied it in the sink, then turned to yank the blankets down. There was no resistance. Annika lay quietly. "Hey, I'd like to sleep in too, but we got to…" She suddenly stopped what she was doing and stared for a moment. It struck her that something was wrong, seriously wrong. Panicking, she abandoned her usual propriety and cried, "Girl, tell me you're sleepin'!" She bent down to check on Annika's breathing. There were no obvious respirations. She felt for a pulse, but finding none, turned and rushed to the nurses' station. Less than a minute elapsed before she was back with the charge-nurse who, after a quick check of Annika's vitals, began CPR. Danisha rushed for the crash cart.

It was too late. The exhausted centenarian- survivor of unimaginable tragedy, witness to some of humanity's darkest deeds- had finally breathed her last.

It was Danisha's job to clean Annika's room, and this she did with the uneasy silence that always seemed to follow the passing of a resident. However familiar that was, the sense of emptiness on this occasion was unlike anything she had ever experienced. Danisha was known and respected for her friendly, outgoing personality, yet she rarely developed close bonds with any of the patients for whom she was responsible. With Annika, things were different. Theirs was a resonance that for all intents and purposes defied description. It wasn't a friendship in the ordinary sense, one based on mutual religion, parallel socio-economic background or even common neighborhood. No, those realities were as vastly different as their respective ages and skin color. In fact, with the exception of gender, Annika and Danisha had shared no observable similarities at all. Inwardly, though, there was an ineffable sense that down deep each understood the other. They had sensed from the first time they met that despite all their apparent differences, they were kindred spirits.

Though it was never discussed, their link was a sensitivity born out of deprivation, discrimination and suffering. Ironically, Annika's death and the palpable sense of loss that Danisha felt would breathe even more life into their brief but meaningful kinship.

As she began removing items from the armoire, Danisha spied two bulging brown folders perched high on the shelf. *Could these be the journals Doctor T. had mentioned,* she wondered? Thicker and heavier than she might have expected, she balanced them in both arms and laid them on the bedside. She was overcome with an unexpected feeling of reverence as she gently freed the assortment of papers, some bound, some loose-leaf, from the antiquated binders. There was no question; these were the dog-eared journals that Annika had bequeathed to her. It was then that Danisha noticed on the nightstand another notebook, the one Annika seemed to carry with her wherever she went. It was open, a ballpoint pen laying on top as if Annika had only recently written in it. Danisha leaned over to retrieve it and found herself mesmerized in reading what was obviously her friend's last entry.

18 Feb, 2016

To Danisha: As you read through my journals and piece together the various stages of my life, I want to add a personal note that would never be obvious from my writings alone. It's probably nothing you'd have thought, maybe not even be interested in, but for what it's worth, I'll share it anyway. Last night, I had a vivid dream, one which illuminated something that has always vexed me. Throughout my life, even beginning in early childhood, I've had an uncanny obsession with the four horses that stand triumphantly over the Brandenburg Gate in Berlin. The statuary is known as the Quadriga, and I've never been able to pass nearby without gazing up at it. Those four majestic stallions came to life last night in a lucid dream, one that literally revealed their true colors. I now have reason to believe that they have foreshadowed my entire life.

Fräulein

I remember waking up in my mid- to late teens from dreams that so often involved a white horse. I never thought much about it at the time, nor even later when, as a psychiatrist, I simply dismissed them as adolescent ramblings. I now feel that those dreams were more significant- that they presaged the conquest of my community by the Nazis. And then, a few years later, I frequently woke up drenched in sweat, my mind swirling from nightmares that featured a high-spirited red horse. That came around the time Germany descended into war. There was so much going on at the time that I didn't think too much about it, but now, as I look back, I recall that as the years progressed, more and more of my nocturnal meanderings involved chilling images of an imposing black steed. It was the same dream, over and over again, especially when I felt most vulnerable, which was mostly during my confinement at Ravensbrück. There was suffering all around me, a macabre darkness that was embodied by that unnerving stallion. The rider was usually an SS officer who would burst onto the appelplatz, *where in one hand, he held the reins with a ledger-book tucked under his arm, and with his other, he would point a bony finger at the gaunt men and women whom he had selected for execution. "Culling the herd," he would shout to the kapos, who would then yank the doomed out from the weary ranks.*

Bad as that dream was, the most dispiriting of the equine dreams, and sadly the one that has plagued me the longest, has involved a faceless rider mounted atop a pale horse. My first encounters with the apparition occurred around the time Pasha and my parents were murdered. Of course, I did not then know of their deaths, which made the nightmare even more unsettling. The dream faded for a short while, but then burst back into my sleep shortly before Rosenthal and Quernheim ripped a fetus from my womb. The same horse- pale as a snowscape on a damp, overcast day- surfaced again in 1956, only that time a woman was saddled with the rider. For all the world, she resembled my dearest friend, Martyna. Haunted by the dream, I made desperate attempts to communicate with her, though none of them were successful. Eventually, with the help of an acquaintance at a

393

local university (whom, for their own security, I will not mention), we learned, after a great deal of digging, that she had been arrested by the SB, *Poland's secret police, and held at the infamous Mokotów prison outside of Warsaw. Apparently, she (of all people!) had long been suspected of having cooperated with the Germans, simply because she had spent time in Germany, no matter that her tenure in that evil country occurred only because of the horrific death march from Auschwitz. That she survived where so many others did not apparently made her suspect in the eyes of the SB, and that, coupled with both her Judaism and her venerable reputation in the community, no doubt sealed her fate with the Communists.*

Why I have been plagued for so long by those nightmares is undoubtedly the guilt that I still feel- NOT because of my complicity in the rabbi's death, but because of diagnoses I made- innocently- that nevertheless resulted in the deaths of so many of my former patients. I had no idea at the time that accurately recording their disabilities would be used to justify their extermination, and while I have tried and tried throughout my life to atone for it, hardly a day goes by that I don't think of patients like Max and Elsie.

One of my life's greatest ironies is that Martyna survived Auschwitz only to be executed by the very people who had liberated her, an unforgivable crime given her selfless commitment to the sick and infirm. Why she died while I lived is unfathomable. Martyna was a lovely woman: kind, intelligent, sensitive and forgiving, the type of person most are fortunate to meet once in a lifetime, not unlike Dietrich Bonhoeffer, who was also murdered by the Nazis. I never saw Martyna following her return to Poland in 1947. It's been 70 years now, yet Martyna remains a spiritual presence in my psyche to this day.

Many say that God never gives more than one can handle. I lost faith in that belief long ago. In my lifetime, millions of people have struggled with much, much more than they could ever handle, eventually succumbing under the strain. If there is a God, it is certainly not the one that I was taught to believe in. That faith was

*shattered in Ravensbrück when on Sundays I would observe the SS
attending worship services, singing homilies to God while only a
short distance away men were left hanging by wrists tied securely
behind their backs. The SS would offer up prayers to their Savior,
leaving women dangling outside from gallows built by their own
hands. That was the God these monsters worshipped, and not just in
the camps, but in towns and villages all throughout Germany and
Europe. Theirs was a god not just of warfare and conquest, but
slavery, torture and, in the end, genocide.*

*So in my final moments, I am left wondering, who is this god of
love who would abandon those who suffocated in cattle cars, or those
shot in the neck at the edge of gaping pits overflowing with the bodies
of friends and neighbors? And what kind of god shows no mercy to
victims, yet allows torturers and executioners, heartless industrialists
and racist doctors, to live comfortably and self-righteously in post-
war lives as if they were guilty of nothing?*

*I've searched all these years for answers, and now, on what
promises to be my deathbed, I realize that 'people are people' and
probably always will be. We all have our dark sides, even me, and I
can't see that this will ever change. Dostoevsky said,* "People speak
sometimes about the "bestial" cruelty of man, but that is terribly
unjust and offensive to beasts. No animal could ever be so cruel as a
man, so artfully, so artistically cruel." *And In my view, that will never
change. People will continue to be seduced by villainous charlatans-
vainglorious and full of deceitful promises. They will follow them to
hell and back, realizing only when it's too late that they have been
deceived. Goebbels and Stalin knew what they were talking about
when they said that truth was the enemy of the people. And Hegel said
it best in recognizing that "we learn from history that we do not learn
from history."*

*Why is that? I've always thought that the answer lies in education.
Without it, people are easily fooled by would-be demagogues, unable
to see through sophistry and illusion, eager to embrace, even to die
for, the very deceptions that inexorably lead to the followers own*

imprisonment. True socialism, for example, was never "National-Socialism" in the same way that Communism was never what Marx envisioned, despite all the platitudes to the contrary. Karl Marx, then, would never have been a "Marxist," just like Jesus Christ would have never called himself a "Christian." Leave that term to a Church that turned love and salvation by grace into a 400-year crusade involving the horrendous torture and murder of millions whom it called "apostate."

Despite all that, I feel fortunate to have survived the war, to have found a husband who loved me unconditionally, and to have had work that felt meaningful and fulfilling. What has sustained me all these years is the hope that my small efforts have helped at least some to grow and maybe discover a purpose to their lives.

Last night's dream showed me that the four horses of the Quadriga, those which from my very earliest years were sources of mystery and intrigue, have been representations of my own apocalypse. I have accompanied the four horsemen, one by one, as they bespoke the unwitting certainties of my life: conquest, war, famine and death. When last I dreamt of the pale horse, Jerome died. Last night, for the first time in 34 years, it appeared again, and this time the bony finger beckoned to me. I know it is my time, and I welcome it. I can only hope that wherever the rider takes me, it will be to rejoin all those who have loved me, and those who stood up for right.

Danisha heard activity out in the hallway, reminding her of her duties. As she tucked the jumble of mismatched notebooks back in their binders, a small, lightly-creased paper, yellowed with age, fluttered to the floor. It was undated, yet in the faded black ink of a fountain pen, it had obviously been written years, perhaps decades, before. She took a moment to read through what was obviously a poem. The short stanzas were written in the elementary style of a schoolgirl, yet by the time Danisha reached the ending, she sensed that the verses were more profound and reflective of Annika's personal philosophy than the reams of paper from which it had escaped.

Ode to a Charlatan

The people are needy, they thirst for reprieve,
when along comes a charlatan with lies up his sleeve.
He senses their weakness and is ready to deceive
the vulnerable, the ignorant, the weak and naïve.

They thrive on his promises, wanting to believe.
He courts them with lies, hard to perceive.
A new world order they're sure he'll achieve.
They trust and they cheer, his vision they receive.

Hyperbole and truth can never interweave.
Disciples and adversaries vow never to cleave.
But with mayhem and suffering, even his acolytes grieve.
Through loss and destruction, all will bereave.

It was a masquerade, the truth we now conceive.
The people are wiser, their wisdom they retrieve.
He was a prophet of illusion, now given the heave.
But for those still alive, their pain will never leave.

In May, 2017, Danisha Jackson, former aide at the Bayshore Nursing Home, was awarded the degree of Doctor of Philosophy in Sociology after successfully defending a dissertation entitled, *The Impact of Nazi Concentration Camps on Women Survivors.* Her thesis was dedicated to the inspirational sacrifices of *Doctor* Annika Tritzchler, someone with whom Danisha acknowledged a deep kinship. Within a year, her research made its way to Annika's beloved New York Psychoanalytic Society, which until then knew almost nothing of its self-effacing member. There, in a special ceremony hosted by Danisha, herself, the organization honored the sacrifices of one they called "their own," an erstwhile German psychiatrist who, at great personal expense, refused to participate with influential colleagues in cold-blooded actions that brought shame and disgrace to an entire profession. In that forum, Annika Tritzchler achieved posthumously a recognition that had eluded her in life: being hailed for her role in restoring to psychiatry and psychoanalysis a credibility once considered lost forever.

Acknowledgements

Over four years and more than one hundred books* have gone into the formulation of this novel, yet nothing has been more valuable to me than ongoing encouragement from so many voices along the way. That people- friends and strangers alike- would take the time to discuss my ideas and/or read through chapter excerpts has been humbling in the extreme. In no particular order, I am sincerely grateful for the support of Nick Rehagen, Jim Pickrell, Tony Campolo, Bruce Gallup, Ron Hyde, Bernie Fortier, James and Ron Standerfer, John and Joanna Carr, and Peter and Irene Genco. Their involvement has invigorated what would otherwise have been a lonely and unfulfilling journey.

In coming to a more realistic appreciation of life in mid-century Germany, I am indebted to Charles Rotmil for sharing several hours talking with me about his experiences as a survivor of the holocaust. My cycling buddy, Erich Reitenbach, added valuable recollections of his early years in an Austrian Displaced Persons (DP) camp. Visualizing those circumstances was enriched by touring some of the notorious concentration camps, but also through my son, Chris, who spent many days showing me around his adopted city of Berlin. Beyond that, his association with the venerable Charité Hospital, first as a medical student and later as a physician, figured prominently in the backdrop to my story.

I am enormously flattered that Jesùs Leguizamo, a highly talented artist in Colombia, has donated his masterpiece ("Plasma") to grace the cover of this book. Nothing could have so hauntingly captured the fractured identity of my main character.

Those who went above and beyond in editing parts or all of my manuscript included Bruce Spang, Jack Morrison, Jonathan Borkum,

Tom Holbrook, Kellsey Metzger, and Dick Taylor. My novel, for all its limitations, has benefitted enormously from their magnanimity.

Lastly, but most importantly, was the abiding support from my wife, Dionna, who spent countless hours reading, listening to, and critiquing my work. On those many occasions when I myself began to doubt- when I was prepared, in fact, to scrap the entire exercise-she stood resolute with unwavering reassurance. In speaking of his own wife, Stephen King (Maine's most prolific novelist) said, "having someone who believes in you makes a lot of difference." For me, Dionna's belief made *all* the difference. Without it, my manuscript would probably be collecting dust in some forgotten file, forever unfinished.

Honoré de Balzac, the renowned French novelist and playwright, was said to have expressed concern, while on his deathbed, about the well-being of characters in his books, as if they were alive. I am no Balzac, but I can certainly resonate with his concerns. For me and my wife, the chief protagonist in my own story was more than a figment of my imagination. Annika invaded our lives as if part of our family; someone whose tears we tasted, whose triumphs we celebrated, and whose passing we mourned.

The renowned Russian philosopher, Nicolai Berdyaev, once said, "the anguish of every parting, of every severance in space and time, is the experience of death." Through Annika, we learned that death, like life, need not be meaningless. Her sufferings spoke volumes not just about resilience and survival, but also responsibility and free-will; the existential hallmarks of what Sartre termed "authenticity."

Annika took on many roles in her lifelong struggle for identity, but the one that truly defined her was a role of which she herself would have been unaware: *eine Lehrerin*. As a teacher, her lessons were profound, and like any serious student, I am changed by them, forever.

*Bibliography available on request by emailing the author at
frauleinnovel@gmail.com

CPSIA information can be obtained
at www.ICGtesting.com
Printed in the USA
BVHW081450300321
603710BV00001B/48

9 781950 381739